EVERYMAN, I will go with thee,

and be thy guide,

In thy most need to go by thy side

FRANCIS TURNER PALGRAVE

Born 1824, son of Sir Francis Palgrave the historian. Examiner and assistant-secretary of the Education Department, 1855–84; Professor of Poetry at Oxford, 1885–95. Died in 1897.

PALGRAVE

The Golden Treasury
of English Songs
and Lyrics

WITH A SUPPLEMENTARY BOOK
OF MORE MODERN POETRY

DENT: LONDON, MELBOURNE AND TORONTO
EVERYMAN'S LIBRARY

No. 96   Hardback ISBN 0 460 00096 9
No. 1096   Paperback ISBN 0 460 01096 4

PREFACE TO THE ORIGINAL EDITION

THIS little Collection differs, it is believed, from others in the attempt made to include in it all the best original Lyrical pieces and Songs in our language, by writers not living,—and none beside the best. Many familiar verses will hence be met with; many also which should be familiar:—the Editor will regard as his fittest readers those who love Poetry so well, that he can offer them nothing not already known and valued.

The Editor is acquainted with no strict and exhaustive definition of Lyrical Poetry; but he has found the task of practical decision increase in clearness and in facility as he advanced with the work, whilst keeping in view a few simple principles. Lyrical has been here held essentially to imply that each Poem shall turn on some single thought, feeling, or situation. In accordance with this, narrative, descriptive, and didactic poems,—unless accompanied by rapidity of movement, brevity, and the colouring of human passion,—have been excluded. Humorous poetry, except in the very unfrequent instances where a truly poetical tone pervades the whole, with what is strictly personal, occasional, and religious, has been considered foreign to the idea of the book. Blank verse and the ten-syllable couplet, with all pieces markedly dramatic, have been rejected as alien from what is commonly understood by Song, and rarely conforming to Lyrical conditions in treatment. But it is not anticipated, nor is it possible, that all readers shall think the line accurately drawn. Some poems, as Gray's Elegy, the Allegro and Penseroso, Wordsworth's Ruth or Campbell's Lord Ullin, might be claimed with perhaps equal justice for a narrative or descriptive selection: whilst with reference especially to Ballads and Sonnets, the Editor can only state that he has taken his utmost pains to decide without caprice or partiality.

This also is all he can plead in regard to a point even more liable to question;—what degree of merit should give rank among the Best. That a Poem shall be worthy of the writer's genius,—that it shall reach a perfection commensurate with its aim,—that we should require finish in proportion to brevity,—that passion, colour, and originality cannot atone for serious imperfections in clearness, unity, or truth,—that a few good lines do not make a good poem,—that popular estimate is serviceable as a guidepost more than as a compass,—above all, that Excellence should be looked for rather in the Whole than in the Parts,—such and other such canons have been always steadily regarded. He may however add that the pieces chosen, and a far larger number rejected, have been carefully and repeatedly considered; and that he has been aided throughout by two friends of independent and exercised judgment, besides the distinguished person addressed in the Dedication. It is hoped that by this procedure the volume has been freed from that one-sidedness which must beset individual decisions:—but for the final choice the Editor is alone responsible.

It would obviously have been invidious to apply the standard aimed at in this Collection to the Living. Nor, even in the cases where this might be done without offence, does it appear wise to attempt to anticipate the verdict of the Future on our contemporaries. Should the book last, poems by Tennyson, Bryant, Clare, Lowell, and others, will no doubt claim and obtain their place among the best. But the Editor trusts that this will be effected by other hands, and in days far distant.

Chalmers' vast collection, with the whole works of all accessible poets not contained in it, and the best Anthologies of different periods, have been twice systematically read through: and it is hence improbable that any omissions which may be regretted are due to oversight. The poems are printed entire, except in a very few instances where a stanza has been omitted. The omissions have been risked only when the piece could be thus brought to a closer lyrical unity: and, as essentially opposed to this unity, extracts, obviously such, are excluded. In regard to the text, the purpose of the book has appeared to justify the choice of the most poetical version, wherever more than one exists: and much labour has been given to present each poem, in disposition, spelling, and punctuation, to the greatest advantage.

For the permission under which the copyright pieces are inserted, thanks are due to the respective Proprietors, without whose liberal concurrence the scheme of the collection would have been defeated.

In the arrangement, the most poetically-effective order has been attempted. The English mind has passed through phases of thought and cultivation so various and so opposed during these three centuries of Poetry, that a rapid passage between Old and New, like rapid alteration of the eye's focus in looking at the landscape, will always be wearisome and hurtful to the sense of Beauty. The poems have been therefore distributed into Books corresponding,

I to the ninety years closing about 1616, II thence
to 1700, III to 1800, IV to the half century just
ended. Or, looking at the Poets who more or less
give each portion its distinctive character, they
might be called the Books of Shakespeare, Milton,
Gray, and Wordsworth. The volume, in this respect,
so far as the limitations of its range allow, accurately
reflects the natural growth and evolution of our
Poetry. A rigidly chronological sequence, however,
rather fits a collection aiming at instruction than
at pleasure, and the Wisdom which comes through
Pleasure:—within each book the pieces have therefore been arranged in gradations of feeling or subject.
The development of the symphonies of Mozart and
Beethoven has been here thought of as a model, and
nothing placed without careful consideration. And
it is hoped that the contents of this Anthology will
thus be found to present a certain unity, 'as episodes',
in the noble language of Shelley, 'to that great Poem
which all poets, like the cooperating thoughts of one
great mind, have built up since the beginning of
the world'.

As he closes his long survey, the Editor trusts he
may add without egotism, that he has found the
vague general verdict of popular Fame more just
than those have thought, who, with too severe a
criticism, would confine judgments on Poetry to 'the
selected few of many generations'. Not many appear
to have gained reputation without some gift or per-
formance that, in due degree, deserved it: and if no
verses by certain writers who show less strength than
sweetness, or more thought than mastery in expres-
sion, are printed in this volume, it should not be
imagined that they have been excluded without much
hesitation and regret,—far less that they have been

slighted. Throughout this vast and pathetic array of Singers now silent, few have been honoured with the name Poet, and have not possessed a skill in words, a sympathy with beauty, a tenderness of feeling, or seriousness in reflection, which render their works, although never perhaps attaining that loftier and finer excellence here required,—better worth reading than much of what fills the scanty hours that most men spare for self-improvement, or for pleasure in any of its more elevated and permanent forms.—And if this be true of even mediocre poetry, for how much more are we indebted to the best! Like the fabled fountain of the Azores, but with a more various power, the magic of this Art can confer on each period of life its appropriate blessing: on early years Experience, on maturity Calm, on age, Youthfulness. Poetry gives treasures 'more golden than gold', leading us in higher and healthier ways than those of the world, and interpreting to us the lessons of Nature. But she speaks best for herself. Her true accents, if the plan has been executed with success, may be heard throughout the following pages:—wherever the Poets of England are honoured, wherever the dominant language of the world is spoken, it is hoped that they will find fit audience.

SELECT BIBLIOGRAPHY

WORKS: *Preciosa, a Tale*, 1852; *Idylls and Songs*, 1854; *The Works of Alfred de Musset* (Oxford Essays), 1855; *The Passionate Pilgrim* (prose), 1858; *The Golden Treasury of English Songs and Lyrics*, 1861 (second series, 1897); *Memoir of Clough* (with edition of poems), 1862; *Handbook to the Fine Art Collection in the International Exhibition of 1862*, 1862; Edition of Shakespeare's Poems, 1865; *Essays on Art*, 1866; *Biographical and Critical Memoir of Scott* (prefixed to poems), 1866; *Hymns*, 1867, 1868; *The Five Days' Entertainments at Wentworth Grange* (stories for children), 1868; *Lyrical Poems*, 1871; *A Lyme Garland: Verses mainly written at Lyme Regis*, etc., 1874; *The Children's Treasury of English Song*, 1875, 1876; *Chrysomela* (selections from Herrick), 1877; *The Visions of England* (verse), 1881; *Selections from Tennyson*, 1885; *Ode for the Twenty-first of June, 1887*, 1887; *The Treasury of Sacred Song*, 1889; *Amenophis and other Poems*, 1892; *Landscape in Poetry from Homer to Tennyson* (Oxford Lectures), 1897.

BIOGRAPHY: G. F. Palgrave, *Francis Turner Palgrave. Memoirs by his Daughter*, 1899; B. I. Evans, 'Tennyson and the Origins of the Golden Treasury', *The Times Literary Supplement*, 8th Dec. 1932; C. J. Horne, 'Palgrave's Golden Treasury', *English Studies*, ii, 1949; N. Lewis, 'Palgrave and his Golden Treasury', *The Listener*, 4th Jan. 1962.

PUBLISHERS' NOTE

In the present Everyman edition of *Palgrave's Golden Treasury* a group of additional poems has been selected to represent the period that has elapsed since Palgrave's selection was made, though the work of no poet appears who was born later than the end of the nineteenth century. A very few of the earlier poems in this additional group fall within the later years of Palgrave's own selection. The poems are printed in the chronological order of the birth of the poets.

Acknowledgments for permission to include copyright poems are made to the following:

The Society of Authors and Mrs Lascelles Abercrombie for 'The Stream's Song' by Lascelles Abercrombie; Messrs Macmillan & Co. Ltd and Diarmuid Russell for 'By the margin of the great deep' from *The Selected Poems of Æ.*; the Clarendon Press, Oxford for 'Nightingales' and 'A Passer-by' from *The Shorter Poems of Robert Bridges*; Messrs Sidgwick & Jackson Ltd for 'The Soldier' and 'Clouds' by Rupert Brooke; The Society of Authors and Mrs Cicely Binyon for 'For the Fallen' by Laurence Binyon; the author's representative for 'The Old Woman' by Joseph Campbell; Messrs Burns Oates & Washbourne Ltd for 'O God of Earth and Altar' by G. K. Chesterton; Messrs J. M. Dent & Sons Ltd for 'The Donkey' by G. K. Chesterton; Messrs Gerald Duckworth & Co. Ltd for 'The South Country' by Hilaire Belloc; Messrs Jonathan Cape Ltd for 'Leisure' by W. H. Davies; Walter de la Mare for 'The Listeners' and 'Many a Mickle'; the author's executors and the Oxford University Press for 'A Garden Song' by Austin Dobson; Messrs Macmillan & Co. Ltd and the Trustees of the Hardy Estate for 'The Oxen' and 'When I set out for Lyonesse' from *The Collected Poems of Thomas Hardy*; The Society of Authors as the Literary Representative of the Trustees of the Estate of the late A. E. Housman and Messrs Jonathan Cape Ltd for 'Reveille,' 'Loveliest of Trees,' and 'On the idle hill of summer' from *The Collected Poems of A. E. Housman*; The Oxford University Press for 'Pied Beauty' from *The Poems of Gerard Manley Hopkins*; Messrs Macmillan & Co. Ltd and Mrs George Bambridge for 'If' by Rudyard Kipling, and Messrs Methuen & Co. Ltd and Mrs George Bambridge for 'Recessional' by Rudyard Kipling; The Society of Authors and Dr John Masefield, O.M., for 'Spanish Waters' and 'Sea Fever'; Wilfrid Meynell for 'The Shepherdess' by Alice Meynell; Messrs John Murray Ltd and the Executors of the late Sir Henry Newbolt for 'Drake's Drum' and 'Vitaï Lampada' from *Poems New and Old*; Messrs Macmillan & Co. Ltd and Mrs Stephens for 'The Snare' and 'Little Things' from *The Collected Poems of James Stephens*; The Hon. V. Sackville-West for 'A Saxon Song'; Messrs Ernest Benn Ltd for 'The Call of the Wild' by R. W. Service; Messrs William Heinemann Ltd for 'Itylus,' 'The Hounds of Spring,' and 'The Garden of Proserpine' by A. C. Swinburne; Mrs Helen Thomas for 'The New House' by Edward Thomas; Messrs Burns Oates and Washbourne Ltd for 'Daisy' and 'In no strange land' by Francis Thompson; Messrs Macmillan & Co. Ltd and Mrs W. B. Yeats for 'Down by the Salley Gardens,' 'The Lake Isle of Innisfree,' and 'When you are old and gray.'

BOOK FIRST

I
SPRING

Spring, the sweet Spring, is the year's pleasant king;
Then blooms each thing, then maids dance in a ring,
Cold doth not sting, the pretty birds do sing,
    Cuckoo, jug-jug, pu-we, to-witta-woo!

The palm and may make country houses gay,
Lambs frisk and play, the shepherds pipe all day,
And we hear aye birds tune this merry lay,
    Cuckoo, jug-jug, pu-we, to-witta-woo.

The fields breathe sweet, the daisies kiss our feet,
Young lovers meet, old wives a-sunning sit,
In every street these tunes our ears do greet,
    Cuckoo, jug-jug, pu-we, to-witta-woo!
        Spring! the sweet Spring!

                                    T. NASH

II
SUMMONS TO LOVE

Phoebus, arise!
And paint the sable skies
With azure, white, and red:
Rouse Memnon's mother from her Tithon's bed
That she may thy career with roses spread:
The nightingales thy coming eachwhere sing:
Make an eternal Spring!
Give life to this dark world which lieth dead;
Spread forth thy golden hair

In larger locks than thou wast wont before
And emperor-like decore
With diadem of pearl thy temples fair:
Chase hence the ugly night
Which serves but to make dear thy glorious light.

—This is that happy morn,
That day, long-wishéd day
Of all my life so dark,
(If cruel stars have not my ruin sworn
And fates my hopes betray),
Which, purely white, deserves
An everlasting diamond should it mark.
This is the morn should bring unto this grove
My Love, to hear and recompense my love.
Fair King, who all preserves,
But show thy blushing beams,
And thou two sweeter eyes
Shalt see than those which by Penéus' streams
Did once thy heart surprize.
Now, Flora, deck thyself in fairest guise:
If that ye winds would hear
A voice surpassing far Amphion's lyre,
Your furious chiding stay;
Let Zephyr only breathe,
And with her tresses play.
—The winds all silent are,
And Phoebus in his chair
Ensaffroning sea and air
Makes vanish every star:
Night like a drunkard reels
Beyond the hills, to shun his flaming wheels:
The fields with flowers are deck'd in every hue,
The clouds with orient gold spangle their blue;
Here is the pleasant place—
And nothing wanting is, save She, alas!

                    W. DRUMMOND OF HAWTHORNDEN

III
TIME AND LOVE

I

When I have seen by Time's fell hand defaced
The rich proud cost of out-worn buried age;
When sometime lofty towers I see down-razed,
And brass eternal slave to mortal rage;

When I have seen the hungry ocean gain
Advantage on the kingdom of the shore,
And the firm soil win of the watery main,
Increasing store with loss, and loss with store;

When I have seen such interchange of state,
Or state itself confounded to decay,
Ruin hath taught me thus to ruminate—
That Time will come and take my Love away:

—This thought is as a death, which cannot choose
But weep to have that which it fears to lose.

W. Shakespeare

IV

2

Since brass, nor stone, nor earth, nor boundless sea,
But sad mortality o'ersways their power,
How with this rage shall beauty hold a plea,
Whose action is no stronger than a flower?

O how shall summer's honey breath hold out
Against the wreckful siege of battering days,
When rocks impregnable are not so stout
Nor gates of steel so strong, but time decays?

O fearful meditation! where, alack!
Shall Time's best jewel from Time's chest lie hid?

Or what strong hand can hold his swift foot back,
Or who his spoil of beauty can forbid?

O! none, unless this miracle have might,
That in black ink my love may still shine bright.

W. SHAKESPEARE

v

THE PASSIONATE SHEPHERD TO HIS LOVE

Come live with me and be my Love,
And we will all the pleasures prove
That hills and valleys, dale and field,
And all the craggy mountains yield.

There will we sit upon the rocks
And see the shepherds feed their flocks,
By shallow rivers, to whose falls
Melodious birds sing madrigals.

There will I make thee beds of roses
And a thousand fragrant posies,
A cap of flowers, and a kirtle
Embroider'd all with leaves of myrtle.

A gown made of the finest wool,
Which from our pretty lambs we pull,
Fair linéd slippers for the cold,
With buckles of the purest gold.

A belt of straw and ivy buds
With coral clasps and amber studs:
And if these pleasures may thee move,
Come live with me and be my Love.

Thy silver dishes for thy meat
As precious as the gods do eat,
Shall on an ivory table be
Prepared each day for thee and me.

The shepherd swains shall dance and sing
For thy delight each May-morning:
If these delights thy mind may move,
Then live with me and be my Love.

C. MARLOWE

VI

A MADRIGAL

Crabbed Age and Youth
Cannot live together:
Youth is full of pleasance,
Age is full of care;
Youth like summer morn,
Age like winter weather,
Youth like summer brave,
Age like winter bare:
Youth is full of sport,
Age's breath is short,
Youth is nimble, Age is lame:
Youth is hot and bold,
Age is weak and cold,
Youth is wild, and Age is tame:—
Age, I do abhor thee,
Youth, I do adore thee;
O! my Love, my Love is young!
Age, I do defy thee—
O sweet shepherd, hie thee,
For methinks thou stay'st too long.

W. SHAKESPEARE

VII

Under the greenwood tree
Who loves to lie with me,
And tune his merry note
Unto the sweet bird's throat—

Come hither, come hither, come hither!
　　　Here shall he see
　　　No enemy
But winter and rough weather.

　　Who doth ambition shun
　　And loves to live i' the sun,
　　Seeking the food he eats
　　And pleased with what he gets—
Come hither, come hither, come hither!
　　　Here shall he see
　　　No enemy
But winter and rough weather.

　　　　　　　　　W. SHAKESPEARE

VIII

It was a lover and his lass
　With a hey and a ho, and a hey-nonino!
That o'er the green corn-field did pass
In the spring time, the only pretty ring time,
When birds do sing hey ding a ding:
　Sweet lovers love the Spring.

Between the acres of the rye
These pretty country folks would lie:
This carol they began that hour,
How that life was but a flower:

And therefore take the present time
　With a hey and a ho and a hey-nonino!
For love is crownéd with the prime
In the spring time, the only pretty ring time,
When birds do sing hey ding a ding:
　Sweet lovers love the Spring.

　　　　　　　　　W. SHAKESPEARE

IX

PRESENT IN ABSENCE

Absence, hear thou my protestation
 Against thy strength,
 Distance, and length;
Do what thou canst for alteration:
 For hearts of truest mettle
Absence doth join, and Time doth settle.

Who loves a mistress of such quality,
 His mind hath found
 Affection's ground
Beyond time, place, and all mortality.
 To hearts that cannot vary
Absence is present, Time doth tarry.

By absence this good means I gain,
 That I can catch her,
 Where none can watch her,
In some close corner of my brain:
 There I embrace and kiss her:
And so enjoy her and none miss her.

ANON.

X

ABSENCE

Being your slave, what should I do but tend
Upon the hours and times of your desire?
I have no precious time at ail to spend
Nor services to do, till you require:

Nor dare I chide the world-without-end-hour
Whilst I, my sovereign, watch the clock for you,
Nor think the bitterness of absence sour
When you have bid your servant once adieu:

Nor dare I question with my jealous thought
Where you may be, or your affairs suppose,
But like a sad slave, stay and think of nought
Save, where you are, how happy you make those;—

So true a fool is love, that in your will
Though you do anything, he thinks no ill.

W. SHAKESPEARE

XI

How like a winter hath my absence been
From Thee, the pleasure of the fleeting year!
What freezings have I felt, what dark days seen,
What old December's bareness everywhere!

And yet this time removed was summer's time:
The teeming autumn, big with rich increase,
Bearing the wanton burden of the prime
Like widow'd wombs after their lords' decease:

Yet this abundant issue seem'd to me
But hope of orphans, and unfather'd fruit;
For summer and his pleasures wait on thee,
And, thou away, the very birds are mute;

Or if they sing, 'tis with so dull a cheer,
That leaves look pale, dreading the winter's near.

W. SHAKESPEARE

XII

A CONSOLATION

When in disgrace with fortune and men's eyes
I all alone beweep my outcast state,
And trouble deaf heaven with my bootless cries,
And look upon myself, and curse my fate;

Wishing me like to one more rich in hope,
Featured like him, like him with friends possest,
Desiring this man's art, and that man's scope,
With what I most enjoy contented least;

Yet in these thoughts myself almost despising,
Haply I think on Thee—and then my state,
Like to the lark at break of day arising
From sullen earth, sings hymns at heaven's gate;

For thy sweet love remember'd, such wealth brings
That then I scorn to change my state with kings.

W. Shakespeare

XIII

THE UNCHANGEABLE

O never say that I was false of heart,
Though absence seem'd my flame to qualify:
As easy might I from myself depart
As from my soul, which in thy breast doth lie;

That is my home of love; if I have ranged,
Like him that travels, I return again,
Just to the time, not with the time exchanged,
So that myself bring water for my stain.

Never believe, though in my nature reign'd
All frailties that besiege all kinds of blood,
That it could so preposterously be stain'd
To leave for nothing all thy sum of good:

For nothing this wide universe I call,
Save thou, my rose: in it thou art my all.

W. Shakespeare

XIV

To me, fair Friend, you never can be old,
For as you were when first your eye I eyed
Such seems your beauty still.   Three winters' cold
Have from the forests shook three summers' pride;

Three beauteous springs to yellow autumn turn'd
In process of the seasons have I seen,
Three April perfumes in three hot Junes burn'd,
Since first I saw you fresh, which yet are green.

Ah! yet doth beauty, like a dial-hand,
Steal from his figure, and no pace perceived;
So your sweet hue, which methinks still doth stand,
Hath motion, and mine eye may be deceived:

For fear of which, hear this, thou age unbred,—
Ere you were born, was beauty's summer dead.

W. SHAKESPEARE

XV
DIAPHENIA

Diaphenia like the daffadowndilly,
White as the sun, fair as the lily,
Heigh ho, how I do love thee!
I do love thee as my lambs
Are belovéd of their dams;
How blest were I if thou would'st prove me.

Diaphenia like the spreading roses,
That in thy sweets all sweets encloses,
Fair sweet, how I do love thee!
I do love thee as each flower
Loves the sun's life-giving power;
For dead, thy breath to life might move me.

Diaphenia like to all things blesséd,
When all thy praises are expresséd,

Dear joy, how I do love thee!
As the birds do love the spring,
Or the bees their careful king:
Then in requite, sweet virgin, love me!

H. Constable

XVI
ROSALINE

Like to the clear in highest sphere
Where all imperial glory shines,
Of selfsame colour is her hair
Whether unfolded, or in twines:
   Heigh ho, fair Rosaline!
Her eyes are sapphires set in snow
Resembling heaven by every wink;
The Gods do fear whenas they glow,
And I do tremble when I think
   Heigh ho, would she were mine!

Her cheeks are like the blushing cloud
That beautifies Aurora's face,
Or like the silver crimson shroud
That Phœbus' smiling looks doth grace
   Heigh ho, fair Rosaline!
Her lips are like two budded roses
Whom ranks of lilies neighbour nigh,
Within which bounds she balm encloses
Apt to entice a deity:
   Heigh ho, would she were mine!

Her neck is like a stately tower
Where Love himself imprison'd lies,
To watch for glances every hour
From her divine and sacred eyes:
   Heigh ho, for Rosaline!
Her paps are centres of delight,
Her breasts are orbs of heavenly frame,
Where Nature moulds the dew of light

To feed perfection with the same:
    Heigh ho, would she were mine!

With orient pearl, with ruby red,
With marble white, with sapphire blue
Her body every way is fed,
Yet soft in touch and sweet in view:
    Heigh ho, fair Rosaline!
Nature herself her shape admires;
The Gods are wounded in her sight;
And Love forsakes his heavenly fires
And at her eyes his brand doth light:
    Heigh ho, would she were mine!

Then muse not, Nymphs, though I bemoan
The absence of fair Rosaline,
Since for a fair there's fairer none,
Nor for her virtues so divine:
    Heigh ho, fair Rosaline;
Heigh ho, my heart! would God that she were mine!

                       T. LODGE

XVII
COLIN

Beauty sat bathing by a spring
    Where fairest shades did hide her;
The winds blew calm, the birds did sing,
    The cool streams ran beside her.
My wanton thoughts enticed mine eye
    To see what was forbidden:
But better memory said, fie!
    So vain desire was chidden:—
        Hey nonny nonny O!
        Hey nonny nonny!

Into a slumber then I fell,
    When fond imagination
Seeméd to see, but could not tell
    Her feature or her fashion.

But ev'n as babes in dreams do smile,
   And sometimes fall a-weeping,
So I awaked, as wise this while
   As when I fell a-sleeping:—
      Hey nonny nonny O!
      Hey nonny nonny!
            THE SHEPHERD TONIE

XVIII
TO HIS LOVE

Shall I compare thee to a summer's day?
Thou art more lovely and more temperate;
Rough winds do shake the darling buds of May,
And summer's lease hath all too short a date:

Sometimes too hot the eye of heaven shines,
And often is his gold complexion dimm'd:
And every fair from fair sometime declines,
By chance, or nature's changing course, untrimm'd:

But thy eternal summer shall not fade
Nor lose possession of that fair thou owest;
Nor shall Death brag thou wanderest in his shade
When in eternal lines to time thou growest.

So long as men can breathe, or eyes can see
So long lives this, and this gives life to thee.
            W. SHAKESPEARE

XIX
TO HIS LOVE

When in the chronicle of wasted time
I see descriptions of the fairest wights,
And beauty making beautiful old rhyme
In praise of ladies dead, and lovely knights;

Then in the blazon of sweet beauty's best
Of hand, of foot, of lip, of eye, of brow,
I see their antique pen would have exprest
Ev'n such a beauty as you master now.

So all their praises are but prophecies
Of this our time, all, you prefiguring;
And for they look'd but with divining eyes,
They had not skill enough your worth to sing!

For we, which now behold these present days,
Have eyes to wonder, but lack tongues to praise.

W. SHAKESPEARE

XX
LOVE'S PERJURIES

On a day, alack the day!
Love, whose month is ever May,
Spied a blossom passing fair
Playing in the wanton air:
Through the velvet leaves the wind,
All unseen, 'gan passage find;
That the lover, sick to death,
Wish'd himself the heaven's breath.
Air, quoth he, they cheeks may blow;
Air, would I might triumph so!
But, alack, my hand is sworn
Ne'er to pluck thee from thy thorn:
Vow, alack, for youth unmeet;
Youth so apt to pluck a sweet.
Do not call it sin in me
That I am forsworn for thee:
Thou for whom e'en Jove would swear
Juno but an Ethiope were,
And deny himself for Jove,
Turning mortal for thy love.

W. SHAKESPEARE

XXI
A SUPPLICATION

Forget not yet the tried intent
Of such a truth as I have meant;
My great travail so gladly spent,
        Forget not yet!

Forget not yet when first began
The weary life ye know, since whan
The suit, the service none tell can;
      Forget not yet!

Forget not yet the great assays,
The cruel wrong, the scornful ways,
The painful patience in delays,
      Forget not yet!

Forget not! O, forget not this,
How long ago hath been, and is
The mind that never meant amiss—
      Forget not yet!

Forget not then thine own approved
The which so long hath thee so loved,
Whose steadfast faith yet never moved—
      Forget not this!

SIR T. WYAT

XXII

TO AURORA

O if thou knew'st how thou thyself dost harm,
And dost prejudge thy bliss, and spoil my rest;
Then thou would'st melt the ice out of thy breast
And thy relenting heart would kindly warm.

O if thy pride did not our joys controul,
What world of loving wonders should'st thou see!
For if I saw thee once transform'd in me,
Then in thy bosom I would pour my soul;

Then all my thoughts should in thy visage shine,
And if that aught mischanced thou should'st not moan
Nor bear the burthen of thy griefs alone;
No, I would have my share in what were thine:

And whilst we thus should make our sorrows one,
This happy harmony would make them none.

W. ALEXANDER, EARL OF STERLINE

TRUE LOVE

Let me not to the marriage of true minds
Admit impediments.   Love is not love
Which alters when it alteration finds,
Or bends with the remover to remove:—

O no! it is an ever-fixéd mark
That looks on tempests, and is never shaken;
It is the star to every wandering bark,
Whose worth's unknown, although his height be taken.

Love's not Time's fool, though rosy lips and cheeks
Within his bending sickle's compass come;
Love alters not with his brief hours and weeks,
But bears it out ev'n to the edge of doom:—

If this be error, and upon me proved,
I never writ, nor no man ever loved.
                              W. SHAKESPEARE

A DITTY

My true-love hath my heart, and I have his,
By just exchange one for another given:
I hold his dear, and mine he cannot miss,
There never was a better bargain driven:
    My true-love hath my heart, and I have his.

His heart in me keeps him and me in one,
My heart in him his thoughts and senses guides:
He loves my heart, for once it was his own,
I cherish his because in me it bides:
    My true-love hath my heart, and I have his.
                              SIR P. SIDNEY

XXV
LOVE'S OMNIPRESENCE

Were I as base as is the lowly plain,
And you, my Love, as high as heaven above,
Yet should the thoughts of me your humble swain
Ascend to heaven, in honour of my Love.

Were I as high as heaven above the plain,
And you, my Love, as humble and as low
As are the deepest bottoms of the main,
Whereso'er you were, with you my love should go.

Were you the earth, dear Love, and I the skies,
My love should shine on you like to the sun,
And look upon you with ten thousand eyes
Till heaven wax'd blind, and till the world were done.

Whereso'er I am, below, or else above you,
Whereso'er you are, my heart shall truly love you.
J. SYLVESTER

XXVI
CARPE DIEM

O Mistress mine, where are you roaming?
O stay and hear! your true-love's coming
That can sing both high and low;
Trip no further, pretty sweeting,
Journeys end in lovers' meeting—
Every wise man's son doth know.

What is love? 'tis not hereafter;
Present mirth hath present laughter;
What's to come is still unsure:
In delay there lies no plenty,—
Then come kiss me, Sweet-and-twenty,
Youth's a stuff will not endure.
W. SHAKESPEARE

XXVII
WINTER

When icicles hang by the wall
   And Dick the shepherd blows his nail,
And Tom bears logs into the hall,
   And milk comes frozen home in pail;
When blood is nipt, and ways be foul,
Then nightly sings the staring owl
          Tu-whoo!
To-whit, Tu-whoo!   A merry note!
While greasy Joan doth keel the pot.

When all about the wind doth blow,
   And coughing drowns the parson's saw,
And birds sit brooding in the snow,
   And Marian's nose looks red and raw;
When roasted crabs hiss in the bowl—
Then nightly sings the staring owl
          Tu-whoo!
To-whit, Tu-whoo!   A merry note!
While greasy Joan doth keel the pot.

W. SHAKESPEARE

XXVIII

That time of year thou may'st in me behold
When yellow leaves, or none, or few, do hang
Upon those boughs which shake against the cold,
Bare ruin'd choirs, where late the sweet birds sang:

In me thou see'st the twilight of such day
As after sunset fadeth in the west,
Which by and by black night doth take away,
Death's second self, that seals up all in rest:

In me thou seest the glowing of such fire,
That on the ashes of his youth doth lie
As the deathbed whereon it must expire,
Consumed with that which it was nourish'd by:

—This thou perceiv'st, which makes thy love more
    strong,
To love that well which thou must leave ere long.
W. Shakespeare

xxix
REMEMBRANCE

When to the sessions of sweet silent thought
I summon up remembrance of things past,
I sigh the lack of many a thing I sought,
And with old woes new wail my dear time's waste;

Then can I drown an eye, unused to flow,
For precious friends hid in death's dateless night,
And weep afresh love's long-since-cancell'd woe,
And moan the expense of many a vanish'd sight.

Then can I grieve at grievances foregone,
And heavily from woe to woe tell o'er
The sad account of fore-bemoanéd moan,
Which I new pay as if not paid before:

—But if the while I think on thee, dear friend,
All losses are restored, and sorrows end.
W. Shakespeare

xxx
REVOLUTIONS

Like as the waves make towards the pebbled shore
So do our minutes hasten to their end;
Each changing place with that which goes before,
In sequent toil all forwards do contend.

Nativity once in the main of light,
Crawls to maturity, wherewith being crown'd,
Crooked eclipses 'gainst his glory fight,
And Time that gave, doth now his gift confound.

Time doth transfix the flourish set on youth,
And delves the parallels in beauty's brow;
Feeds on the rarities of nature's truth,
And nothing stands but for his scythe to mow:—

And yet, to times in hope, my verse shall stand
Praising Thy worth, despite his cruel hand.

W. SHAKESPEARE

XXXI

Farewell! thou art too dear for my possessing,
And like enough thou know'st thy estimate:
The charter of thy worth gives thee releasing;
My bonds in thee are all determinate.

For how do I hold thee but by thy granting?
And for that riches where is my deserving?
The cause of this fair gift in me is wanting,
And so my patent back again is swerving.

Thyself thou gav'st, thy own worth then not knowing,
Or me, to whom thou gav'st it, else mistaking;
So thy great gift, upon misprision growing,
Comes home again, on better judgment making.

Thus have I had thee as a dream doth flatter;
In sleep, a king; but waking, no such matter.

W. SHAKESPEARE

XXXII

THE LIFE WITHOUT PASSION

They that have power to hurt, and will do none,
That do not do the thing they most do show,
Who, moving others, are themselves as stone,
Unmovéd, cold, and to temptation slow,—

They rightly do inherit heaven's graces,
And husband nature's riches from expense;
They are the lords and owners of their faces,
Others, but stewards of their excellence.

The summer's flower is to the summer sweet
Though to itself it only live and die;
But if that flower with base infection meet,
The basest weed outbraves his dignity:

For sweetest things turn sourest by their deeds;
Lilies that fester smell far worse than weeds.

W. SHAKESPEARE

XXXIII

THE LOVER'S APPEAL

And wilt thou leave me thus?
Say nay! say nay! for shame,
To save thee from the blame
Of all my grief and grame.
And wilt thou leave me thus?
Say nay! say nay!

And wilt thou leave me thus,
That hath loved thee so long
In wealth and woe among:
And is thy heart so strong
As for to leave me thus?
Say nay! say nay!

And wilt thou leave me thus,
That hath given thee my heart
Never for to depart
Neither for pain nor smart:
And wilt thou leave me thus?
Say nay! say nay!

And wilt thou leave me thus,
And have no more pity
Of him that loveth thee?
Alas! thy cruelty!
And wilt thou leave me thus?
Say nay! say nay!

SIR T. WYAT

XXXIV

THE NIGHTINGALE

As it fell upon a day
In the merry month of May,
Sitting in a pleasant shade
Which a grove of myrtles made,
Beasts did leap and birds did sing,
Trees did grow and plants did spring;
Every thing did banish moan
Save the Nightingale alone.
She, poor bird, as all forlorn,
Lean'd her breast against a thorn,
And there sung the dolefull'st ditty
That to hear it was great pity.
Fie, fie, fie, now would she cry;
Tereu, tereu, by and by:
That to hear her so complain
Scarce I could from tears refrain;
For her griefs so lively shown
Made me think upon mine own.
—Ah, thought I, thou mourn'st in vain,
None takes pity on thy pain:
Senseless trees, they cannot hear thee,
Ruthless beasts, they will not cheer thee;
King Pandion, he is dead,
All thy friends are lapp'd in lead:
All thy fellow birds do sing
Careless of thy sorrowing:
Even so, poor bird, like thee
None alive will pity me.

R. Barnefield

XXXV

Care-charmer Sleep, son of the sable Night,
Brother to Death, in silent darkness born,
Relieve my languish, and restore the light;
With dark forgetting of my care return.

And let the day be time enough to mourn
The shipwreck of my illadventured youth:
Let waking eyes suffice to wail their scorn,
Without the torment of the night's untruth.

Cease, dreams, the images of day-desires,
To model forth the passions of the morrow;
Never let rising Sun approve you liars,
To add more grief to aggravate my sorrow:

Still let me sleep, embracing clouds in vain,
And never wake to feel the day's disdain.
S. DANIEL

XXXVI
MADRIGAL

Take, O take those lips away
That so sweetly were forsworn,
And those eyes, the break of day,
Lights that do mislead the morn:
But my kisses bring again,
        Bring again—
Seals of love, but seal'd in vain,
        Seal'd in vain!
W. SHAKESPEARE

XXXVII
LOVE'S FAREWELL

Since there's no help, come let us kiss and part,—
Nay I have done, you get no more of me;
And I am glad, yea, glad with all my heart,
That thus so cleanly I myself can free;

Shake hands for ever, cancel all our vows,
And when we meet at any time again,
Be it not seen in either of our brows
That we one jot of former love retain.

Now at the last gasp of love's latest breath,
When his pulse failing, passion speechless lies,
When faith is kneeling by his bed of death,
And innocence is closing up his eyes,

—Now if thou would'st, when all have given him over,
From death to life thou might'st him yet recover!

M. DRAYTON

XXXVIII
TO HIS LUTE

My lute, be as thou wert when thou didst grow
With thy green mother in some shady grove,
When immelodious winds but made thee move,
And birds their ramage did on thee bestow.

Since that dear Voice which did thy sounds approve,
Which wont in such harmonious strains to flow,
Is reft from Earth to tune those spheres above,
What art thou but a harbinger of woe?

Thy pleasing notes be pleasing notes no more,
But orphans' wailings to the fainting ear;
Each stroke a sigh, each sound draws forth a tear
For which be silent as in woods before:

Or if that any hand to touch thee deign,
Like widow'd turtle still her loss complain.

W. DRUMMOND

XXXIX
BLIND LOVE

O me! what eyes hath love put in my head
Which have no correspondence with true sight:
Or if they have, where is my judgment fled
That censures falsely what they see aright?

If that be fair whereon my false eyes dote,
What means the world to say it is not so?
If it be not, then love doth well denote
Love's eye is not so true as all men's: No,

How can it? O how can love's eye be true,
That is so vex'd with watching and with tears?
No marvel then though I mistake my view:
The sun itself sees not till heaven clears.

O cunning Love! with tears thou keep'st me blind
Lest eyes well-seeing thy foul faults should find!

W. SHAKESPEARE

XL
THE UNFAITHFUL SHEPHERDESS

While that the sun with his beams hot
Scorchéd the fruits in vale and mountain,
Philon the shepherd, late forgot,
Sitting beside a crystal fountain,
  In shadow of a green oak tree
  Upon his pipe this song play'd he:
Adieu Love, adieu Love, untrue Love;
Untrue Love, untrue Love, adieu Love;
Your mind is light, soon lost for new love.

So long as I was in your sight
I was your heart, your soul, and treasure;
And evermore you sobb'd and sigh'd
Burning in flames beyond all measure:
  —Three days endured your love to me,
  And it was lost in other three!
Adieu Love, adieu Love, untrue Love,
Untrue Love, untrue Love, adieu Love
Your mind is light, soon lost for new love.

Another Shepherd you did see
To whom your heart was soon enchainéd;

Full soon your love was leapt from me,
Full soon my place he had obtainéd.
    Soon came a third, your love to win,
    And we were out and he was in.
Adieu Love, adieu Love, untrue Love,
Untrue Love, untrue Love, adieu Love;
Your mind is light, soon lost for new love.

Sure you have made me passing glad
That you your mind so soon removéd,
Before that I the leisure had
To choose you for my best belovéd:
    For all your love was past and done
    Two days before it was begun:—
Adieu Love, adieu Love, untrue Love,
Untrue Love, untrue Love, adieu Love;
Your mind is light, soon lost for new love.

ANON.

XLI

A RENUNCIATION

If women could be fair, and yet not fond,
Or that their love were firm, not fickle still,
I would not marvel that they make men bond
By service long to purchase their good will;
But when I see how frail those creatures are,
I muse that men forget themselves so far.

To mark the choice they make, and how they change,
How oft from Phoebus they do flee to Pan;
Unsettled still, like haggards wild they range,
These gentle birds that fly from man to man;
Who would not scorn and shake them from the fist,
And let them fly, fair fools, which way they list?

Yet for disport we fawn and flatter both,
To pass the time when nothing else can please,

And train them to our lure with subtle oath,
Till, weary of their wiles, ourselves we ease;
And then we say when we their fancy try,
To play with fools, O what a fool was I!

E. VERE, EARL OF OXFORD

XLII

Blow, blow, thou winter wind,
Thou art not so unkind
As man's ingratitude;
Thy tooth is not so keen
Because thou art not seen,
Although thy breath be rude.
Heigh ho! sing heigh ho! unto the green holly:
Most friendship is feigning, most loving mere folly:
Then, heigh ho! the holly!
This life is most jolly.

Freeze, freeze, thou bitter sky,
Thou dost not bite so nigh
As benefits forgot:
Though thou the waters warp,
Thy sting is not so sharp
As friend remember'd not.
Heigh ho! sing heigh ho! unto the green holly:
Most friendship is feigning, most loving mere folly:
Then, heigh ho! the holly!
This life is most jolly.

W. SHAKESPEARE

XLIII
MADRIGAL

My thoughts hold mortal strife;
I do detest my life,
And with lamenting cries
Peace to my soul to bring
Oft call that prince which here doth monarchize:
—But he, grim grinning King,

Who caitiffs scorns, and doth the blest surprize,
Late having deck'd with beauty's rose his tomb,
Disdains to crop a weed, and will not come.

W. DRUMMOND

XLIV
DIRGE OF LOVE

Come away, come away, Death,
And in sad cypres let me be laid;
  Fly away, fly away, breath;
I am slain by a fair cruel maid.
My shroud of white, stuck all with yew,
        O prepare it!
My part of death no one so true
        Did share it.

  Not a flower, not a flower sweet
On my black coffin let there be strown;
  Not a friend, not a friend greet
My poor corpse, where my bones shall be thrown;
A thousand thousand sighs to save,
        Lay me, O where
Sad true lover never find my grave,
        To weep there.

W. SHAKESPEARE

XLV
FIDELE

Fear no more the heat o' the sun
        Nor the furious winter's rages;
Thou thy worldly task hast done,
        Home art gone and ta'en thy wages:
Golden lads and girls all must,
As chimney-sweepers, come to dust.

Fear no more the frown o' the great,
        Thou art past the tyrant's stroke;

Care no more to clothe and eat;
    To thee the reed is as the oak:
The sceptre, learning, physic, must
All follow this, and come to dust.

Fear no more the lightning-flash
    Nor the all-dreaded thunder-stone;
Fear not slander, censure rash;
    Thou hast finish'd joy and moan:
All lovers young, all lovers must
Consign to thee, and come to dust.

W. Shakespeare

XLVI

A SEA DIRGE

Full fathom five thy father lies:
    Of his bones are coral made;
Those are pearls that were his eyes:
    Nothing of him that doth fade,
But doth suffer a sea-change
Into something rich and strange.
Sea-nymphs hourly ring his knell:
    Hark! now I hear them,—
        Ding, dong, Bell.

W. Shakespeare

XLVII

A LAND DIRGE

Call for the robin-redbreast and the wren,
Since o'er shady groves they hover
And with leaves and flowers do cover
The friendless bodies of unburied men.
Call unto his funeral dole
The ant, the field-mouse, and the mole
To rear him hillocks that shall keep him warm
And (when gay tombs are robb'd) sustain no harm;
But keep the wolf far hence, that's foe to men,
For with his nails he'll dig them up again.

J. Webster

XLVIII
POST MORTEM

If Thou survive my well-contented day
When that churl Death my bones with dust shall cover,
And shalt by fortune once more re-survey
These poor rude lines of thy deceaséd lover;

Compare them with the bettering of the time,
And though they be outstripp'd be every pen,
Reserve them for my love, not for their rhyme
Exceeded by the height of happier men.

O then vouchsafe me but this loving thought—
'Had my friend's muse grown with this growing age,
A dearer birth than this his love had brought,
To march in ranks of better equipage:

But since he died, and poets better prove,
Theirs for their style I'll read, his for his love.'

W. Shakespeare

XLIX
THE TRIUMPH OF DEATH

No longer mourn for me when I am dead
Than you shall hear the surly sullen bell
Give warning to the world, that I am fled
From this vile world, with vilest worms to dwell;

Nay, if you read this line, remember not
The hand that writ it; for I love you so,
That I in your sweet thoughts would be forgot
If thinking on me then should make you woe.

O if, I say, you look upon this verse
When I perhaps compounded am with clay,
Do not so much as my poor name rehearse,
But let your love even with my life decay;

Lest the wise world should look into your moan,
And mock you with me after I am gone.

W. Shakespeare

L

MADRIGAL

Tell me where is Fancy bred,
Or in the heart, or in the head?
How begot, how nourishéd?
      Reply, reply.

It is engender'd in the eyes;
With gazing fed; and Fancy dies
In the cradle where it lies:
Let us all ring Fancy's knell;
I'll begin it,—Ding, dong, bell.
      —Ding, dong, bell.
          W. SHAKESPEARE

LI

CUPID AND CAMPASPE

Cupid and my Campaspe play'd
At cards for kisses; Cupid paid:
He stakes his quiver, bow, and arrows,
His mother's doves, and team of sparrows;
Loses them too; then down he throws
The coral of his lip, the rose
Growing on's cheek (but none knows how);
With these, the crystal of his brow,
And then the dimple on his chin;
All these did my Campaspe win:
And last he set her both his eyes—
She won, and Cupid blind did rise.
    O Love! has she done this to thee?
    What shall, alas! become of me?
          J. LYLYE

LII

Pack, clouds, away, and welcome day,
    With night we banish sorrow;

Sweet air blow soft, mount larks aloft
    To give my Love good-morrow!
Wings from the wind to please her mind
    Notes from the lark I'll borrow;
Bird, prune thy wing, nightingale sing,
    To give my Love good-morrow;
      To give my Love good-morrow
      Notes from them both I'll borrow.

Wake from thy nest, Robin-red-breast,
    Sing, birds, in every furrow;
And from each hill, let music shrill
    Give my fair Love good-morrow!
Blackbird and thrush in every bush,
    Stare, linnet, and cock-sparrow!
You pretty elves, amongst yourselves
    Sing my fair Love good-morrow;
      To give my Love good-morrow
      Sing, birds, in every furrow!

               T. Heywood

LIII

PROTHALAMION

Calm was the day, and through the trembling air
Sweet-breathing Zephyrus did softly play—
A gentle spirit, that lightly did delay
Hot Titan's beams, which then did glister fair;
When I, (whom sullen care,
Through discontent of my long fruitless stay
In princes' court, and expectation vain
Of idle hopes, which still do fly away
Like empty shadows, did afflict my brain)
Walk'd forth to ease my pain
Along the shore of silver-streaming Thames;
Whose rutty bank, the which his river hems,
Was painted all with variable flowers,
And all the meads adorn'd with dainty gems

Fit to deck maidens' bowers,
And crown their paramours
Against the bridal day, which is not long:
  Sweet Thames! run softly, till I end my song.

There in a meadow by the river's side
A flock of nymphs I chancéd to espy,
All lovely daughters of the flood thereby,
With goodly greenish locks all loose untied
As each had been a bride;
And each one had a little wicker basket
Made of fine twigs, entrailéd curiously,
In which they gather'd flowers to fill their flasket,
And with fine fingers cropt full feateously
The tender stalks on high.
Of every sort which in that meadow grew
They gather'd some; the violet, pallid blue,
The little daisy that at evening closes,
The virgin lily and the primrose true:
With store of vermeil roses,
To deck their bridegrooms' posies
Against the bridal day, which was not long:
  Sweet Thames! run softly, till I end my song.

With that I saw two swans of goodly hue
Come softly swimming down along the lee;
Two fairer birds I yet did never see;
The snow which doth the top of Pindus strow
Did never whiter show,
Nor Jove himself, when he a swan would be
For love of Leda, whiter did appear;
Yet Leda was (they say) as white as he,
Yet not so white as these, nor nothing near;
So purely white they were
That even the gentle stream, the which them bare,
Seem'd foul to them, and bade his billows spare
To wet their silken feathers, lest they might

Soil their fair plumes with water not so fair,
And mar their beauties bright
That shone as Heaven's light
Against their bridal day, which was not long:
Sweet Thames! run softly, till I end my song.

Eftsoons the nymphs, which now had flowers their fill,
Ran all in haste to see that silver brood
As they came floating on the crystal flood;
Whom when they saw, they stood amazéd still
Their wondering eyes to fill;
Them seem'd they never saw a sight so fair
Of fowls, so lovely, that they sure did deem
Them heavenly born, or to be that same pair
Which through the sky draw Venus' silver team;
For sure they did not seem
To be begot of any earthly seed,
But rather angels, or of angels' breed;
Yet were they bred of summer's heat, they say,
In sweetest season, when each flower and weed
The earth did fresh array;
So fresh they seem'd as day,
Ev'n as their bridal day, which was not long:
Sweet Thames! run softly, till I end my song.

Then forth they all out of their baskets drew
Great store of flowers, the honour of the field,
That to the sense did fragrant odours yield,
All which upon those goodly birds they threw
And all the waves did strew,
That like old Peneus' waters they did seem
When down along by pleasant Tempe's shore
Scatter'd with flowers, through Thessaly they stream.
That they appear, through lilies' plenteous store,
Like a bride's chamber-floor.
Two of those nymphs meanwhile two garlands bound
Of freshest flowers which in that mead they found,

The which presenting all in trim array,
Their snowy foreheads therewithal they crown'd;
Whilst one did sing this lay
Prepared against that day,
Against their bridal day, which was not long:
    Sweet Thames! run softly till I end my song.

'Ye gentle birds! the world's fair ornament,
And Heaven's glory, whom this happy hour
Doth lead unto your lovers' blissful bower,
Joy may you have, and gentle heart's content
Of your love's complement;
And let fair Venus, that is queen of love,
With her heart-quelling son upon you smile,
Whose smile, they say, hath virtue to remove
All love's dislike, and friendship's faulty guile
For ever to assoil.
Let endless peace your steadfast hearts accord,
And blessed plenty wait upon your board;
And let your bed with pleasures chaste abound,
That fruitful issue may to you afford
Which may your foes confound,
And make your joys redound
Upon your bridal day, which is not long:
    Sweet Thames! run softly, till I end my song.'

So ended she; and all the rest around
To her redoubled that her undersong,
Which said their bridal day should not be long:
And gentle Echo from the neighbour ground
Their accents did resound.
So forth those joyous birds did pass along
Adown the lee that to them murmur'd low,
As he would speak but that he lack'd a tongue;
Yet did by signs his glad affection show,
Making his stream run slow.
And all the fowl which in his flood did dwell

'Gan flock about these twain, that did excel
The rest, so far as Cynthia doth shend
The lesser stars.   So they, enrangéd well,
Did on those two attend,
And their best service lend
Against their wedding day, which was not long:
    Sweet Thames! run softly, till I end my song.

At length they all to merry London came,
To merry London, my most kindly nurse,
That to me gave this life's first native source,
Though from another place I take my name,
An house of ancient fame:
There when they came whereas those bricky towers
The which on Thames' broad aged back do ride,
Where now the studious lawyers have their bowers,
Their whilome wont the Templar-knights to bide,
Till they decay'd through pride;
Next whereunto there stands a stately place,
Where oft I gainéd gifts and goodly grace
Of that great lord, which therein wont to dwell,
Whose want too well now feels my friendless case;
But ah! here fits not well
Old woes, but joys to tell
Against the bridal day, which is not long:
    Sweet Thames! run softly, till I end my song.

Yet therein now doth lodge a noble peer,
Great England's glory and the world's wide wonder,
Whose dreadful name late through all Spain did
     thunder,
And Hercules' two pillars standing near
Did make to quake and fear:
Fair branch of honour, flower of chivalry!
That fillest England with thy triumphs' fame
Joy have thou of thy noble victory,
And endless happiness of thine own name

That promiseth the same;
That through thy prowess and victorious arms
Thy country may be freed from foreign harms,
And great Elisa's glorious name may ring
Through all the world, fill'd with thy wide alarms,
Which some brave Muse may sing
To ages following:
Upon the bridal day, which is not long:
  Sweet Thames! run softly, till I end my song.

From those high towers this noble lord issúing
Like radiant Hesper, when his golden hair
In th' ocean billows he hath bathéd fair,
Descended to the river's open viewing
With a great train ensuing.
Above the rest were goodly to be seen
Two gentle knights of lovely face and feature,
Beseeming well the bower of any queen,
With gifts of wit and ornaments of nature,
Fit for so goodly stature,
That like the twins of Jove they seem'd in sight
Which deck the baldric of the Heavens bright;
They two, forth pacing to the river's side,
Received those two fair brides, their love's delight;
Which, at th' appointed tide,
Each one did make his bride
Against their bridal day, which is not long:
  Sweet Thames! run softly, till I end my song.

E. SPENSER

LIV

THE HAPPY HEART

Art thou poor, yet hast thou golden slumbers?
    O sweet content!
Art thou rich, yet is thy mind perplexéd?
    O punishment!
Dost thou laugh to see how fools are vexéd

To add to golden numbers, golden numbers?
O sweet content! O sweet, O sweet content!
   Work apace, apace, apace, apace;
   Honest labour bears a lovely face;
Then hey nonny nonny, hey nonny nonny!

Canst drink the waters of the crispéd spring?
       O sweet content!
Swimm'st thou in wealth, yet sink'st in thine own tears?
       O punishment!
Then he that patiently want's burden bears
No burden bears, but is a king, a king!
O sweet content! O sweet, O sweet content!
   Work apace, apace, apace, apace;
   Honest labour bears a lovely face;
Then hey nonny nonny, hey nonny nonny!

T. DEKKER

LV

   This Life, which seems so fair,
   Is like a bubble blown up in the air
      By sporting children's breath,
   Who chase it everywhere
And strive who can most motion it bequeath.
And though it sometimes seem of its own might
Like to an eye of gold to be fix'd there,
And firm to hover in that empty height,
   That only is because it is so light.
—But in that pomp it doth not long appear;
For when 'tis most admired, in a thought,
Because it erst was nought, it turns to nought.

W. DRUMMOND

LVI

SOUL AND BODY

Poor Soul, the centre of my sinful earth,
Fool'd by those rebel powers that thee array,
Why dost thou pine within, and suffer dearth,
Painting thy outward walls so costly gay?

Why so large cost, having so short a lease,
Dost thou upon thy fading mansion spend?
Shall worms, inheritors of this excess,
Eat up thy charge? is this thy body's end?

Then, Soul, live thou upon thy servant's loss,
And let that pine to aggravate thy store;
Buy terms divine in selling hours of dross;
Within be fed, without be rich no more:—

So shalt thou feed on death, that feeds on men,
And death once dead, there's no more dying then.

W. SHAKESPEARE

LVII
LIFE

The world's a bubble and the Life of Man
   Less than a span
In his conception wretched, from the womb
   So to the tomb;
Curst from his cradle, and brought up to years
   With cares and fears.
Who then to frail mortality shall trust,
But limns on water, or but writes in dust.

Yet whilst with sorrow here we live opprest,
   What life is best?
Courts are but only superficial schools
   To dandle fools:
The rural parts are turn'd into a den
   Of savage men:
And where's a city from foul vice so free,
But may be termed the worst of all the three?

Domestic cares afflict the husband's bed,
   Or pains his head:
Those that live single, take it for a curse
   Or do things worse:

Some would have children: those that have them moan
　　　　Or wish them gone:
What is it, then, to have, or have no wife,
But single thraldom or a double strife?

But our affections still at home to please
　　　　Is a disease:
To cross the seas to any foreign soil,
　　　　Peril and toil:
Wars with their noise affright us: when they cease,
　　　　We are worse in peace;—
What then remains, but that we still should cry
For being born, or being born, to die?

　　　　　　　　　　　　　　　LORD BACON

LVIII

THE LESSONS OF NATURE

Of this fair volume which we World do name
If we the sheets and leaves could turn with care,
Of him who it corrects, and did it frame,
We clear might read the art and wisdom rare:

Find out his power which wildest powers doth tame,
His providence extending everywhere,
His justice which proud rebels doth not spare,
In every page, no period of the same.

But silly we, like foolish children, rest
Well pleased with colour'd vellum, leaves of gold,
Fair dangling ribbands, leaving what is best,
On the great writer's sense ne'er taking hold;

Or if by chance we stay our minds on aught,
It is some picture on the margin wrought.

　　　　　　　　　　　　　　W. DRUMMOND

LIX

Doth then the world go thus, doth all thus move?
Is this the justice which on Earth we find?

Is this that firm decree which all doth bind?
Are these your influences, Powers above?

Those souls which vice's moody mists most blind,
Blind Fortune, blindly, most their friend doth prove;
And they who thee, poor idol Virtue! love,
Ply like a feather toss'd by storm and wind.

Ah! if a Providence doth sway this all
Why should best minds groan under most distress?
Or why should pride humility make thrall,
And injuries the innocent oppress?

Heavens! hinder, stop this fate; or grant a time
When good may have, as well as bad, their prime!
                                        W. DRUMMOND

LX

THE WORLD'S WAY

Tired with all these, for restful death I cry—
As, to behold desert a beggar born,
And needy nothing trimm'd in jollity,
And purest faith unhappily forsworn,

And gilded honour shamefully misplaced,
And maiden virtue rudely strumpeted,
And right perfection wrongfully disgraced,
And strength by limping sway disabled,

And art made tongue-tied by authority,
And folly, doctor-like, controlling skill,
And simple truth miscall'd simplicity,
And captive Good attending captain Ill:—

—Tired with all these, from these would I be gone,
Save that, to die, I leave my Love alone.
                                        W. SHAKESPEARE

SAINT JOHN BAPTIST

The last and greatest Herald of Heaven's King
Girt with rough skins, hies to the deserts wild,
Among that savage brood the woods forth bring,
Which he more harmless found than man, and mild

His food was locusts, and what there doth spring,
With honey that from virgin hives distill'd;
Parch'd body, hollow eyes, some uncouth thing
Made him appear, long since from earth exiled.

There burst he forth: All ye whose hopes rely
On God, with me amidst these deserts mourn,
Repent, repent, and from old errors turn!
—Who listen'd to his voice, obey'd his cry?

Only the echoes, which he made relent,
Rung from their flinty caves, Repent! Repent!

W. DRUMMOND

BOOK SECOND

ODE ON THE MORNING OF CHRIST'S NATIVITY

This is the month, and this the happy morn
Wherein the Son of Heaven's Eternal King
Of wedded maid and virgin mother born,
Our great redemption from above did bring;
For so the holy sages once did sing
That he our deadly forfeit should release,
And with his Father work us a perpetual peace.

That glorious Form, that Light unsufferable,
And that far-beaming blaze of Majesty
Wherewith he wont at Heaven's high council-table
To sit the midst of Trinal Unity,
He laid aside; and, here with us to be,
Forsook the courts of everlasting day,
And chose with us a darksome house of mortal clay.

Say, heavenly Muse, shall not thy sacred vein
Afford a present to the Infant God?
Hast thou no verse, no hymn, or solemn strain
To welcome him to this his new abode,
Now while the heaven, by the sun's team untrod,
Hath took no print of the approaching light,
And all the spangled host keep watch in squadrons
      bright?

See how from far, upon the eastern road,
The star-led wizards haste with odours sweet:
O run, prevent them with thy humble ode
And lay it lowly at his blessed feet;
Have thou the honour first thy Lord to greet,
And join thy voice unto the angel quire
From out his secret altar touch'd with hallow'd fire.

THE HYMN

It was the winter wild
While the heaven-born Child
All meanly wrapt in the rude manger lies;
Nature in awe to Him
Had doff'd her gaudy trim,
With her great Master so to sympathize:
It was no season then for her
To wanton with the sun, her lusty paramour.

Only with speeches fair
She woos the gentle air
To hide her guilty front with innocent snow;
And on her naked shame,
Pollute with sinful blame,
The saintly veil of maiden white to throw;
Confounded, that her Maker's eyes
Should look so near upon her foul deformities.

But he, her fears to cease,
Sent down the meek-eyed Peace;
She, crown'd with olive green, came softly sliding
Down through the turning sphere,
His ready harbinger,
With turtle wing the amorous clouds dividing;
And waving wide her myrtle wand,
She strikes a universal peace through sea and land.

No war, or battle's sound
Was heard the world around:
The idle spear and shield were high uphung;
The hookéd chariot stood
Unstain'd with hostile blood;
The trumpet spake not to the arméd throng;
And kings sat still with awful eye,
As if they surely knew their sovran Lord was by.

But peaceful was the night
Wherein the Prince of Light
His reign of peace upon the earth began:
The winds, with wonder whist,
Smoothly the waters kist
Whispering new joys to the mild oceán—
Who now hath quite forgot to rave,
While birds of calm sit brooding on the charméd wave

The stars, with deep amaze,
Stand fix'd in steadfast gaze,
Bending one way their precious influence;
And will not take their flight
For all the morning light,
Or Lucifer that often warn'd them thence;
But in their glimmering orbs did glow
Until their Lord himself bespake, and bid them go.

And though the shady gloom
Had given day her room,
The sun himself withheld his wonted speed,
And hid his head for shame,
As his inferior flame
The new-enlighten'd world no more should need;
He saw a greater Sun appear
Than his bright throne, or burning axletree, could bear

The shepherds on the lawn
Or ere the point of dawn
Sate simply chatting in a rustic row;
Full little thought they then
That the mighty Pan
Was kindly come to live with them below;
Perhaps their loves, or else their sheep
Was all that did their silly thoughts so busy keep.

When such music sweet
Their hearts and ears did greet
As never was by mortal finger strook—

Divinely-warbled voice
Answering the stringéd noise,
As all their souls in blissful rapture took:
The air, such pleasure loth to lose,
With thousand echoes still prolongs each heavenly close.

Nature, that heard such sound
Beneath the hollow round
Of Cynthia's seat the airy region thrilling,
Now was almost won
To think her part was done,
And that her reign had here its last fulfilling,
She knew such harmony alone
Could hold all heaven and earth in happier union.

At last surrounds their sight
A globe of circular light
That with long beams the shamefaced night array'd;
The helméd Cherubim
And sworded Seraphim
Are seen in glittering ranks with wings display'd,
Harping in loud and solemn quire
With unexpressive notes, to Heaven's new-born Heir.

Such music (as 'tis said)
Before was never made
But when of old the sons of morning sung,
While the Creator great
His constellations set
And the well-balanced world on hinges hung;
And cast the dark foundations deep,
And bid the weltering waves their oozy channel keep.

Ring out, ye crystal spheres!
Once bless our human ears,
If ye have power to touch our senses so;
And let your silver chime
Move in melodious time;
And let the base of heaven's deep organ blow;

And with your ninefold harmony
Make up full consort to the angelic symphony.

For if such holy song
Enwrap our fancy long,
Time will run back, and fetch the age of gold;
And speckled vanity
Will sicken soon and die,
And leprous sin will melt from earthly mould;
And Hell itself will pass away,
And leave her dolorous mansions to the peering day.

Yea, Truth and Justice then
Will down return to men,
Orb'd in a rainbow; and, like glories wearing,
Mercy will sit between
Throned in celestial sheen,
With radiant feet the tissued clouds down steering;
And Heaven, as at some festival,
Will open wide the gates of her high palace hall.

But wisest Fate says No;
This must not yet be so;
The Babe yet lies in smiling infancy
That on the bitter cross
Must redeem our loss;
So both himself and us to glorify:
Yet first, to those ychain'd in sleep
The wakeful trump of doom must thunder through
    the deep;
With such a horrid clang
As on Mount Sinai rang
While the red fire and smouldering clouds outbrake:
The aged Earth aghast
With terror of that blast
Shall from the surface to the centre shake,
When, at the world's last sessión,
The dreadful Judge in middle air shall spread His
    throne.

And then at last our bliss
Full and perfect is,
But now begins; for from this happy day
The old Dragon under ground,
In straiter limits bound,
Not half so far casts his usurpéd sway;
And, wroth to see his kingdom fail,
Swinges the scaly horrour of his folded tail.

The oracles are dumb;
No voice or hideous hum
Runs through the archéd roof in words deceiving.
Apollo from his shrine
Can no more divine,
With hollow shriek the steep of Delphos leaving:
No nightly trance or breathéd spell
Inspires the pale-eyed priest from the prophetic cell.

The lonely mountains o'er
And the resounding shore
A voice of weeping heard, and loud lament;
From haunted spring and dale
Edged with poplar pale
The parting Genius is with sighing sent;
With flower-inwoven tresses torn
The Nymphs in twilight shade of tangled thickets
     mourn.

In consecrated earth
And on the holy hearth
The Lars and Lemurés moan with midnight plaint;
In urns, and altars round
A drear and dying sound
Affrights the Flamens at their service quaint;
And the chill marble seems to sweat,
While each peculiar Power foregoes his wonted seat.

Peor and Baalim
Forsake their temples dim,

With that twice-batter'd god of Palestine
And moonéd Ashtaroth
Heaven's queen and mother both,
Now sits not girt with tapers' holy shine;
The Lybic Hammon shrinks his horn:
In vain the Tyrian maids their wounded Thammuz
    mourn.

And sullen Moloch, fled,
Hath left in shadows dread
His burning idol all of blackest hue;
In vain with cymbals' ring
They call the grisly king,
In dismal dance about the furnace blue;
The brutish gods of Nile as fast,
Isis, and Orus, and the dog Anubis, haste.

Nor is Osiris seen
In Memphian grove, or green,
Trampling the unshower'd grass with lowings loud:
Nor can he be at rest
Within his sacred chest;
Nought but profoundest Hell can be his shroud;
In vain with timbrell'd anthems dark
The sable stoléd sorcerers bear his worshipt ark.

He feels from Juda's land
The dreaded infant's hand;
The rays of Bethlehem blind his dusky eyn;
Nor all the gods beside
Longer dare abide,
Nor Typhon huge ending in snaky twine:
Our Babe, to show his Godhead true,
Can in His swaddling bands control the damnéd crew.

So, when the sun in bed
Curtain'd with cloudy red
Pillows his chin upon an orient wave,
The flocking shadows pale

Troop to the infernal jail,
Each fetter'd ghost slips to his several grave;
And the yellow-skirted fays
Fly after the night-steeds, leaving their moon-loved
  maze.

But see! the Virgin blest
Hath laid her Babe to rest;
Time is, our tedious song should here have ending:
Heaven's youngest-teeméd star
Hath fix'd her polish'd car,
Her sleeping Lord with hand-maid lamp attending:
And all about the courtly stable
Bright-harness'd Angels sit in order serviceable.

J. MILTON

LXIII

SONG FOR ST. CECILIA'S DAY
1687

From Harmony, from heavenly Harmony
  This universal frame began:
 When Nature underneath a heap
  Of jarring atoms lay
 And could not heave her head,
The tuneful voice was heard from high,
  Arise, ye more than dead!
Then cold, and hot, and moist, and dry
In order to their stations leap,
  And Music's power obey.
From harmony, from heavenly harmony
  This universal frame began:
  From harmony to harmony
Through all the compass of the notes it ran,
The diapason closing full in Man.

What passion cannot Music raise and quell?
  When Jubal struck the chorded shell

His listening brethren stood around,
    And, wondering, on their faces fell
To worship that celestial sound.
Less than a god they thought there could not dwell
    Within the hollow of that shell
    That spoke so sweetly and so well.
What passion cannot Music raise and quell?

    The trumpet's loud clangor
        Excites us to arms,
    With shrill notes of anger
        And mortal alarms.
    The double double double beat
        Of the thundering drum
        Cries ' Hark! the foes come;
Charge, charge, 'tis too late to retreat!'

    The soft complaining flute
        In dying notes discovers
    The woes of hopeless lovers,
Whose dirge is whisper'd by the warbling lute.

    Sharp violins proclaim
Their jealous pangs and desperation,
Fury, frantic indignation,
Depth of pains, and height of passion
    For the fair disdainful dame.

But oh! what art can teach,
What human voice can reach
    The sacred organ's praise?
Notes inspiring holy love,
Notes that wing their heavenly ways
    To mend the choirs above.

Orpheus could lead the savage race,
And trees unrooted left their place
    Sequacious of the lyre:
But bright Cecilia raised the wonder higher:

When to her Organ vocal breath was given
An Angel heard, and straight appear'd—
   Mistaking Earth for Heaven.

Grand Chorus

As from the power of sacred lays
   The spheres began to move,
And sung the great Creator's praise
   To all the blest above;
So when the last and dreadful hour
This crumbling pageant shall devour,
The trumpet shall be heard on high,
The dead shall live, the living die,
And Music shall untune the sky.

J. DRYDEN

LXIV

ON THE LATE MASSACRE IN PIEDMONT

Avenge, O Lord! Thy slaughter'd Saints, whose bones
Lie scatter'd on the Alpine mountains cold;
Even them who kept thy truth so pure of old
When all our fathers worshipt stocks and stones,

Forget not: In thy book record their groans
Who were thy sheep, and in their ancient fold
Slain by the bloody Piemontese, that roll'd
Mother with infant down the rocks.   Their moans

The vales redoubled to the hills, and they
To Heaven.   Their martyr'd blood and ashes sow
O'er all the Italian fields, where still doth sway
The triple tyrant: that from these may grow
A hundred-fold, who, having learnt Thy way,
Early may fly the Babylonian woe.

J. MILTON

LXV

HORATIAN ODE UPON CROMWELL'S RETURN FROM IRELAND

The forward youth that would appear,
Must now forsake his Muses dear,
    Nor in the shadows sing
    His numbers languishing.

'Tis time to leave the books in dust,
And oil the unused armour's rust,
    Removing from the wall
    The corslet of the hall.

So restless Cromwell could not cease
In the inglorious arts of peace,
    But through adventurous war
    Urgéd his active star:

And like the three-fork'd lightning first
Breaking the clouds where it was nurst,
    Did thorough his own side
    His fiery way divide:

For 'tis all one to courage high,
The emulous, or enemy;
    And with such, to enclose
    Is more than to oppose;

Then burning through the air he went
And palaces and temples rent;
    And Caesar's head at last
    Did through his laurels blast.

'Tis madness to resist or blame
The face of angry heaven's flame;
    And if we would speak true,
    Much to the Man is due

Who, from his private gardens, where
He lived reservéd and austere,
    (As if his highest plot
    To plant the bergamot,)

Could by industrious valour climb
To ruin the great work of time,
    And cast the Kingdoms old
    Into another mould.

Though Justice against Fate complain,
And plead the ancient Rights in vain—
    But those do hold or break
    As men are strong or weak;

Nature, that hateth emptiness,
Allows of penetration less,
    And therefore must make room
    Where greater spirits come.

What field of all the civil war
Where his were not the deepest scar?
    And Hampton shows what part
    He had of wiser art,

Where, twining subtle fears with hope,
He wove a net of such a scope
    That Charles himself might chase
    To Carisbrook's narrow case,

That thence the Royal actor borne
The tragic scaffold might adorn:
    While round the arméd bands
    Did clap their bloody hands.

He nothing common did or mean
Upon that memorable scene,
    But with his keener eye
    The axe's edge did try;

Nor call'd the Gods, with vulgar spite,
To vindicate his helpless right;

But bow'd his comely head
Down, as upon a bed.

—This was that memorable hour
Which first assured the forcéd power:
    So when they did design
    The Capitol's first line,

A Bleeding Head, where they begun,
Did fright the architects to run;
    And yet in that the State
    Foresaw its happy fate!

And now the Irish are ashamed
To see themselves in one year tamed:
    So much one can man do
    That does both act and know.

They can affirm his praises best,
And have, though overcome, confest
    How good he is, how just
    And fit for highest trust;

Nor yet grown stiffer with command,
But still in the Republic's hand—
    How fit he is to sway
    That can so well obey!

He to the Commons' feet presents
A Kingdom for his first year's rents,
    And (what he may) forbears
    His fame, to make it theirs:

And has his sword and spoils ungirt
To lay them at the Public's skirt.
    So when the falcon high
    Falls heavy from the sky,

She, having kill'd, no more does search
But on the next green bough to perch,
    Where, when he first does lure,
    The falconer has her sure.

—What may not then our Isle presume
While victory his crest does plume?
    What may not others fear
    If thus he crowns each year?

As Caesar he, ere long, to Gaul,
To Italy an Hannibal,
    And to all States not free
    Shall climacteric be.

The Pict no shelter now shall find
Within his parti-colour'd mind,
    But from this valour sad,
    Shrink underneath the plaid—

Happy, if in the tufted brake
The English hunter him mistake,
    Nor lay his hounds in near
    The Caledonian deer.

But Thou, the War's and Fortune's son,
March indefatigably on;
    And for the last effect
    Still keep the sword erect:

Besides the force it has to fright
The spirits of the shady night,
    The same arts that did gain
    A power, must it maintain.

A. Marvell

LXVI

LYCIDAS

Elegy on a Friend drowned in the Irish Channel

Yet once more, O ye laurels, and once more
Ye myrtles brown, with ivy never sere,
I come to pluck your berries harsh and crude,
And with forced fingers rude
Shatter your leaves before the mellowing year.

Bitter constraint and sad occasion dear
Compels me to disturb your season due:
For Lycidas is dead, dead ere his prime,
Young Lycidas, and hath not left his peer:
Who would not sing for Lycidas? he knew
Himself to sing, and build the lofty rhyme.
He must not float upon his watery bier
Unwept, and welter to the parching wind,
Without the meed of some melodious tear.

Begin then, Sisters of the sacred well
That from beneath the seat of Jove doth spring;
Begin, and somewhat loudly sweep the string;
Hence with denial vain and coy excuse:
So may some gentle Muse
With lucky words favour my destined urn;
And as he passes, turn
And bid fair peace be to my sable shroud.

For we were nursed upon the self-same hill,
Fed the same flock by fountain, shade, and rill.
Together both, ere the high lawns appear'd
Under the opening eye-lids of the Morn,
We drove a-field, and both together heard
What time the gray-fly winds her sultry horn,
Battening our flocks with the fresh dews of night;
Oft till the star, that rose at evening bright,
Toward heaven's descent had sloped his westering
    wheel.
Meanwhile the rural ditties were not mute,
Temper'd to the oaten flute;
Rough Satyrs danced, and Fauns with cloven heel
From the glad sound would not be absent long;
And old Damoetas loved to hear our song.

But, O the heavy change, now thou art gone,
Now thou art gone, and never must return!
Thee, Shepherd, thee the woods and desert caves

With wild thyme and the gadding vine o'ergrown,
And all their echoes, mourn:
The willows and the hazel copses green
Shall now no more be seen
Fanning their joyous leaves to thy soft lays:—
As killing as the canker to the rose,
Or taint-worm to the weanling herds that graze,
Or frost to flowers, that their gay wardrobe wear
When first the white-thorn blows;
Such, Lycidas, thy loss to shepherd's ear.

Where were ye, Nymphs, when the remorseless deep
Closed o'er the head of your loved Lycidas?
For neither were ye playing on the steep
Where your old bards, the famous Druids, lie,
Nor on the shaggy top of Mona high,
Nor yet where Deva spreads her wizard stream:
Ay me! I fondly dream—
Had ye been there—for what could that have done
What could the Muse herself that Orpheus bore,
The Muse herself, for her enchanting son,
Whom universal nature did lament,
When by the rout that made the hideous roar
His gory visage down the stream was sent,
Down the swift Hebrus to the Lesbian shore?

Alas! what boots it with uncessant care
To tend the homely, slighted, shepherd's trade
And strictly meditate the thankless Muse?
Were it not better done, as others use,
To sport with Amaryllis in the shade,
Or with the tangles of Neaera's hair?
Fame is the spur that the clear spirit doth raise
(That last infirmity of noble mind)
To scorn delights, and live laborious days;
But the fair guerdon when we hope to find,
And think to burst out into sudden blaze,
Comes the blind Fury with the abhorréd shears

And slits the thin-spun life. 'But not the praise'
Pheobus replied, and touch'd my trembling ears;
'Fame is no plant that grows on mortal soil,
Nor in the glistering foil
Set off to the world, nor in broad rumour lies:
But lives and spreads aloft by those pure eyes
And perfect witness of all-judging Jove;
As he pronounces lastly on each deed,
Of so much fame in heaven expect thy meed.'

O fountain Arethuse, and thou honour'd flood
Smooth-sliding Mincius, crown'd with vocal reeds!
That strain I heard was of a higher mood:
But now my oat proceeds,
And listens to the herald of the sea
That came in Neptune's plea;
He ask'd the waves, and ask'd the felon winds,
What hard mishap hath doom'd this gentle swain?
And question'd every gust of rugged wings
That blows from off each beakéd promontory:
They knew not of his story;
And sage Hippotadés their answer brings,
That not a blast was from his dungeon stray'd;
The air was calm, and on the level brine
Sleek Panopé with all her sisters play'd.
It was that fatal and perfidious bark
Built in the eclipse, and rigg'd with curses dark,
That sunk so low that sacred head of thine.

Next Camus, reverend sire, went footing slow,
His mantle hairy, and his bonnet sedge
Inwrought with figures dim, and on the edge
Like to that sanguine flower inscribed with woe:
'Ah! who hath reft,' quoth he, 'my dearest pledge!
Last came, and last did go
The Pilot of the Galilean lake;
Two massy keys he bore of metals twain
(The golden opes, the iron shuts amain);

He shook his mitred locks, and stern bespake:
' How well could I have spared for thee, young swain,
Enow of such, as for their bellies' sake
Creep and intrude and climb into the fold!
Of other care they little reckoning make
Than how to scramble at the shearers' feast,
And shove away the worthy bidden guest;
Blind mouths! that scarce themselves know how to
　　hold
A sheep-hook, or have learn'd aught else the least
That to the faithful herdman's art belongs!
What recks it them? What need they? They are
　　sped;
And when they list, their lean and flashy songs
Grate on their scrannel pipes of wretched straw;
The hungry sheep look up, and are not fed,
But swoln with wind and the rank mist they draw
Rot inwardly, and foul contagion spread:
Besides what the grim wolf with privy paw
Daily devours apace, and nothing said:
—But that two-handed engine at the door
Stands ready to smite once, and smite no more.'

　　Return, Alphéus; the dread voice is past
That shrunk thy streams; return, Sicilian Muse,
And call the vales, and bid them hither cast
Their bells and flowerets of a thousand hues.
Ye valleys low, where the mild whispers use
Of shades, and wanton winds, and gushing brooks
On whose fresh lap the swart star sparely looks;
Throw hither all your quaint enamell'd eyes
That on the green turf suck the honey'd showers
And purple all the ground with vernal flowers.
Bring the rathe primrose that forsaken dies,
The tufted crow-toe, and pale jessamine,
The white pink, and the pansy freak'd with jet,
The glowing violet,

The musk-rose, and the well-attired woodbine,
With cowslips wan that hang the pensive head,
And every flower that sad embroidery wears:
Bid amarantus all his beauty shed,
And daffadillies fill their cups with tears
To strew the laureat hearse where Lycid lies.
For so to interpose a little ease,
Let our frail thoughts dally with false surmise;
Ay me! whilst thee the shores and sounding seas
Wash far away,—where'er thy bones are hurl'd,
Whether beyond the stormy Hebrides
Where thou perhaps, under the whelming tide,
Visitest the bottom of the monstrous world;
Or whether thou, to our moist vows denied,
Sleep'st by the fable of Bellerus old,
Where the great Vision of the guarded mount
Looks toward Namancos and Bayona's hold,
—Look homeward, Angel, now, and melt with ruth:
—And, O ye dolphins, waft the hapless youth!

Weep no more, woeful shepherds, weep no more,
For Lycidas, your sorrow, is not dead,
Sunk though he be beneath the watery floor;
So sinks the day-star in the ocean bed,
And yet anon repairs his drooping head
And tricks his beams, and with new-spangled ore
Flames in the forehead of the morning sky:
So Lycidas sunk low, but mounted high
Through the dear might of Him that walk'd the
    waves;
Where, other groves and other streams along,
With nectar pure his oozy locks he laves,
And hears the unexpressive nuptial song
In the blest kingdoms meek of joy and love.
There entertain him all the saints above
In solemn troops, and sweet societies,
That sing, and singing, in their glory move,

And wipe the tears for ever from his eyes.
Now, Lycidas, the shepherds weep no more;
Henceforth thou art the Genius of the shore
In thy large recompense, and shalt be good
To all that wander in that perilous flood.

    Thus sang the uncouth swain to the oaks and rills,
While the still morn went out with sandals gray;
He touch'd the tender stops of various quills,
With eager thought warbling his Doric lay:
And now the sun had stretch'd out all the hills,
And now was dropt into the western bay:
At last he rose, and twitch'd his mantle blue:
To-morrow to fresh woods, and pastures new.

J. MILTON

LXVII

ON THE TOMBS IN WESTMINSTER ABBEY

    Mortality, behold and fear
What a change of flesh is here!
Think how many royal bones
Sleep within these heaps of stones;
Here they lie, had realms and lands,
Who now want strength to stir their hands,
Where from their pulpits seal'd with dust
They preach, ' In greatness is no trust.'
Here's an acre sown indeed
With the richest royallest seed
That the earth did e'er suck in
Since the first man died for sin:
Here the bones of birth have cried
' Though gods they were, as men they died!'
Here are sands, ignoble things,
Dropt from the ruin'd sides of kings:
Here's a world of pomp and state
Buried in dust, once dead by fate.

F. BEAUMONT

THE LAST CONQUEROR

Victorious men of earth, no more
   Proclaim how wide your empires are;
Though you bind-in every shore
   And your triumphs reach as far
     As night or day,
   Yet you, proud monarchs, must obey
And mingle with forgotten ashes, when
Death calls ye to the crowd of common men.

Devouring Famine, Plague, and War,
   Each able to undo mankind,
Death's servile emissaries are;
   Nor to these alone confined,
     He hath at will
   More quaint and subtle ways to kill;
A smile or kiss, as he will use the art,
Shall have the cunning skill to break a heart.
J. Shirley

DEATH THE LEVELLER

The glories of our blood and state
   Are shadows, not substantial things;
There is no armour against fate;
   Death lays his icy hand on kings:
     Sceptre and Crown
     Must tumble down,
And in the dust be equal made
With the poor crooked scythe and spade.

Some men with swords may reap the field,
   And plant fresh laurels where they kill:
But their strong nerves at last must yield;
   They tame but one another still:
     Early or late
     They stoop to fate,

And must give up their murmuring breath
When they, pale captives, creep to death.

The garlands wither on your brow;
    Then boast no more your mighty deeds;
Upon Death's purple altar now
    See where the victor-victim bleeds:
      Your heads must come
      To the cold tomb;
Only the actions of the just
Smell sweet, and blossom in their dust.

J. SHIRLEY

LXX

WHEN THE ASSAULT WAS INTENDED TO THE CITY

Captain, or Colonel, or Knight in arms,
Whose chance on these defenceless doors may seize,
If deed of honour did thee ever please,
Guard them, and him within protect from harms.

He can requite thee; for he knows the charms
That call fame on such gentle acts as these,
And he can spread thy name o'er lands and seas,
Whatever clime the sun's bright circle warms.

Lift not thy spear against the Muses' bower:
The great Emathian conqueror bid spare
The house of Pindarus, when temple and tower
Went to the ground: and the repeated air
Of sad Electra's poet had the power
To save the Athenian walls from ruin bare.

J. MILTON

LXXI

ON HIS BLINDNESS

When I consider how my light is spent
Ere half my days, in this dark world and wide,
And that one talent which is death to hide
Lodged with me useless, though my soul more bent

To serve therewith my Maker, and present
My true account, lest he returning chide,—
Doth God exact day-labour, light denied?
I fondly ask:—But Patience, to prevent

That murmur, soon replies; God doth not need
Either man's work, or his own gifts: who best
Bear his mild yoke, they serve him best: His state

Is kingly; thousands at his bidding speed
And post o'er land and ocean without rest:—
They also serve who only stand and wait.

J. Milton

LXXII

CHARACTER OF A HAPPY LIFE

How happy is he born and taught
That serveth not another's will;
Whose armour is his honest thought
And simple truth his utmost skill!

Whose passions not his masters are,
Whose soul is still prepared for death,
Not tied unto the world with care
Of public fame, or private breath;

Who envies none that chance doth raise
Or vice; Who never understood
How deepest wounds are given by praise;
Nor rules of state, but rules of good:

Who hath his life from rumours freed,
Whose conscience is his strong retreat;
Whose state can neither flatterers feed,
Nor ruin make oppressors great;

Who God doth late and early pray
More of his grace than gifts to lend;
And entertains the harmless day
With a well-chosen book or friend;

—This man is freed from servile bands
Of hope to rise, or fear to fall;
Lord of himself, though not of lands;
And having nothing, yet hath all.

Sir H. Wotton

LXXIII
THE NOBLE NATURE

It is not growing like a tree
In bulk, doth make Man better be;
Or standing long an oak, three hundred year,
To fall a log at last, dry, bald, and sere:
   A lily of a day
   Is fairer far in May,
  Although it fall and die that night—
  It was the plant and flower of Light.
In small proportions we just beauties see;
And in short measures life may perfect be.

B. Jonson

LXXIV
THE GIFTS OF GOD

When God at first made Man,
Having a glass of blessings standing by;
Let us (said he) pour on him all we can:
Let the world's riches, which dispersèd lie,
  Contract into a span.

So strength first made a way;
Then beauty flow'd, then wisdom, honour, pleasure:
When almost all was out, God made a stay,
Perceiving that alone, of all his treasure,
  Rest in the bottom lay.

For if I should (said he)
Bestow this jewel also on my creature,
He would adore my gifts instead of me,
And rest in Nature, not the God of Nature,
  So both should losers be.

Yet let him keep the rest,
But keep them with repining restlessness:
Let him be rich and weary, that at least,
If goodness lead him not, yet weariness
      May toss him to my breast.

G. HERBERT

LXXV

THE RETREAT

Happy those early days, when I
Shined in my Angel-infancy!
Before I understood this place
Appointed for my second race,
Or taught my soul to fancy aught
But a white, celestial thought;
When yet I had not walk'd above
A mile or two from my first Love,
And looking back, at that short space
Could see a glimpse of his bright face
When on some gilded cloud or flower
My gazing soul would dwell an hour,
And in those weaker glories spy
Some shadows of eternity;
Before I taught my tongue to wound
My conscience with a sinful sound,
Or had the black art to dispense
A several sin to every sense,
But felt through all this fleshly dress
Bright shoots of everlastingness.

O how I long to travel back,
And tread again that ancient track!
That I might once more reach that plain
Where first I felt my glorious train;
From whence th' enlighten'd spirit sees
That shady City of Palm trees!
But ah! my soul with too much stay
Is drunk, and staggers in the way:—

Some men a forward motion love,
But I by backward steps would move;
And when this dust falls to the urn,
In that state I came, return.

H. VAUGHAN

LXXVI
TO MR. LAWRENCE

Lawrence, of virtuous father virtuous son,
Now that the fields are dank and ways are mire,
Where shall we sometimes meet, and by the fire
Help waste a sullen day, what may be won

From the hard season gaining?   Time will run
On smoother, till Favonius re-inspire
The frozen earth, and clothe in fresh attire
The lily and rose, that neither sow'd nor spun.

What neat repast shall feast us, light and choice,
Of Attic taste, with wine, whence we may rise
To hear the lute well touch'd, or artful voice

Warble immortal notes and Tuscan air?
He who of those delights can judge, and spare
To interpose them oft, is not unwise.

J. MILTON

LXXVII
TO CYRIACK SKINNER

Cyriack, whose grandsire, on the royal bench
Of British Themis, with no mean applause
Pronounced, and in his volumes taught, our laws,
Which others at their bar so often wrench;

To-day deep thoughts resolve with me to drench
In mirth, that after no repenting draws;
Let Euclid rest, and Archimedes pause,
And what the Swede intends, and what the French.

To measure life learn thou betimes, and know
Toward solid good what leads the nearest way;
For other things mild Heaven a time ordains,

And disapproves that care, though wise in show,
That with superfluous burden loads the day,
And, when God sends a cheerful hour, refrains.

J. MILTON

LXXVIII

HYMN TO DIANA

Queen and Huntress, chaste and fair,
    Now the sun is laid to sleep,
Seated in thy silver chair
      State in wonted manner keep:
        Hesperus entreats thy light,
        Goddess excellently bright.

Earth, let not thy envious shade
    Dare itself to interpose;
Cynthia's shining orb was made
      Heaven to clear when day did close:
        Bless us then with wishéd sight,
        Goddess excellently bright.

Lay thy bow of pearl apart
    And thy crystal-shining quiver;
Give unto the flying hart
      Space to breathe, how short soever:
        Thou that mak'st a day of night,
        Goddess excellently bright!

B. JONSON

LXXIX

WISHES FOR THE SUPPOSED MISTRESS

    Whoe'er she be,
    That not impossible She
    That shall command my heart and me;

    Where'er she lie,
    Lock'd up from mortal eye
    In shady leaves of destiny:

Till that ripe birth
Of studied Fate stand forth,
And teach her fair steps tread our earth

Till that divine
Idea take a shrine
Of crystal flesh, through which to shine:

—Meet you her, my Wishes,
Bespeak her to my blisses,
And be ye call'd, my absent kisses.

I wish her beauty
That owes not all its duty
To gaudy tire, or glist'ring shoe-tie:

Something more than
Taffata or tissue can,
Or rampant feather, or rich fan.

A face that's best
By its own beauty drest,
And can alone commend the rest:

A face made up
Out of no other shop
Than what Nature's white hand sets ope.

Sydneian showers
Of sweet discourse, whose powers
Can crown old Winter's head with flowers.

Whate'er delight
Can make day's forehead bright
Or give down to the wings of night.

Soft silken hours,
Open suns, shady bowers;
'Bove all, nothing within that lowers.

Days, that need borrow
No part of their good morrow
From a fore-spent night of sorrow:

Days, that in spite
Of darkness, by the light
Of a clear mind are day all night.

Life, that dares send
A challenge to his end,
And when it comes, say, 'Welcome, friend.'

I wish her store
Of worth may leave her poor
Of wishes; and I wish——no more.

—Now, if Time knows
That Her, whose radiant brows
Weave them a garland of my vows;

Her that dares be
What these lines wish to see:
I seek no further, it is She.

'Tis She, and here
Lo! I unclothe and clear
My wishes' cloudy character.

Such worth as this is
Shall fix my flying wishes,
And determine them to kisses.

Let her full glory,
My fancies, fly before ye;
Be ye my fictions:—but her story.

R. Crashaw

LXXX

THE GREAT ADVENTURER

Over the mountains
And over the waves,
Under the fountains
And under the graves;

Under floods that are deepest,
Which Neptune obey;
Over rocks that are steepest
Love will find out the way.

Where there is no place
For the glow-worm to lie;
Where there is no space
For receipt of a fly;
Where the midge dares not venture
Lest herself fast she lay;
If love come, he will enter
And soon find out his way.

You may esteem him
A child for his might;
Or you may deem him
A coward from his flight;
But if she whom love doth honour
Be conceal'd from the day,
Set a thousand guards upon her,
Love will find out the way.

Some think to lose him
By having him confined;
And some do suppose him,
Poor thing, to be blind;
But if ne'er so close ye wall him,
Do the best that you may,
Blind love, if so ye call him,
Will find out his way.

You may train the eagle
To stoop to your fist;
Or you may inveigle
The phoenix of the east;
The lioness, ye may move her

To give o'er her prey;
But you'll ne'er stop a lover:
He will find out his way.   ANON.

LXXXI
CHILD AND MAIDEN

Ah, Chloris! could I now but sit
  As unconcern'd as when
Your infant beauty could beget
  No happiness or pain!
When I the dawn used to admire,
  And praised the coming day,
I little thought the rising fire
  Would take my rest away.

Your charms in harmless childhood lay
  Like metals in a mine;
Age from no face takes more away
  Than youth conceal'd in thine.
But as your charms insensibly
  To their perfection prest,
So love as unperceived did fly,
  And center'd in my breast.

My passion with your beauty grew,
  While Cupid at my heart
Still as his mother favour'd you
  Threw a new flaming dart:
Each gloried in their wanton part;
  To make a lover, he
Employ'd the utmost of his art—
  To make a beauty, she.

                        SIR C. SEDLEY

LXXXII
COUNSEL TO GIRLS

Gather ye rose-buds while ye may,
  Old Time is still a-flying:
And this same flower that smiles to-day,
  To-morrow will be dying.

The glorious Lamp of Heaven, the Sun,
  The higher he's a-getting
The sooner will his race be run,
  And nearer he's to setting.

That age is best which is the first,
  When youth and blood are warmer;
But being spent, the worse, and worst
  Times, still succeed the former.

Then be not coy, but use your time;
  And while ye may, go marry:
For having lost but once your prime,
  You may for ever tarry.

R. HERRICK

LXXXIII

TO LUCASTA, ON GOING TO THE WARS

Tell me not, Sweet, I am unkind
  That from the nunnery
Of thy chaste breast and quiet mind,
  To war and arms I fly.

True, a new mistress now I chase,
  The first foe in the field;
And with a stronger faith embrace
  A sword, a horse, a shield.

Yet this inconstancy is such
  As you too shall adore;
I could not love thee, Dear, so much,
  Loved I not Honour more.

COLONEL LOVELACE

LXXXIV

ELIZABETH OF BOHEMIA

You meaner beauties of the night,
  That poorly satisfy our eyes
More by your number than your light,
  You common people of the skies,
What are you, when the Moon shall rise?

Ye violets that first appear,
  By your pure purple mantles known
Like the proud virgins of the year,
  As if the spring were all your own,—
What are you, when the Rose is blown?

Ye curious chanters of the wood
  That warble forth dame Nature's lays,
Thinking your passions understood
  By your weak accents; what's your praise
When Philomel her voice doth raise?

So when my Mistress shall be seen
  In sweetness of her looks and mind,
By virtue first, then choice, a Queen,
  Tell me, if she were not design'd
Th' eclipse and glory of her kind?

SIR H. WOTTON

LXXXV

TO THE LADY MARGARET LEY

Daughter to that good Earl, once President
Of England's council and her treasury,
Who lived in both, unstain'd with gold or fee,
And left them both, more in himself content,

Till the sad breaking of that parliament
Broke him, as that dishonest victory
At Chaeronea, fatal to liberty,
Kill'd with report that old man eloquent;—

Though later born than to have known the days
Wherein your father flourish'd, yet by you,
Madam, methinks I see him living yet;

So well your words his noble virtues praise,
That all both judge you to relate them true,
And to possess them, honour'd Margaret.

J. MILTON

THE LOVELINESS OF LOVE

It is not Beauty I demand,
　A crystal brow, the moon's despair,
Nor the snow's daughter, a white hand,
　Nor mermaid's yellow pride of hair:

Tell me not of your starry eyes,
　Your lips that seem on roses fed,
Your breasts, where Cupid tumbling lies
　Nor sleep for kissing of his bed:—

A bloomy pair of vermeil cheeks
　Like Hebe's in her ruddiest hours,
A breath that softer music speaks
　Than summer winds a-wooing flowers,

These are but gauds: nay, what are lips?
　Coral beneath the ocean-stream,
Whose brink when your adventurer slips
　Full oft he perisheth on them.

And what are cheeks but ensigns oft
　That wave hot youth to fields of blood?
Did Helen's breast, though ne'er so soft,
　Do Greece or Ilium any good?

Eyes can with baleful ardour burn;
　Poison can breathe, than erst perfumed;
There's many a white hand holds an urn
　With lovers' hearts to dust consumed.

For crystal brows there's nought within;
　They are but empty cells for pride;
He who the Syren's hair would win
　Is mostly strangled in the tide.

Give me, instead of Beauty's bust,
　A tender heart, a loyal mind

Which with temptation I would trust,
  Yet never link'd with error find,—

One in whose gentle bosom I
  Could pour my secret heart of woes,
Like the case-burthen'd honey-fly
  That hides his murmurs in the rose—

My earthly Comforter! whose love
  So indefeasible might be
That, when my spirit wonn'd above
  Hers could not stay, for sympathy.

                              G. Darley

LXXXVII
THE TRUE BEAUTY

He that loves a rosy cheek
  Or a coral lip admires,
Or from star-like eyes doth seek
  Fuel to maintain his fires;
As old Time makes these decay,
So his flames must waste away.

But a smooth and steadfast mind,
  Gentle thoughts, and calm desires,
Hearts with equal love combined,
  Kindle never-dying fires:—
Where these are not, I despise
Lovely cheeks or lips or eyes.

                              T. Carew

LXXXVIII
TO DIANEME

Sweet, be not proud of those two eyes
Which starlike sparkle in their skies;
Nor be you proud, that you can see
All hearts your captives; yours yet free:
Be you not proud of that rich hair
Which wantons with the lovesick air;

Whenas that ruby which you wear,
Sunk from the tip of your soft ear,
Will last to be a precious stone
When all your world of beauty's gone.

R. Herrick

LXXXIX

Go, lovely Rose!
Tell her, that wastes her time and me,
That now she knows,
When I resemble her to thee,
How sweet and fair she seems to be.

Tell her that's young
And shuns to have her graces spied,
That hadst thou sprung
In deserts, where no men abide,
Thou must have uncommended died.

Small is the worth
Of beauty from the light retired:
Bid her come forth,
Suffer herself to be desired,
And not blush so to be admired.

Then die! that she
The common fate of all things rare
May read in thee:
How small a part of time they share
That are so wondrous sweet and fair!

E. Waller

XC

TO CELIA

Drink to me only with thine eyes,
And I will pledge with mine;
Or leave a kiss but in the cup
And I'll not look for wine.
The thirst that from the soul doth rise
Doth ask a drink divine;

But might I of Jove's nectar sup,
   I would not change for thine.

I sent thee late a rosy wreath,
   Not so much honouring thee
As giving it a hope that there
   It could not wither'd be;
But thou thereon didst only breathe
   And sent'st it back to me;
Since when it grows, and smells, I swear,
   Not of itself but thee!

B. Jonson

XCI

CHERRY-RIPE

There is a garden in her face
   Where roses and white lilies blow;
A heavenly paradise is that place,
   Wherein all pleasant fruits do grow;
There cherries grow that none may buy,
Till Cherry-Ripe themselves do cry.

Those cherries fairly do enclose
   Of orient pearl a double row,
Which when her lovely laughter shows,
   They look like rose-buds fill'd with snow:
Yet them no peer nor prince may buy,
Till Cherry-Ripe themselves do cry.

Her eyes like angels watch them still;
   Her brows like bended bows do stand,
Threat'ning with piercing frowns to kill
   All that approach with eye or hand
These sacred cherries to come nigh,
Till Cherry-Ripe themselves do cry!

T. Campion

XCII

THE POETRY OF DRESS

I

A sweet disorder in the dress
Kindles in clothes a wantonness:—
A lawn about the shoulders thrown
Into a fine distractión,—
An erring lace, which here and there
Enthrals the crimson stomacher,—
A cuff neglectful, and thereby
Ribbands to flow confusedly,—
A winning wave, deserving note,
In the tempestuous petticoat,—
A careless shoe-string, in whose tie
I see a wild civility,—
Do more bewitch me, than when art
Is too precise in every part.

R. HERRICK

XCIII

2

Whenas in silks my Julia goes
Then, then (methinks) how sweetly flows
That liquefaction of her clothes.

Next, when I cast mine eyes and see
That brave vibration each way free;
O how that glittering taketh me!

R. HERRICK

XCIV

3

My Love in her attire doth shew her wit,
    It doth so well become her:
For every season she hath dressings fit,
    For Winter, Spring, and Summer.

No beauty she doth miss
When all her robes are on:
But Beauty's self she is
When all her robes are gone.   ANON.

XCV
ON A GIRDLE

That which her slender waist confined
Shall now my joyful temples bind:
No monarch but would give his crown
His arms might do what this has done.

It was my Heaven's extremest sphere,
The pale which held that lovely deer:
My joy, my grief, my hope, my love
Did all within this circle move.

A narrow compass! and yet there
Dwelt all that's good, and all that's fair:
Give me but what this ribband bound,
Take all the rest the Sun goes round.

E. WALLER

XCVI
TO ANTHEA WHO MAY COMMAND HIM ANY THING

Bid me to live, and I will live
　Thy Protestant to be:
Or bid me love, and I will give
　A loving heart to thee.

A heart as soft, a heart as kind,
　A heart as sound and free
As in the whole world thou canst find,
　That heart I'll give to thee.

Bid that heart stay, and it will stay,
　To honour thy decree:
Or bid it languish quite away,
　And 't shall do so for thee.

Bid me to weep, and I will weep
  While I have eyes to see:
And having none, yet I will keep
  A heart to weep for thee.

Bid me despair, and I'll despair,
  Under that cypress tree:
Or bid me die, and I will dare
  E'en Death, to die for thee.

Thou art my life, my love, my heart,
  The very eyes of me,
And hast command of every part,
  To live and die for thee.

R. HERRICK

XCVII

Love not me for comely grace,
For my pleasing eye or face,
Nor for any outward part,
No, nor for my constant heart,—
  For those may fail, or turn to ill,
    So thou and I shall sever:
Keep therefore a true woman's eye,
And love me still, but know not why—
  So hast thou the same reason still
    To doat upon me ever!

ANON.

XCVIII

Not, Celia, that I juster am
  Or better than the rest;
For I would change each hour, like them,
  Were not my heart at rest.

But I am tied to very thee
  By every thought I have;
Thy face I only care to see,
  Thy heart I only crave.

All that in woman is adored
  In thy dear self I find—
For the whole sex can but afford
  The handsome and the kind.

Why then should I seek further store,
  And still make love anew?
When change itself can give no more,
  'Tis easy to be true.

Sir C. Sedley

xcix

TO ALTHEA FROM PRISON

When Love with unconfinéd wings
  Hovers within my gates,
And my divine Althea brings
  To whisper at the grates;
When I lie tangled in her hair
  And fetter'd to her eye,
The birds that wanton in the air
  Know no such liberty.

When flowing cups run swiftly round
  With no allaying Thames,
Our careless heads with roses crown'd,
  Our hearts with loyal flames;
When thirsty grief in wine we steep,
  When healths and draughts go free—
Fishes that tipple in the deep
  Know no such liberty.

When, linnet-like confinèd I
  With shriller throat shall sing
The sweetness, mercy, majesty
  And glories of my King;
When I shall voice aloud how good
  He is, how great should be,
Enlargéd winds, that curl the flood,
  Know no such liberty.

Stone walls do not a prison make,
    Nor iron bars a cage;
Minds innocent and quiet take
    That for an hermitage;
If I have freedom in my love
    And in my soul am free,
Angels alone, that soar above,
    Enjoy such liberty.

COLONEL LOVELACE

C

TO LUCASTA, GOING BEYOND THE SEAS

If to be absent were to be
    Away from thee;
Or that when I am gone
    You or I were alone;
Then, my Lucasta, might I crave
Pity from blustering wind, or swallowing wave.

Though seas and land betwixt us both,
    Our faith and troth,
Like separated souls,
    All time and space coutrols:
Above the highest sphere we meet
Unseen, unknown, and greet as Angels greet.

So then we do anticipate
    Our after-fate,
And are alive i' the skies,
    If thus our lips and eyes
Can speak like spirits unconfined
In Heaven, their earthy bodies left behind.

COLONEL LOVELACE

CI

ENCOURAGEMENTS TO A LOVER

Why so pale and wan, fond lover?
    Prythee, why so pale?
Will, if looking well can't move her,

        Looking ill prevail?
        Prythee, why so pale?

Why so dull and mute, young sinner?
        Prythee, why so mute?
Will, when speaking well can't win her,
        Saying nothing do't?
        Prythee, why so mute?

Quit, quit, for shame! this will not move,
        This cannot take her;
If of herself she will not love,
        Nothing can make her:
        The D—l take her!

                   Sir J. Suckling

CII

A SUPPLICATION

    Awake, awake, my Lyre!
And tell thy silent master's humble tale
    In sounds that may prevail;
  Sounds that gentle thoughts inspire
    Though so exalted she
    And I so lowly be
Tell her, such different notes make all thy harmony.

    Hark, how the strings awake:
And, though the moving hand approach not near,
    Themselves with awful fear
  A kind of numerous trembling make.
    Now all thy forces try;
    Now all thy charms apply;
Revenge upon her ear the conquests of her eye.

    Weak Lyre! thy virtue sure
Is useless here, since thou art only found
    To cure, but not to wound,
  And she to wound, but not to cure.

Too weak too wilt thou prove
My passion to remove;
Physic to other ills, thou'rt nourishment to love.

Sleep, sleep again, my Lyre!
For thou canst never tell my humble tale
In sounds that will prevail,
Nor gentle thoughts in her inspire;
All thy vain mirth lay by,
Bid thy strings silent lie,
Sleep, sleep again, my Lyre, and let thy master die
A. COWLEY

CIII
THE MANLY HEART

Shall I, wasting in despair,
Die because a woman's fair?
Or my cheeks make pale with care
'Cause another's rosy are?
Be she fairer than the day
Or the flowery meads in May—
If she be not so to me
What care I how fair she be?

Shall my foolish heart be pined
'Cause I see a woman kind;
Or a well disposéd nature
Joinéd with a lovely feature?
Be she meeker, kinder, than
Turtle-dove or pelican,
If she be not so to me
What care I how kind she be?

Shall a woman's virtues move
Me to perish for her love?
Or her merits' value known
Make me quite forget mine own?

Be she with that goodness blest
Which may gain her name of Best;
    If she seem not such to me,
    What care I how good she be?

'Cause her fortune seems too high,
Shall I play the fool and die?
Those that bear a noble mind
Where they want of riches find,
Think what with them they would do
Who without them dare to woo;
    And unless that mind I see,
    What care I how great she be?

Great or good, or kind or fair,
I will ne'er the more despair;
If she love me, this believe,
I will die ere she shall grieve;
If she slight me when I woo,
I can scorn and let her go;
    For if she be not for me,
    What care I for whom she be?

G. WITHER

CIV

MELANCHOLY

Hence, all you vain delights,
As short as are the nights,
Wherein you spend your folly:
There's nought in this life sweet
If man were wise to see't,
But only melancholy,
O sweetest Melancholy!
Welcome, folded arms, and fixéd eyes,
A sigh that piercing mortifies,
A look that's fasten'd to the ground,
A tongue chain'd up without a sound!
Fountain heads and pathless groves,

Places which pale passion loves!
Moonlight walks, when all the fowls
Are warmly housed save bats and owls!
A midnight bell, a parting groan!
These are the sounds we feed upon;
Then stretch our bones in a still gloomy valley;
Nothing's so dainty sweet as lovely melancholy.

J. FLETCHER

cv

TO A LOCK OF HAIR

Thy hue, dear pledge, is pure and bright
As in that well-remember'd night
When first thy mystic braid was wore,
And first my Agnes whisper'd love.

Since then how often hast thou prest
The torrid zone of this wild breast,
Whose wrath and hate have sworn to dwell
With the first sin that peopled hell;
A breast whose blood's a troubled ocean,
Each throb the earthquake's wild commotion!
O if such clime thou canst endure
Yet keep thy hue unstain'd and pure,
What conquest o'er each erring thought
Of that fierce realm had Agnes wrought!
I had not wander'd far and wide
With such an angel for my guide;
Nor heaven nor earth could then reprove me
If she had lived and lived to love me.

Not then this world's wild joys had been
To me one savage hunting scene,
My sole delight the headlong race
And frantic hurry of the chase;
To start, pursue, and bring to bay,
Rush in, drag down, and rend my prey,
Then—from the carcass turn away!

Mine ireful mood had sweetness tamed,
And soothed each wound which pride inflamed:—
Yes, God and man might now approve me
If thou hadst lived and lived to love me!

Sir W. Scott

CVI

FORSAKEN

O waly waly up the bank,
 And waly waly down the brae,
And waly waly yon burn-side
 Where I and my Love wont to gae!
I leant my back unto an aik,
 I thought it was a trusty tree;
But first it bow'd, and syne it brak,
 Sae my true Love did lichtly me.

O waly waly, but love be bonny
 A little time while it is new;
But when 'tis auld, it waxeth cauld
 And fades awa' like morning dew.
O wherefore should I busk my head?
 Or wherefore should I kame my hair?
For my true Love has me forsook,
 And says he'll never loe me mair.

Now Arthur-seat sall be my bed;
 The sheets shall ne'er be prest by me:
Saint Anton's well sall be my drink,
 Since my true Love has forsaken me.
Marti'mas wind, when wilt thou blaw
 And shake the green leaves aff the tree?
O gentle Death, when wilt thou come?
 For of my life I am wearie.

'Tis not the frost, that freezes fell,
 Nor blawing snaw's inclemencie;
'Tis not sic cauld that makes me cry,
 But my Love's heart grown cauld to me.

When we came in by Glasgow town
    We were a comely sight to see;
My Love was clad in the black velvét,
    And I mysell in cramasie.

But had I wist, before I kist,
    That love had been sae ill to win;
I had lockt my heart in a case of gowd
    And pinn'd it with a siller pin.
And, O! if my young babe were born,
    And set upon the nurse's knee,
And I mysell were dead and gone,
    And the green grass growing over me!

ANON.

CVII

FAIR HELEN

I wish I were where Helen lies;
Night and day on me she cries;
O that I were where Helen lies
    On fair Kirconnell lea!

Curst be the heart that thought the thought,
And curst the hand that fired the shot,
When in my arms burd Helen dropt,
    And died to succour me!

O think na but my heart was sair
When my Love dropt down and spak nae mair!
I laid her down wi' meikle care
    On fair Kirconnell lea.

As I went down the water-side,
None but my foe to be my guide,
None but my foe to be my guide,
    On fair Kirconnell lea;

I lighted down my sword to draw,
I hackéd him in pieces sma',
I hackéd him in pieces sma',
    For her sake that died for me.

O Helen fair, beyond compare!
I'll make a garland of thy hair
Shall bind my heart for evermair
    Until the day I die.

O that I were where Helen lies!
Night and day on me she cries;
Out of my bed she bids me rise,
    Says, 'Haste and come to me!'

O Helen fair! O Helen chaste!
If I were with thee, I were blest,
Where thou lies low and takes thy rest
    On fair Kirconnell lea.

I wish my grave were growing green,
A winding-sheet drawn ower my een,
And I in Helen's arms lying,
    On fair Kirconnell lea.

I wish I were where Helen lies;
Night and day on me she cries;
And I am weary of the skies,
    Since my Love died for me.   ANON.

CVIII
THE TWA CORBIES

As I was walking all alane
I heard twa corbies making a mane;
The tane unto the t'other say,
'Where sall we gang and dine today?

'—In behint yon auld fail dyke
I wot there lies a new-slain Knight;
And naebody kens that he lies there,
But his hawk, his hound, and lady fair.

'His hound is to the hunting gane,
His hawk to fetch the wild-fowl hame,
His lady's ta'en another mate,
So we may mak our dinner sweet.

' Ye'll sit on his white hause-bane,
And I'll pick out his bonnie blue een:
Wi' ae lock o' his gowden hair
We'll theek our nest when it grows bare.

' Mony a one for him makes mane,
But nane sall ken where he is gane;
O'er his white banes, when they are bare,
The wind sall blaw for evermair.'   ANON.

CIX
TO BLOSSOMS

Fair pledges of a fruitful tree,
    Why do ye fall so fast?
    Your date is not so past,
But you may stay yet here awhile
    To blush and gently smile,
      And go at last.

What, were ye born to be
    An hour or half's delight,
    And so to bid good-night?
'Twas pity Nature brought ye forth
    Merely to show your worth,
      And lose you quite.

But you are lovely leaves, where we
    May read how soon things have
    Their end, though ne'er so brave:
And after they have shown their pride
    Like you, awhile, they glide
      Into the grave.   R. HERRICK

CX
TO DAFFODILS

Fair Daffodils, we weep to see
    You haste away so soon:
As yet the early-rising Sun
    Has not attain'd his noon.

Stay, stay,
Until the hasting day
Has run
But to the even-song;
And, having pray'd together, we
Will go with you along.

We have short time to stay, as you,
We have as short a Spring!
As quick a growth to meet decay
As you, or any thing.
We die,
As your hours do, and dry
Away
Like to the Summer's rain;
Or as the pearls of morning's dew
Ne'er to be found again.

R. HERRICK

CXI

THOUGHTS IN A GARDEN

How vainly men themselves amaze
To win the palm, the oak, or bays,
And their incessant labours see
Crown'd from some single herb or tree,
Whose short and narrow-vergéd shade
Does prudently their toils upbraid;
While all the flowers and trees do close
To weave the garlands of Repose.

Fair Quiet, have I found thee here,
And Innocence thy sister dear!
Mistaken long, I sought you then
In busy companies of men:
Your sacred plants, if here below,
Only among the plants will grow:
Society is all but rude
To this delicious solitude.

No white nor red was ever seen
So amorous as this lovely green.
Fond lovers, cruel as their flame,
Cut in these trees their mistress' name:
Little, alas, they know or heed
How far these beauties her exceed!
Fair trees! where'er your barks I wound,
No name shall but your own be found.

When we have run our passions' heat
Love hither makes his best retreat:
The gods, who mortal beauty chase,
Still in a tree did end their race;
Apollo hunted Daphne so
Only that she might laurel grow;
And Pan did after Syrinx speed
Not as a nymph, but for a reed.

What wondrous life is this I lead
Ripe apples drop about my head;
The luscious clusters of the vine
Upon my mouth do crush their wine;
The nectarine and curious peach
Into my hands themselves do reach;
Stumbling on melons, as I pass,
Ensnared with flowers, I fall on grass.

Meanwhile the mind from pleasure less
Withdraws into its happiness;
The mind, that ocean where each kind
Does straight its own resemblance find;
Yet it creates, transcending these,
Far other worlds, and other seas;
Annihilating all that's made
To a green thought in a green shade.

Here at the fountain's sliding foot
Or at some fruit-tree's mossy root,
Casting the body's vest aside

My soul into the boughs does glide;
There, like a bird, it sits and sings,
Then whets and claps its silver wings,
And, till prepared for longer flight,
Waves in its plumes the various light.

Such was that happy Garden-state
While man there walk'd without a mate:
After a place so pure and sweet,
What other help could yet be meet!
But 'twas beyond a mortal's share
To wander solitary there:
Two paradises 'twere in one,
To live in Paradise alone.

How well the skilful gardener drew
Of flowers and herbs this dial new!
Where, from above, the milder sun
Does through a fragrant zodiac run:
And, as it works, th' industrious bee
Computes its time as well as we.
How could such sweet and wholesome hours
Be reckon'd, but with herbs and flowers!

A. MARVELL

CXII

L'ALLEGRO

Hence, loathéd Melancholy,
  Of Cerberus and blackest Midnight born
In Stygian cave forlorn
  'Mongst horrid shapes, and shrieks, and sights
      unholy!
Find out some uncouth cell
  Where brooding Darkness spreads his jealous wings
And the night-raven sings;
  There under ebon shades, and low-brow'd rocks
As ragged as thy locks,
  In dark Cimmerian desert ever dwell.

But come, thou goddess fair and free,
In heaven yclept Euphrosyne,
And by men, heart-easing Mirth,
Whom lovely Venus at a birth
With two sister Graces more
To ivy-crownéd Bacchus bore;
Or whether (as some sager sing)
The frolic wind that breathes the spring
Zephyr, with Aurora playing,
As he met her once a-Maying—
There on beds of violets blue
And fresh-blown roses wash'd in dew
Fill'd her with thee, a daughter fair,
So buxom, blithe, and debonair.
  Haste thee, Nymph, and bring with thee
Jest, and youthful jollity,
Quips, and cranks, and wanton wiles,
Nods, and becks, and wreathéd smiles
Such as hang on Hebe's cheek,
And love to live in dimple sleek;
Sport that wrinkled Care derides,
And Laughter holding both his sides:—
Come, and trip it as you go
On the light fantastic toe;
And in thy right hand lead with thee
The mountain-nymph, sweet Liberty;
And if I give thee honour due
Mirth, admit me of thy crew,
To live with her, and live with thee
In unreprovéd pleasures free;
To hear the lark begin his flight
And singing startle the dull night
From his watch-tower in the skies,
Till the dappled dawn doth rise;
Then to come, in spite of sorrow,
And at my window bid good-morrow
Through the sweetbriar, or the vine,

Or the twisted eglantine:
While the cock with lively din
Scatters the rear of darkness thin,
And to the stack, or the barn-door,
Stoutly struts his dames before:
Oft listening how the hounds and horn
Cheerly rouse the slumbering morn,
From the side of some hoar hill,
Through the high wood echoing shrill;
Sometime walking, not unseen,
By hedge-row elms, on hillocks green,
Right against the eastern gate
Where the great Sun begins his state
Robed in flames and amber light,
The clouds in thousand liveries dight;
While the ploughman, near at hand,
Whistles o'er the furrow'd land,
And the milkmaid singeth blithe,
And the mower whets his scythe,
And every shepherd tells his tale
Under the hawthorn in the dale.
　　Straight mine eye hath caught new pleasures
Whilst the landscape round it measures;
Russet lawns, and fallows gray,
Where the nibbling flocks do stray;
Mountains, on whose barren breast
The labouring clouds do often rest;
Meadows trim with daisies pied,
Shallow brooks, and rivers wide;
Towers and battlements it sees
Bosom'd high in tufted trees,
Where perhaps some Beauty lies,
The Cynosure of neighbouring eyes.
　　Hard by, a cottage chimney smokes
From betwixt two aged oaks,
Where Corydon and Thyrsis, met,
Are at their savoury dinner set

Of herbs, and other country messes
Which the neat-handed Phillis dresses;
And then in haste her bower she leaves
With Thestylis to bind the sheaves;
Or, if the earlier season lead,
To the tann'd haycock in the mead.
  Sometimes with secure delight
The upland hamlets will invite,
When the merry bells ring round,
And the jocund rebecks sound
To many a youth and many a maid,
Dancing in the chequer'd shade;
And young and old come forth to play
On a sun-shine holy-day,
Till the live-long day-light fail:
Then to the spicy nut-brown ale,
With stories told of many a feat,
How faery Mab the junkets eat:—
She was pinch'd, and pull'd, she said;
And he, by friar's lantern led;
Tells how the drudging Goblin sweat
To earn his cream-bowl duly set,
When in one night, ere glimpse of morn,
His shadowy flail hath thresh'd the corn
That ten day-labourers could not end;
Then lies him down the lubber fiend,
And, stretch'd out all the chimney's length,
Basks at the fire his hairy strength;
And crop-full out of doors he flings,
Ere the first cock his matin rings.
   Thus done the tales, to bed they creep,
By whispering winds soon lull'd asleep.
   Tower'd cities please us then
And the busy hum of men,
Where throngs of knights and barons bold,
In weeds of peace, high triumphs hold,
With store of ladies, whose bright eyes

Rain influence, and judge the prize
Of wit or arms, while both contend
To win her grace, whom all commend.
There let Hymen oft appear
In saffron robe, with taper clear,
And pomp, and feast, and revelry,
With mask, and antique pageantry;
Such sights as youthful poets dream
On summer eves by haunted stream.
Then to the well-trod stage anon,
If Jonson's learned sock be on,
Or sweetest Shakespeare, Fancy's child,
Warble his native wood-notes wild.

And ever against eating cares
Lap me in soft Lydian airs
Married to immortal verse,
Such as the meeting soul may pierce
In notes, with many a winding bout
Of linkéd sweetness long drawn out,
With wanton heed and giddy cunning,
The melting voice through mazes running,
Untwisting all the chains that tie
The hidden soul of harmony;
That Orpheus' self may heave his head
From golden slumber, on a bed
Of heap'd Elysian flowers, and hear
Such strains as would have won the ear
Of Pluto, to have quite set free
His half-regain'd Eurydice.

These delights if thou canst give,
Mirth, with thee I mean to live.   J. MILTON

CXIII

IL PENSEROSO

Hence, vain deluding Joys,
   The brood of Folly without father bred!
How little you bestead
   Or fill the fixéd mind with all your toys!

Dwell in some idle brain,
   And fancies fond with gaudy shapes possess
As thick and numberless
   As the gay motes that people the sunbeams,
Or likest hovering dreams,
   The fickle pensioners of Morpheus' train.

   But hail, thou goddess sage and holy,
Hail, divinest Melancholy!
Whose saintly visage is too bright
To hit the sense of human sight,
And therefore to our weaker view
O'erlaid with black, staid Wisdom's hue;
Black, but such as in esteem
Prince Memnon's sister might beseem,
Or that starr'd Ethiop queen that strove
To set her beauty's praise above
The sea-nymphs, and their powers offended:
Yet thou art higher far descended:
Thee bright-hair'd Vesta, long of yore,
To solitary Saturn bore;
His daughter she; in Saturn's reign
Such mixture was not held a stain:
Oft in glimmering bowers and glades
He met her, and in secret shades
Of woody Ida's inmost grove,
While yet there was no fear of Jove.
   Come, pensive Nun, devout and pure,
Sober, steadfast, and demure,
All in a robe of darkest grain
Flowing with majestic train,
And sable stole of cypres lawn
Over thy decent shoulders drawn:
Come, but keep thy wonted state,
With even step, and musing gait,
And looks commercing with the skies,
Thy rapt soul sitting in thine eyes:

There, held in holy passion still,
Forget thyself to marble, till
With a sad leaden downward cast
Thou fix them on the earth as fast:
And join with thee calm Peace, and Quiet,
Spare Fast, that oft with gods doth diet,
And hears the Muses in a ring
Aye round about Jove's altar sing:
And add to these retired Leisure
That in trim gardens takes his pleasure:—
But first and chiefest, with thee bring
Him that yon soars on golden wing
Guiding the fiery-wheeléd throne,
The cherub Contemplatión;
And the mute Silence hist along,
'Less Philomel will deign a song
In her sweetest saddest plight
Smoothing the rugged brow of Night,
While Cynthia checks her dragon yoke
Gently o'er the accustom'd oak.
—Sweet bird, that shunn'st the noise of folly,
Most musical, most melancholy!
Thee, chauntress, oft, the woods among
I woo, to hear thy even-song;
And missing thee, I walk unseen
On the dry smooth-shaven green,
To behold the wandering Moon
Riding near her highest noon,
Like one that had been led astray
Through the heaven's wide pathless way,
And oft, as if her head she bow'd,
Stooping through a fleecy cloud.
  Oft, on a plat of rising ground
I hear the far-off curfeu sound
Over some wide-water'd shore,
Swinging slow with sullen roar:
Or, if the air will not permit,

Some still removéd place will fit,
Where glowing embers through the room
Teach light to counterfeit a gloom;
Far from all resort of mirth,
Save the cricket on the hearth,
Or the bellman's drowsy charm
To bless the doors from nightly harm.

　　Or let my lamp at midnight hour
Be seen in some high lonely tower,
Where I may oft out-watch the Bear
With thrice-great Hermes, or unsphere
The spirit of Plato, to unfold
What worlds or what vast regions hold
The immortal mind, that hath forsook
Her mansion in this fleshly nook:
And of those demons that are found
In fire, air, flood, or under ground,
Whose power hath a true consent
With planet, or with element.
Sometime let gorgeous Tragedy
In scepter'd pall come sweeping by,
Presenting Thebes, or Pelops' line,
Or the tale of Troy divine;
Or what (though rare) of later age
Ennobled hath the buskin'd stage.

　　But, O sad Virgin, that thy power,
Might raise Musaeus from his bower,
Or bid the soul of Orpheus sing
Such notes as, warbled to the string,
Drew iron tears down Pluto's cheek
And made Hell grant what Love did seek!
Or call up him that left half-told
The story of Cambuscan bold,
Of Camball, and of Algarsife,
And who had Canacé to wife
That own'd the virtuous ring and glass;
And of the wondrous horse of brass

On which the Tartar king did ride:
And if aught else great bards beside
In sage and solemn tunes have sung
Of turneys, and of trophies hung,
Of forests, and enchantments drear,
Where more is meant than meets the ear.
  Thus, Night, oft see me in thy pale career,
Till civil-suited Morn appear,
Not trick'd and frounced as she was wont
With the Attic Boy to hunt,
But kercheft in a comely cloud
While rocking winds are piping loud,
Or usher'd with a shower still,
When the gust hath blown his fill,
Ending on the rustling leaves
With minute drops from off the eaves.
And when the sun begins to fling
His flaring beams, me, goddess, bring
To archéd walks of twilight groves,
And shadows brown, that Sylvan loves,
Of pine, or monumental oak,
Where the rude axe, with heavéd stroke,
Was never heard the nymphs to daunt
Or fright them from their hallow'd haunt.
There in close covert by some brook
Where no profaner eye may look,
Hide me from day's garish eye,
While the bee with honey'd thigh
That at her flowery work doth sing,
And the waters murmuring,
With such consort as they keep
Entice the dewy-feather'd Sleep;
And let some strange mysterious dream
Wave at his wings in aery stream
Of lively portraiture display'd,
Softly on my eyelids laid:
And, as I wake, sweet music breathe

Above, about, or underneath,
Sent by some spirit to mortals good,
Or the unseen Genius of the wood.
    But let my due feet never fail
To walk the studious cloister's pale
And love the high-embowéd roof,
With antique pillars massy proof
And storied windows richly dight
Casting a dim religious light:
There let the pealing organ blow
To the full-voiced quire below
In service high and anthems clear,
As may with sweetness, through mine ear,
Dissolve me into ecstasies,
And bring all Heaven before mine eyes.
    And may at last my weary age
Find out the peaceful hermitage,
The hairy gown and mossy cell
Where I may sit and rightly spell
Of every star that heaven doth shew,
And every herb that sips the dew;
Till old experience do attain
To something like prophetic strain.

    These pleasures, Melancholy, give,
And I with thee will choose to live.
                                J. Milton

CXIV

SONG OF THE EMIGRANTS IN BERMUDA

Where the remote Bermudas ride
In the ocean's bosom unespied,
From a small boat that row'd along
The listening winds received this song.
    'What should we do but sing His praise
That led us through the watery maze
Where He the huge sea-monsters wracks,

That lift the deep upon their backs,
Unto an isle so long unknown,
And yet far kinder than our own?
He lands us on a grassy stage,
Safe from the storms, and prelate's rage:
He gave us this eternal spring
Which here enamels everything,
And sends the fowls to us in care
On daily visits through the air.
He hangs in shades the orange bright
Like golden lamps in a green night,
And does in the pomegranates close
Jewels more rich than Ormus shows:
He makes the figs our mouths to meet
And throws the melons at our feet;
But apples plants of such a price,
No tree could ever bear them twice.
With cedars chosen by his hand
From Lebanon he stores the land;
And makes the hollow seas that roar
Proclaim the ambergris on shore.
He cast (of which we rather boast)
The Gospel's pearl upon our coast;
And in these rocks for us did frame
A temple where to sound His name.
Oh! let our voice His praise exalt
Till it arrive at Heaven's vault,
Which then perhaps rebounding may
Echo beyond the Mexique bay!'
—Thus sung they in the English boat
A holy and a cheerful note:
And all the way, to guide their chime,
With falling oars they kept the time.

A. MARVELL

CXV

AT A SOLEMN MUSIC

Blest pair of Sirens, pledges of Heaven's joy
Sphere-born harmonious Sisters, Voice and Verse!
Wed your divine sounds, and mixt power employ,
Dead things with inbreathed sense able to pierce;
And to our high-raised phantasy present
That undisturbéd Song of pure concent
Aye sung before the sapphire-colour'd throne
     To Him that sits thereon,

With saintly shout and solemn jubilee;
Where the bright Seraphim in burning row
Their loud uplifted angel-trumpets blow;
And the Cherubic host in thousand quires
Touch their immortal harps of golden wires,
With those just Spirits that wear victorious palms,
     Hymns devout and holy psalms
     Singing everlastingly:
That we on earth, with undiscording voice
May rightly answer the melodious noise;
As once we did, till disproportion'd sin
Jarr'd against nature's chime, and with harsh din
Broke the fair music that all creatures made
To their great Lord, whose love their motion sway'd
In perfect diapason, whilst they stood
In first obedience, and their state of good.
O may we soon again renew that Song,
And keep in tune with Heaven, till God ere long
To his celestial consort us unite,
To live with him, and sing in endless morn of light!
                  J. MILTON

CXVI

ALEXANDER'S FEAST, OR, THE POWER OF MUSIC

'Twas at the royal feast for Persia won
  By Philip's warlike son—
  Aloft in awful state
  The godlike hero sate
  On his imperial throne;
His valiant peers were placed around,
Their brows with roses and with myrtles bound,
(So should desert in arms be crown'd);
  The lovely Thais by his side
  Sate like a blooming eastern bride
  In flower of youth and beauty's pride:—
  Happy, happy, happy pair!
    None but the brave
    None but the brave
    None but the brave deserves the fair!

  Timotheus placed on high
Amid the tuneful quire
With flying fingers touch'd the lyre:
The trembling notes ascend the sky
And heavenly joys inspire.
The song began from Jove
Who left his blissful seats above—
Such is the power of mighty love!
A dragon's fiery form belied the god;
Sublime on radiant spires he rode
When he to fair Olympia prest,
And while he sought her snowy breast,
Then round her slender waist he curl'd,
And stamp'd an image of himself, a sovereign of the
        world.
—The listening crowd admire the lofty sound!
A present deity! they shout around:
A present deity! the vaulted roofs rebound!

With ravish'd ears
The monarch hears,
Assumes the god;
Affects to nod
And seems to shake the spheres.

The praise of Bacchus then the sweet musician sung,
Of Bacchus ever fair and ever young:
The jolly god in triumph comes!
Sound the trumpets, beat the drums!
Flush'd with a purple grace
He shows his honest face;
Now give the hautboys breath; he comes, he comes!
Bacchus, ever fair and young,
Drinking joys did first ordain;
Bacchus' blessings are a treasure,
Drinking is the soldier's pleasure:
Rich the treasure,
Sweet the pleasure,
Sweet is pleasure after pain.

Soothed with the sound, the king grew vain;
Fought all his battles o'er again,
And thrice he routed all his foes, and thrice he slew
    the slain!
The master saw the madness rise,
His glowing cheeks, his ardent eyes;
And while he Heaven and Earth defied
Changed his hand and check'd his pride.
He chose a mournful Muse
Soft pity to infuse:
He sung Darius great and good,
By too severe a fate
Fallen, fallen, fallen, fallen,
Fallen from his high estate,
And weltering in his blood;
Deserted at his utmost need
By those his former bounty fed;
On the bare earth exposed he lies

With not a friend to close his eyes.
—With downcast looks the joyless victor sate,
Revolving in his alter'd soul
The various turns of Chance below;
And now and then a sigh he stole,
And tears began to flow.

The mighty master smiled to see
That love was in the next degree;
'Twas but a kindred-sound to move,
For pity melts the mind to love.
Softly sweet, in Lydian measures
Soon he soothed his soul to pleasures.
War, he sung, is toil and trouble,
Honour but an empty bubble;
Never ending, still beginning,
Fighting still, and still destroying;
If the world be worth thy winning,
Think, O think, it worth enjoying:
Lovely Thais sits beside thee,
Take the good the gods provide thee!
—The many rend the skies with loud applause;
So Love was crown'd, but Music won the cause.
The prince, unable to conceal his pain,
Gazed on the fair
Who caused his care,
And sigh'd and look'd, sigh'd and look'd again:
Sigh'd and look'd, and sigh'd again:
At length with love and wine at once opprest
The vanquish'd victor sunk upon her breast.

Now strike the golden lyre again:
A louder yet, and yet a louder strain!
Break his bands of sleep asunder
And rouse him like a rattling peal of thunder.
Hark, hark! the horrid sound
Has raised up his head:
As awaked from the dead

And amazed he stares around.
Revenge, revenge, Timotheus cries,
See the Furies arise!
See the snakes that they rear
How they hiss in their hair,
And the sparkles that flash from their eyes!
Behold a ghastly band,
Each a torch in his hand!
Those are Grecian ghosts, that in battle were slain
And unburied remain
Inglorious on the plain:
Give the vengeance due
To the valiant crew!
Behold how they toss their torches on high,
How they point to the Persian abodes
And glittering temples of their hostile gods.
—The princes applaud with a furious joy:
And the King seized a flambeau with zeal to destroy;
Thais led the way
To light him to his prey,
And like another Helen, fired another Troy!

   —Thus, long ago,
Ere heaving bellows learn'd to blow,
While organs yet were mute,
Timotheus, to his breathing flute
And sounding lyre
Could swell the soul to rage, or kindle soft desire.
At last divine Cecilia came,
Inventress of the vocal frame;
The sweet enthusiast from her sacred store
Enlarged the former narrow bounds,
And added length to solemn sounds,
With Nature's mother-wit, and arts unknown before.
—Let old Timotheus yield the prize
Or both divide the crown;
He raised a mortal to the skies;
She drew an angel down!   J. DRYDEN

BOOK THIRD

ODE ON THE PLEASURE ARISING FROM VICISSITUDE

Now the golden Morn aloft
    Waves her dew-bespangled wing,
With vermeil cheek and whisper soft
    She woos the tardy Spring:
Till April starts, and calls around
The sleeping fragrance from the ground,
And lightly o'er the living scene
Scatters his freshest, tenderest green.

New-born flocks, in rustic dance,
    Frisking ply their feeble feet;
Forgetful of their wintry trance
    The birds his presence greet:
But chief, the sky-lark warbles high
His trembling thrilling ecstasy;
And lessening from the dazzled sight,
Melts into air and liquid light.

Yesterday the sullen year
    Saw the snowy whirlwind fly;
Mute was the music of the air,
    The herd stood drooping by:
Their raptures now that wildly flow
No yesterday nor morrow know;
'Tis Man alone that joy descries
With forward and reverted eyes.

Smiles on past Misfortune's brow
    Soft Reflection's hand can trace,
And o'er the cheek of Sorrow throw
    A melancholy grace;

While Hope prolongs our happier hour,
Or deepest shades, that dimly lour
And blacken round our weary way,
Gilds with a gleam of distant day.

Still, where rosy Pleasure leads,
   See a kindred Grief pursue;
Behind the steps that Misery treads
   Approaching Comfort view:
The hues of bliss more brightly glow
Chastised by sabler tints of woe,
And blended form, with artful strife,
The strength and harmony of life.

See the wretch that long has tost
   On the thorny bed of pain,
At length repair his vigour lost
   And breathe and walk again:
The meanest floweret of the vale,
The simplest note that swells the gale,
The common sun, the air, the skies,
To him are opening Paradise.

T. GRAY

CXVIII

SOLITUDE

Happy the man, whose wish and care
A few paternal acres bound,
Content to breathe his native air
          In his own ground.

Whose herds with milk, whose fields with bread
Whose flocks supply him with attire;
Whose trees in summer yield him shade,
          In winter fire.

Blest, who can unconcern'dly find
Hours, days, and years, slide soft away
In health of body, peace of mind,
          Quiet by day.

Sound sleep by night; study and ease
Together mix'd, sweet recreation,
And innocence, which most does please
        With meditation.

Thus let me live, unseen, unknown;
Thus unlamented let me die;
Steal from the world, and not a stone
        Tell where I lie.

                A. POPE

CXIX

THE BLIND BOY

O say what is that thing call'd Light,
    Which I must ne'er enjoy;
What are the blessings of the sight,
    O tell your poor blind boy!

You talk of wondrous things you see,
    You say the sun shines bright;
I feel him warm, but how can he
    Or make it day or night?

My day or night myself I make
    Whene'er I sleep or play;
And could I ever keep awake
    With me 'twere always day.

With heavy sighs I often hear
    You mourn my hapless woe;
But sure with patience I can bear
    A loss I ne'er can know.

Then let not what I cannot have
    My cheer of mind destroy:
Whilst thus I sing, I am a king,
    Although a poor blind boy.

                C. CIBBER

CXX

ON A FAVOURITE CAT, DROWNED IN A TUB OF GOLD FISHES

'Twas on a lofty vase's side,
Where China's gayest art had dyed
The azure flowers that blow,
Demurest of the tabby kind
The pensive Selima, reclined,
Gazed on the lake below.

Her conscious tail her joy declared:
The fair round face, the snowy beard,
The velvet of her paws,
Her coat that with the tortoise vies,
Her ears of jet, and emerald eyes—
She saw, and purr'd applause.

Still had she gazed, but 'midst the tide
Two angel forms were seen to glide,
The Genii of the stream:
Their scaly armour's Tyrian hue
Through richest purple, to the view
Betray'd a golden gleam.

The hapless Nymph with wonder saw:
A whisker first, and then a claw
With many an ardent wish
She stretch'd, in vain, to reach the prize—
What female heart can gold despise?
What Cat's averse to fish?

Presumptuous maid! with looks intent
Again she stretch'd, again she bent,
Nor knew the gulf between—
Malignant Fate sat by and smiled—
The slippery verge her feet beguiled;
She tumbled headlong in!

Eight times emerging from the flood
She mew'd to every watery God
Some speedy aid to send:—
No Dolphin came, no Nereid stirr'd,
Nor cruel Tom nor Susan heard—
A favourite has no friend!

From hence, ye Beauties! undeceived
Know one false step is ne'er retrieved,
And be with caution bold:
Not all that tempts your wandering eyes
And heedless hearts, is lawful prize,
Nor all that glisters, gold!

T. GRAY

CXXI

TO CHARLOTTE PULTENEY

Timely blossom, Infant fair,
Fondling of a happy pair,
Every morn and every night
Their solicitous delight,
Sleeping, waking, still at ease,
Pleasing, without skill to please;
Little gossip, blithe and hale,
Tattling many a broken tale,
Singing many a tuneless song,
Lavish of a heedless tongue;
Simple maiden, void of art,
Babbling out the very heart,
Yet abandon'd to thy will,
Yet imagining no ill,
Yet too innocent to blush;
Like the linnet in the bush
To the mother-linnet's note
Moduling her slender throat;
Chirping forth thy petty joys,
Wanton in the change of toys,

Like the linnet green, in May
Flitting to each bloomy spray;
Wearied then and glad of rest,
Like the linnet in the nest:—
This thy present happy lot
This, in time will be forgot:
Other pleasures, other cares,
Ever-busy Time prepares;
And thou shalt in thy daughter see,
This picture, once, resembled thee.

A. Philips

CXXII

RULE, BRITANNIA

When Britain first at Heaven's command
    Arose from out the azure main,
This was the charter of her land,
    And guardian angels sung the strain:
Rule, Britannia! Britannia rules the waves!
    Britons never shall be slaves.

The nations not so blest as thee
    Must in their turn to tyrants fall,
Whilst thou shalt flourish great and free
    The dread and envy of them all.

Still more majestic shalt thou rise,
    More dreadful from each foreign stroke;
As the loud blast that tears the skies
    Serves but to root thy native oak.

Thee haughty tyrants ne'er shall tame;
    All their attempts to bend thee down
Will but arouse thy generous flame,
    And work their woe and thy renown.

To thee belongs the rural reign;
    Thy cities shall with commerce shine;
All thine shall be the subject main,
    And every shore it circles thine!

The Muses, still with Freedom found,
  Shall to thy happy coast repair;
Blest Isle, with matchless beauty crown'd
  And manly hearts to guard the fair:—
Rule, Britannia! Britannia rules the waves;
  Britons never shall be slaves!

J. THOMSON

CXXIII

THE BARD

Pindaric Ode

'Ruin seize thee, ruthless King!
  Confusion on thy banners wait!
Tho' fann'd by Conquest's crimson wing
  They mock the air with idle state.
Helm, nor hauberk's twisted mail
Nor e'en thy virtues, tyrant, shall avail
To save thy secret soul from nightly fears,
From Cambria's curse, from Cambria's tears!'
—Such were the sounds that o'er the crested pride
  Of the first Edward scatter'd wild dismay,
As down the steep of Snowdon's shaggy side
  He wound with toilsome march his long array:—
Stout Glo'ster stood aghast in speechless trance;
'To arms!' cried Mortimer, and couch'd his quivering
    lance.

On a rock, whose haughty brow
Frowns o'er old Conway's foaming flood,
  Robed in the sable garb of woe
With haggard eyes the Poet stood;
(Loose his beard and hoary hair
Stream'd like a meteor to the troubled air)
And with a master's hand and prophet's fire
Struck the deep sorrows of his lyre:
'Hark, how each giant-oak and desert-cave
Sighs to the torrent's awful voice beneath!

O'er thee, O King! their hundred arms they wave
　　Revenge on thee in hoarser murmurs breathe;
Vocal no more, since Cambria's fatal day,
To high-born Hoel's harp, or soft Llewellyn's lay.

　'Cold is Cadwallo's tongue,
　　That hush'd the stormy main:
Brave Urien sleeps upon his craggy bed:
　　Mountains, ye mourn in vain
　　Modred, whose magic song
Made huge Plinlimmon bow his cloud-topt head.
　　On dreary Arvon's shore they lie
Smear'd with gore and ghastly pale:
　　Far, far aloof the affrighted ravens sail;
　　The famish'd eagle screams, and passes by.
Dear lost companions of my tuneful art,
　　Dear as the light that visits these sad eyes,
Dear as the ruddy drops that warm my heart,
　　Ye died amidst your dying country's cries—
No more I weep; They do not sleep;
　　On yonder cliffs, a griesly band,
I see them sit; They linger yet,
　　Avengers of their native land:
With me in dreadful harmony they join,
And weave with bloody hands the tissue of thy line.'

Weave the warp and weave the woof
　　The winding sheet of Edward's race:
Give ample room and verge enough
　　The characters of hell to trace.
Mark the year, and mark the night,
When Severn shall re-echo with affright
The shrieks of death thro' Berkley's roof that ring,
Shrieks of an agonising king!
　　She-wolf of France, with unrelenting fangs
That tear'st the bowels of thy mangled mate,
　　From thee be born, who o'er thy country hangs
The scourge of Heaven! What terrors round him wait!

Amazement in his van, with Flight combined,
And Sorrow's faded form, and Solitude behind.

'Mighty victor, mighty lord,
　　Low on his funeral couch he lies!
No pitying heart, no eye, afford
　　A tear to grace his obsequies.
Is the sable warrior fled?
Thy son is gone. He rests among the dead.
The swarm that in thy noon-tide beam were born?
—Gone to salute the rising morn.
Fair laughs the Morn, and soft the zephyr blows,
　　While proudly riding o'er the azure realm
In gallant trim the gilded Vessel goes:
　　Youth on the prow, and Pleasure at the helm:
Regardless of the sweeping Whirlwind's sway,
That hush'd in grim repose expects his evening prey.

'Fill high the sparkling bowl,
The rich repast prepare;
　　Reft of a crown, he yet may share the feast:
Close by the regal chair
　　Fell Thirst and Famine scowl
　　A baleful smile upon their baffled guest.
Heard ye the din of battle bray,
　　Lance to lance, and horse to horse?
　　Long years of havock urge their destined course,
And thro' the kindred squadrons mow their way.
　　Ye towers of Julius, London's lasting shame,
With many a foul and midnight murder fed,
　　Revere his Consort's faith, his Father's fame,
And spare the meek usurper's holy head!
Above, below, the rose of snow,
　　Twined with her blushing foe, we spread:
The bristled boar in infant-gore
　　Wallows beneath the thorny shade.
Now, brothers, bending o'er the accursèd loom,
Stamp we our vengeance deep, and ratify his doom.

' Edward, lo! to sudden fate
   (Weave we the woof; The thread is spun;)
Half of thy heart we consecrate.
   (The web is wove; The work is done.)
—Stay, oh stay! nor thus forlorn
Leave me unbless'd, unpitied, here to mourn:
In yon bright track that fires the western skies
They melt, they vanish from my eyes.
But O! what solemn scenes on Snowdon's height
   Descending slow their glittering skirts unroll?
Visions of glory, spare my aching sight,
Ye unborn ages, crowd not on my soul!
No more our long-lost Arthur we bewail:—
All hail, ye genuine kings! Britannia's issue, hail

  ' Girt with many a baron bold
Sublime their starry fronts they rear;
   And gorgeous dames, and statesmen old
In bearded majesty, appear.
In the midst a form divine!
Her eye proclaims her of the Briton-Line:
Her lion-port, her awe-commanding face
Attemper'd sweet to virgin-grace.
What strings symphonious tremble in the air,
   What strains of vocal transport round her play?
Hear from the grave, great Taliessin, hear;
   They breathe a soul to animate thy clay.
Bright Rapture calls, and soaring as she sings,
Waves in the eye of Heaven her many-coloured wing

' The verse adorn again
   Fierce War, and faithful Love,
And Truth severe, by fairy Fiction drest.
   In buskin'd measures move
Pale Grief, and pleasing Pain,
With Horror, tyrant of the throbbing breast.
A voice as of the cherub-choir

Gales from blooming Eden bear,
  And distant warblings lessen on my ear
That lost in long futurity expire.
Fond impious man, think'st thou yon sanguine cloud
  Raised by thy breath, has quench'd the orb of day?
To-morrow he repairs the golden flood
  And warms the nations with redoubled ray.
Enough for me: with joy I see
  The different doom our fates assign:
Be thine Despair and sceptred Care,
  To triumph and to die are mine.'
—He spoke, and headlong from the mountain's height
Deep in the roaring tide he plunged to endless night.

T. Gray

CXXIV

ODE WRITTEN IN MDCCXLVI

How sleep the Brave, who sink to rest
By all their Country's wishes blest!
When Spring, with dewy fingers cold,
Returns to deck their hallow'd mould,
She there shall dress a sweeter sod
Than Fancy's feet have ever trod.

By fairy hands their knell is rung,
By forms unseen their dirge is sung:
There Honour comes, a pilgrim gray,
To bless the turf that wraps their clay;
And Freedom shall awhile repair
To dwell a weeping hermit there!

W. Collins

CXXV

LAMENT FOR CULLODEN

The lovely lass o' Inverness,
Nae joy nor pleasure can she see;
For e'en and morn she cries, Alas!
And aye the saut tear blins her ee:

Drumossie moor—Drumossie day—
A waefu' day it was to me!
For there I lost my father dear,
My father dear, and brethren three.

Their winding-sheet the bluidy clay,
Their graves are growing green to see:
And by them lies the dearest lad
That ever blest a woman's ee!
Now wae to thee, thou cruel lord,
A bluidy man I trow thou be;
For mony a heart thou hast made sair
That ne'er did wrang to thine or thee.

R. BURNS

CXXVI

LAMENT FOR FLODDEN

I've heard them lilting at our ewe-milking,
   Lasses a' lilting before dawn o' day;
But now they are moaning on ilka green loaning—
   The Flowers of the Forest are a' wede away.

At bughts, in the morning, nae blythe lads are
    scorning,
   Lasses are lonely and dowie and wae;
Nae daffin', nae gabbin', but sighing and sabbing,
   Ilk ane lifts her leglin and hies her away.

In har'st, at the shearing, nae youths now are jeering,
   Bandsters are lyart, and runkled, and gray;
At fair or at preaching, nae wooing, nae fleeching—
   The Flowers of the Forest are a' wede away.

At e'en, in the gloaming, nae younkers are roaming
   'Bout stacks wi' the lasses at bogle to play;
But ilk ane sits drearie, lamenting her dearie—
   The Flowers of the Forest are weded away.

Dool and wae for the order, sent our lads to the Border:
  The English, for ance, by guile wan the day;
The Flowers of the Forest, that fought aye the fore-
      most,
  The prime of our land, are cauld in the clay.

We'll hear nae mair lilting at the ewe-milking;
  Women and bairns are heartless and wae;
Sighing and moaning on ilka green loaning—
  The Flowers of the Forest are a' wede away.

                            J. Elliott

CXXVII

THE BRAES OF YARROW

Thy braes were bonny, Yarrow stream,
  When first on them I met my lover;
Thy braes how dreary, Yarrow stream,
  When now thy waves his body cover!
For ever now, O Yarrow stream!
  Thou art to me a stream of sorrow;
For never on thy banks shall I
  Behold my Love, the flower of Yarrow.

He promised me a milk-white steed
  To bear me to his father's bowers;
He promised me a little page
  To squire me to his father's towers;
He promised me a wedding-ring,—
  The wedding-day was fix'd to-morrow;—
Now he is wedded to his grave,
  Alas, his watery grave, in Yarrow!

Sweet were his words when last we met;
  My passion I as freely told him;
Clasp'd in his arms, I little thought
  That I should never more behold him!
Scarce was he gone, I saw his ghost;
  It vanish'd with a shriek of sorrow;

Thrice did the water-wraith ascend,
And gave a doleful groan thro' Yarrow.

His mother from the window look'd
With all the longing of a mother;
His little sister weeping walk'd
The green-wood path to meet her brother;
They sought him east, they sought him west,
They sought him all the forest thorough;
They only saw the cloud of night,
They only heard the roar of Yarrow.

No longer from thy window look—
Thou hast no son, thou tender mother!
No longer walk, thou lovely maid;
Alas, thou hast no more a brother!
No longer seek him east or west
And search no more the forest thorough;
For, wandering in the night so dark,
He fell a lifeless corpse in Yarrow.

The tear shall never leave my cheek,
No other youth shall be my marrow—
I'll seek thy body in the stream,
And then with thee I'll sleep in Yarrow.
—The tear did never leave her cheek,
No other youth became her marrow;
She found his body in the stream,
And now with him she sleeps in Yarrow.

J. LOGAN

CXXVIII

WILLY DROWNED IN YARROW

Down in yon garden sweet and gay
   Where bonnie grows the lily,
I heard a fair maid sighing say,
   ' My wish be wi' sweet Willie!

' Willie's rare, and Willie's fair,
   And Willie's wondrous bonny;
And Willie hecht to marry me
   Gin e'er he married ony.

' O gentle wind, that bloweth south,
   From where my Love repaireth,
Convey a kiss frae his dear mouth
   And tell me how he fareth!

' O tell sweet Willie to come doun
   And hear the mavis singing,
And see the birds on ilka bush
   And leaves around them hinging.

' The lav'rock there, wi' her white breast
   And gentle throat sae narrow;
There's sport eneuch for gentlemen
   On Leader haughs and Yarrow.

' O Leader haughs are wide and braid
   And Yarrow haughs are bonny;
There Willie hecht to marry me
   If e'er he married ony.

' But Willie's gone, whom I thought on,
   And does not hear me weeping;
Draws many a tear frae true love's e'e
   When other maids are sleeping.

' Yestreen I made my bed fu' braid,
   The night I'll mak' it narrow,
For a' the live-lang winter night
   I lie twined o' my marrow.

' O came ye by yon water-side?
   Pou'd you the rose or lily?
Or came you by yon meadow green
   Or saw you my sweet Willie?'

She sought him up, she sought him down,
　She sought him braid and narrow;
Syne, in the cleaving of a craig,
　She found him drown'd in Yarrow!

ANON.

CXXIX
LOSS OF THE ROYAL GEORGE

Toll for the Brave!
The brave that are no more!
All sunk beneath the wave
Fast by their native shore!

Eight hundred of the brave
Whose courage well was tried,
Had made the vessel heel
And laid her on her side.

A land-breeze shook the shrouds
And she was overset;
Down went the Royal George,
With all her crew complete.

Toll for the brave!
Brave Kempenfelt is gone;
His last sea-fight is fought,
His work of glory done.

It was not in the battle;
No tempest gave the shock;
She sprang no fatal leak,
She ran upon no rock.

His sword was in its sheath,
His fingers held the pen,
When Kempenfelt went down
With twice four hundred men.

Weigh the vessel up
Once dreaded by our foes!

And mingle with our cup
The tears that England owes.

Her timbers yet are sound,
And she may float again
Full charged with England's thunder,
And plough the distant main:

But Kempenfelt is gone,
His victories are o'er;
And he and his eight hundred
Shall plough the waves no more.

W. COWPER

CXXX

BLACK-EYED SUSAN

All in the Downs the fleet was moor'd,
    The streamers waving in the wind,
When black-eyed Susan came aboard;
    'O! where shall I my true-love find?
Tell me, ye jovial sailors, tell me true
If my sweet William sails among the crew.'

William, who high upon the yard
    Rock'd with the billow to and fro,
Soon as her well-known voice he heard
    He sigh'd, and cast his eyes below:
The cord slides swiftly through his glowing hands,
And quick as lightning on the deck he stands.

So the sweet lark, high poised in air,
    Shuts close his pinions to his breast
If chance his mate's shrill call he hear,
    And drops at once into her nest:—
The noblest captain in the British fleet
Might envy William's lip those kisses sweet.

'O Susan, Susan, lovely dear,
    My vows shall ever true remain;

Let me kiss off that falling tear;
   We only part to meet again.
Change as ye list, ye winds; my heart shall be
The faithful compass that still points to thee.

' Believe not what the landmen say
   Who tempt with doubts thy constant mind:
They'll tell thee, sailors, when away,
   In every port a mistress find:
Yes, yes, believe them when they tell thee so,
For Thou art present wheresoe'er I go.

' If to fair India's coast we sail,
   Thy eyes are seen in diamonds bright,
Thy breath is Afric's spicy gale,
   Thy skin is ivory so white.
Thus every beauteous object that I view
Wakes in my soul some charm of lovely Sue.

' Though battle call me from thy arms
   Let not my pretty Susan mourn;
Though cannons roar, yet safe from harms
   William shall to his Dear return.
Love turns aside the balls that round me fly,
Lest precious tears should drop from Susan's eye.'

The boatswain gave the dreadful word,
   The sails their swelling bosom spread,
No longer must she stay aboard;
   They kiss'd, she sigh'd, he hung his head.
Her lessening boat unwilling rows to land;
' Adieu!' she cries; and waved her lily hand.

J. GAY

CXXXI

SALLY IN OUR ALLEY

Of all the girls that are so smart
   There's none like pretty Sally;
She is the darling of my heart,
   And she lives in our alley.

There is no lady in the land
   Is half so sweet as Sally;
She is the darling of my heart,
   And she lives in our alley.

Her father he makes cabbage-nets
   And through the streets does cry 'em;
Her mother she sells laces long
   To such as please to buy 'em:
But sure such folks could ne'er beget
   So sweet a girl as Sally!
She is the darling of my heart,
   And she lives in our alley.

When she is by, I leave my work,
   I love her so sincerely;
My master comes like any Turk,
   And bangs me most severely—
But let him bang his bellyfull,
   I'll bear it all for Sally;
She is the darling of my heart,
   And she lives in our alley.

Of all the days that's in the week
   I dearly love but one day—
And that's the day that comes betwixt
   A Saturday and Monday;
For then I'm drest all in my best
   To walk abroad with Sally
She is the darling of my heart,
   And she lives in our alley.

My master carries me to church,
   And often am I blamed
Because I leave him in the lurch
   As soon as text is named;
I leave the church in sermon-time
   And slink away to Sally;

She is the darling of my heart,
  And she lives in our alley.

When Christmas comes about again
  O then I shall have money;
I'll hoard it up, and box it all,
  I'll give it to my honey;
I would it were ten thousand pound,
  I'd give it all to Sally;
She is the darling of my heart,
  And she lives in our alley.

My master and the neighbours all
  Make game of me and Sally,
And, but for her, I'd better be
  A slave and row a galley;
But when my seven long years are out
  O then I'll marry Sally,—
O then we'll wed, and then we'll bed,
  But not in our alley!

                                    H. CAREY

CXXXII
A FAREWELL

Go fetch to me a pint o' wine,
  An' fill it in a silver tassie;
That I may drink before I go
  A service to my bonnie lassie:
The boat rocks at the pier o' Leith,
  Fu' loud the wind blaws frae the Ferry,
The ship rides by the Berwick-law,
  And I maun leave my bonnie Mary.

The trumpets sound, the banners fly,
  The glittering spears are rankéd ready;
The shouts o' war are heard afar,
  The battle closes thick and bloody;

But it's not the roar o' sea or shore
   Wad make me langer wish to tarry
Nor shout o' war that's heard afar—
   It's leaving thee, my bonnie Mary.

                  R. BURNS

CXXXIII

If doughty deeds my lady please
   Right soon I'll mount my steed;
And strong his arm, and fast his seat
   That bears frae me the meed.
I'll wear thy colours in my cap,
   Thy picture at my heart;
And he that bends not to thine eye
   Shall rue it to his smart!
     Then tell me how to woo thee, Love;
      O tell me how to woo thee!
      For thy dear sake, nae care I'll take
      Tho' ne'er another trow me.

If gay attire delight thine eye
   I'll dight me in array;
I'll tend thy chamber door all night,
   And squire thee all the day.
If sweetest sounds can win thine ear,
   These sounds I'll strive to catch;
Thy voice I'll steal to woo thysell,
   That voice that nane can match.

But if fond love thy heart can gain,
   I never broke a vow;
Nae maiden lays her skaith to me,
   I never loved but you.
For you alone I ride the ring,
   For you I wear the blue;
For you alone I strive to sing,
   O tell me how to woo!

Then tell me how to woo thee, Love
O tell me how to woo thee!
For thy dear sake, nae care I'll take,
Tho' ne'er another trow me.
                    R. GRAHAM OF GARTMORE

CXXXIV

TO A YOUNG LADY

Sweet stream, that winds through yonder glade,
Apt emblem of a virtuous maid—
Silent and chaste she steals along,
Far from the world's gay busy throng:
With gentle yet prevailing force,
Intent upon her destined course;
Graceful and useful all she does,
Blessing and blest where'er she goes;
Pure-bosom'd as that watery glass,
And Heaven reflected in her face.
                    W. COWPER

CXXXV

THE SLEEPING BEAUTY

Sleep on, and dream of Heaven awhile—
Tho' shut so close thy laughing eyes,
Thy rosy lips still wear a smile
And move, and breathe delicious sighs!

Ah, now soft blushes tinge her cheeks
And mantle o'er her neck of snow:
Ah, now she murmurs, now she speaks
What most I wish—and fear to know!

She starts, she trembles, and she weeps!
Her fair hands folded on her breast:
—And now, how like a saint she sleeps!
A seraph in the realms of rest!

Sleep on secure!   Above controul
Thy thoughts belong to Heaven and thee:
And may the secret of thy soul
Remain within its sanctuary!

S. ROGERS

CXXXVI

For ever, Fortune, wilt thou prove
An unrelenting foe to Love,
And when we meet a mutual heart
Come in between, and bid us part?

Bid us sigh on from day to day,
And wish and wish the soul away;
Till youth and genial years are flown,
And all the life of life is gone?

But busy, busy, still art thou,
To bind the loveless joyless vow,
The heart from pleasure to delude,
To join the gentle to the rude.

For once, O Fortune, hear my prayer,
And I absolve thy future care;
All other blessings I resign,
Make but the dear Amanda mine.

J. THOMSON

CXXXVII

The merchant, to secure his treasure,
    Conveys it in a borrow'd name:
Euphelia serves to grace my measure,
    But Cloe is my real flame.

My softest verse, my darling lyre
    Upon Euphelia's toilet lay—
When Cloe noted her desire
    That I should sing, that I should play.

My lyre I tune, my voice I raise,
    But with my numbers mix my sighs;

And whilst I sing Euphelia's praise,
    I fix my soul on Cloe's eyes.

Fair Cloe blush'd; Euphelia frown'd:
    I sung, and gazed; I play'd, and trembled:
And Venus to the Loves around
    Remark'd how ill we all dissembled.

M. Prior

CXXXVIII

When lovely woman stoops to folly
    And finds too late that men betray,—
What charm can soothe her melancholy,
    What art can wash her guilt away?

The only art her guilt to cover,
    To hide her shame from every eye,
To give repentance to her lover
    And wring his bosom, is—to die.

O. Goldsmith

CXXXIX

Ye banks and braes o' bonnie Doon,
    How can ye blume sae fair!
How can ye chant, ye little birds,
    And I sae fu' o' care!

Thou'll break my heart, thou bonnie bird
    That sings upon the bough;
Thou minds me o' the happy days
    When my fause Luve was true.

Thou'll break my heart, thou bonnie bird
    That sings beside thy mate;
For sae I sat, and sae I sang,
    And wist na o' my fate.

Aft hae I roved by bonnie Doon
    To see the woodbine twine,
And ilka bird sang o' its love;
    And sae did I o' mine.

Wi' lightsome heart I pu'd a rose,
  Frae aff its thorny tree;
And my fause luver staw the rose,
  But left the thorn wi' me.

R. Burns

CXL

THE PROGRESS OF POESY

A Pindaric Ode

Awake, Aeolian lyre, awake,
And give to rapture all thy trembling strings.
From Helicon's harmonious springs
    A thousand rills their mazy progress take:
The laughing flowers that round them blow
Drink life and fragrance as they flow.
Now the rich stream of Music winds along
Deep, majestic, smooth, and strong,
Through verdant vales, and Ceres' golden reign;
Now rolling down the steep amain
Headlong, impetuous, see it pour:
The rocks and nodding groves re-bellow to the roar.

O Sovereign of the willing soul,
Parent of sweet and solemn-breathing airs,
Enchanting shell! the sullen Cares
    And frantic Passions hear thy soft control.
On Thracia's hills the Lord of War
Has curb'd the fury of his car
And dropt his thirsty lance at thy command.
Perching on the sceptred hand
Of Jove, thy magic lulls the feather'd king
With ruffled plumes, and flagging wing:
Quench'd in dark clouds of slumber lie
The terror of his beak, and lightnings of his eye.
Thee the voice, the dance, obey
Temper'd to thy warbled lay.
O'er Idalia's velvet-green

The rosy-crownéd Loves are seen
On Cytherea's day,
With antic Sport, and blue-eyed Pleasures,
Frisking light in frolic measures;
Now pursuing, now retreating,
   Now in circling troops they meet:
To brisk notes in cadence beating
   Glance their many-twinkling feet.
Slow melting strains their Queen's approach declare:
   Where'er she turns, the Graces homage pay:
With arms sublime that float upon the air
   In gliding state she wins her easy way:
O'er her warm cheek and rising bosom move
The bloom of young Desire and purple light of Love.

   Man's feeble race what ills await!
Labour, and Penury, the racks of Pain,
Disease, and Sorrow's weeping train,
   And Death, sad refuge from the storms of Fate!
The fond complaint, my song, disprove,
And justify the laws of Jove.
Say, has he given in vain the heavenly Muse?
Night, and all her sickly dews,
Her spectres wan, and birds of boding cry
He gives to range the dreary sky:
Till down the eastern cliffs afar
Hyperion's march they spy, and glittering shafts of
    war.

   In climes beyond the solar road
Where shaggy forms o'er ice-built mountains roam,
The Muse has broke the twilight gloom
   To cheer the shivering native's dull abode.
And oft, beneath the odorous shade
Of Chili's boundless forests laid,
She deigns to hear the savage youth repeat
In loose numbers wildly sweet
Their feather-cinctured chiefs, and dusky loves.

Her track, where'er the Goddess roves,
Glory pursue, and generous Shame,
Th' unconquerable Mind, and Freedom's holy flame.

Woods, that wave o'er Delphi's steep,
Isles, that crown th' Aegean deep,
Fields that cool Ilissus laves,
Or where Maeander's amber waves
In lingering lab'rinths creep,
How do your tuneful echoes languish,
Mute, but to the voice of anguish!
Where each old poetic mountain
    Inspiration breathed around;
Every shade and hallow'd fountain
    Murmur'd deep a solemn sound:
Till the sad Nine, in Greece's evil hour
    Left their Parnassus for the Latian plains.
Alike they scorn the pomp of tyrant Power,
    And coward Vice, that revels in her chains.
When Latium had her lofty spirit lost,
They sought, O Albion! next, thy sea-encircled coast.

    Far from the sun and summer-gale
In thy green lap was Nature's Darling laid,
What time, where lucid Avon stray'd,
    To him the mighty Mother did unveil
Her awful face: the dauntless Child
Stretch'd forth his little arms, and smiled.
This pencil take (she said), whose colours clear
Richly paint the vernal year:
Thine, too, these golden keys, immortal Boy!
This can unlock the gates of Joy;
Of Horror that, and thrilling Fears,
Or ope the sacred source of sympathetic Tears.

    Nor second He, that rode sublime
Upon the seraph-wings of Ecstasy
The secrets of the Abyss to spy:
    He pass'd the flaming bounds of Place and Time

The living Throne, the sapphire-blaze
Where Angels tremble while they gaze,
He saw; but blasted with excess of light,
Closed his eyes in endless night.
Behold where Dryden's less presumptuous car
Wide o'er the fields of Glory bear
Two coursers of ethereal race,
With necks in thunder clothed, and long-resounding
    pace.

Hark, his hands the lyre explore!
Bright-eyed Fancy, hovering o'er,
Scatters from her pictured urn
Thoughts that breathe, and words that burn.
But ah! 'tis heard no more—
Oh! Lyre divine, what daring Spirit
Wakes thee now! Tho' he inherit
Nor the pride, nor ample pinion,
   That the Theban Eagle bear,
Sailing with supreme dominion
   Thro' the azure deep of air:
Yet oft before his infant eyes would run
   Such forms as glitter in the Muse's ray
With orient hues, unborrow'd of the sun:
   Yet shall he mount, and keep his distant way
Beyond the limits of a vulgar fate:
Beneath the Good how far—but far above the Great
                      T. Gray

CXLI

THE PASSIONS

An Ode for Music

When Music, heavenly maid, was young,
While yet in early Greece she sung,
The Passions oft, to hear her shell,
Throng'd around her magic cell
Exulting, trembling, raging, fainting,
Possest beyond the Muse's painting;

By turns they felt the glowing mind
Disturb'd, delighted, raised, refined:
'Till once, 'tis said, when all were fired,
Fill'd with fury, rapt, inspired,
From the supporting myrtles round
They snatch'd her instruments of sound,
And, as they oft had heard apart
Sweet lessons of her forceful art,
Each, for Madness ruled the hour,
Would prove his own expressive power.

First Fear his hand, its skill to try,
  Amid the chords bewilder'd laid,
And back recoil'd, he knew not why,
  E'en at the sound himself had made.

Next Anger rush'd, his eyes on fire,
  In lightnings own'd his secret stings;
In one rude clash he struck the lyre
  And swept with hurried hand the strings.

With woeful measures wan Despair,
  Low sullen sounds, his grief beguiled;
A solemn, strange, and mingled air,
  'Twas sad by fits, by starts 'twas wild.
But thou, O Hope, with eyes so fair,
  What was thy delighted measure?
Still it whisper'd promised pleasure
  And bade the lovely scenes at distance hail!
Still would her touch the strain prolong;
  And from the rocks, the woods, the vale
She call'd on Echo still through all the song;
  And, where her sweetest theme she chose,
  A soft responsive voice was heard at every close;
And Hope enchanted smiled, and waved her golden
    hair;—

And longer had she sung:—but with a frown
  Revenge impatient rose:

He threw his blood-stain'd sword in thunder down;
    And with a withering look
  The war-denouncing trumpet took
And blew a blast so loud and dread,
Were ne'er prophetic sounds so full of woe!
    And ever and anon he beat
    The doubling drum with furious heat;
And, though sometimes, each dreary pause between,
    Dejected Pity at his side
    Her soul-subduing voice applied,
  Yet still he kept his wild unalter'd mien,
While each strain'd ball of sight seem'd bursting from
    his head.

Thy numbers, Jealousy, to nought were fix'd:
  Sad proof of thy distressful state!
Of differing themes the veering song was mix'd;
  And now it courted Love, now raving call'd on
    Hate.

With eyes up-raised, as one inspired,
Pale Melancholy sat retired;
And from her wild sequester'd seat,
In notes by distance made more sweet,
Pour'd through the mellow horn her pensive soul:
    And dashing soft from rocks around
    Bubbling runnels join'd the sound;
Through glades and glooms the mingled measure
    stole,
  Or, o'er some haunted stream, with fond delay,
    Round an holy calm diffusing,
    Love of peace, and lonely musing,
  In hollow murmurs died away.

But O! how alter'd was its sprightlier tone
When Cheerfulness, a nymph of healthiest hue,
  Her bow across her shoulder flung,
  Her buskins gemm'd with morning dew,

Blew an inspiring air, that dale and thicket rung,
   The hunter's call to Faun and Dryad known!
The oak-crown'd Sisters and their chaste-eyed Queen,
   Satyrs and Sylvan Boys, were seen
   Peeping from forth their alleys green:
Brown Exercise rejoiced to hear;
   And Sport leapt up, and seized his beechen spear.

Last came Joy's ecstatic trial:
He, with viny crown advancing,
   First to the lively pipe his hand addrest:
But soon he saw the brisk awakening viol
   Whose sweet entrancing voice he loved the best:
They would have thought who heard the strain
      They saw, in Tempe's vale, her native maids
      Amidst the festal-sounding shades
To some unwearied minstrel dancing;
While, as his flying fingers kiss'd the strings,
   Love framed with Mirth a gay fantastic round:
   Loose were her tresses seen, her zone unbound;
   And he, amidst his frolic play,
   As if he would the charming air repay,
Shook thousand odours from his dewy wings.

   O Music! sphere-descended maid,
   Friend of Pleasure, Wisdom's aid!
   Why, goddess, why, to us denied,
   Lay'st thou thy ancient lyre aside?
   As in that loved Athenian bower
   You learn'd an all-commanding power,
   Thy mimic soul, O nymph endear'd!
   Can well recall what then it heard.
   Where is thy native simple heart
   Devote to Virtue, Fancy, Art?
   Arise, as in that elder time,
   Warm, energetic, chaste, sublime!
   Thy wonders, in that god-like age,
   Fill thy recording Sister's page;—

'Tis said, and I believe the tale,
Thy humblest reed could more prevail,
Had more of strength, diviner rage,
Than all which charms this laggard age,
E'en all at once together found
Cecilia's mingled world of sound:—
O bid our vain endeavours cease:
Revive the just designs of Greece:
Return in all thy simple state!
Confirm the tales her sons relate!

W. COLLINS

CXLII
ODE ON THE SPRING

Lo! where the rosy-bosom'd Hours,
    Fair Venus' train, appear,
Disclose the long-expecting flowers
    And wake the purple year!
The Attic warbler pours her throat
Responsive to the cuckoo's note,
The untaught harmony of Spring:
While, whispering pleasure as they fly,
Cool Zephyrs thro' the clear blue sky
    Their gather'd fragrance fling.

Where'er the oak's thick branches stretch
    A broader, browner shade,
Where'er the rude and moss-grown beech
    O'er-canopies the glade,
Beside some water's rushy brink
With me the Muse shall sit, and think
(At ease reclined in rustic state)
How vain the ardour of the Crowd,
How low, how little are the Proud,
    How indigent the Great!

Still is the toiling hand of Care;
    The panting herds repose:

Yet hark, how thro' the peopled air
  The busy murmur glows!
The insect youth are on the wing,
Eager to taste the honied spring
And float amid the liquid noon:
Some lightly o'er the current skim,
Some show their gaily-gilded trim
  Quick-glancing to the sun.

To Contemplation's sober eye
  Such is the race of Man:
And they that creep, and they that fly
  Shall end where they began.
Alike the busy and the gay
But flutter thro' life's little day,
In Fortune's varying colours drest:
Brush'd by the hand of rough Mischance,
Or chill'd by Age, their airy dance
  They leave, in dust to rest.

Methinks I hear in accents low
  The sportive kind reply:
Poor moralist; and what art thou?
  A solitary fly!
Thy joys no glittering female meets,
No hive hast thou of hoarded sweets,
No painted plumage to display:
On hasty wings thy youth is flown;
Thy sun is set, thy spring is gone—
  We frolic while 'tis May.

T. GRAY

CXLIII

THE POPLAR FIELD

The poplars are fell'd, farewell to the shade
And the whispering sound of the cool colonnade;
The winds play no longer and sing in the leaves,
Nor Ouse on his bosom their image receives.

Twelve years have elapsed since I first took a view
Of my favourite field, and the bank where they grew:
And now in the grass behold they are laid,
And the tree is my seat that once lent me a shade.

The blackbird has fled to another retreat
Where the hazels afford him a screen from the heat;
And the scene where his melody charm'd me before
Resounds with his sweet-flowing ditty no more.

My fugitive years are all hasting away,
And I must ere long lie as lowly as they,
With a turf on my breast and a stone at my head
Ere another such grove shall arise in its stead.

'Tis a sight to engage me, if anything can,
To muse on the perishing pleasures of man;
Short-lived as we are, our enjoyments, I see,
Have a still shorter date; and die sooner than we.

W. COWPER

CXLIV

TO A FIELD-MOUSE

Wee, sleekit, cow'rin', tim'rous beastie,
O what a panic's in thy breastie!
Thou need na start awa sae hasty,
Wi' bickering brattle!
I wad be laith to rin and chase thee
Wi' murd'ring pattle!

I'm truly sorry man's dominion
Has broken nature's social union,
An' justifies that ill opinion
Which makes thee startle
At me, thy poor earth-born companion,
An' fellow-mortal!

I doubt na, whyles, but thou may thieve;
What then? poor beastie, thou maun live!

A daimen icker in a thrave
'S a sma' request:
I'll get a blessin' wi' the lave,
And never miss 't!

Thy wee bit housie, too, in ruin!
Its silly wa's the win's are strewin':
And naething, now, to big a new ane,
O' foggage green!
And bleak December's winds ensuin'
Baith snell an' keen!

Thou saw the fields laid bare and waste
And weary winter comin' fast,
And cozie here, beneath the blast,
Thou thought to dwell,
Till, crash! the cruel coulter past
Out thro' thy cell.

That wee bit heap o' leaves an' stibble
Has cost thee mony a weary nibble!
Now thou's turn'd out, for a' thy trouble,
But house or hald,
To thole the winter's sleety dribble
An' cranreuch cauld!

But, Mousie, thou art no thy lane
In proving foresight may be vain:
The best laid schemes o' mice an' men
Gang aft a-gley,
An' lea'e us nought but grief an' pain,
For promised joy.

Still thou art blest, compared wi' me!
The present only toucheth thee:
But, och! I backward cast my e'e
On prospects drear!
An' forward, tho' I canna see,
I guess and fear!

R. Burns

CXLV

A WISH

Mine be a cot beside the hill;
A bee-hive's hum shall soothe my ear;
A willowy brook that turns a mill,
With many a fall shall linger near.

The swallow, oft, beneath my thatch
Shall twitter from her clay-built nest;
Oft shall the pilgrim lift the latch,
And share my meal, a welcome guest.

Around my ivied porch shall spring
Each fragrant flower that drinks the dew;
And Lucy, at her wheel, shall sing
In russet-gown and apron blue.

The village-church among the trees,
Where first our marriage-vows were given,
With merry peals shall swell the breeze
And point with taper spire to Heaven.

S. Rogers

CXLVI

TO EVENING

If aught of oaten stop or pastoral song
May hope, chaste Eve, to soothe thy modest ear
    Like thy own solemn springs,
    Thy springs, and dying gales;

O Nymph reserved,—while now the bright-hair'd sun
Sits in yon western tent, whose cloudy skirts,
    With brede ethereal wove,
    O'erhang his wavy bed,

Now air is hush'd, save where the weak-eyed bat
With short shrill shriek flits by on leathern wing,
    Or where the beetle winds
    His small but sullen horn,

As oft he rises midst the twilight path,
Against the pilgrim borne in heedless hum,—
  Now teach me, maid composed,
   To breathe some soften'd strain

Whose numbers, stealing through thy darkening vale,
May not unseemly with its stillness suit;
  As, musing slow I hail
   Thy genial loved return.

For when thy folding-star arising shows
His paly circlet, at his warning lamp
  The fragrant Hours, and Elves
   Who slept in buds the day,

And many a Nymph who wreathes her brows with sedge
And sheds the freshening dew, and, lovelier still,
  The pensive Pleasures sweet,
   Prepare thy shadowy car.

Then let me rove some wild and heathy scene;
Or find some ruin midst its dreary dells,
  Whose walls more awful nod
   By thy religious gleams.

Or, if chill blustering winds or driving rain
Prevent my willing feet, be mine the hut
  That, from the mountain's side,
   Views wilds and swelling floods,

And hamlets brown, and dim-discover'd spires;
And hears their simple bell; and marks o'er all
  Thy dewy fingers draw
   The gradual dusky veil.

While Spring shall pour his showers, as oft he wont,
And bathe thy breathing tresses, meekest Eve!
  While Summer loves to sport
   Beneath thy lingering light;

While sallow Autumn fills thy lap with leaves;
Or Winter, yelling through the troublous air,
 Affrights thy shrinking train
 And rudely rends thy robes;

So long, regardful of thy quiet rule,
Shall Fancy, Friendship, Science, smiling Peace,
 Thy gentlest influence own,
 And love thy favourite name!

W. COLLINS

CXLVII

ELEGY

WRITTEN IN A COUNTRY CHURCHYARD

The curfew tolls the knell of parting day,
The lowing herd winds slowly o'er the lea,
The ploughman homeward plods his weary way,
And leaves the world to darkness and to me.

Now fades the glimmering landscape on the sight,
And all the air a solemn stillness holds,
Save where the beetle wheels his droning flight,
And drowsy tinklings lull the distant folds:

Save that from yonder ivy-mantled tower
The moping owl does to the moon complain
Of such as, wandering near her secret bower,
Molest her ancient solitary reign.

Beneath those rugged elms, that yew-tree's shade
Where heaves the turf in many a mouldering heap,
Each in his narrow cell for ever laid,
The rude Forefathers of the hamlet sleep.

The breezy call of incense-breathing morn,
The swallow twittering from the straw-built shed,
The cock's shrill clarion, or the echoing horn,
No more shall rouse them from their lowly bed.

For them no more the blazing hearth shall burn
Or busy housewife ply her evening care:

No children run to lisp their sire's return,
Or climb his knees the envied kiss to share.

Oft did the harvest to their sickle yield,
Their furrow oft the stubborn glebe has broke;
How jocund did they drive their team afield!
How bow'd the woods beneath their sturdy stroke!

Let not Ambition mock their useful toil,
Their homely joys, and destiny obscure;
Nor Grandeur hear with a disdainful smile
The short and simple annals of the Poor.

The boast of heraldry, the pomp of power,
And all that beauty, all that wealth e'er gave
Awaits alike th' inevitable hour:—
The paths of glory lead but to the grave.

Nor you, ye Proud, impute to these the fault
If Memory o'er their tomb no trophies raise,
Where through the long-drawn aisle and fretted vault
The pealing anthem swells the note of praise.

Can storied urn or animated bust
Back to its mansion call the fleeting breath?
Can Honour's voice provoke the silent dust,
Or Flattery soothe the dull cold ear of Death?

Perhaps in this neglected spot is laid
Some heart once pregnant with celestial fire;
Hands, that the rod of empire might have sway'd,
Or waked to ecstasy the living lyre:

But Knowledge to their eyes her ample page,
Rich with the spoils of time, did ne'er unroll;
Chill Penury repress'd their noble rage,
And froze the genial current of the soul.

Full many a gem of purest ray serene
The dark unfathom'd caves of ocean bear:
Full many a flower is born to blush unseen,
And waste its sweetness on the desert air.

Some village-Hampden, that with dauntless breast
The little tyrant of his fields withstood,
Some mute inglorious Milton here may rest,
Some Cromwell, guiltless of his country's blood.

Th' applause of listening senates to command,
The threats of pain and ruin to despise,
To scatter plenty o'er a smiling land,
And read their history in a nation's eyes

Their lot forbad: nor circumscribed alone
Their growing virtues, but their crimes confined;
Forbad to wade through slaughter to a throne,
And shut the gates of mercy on mankind;

The struggling pangs of conscious truth to hide,
To quench the blushes of ingenuous shame,
Or heap the shrine of Luxury and Pride
With incense kindled at the Muse's flame.

Far from the madding crowd's ignoble strife
Their sober wishes never learn'd to stray;
Along the cool sequester'd vale of life
They kept the noiseless tenour of their way.

Yet e'en these bones from insult to protect
Some frail memorial still erected nigh,
With uncouth rhymes and shapeless sculpture deck'd,
Implores the passing tribute of a sigh.

Their name, their years, spelt by th' unletter'd Muse,
The place of fame and elegy supply:
And many a holy text around she strews,
That teach the rustic moralist to die.

For who, to dumb forgetfulness a prey,
This pleasing anxious being e'er resign'd,
Left the warm precincts of the cheerful day,
Nor cast one longing lingering look behind?

On some fond breast the parting soul relies,
Some pious drops the closing eye requires;
E'en from the tomb the voice of Nature cries,
E'en in our ashes live their wonted fires.

For thee, who, mindful of th' unhonour'd dead,
Dost in these lines their artless tale relate;
If chance, by lonely Contemplation led,
Some kindred spirit shall Enquire thy fate,—

Haply some hoary-headed swain may say,
Oft have we seen him at the peep of dawn
Brushing with hasty steps the dews away,
To meet the sun upon the upland lawn;

There at the foot of yonder nodding beech
That wreathes its old fantastic roots so high,
His listless length at noon-tide would he stretch,
And pore upon the brook that babbles by.

Hard by yon wood, now smiling as in scorn,
Muttering his wayward fancies he would rove;
Now drooping, woeful-wan, like one forlorn,
Or crazed with care, or cross'd in hopeless love.

One morn I miss'd him on the custom'd hill,
Along the heath, and near his favourite tree;
Another came; nor yet beside the rill,
Nor up the lawn, nor at the wood was he;

The next with dirges due in sad array
Slow through the church-way path we saw him borne,—
Approach and read (for thou canst read) the lay
Graved on the stone beneath yon aged thorn.

THE EPITAPH

Here rests his head upon the lap of Earth
A youth, to Fortune and to Fame unknown;
Fair Science frown'd not on his humble birth
And Melancholy mark'd him for her own.

Large was his bounty, and his soul sincere;
Heaven did a recompense as largely send:
He gave to Misery all he had, a tear,
He gain'd from Heaven, 'twas all he wish'd, a friend.

No farther seek his merits to disclose,
Or draw his frailties from their dread abode,
(There they alike in trembling hope repose,)
The bosom of his Father and his God.

T. GRAY

CXLVIII

MARY MORISON

O Mary, at thy window be,
It is the wish'd, the trysted hour!
Those smiles and glances let me see
That make the miser's treasure poor:
How blythely wad I bide the stoure,
A weary slave frae sun to sun,
Could I the rich reward secure,
The lovely Mary Morison.

Yestreen when to the trembling string
The dance gaed thro' the lighted ha',
To thee my fancy took its wing,—
I sat, but neither heard nor saw:
Tho' this was fair, and that was braw,
And yon the toast of a' the town,
I sigh'd, and said amang them a',
' Ye are na Mary Morison.'

O Mary, canst thou wreck his peace
Wha for thy sake wad gladly dee?
Or canst thou break that heart of his,
Whase only faut is loving thee?
If love for love thou wilt na gie,
At least be pity to me shown;
A thought ungentle canna be
The thought o' Mary Morison.   R. BURNS

CXLIX
BONNIE LESLEY

O saw ye bonnie Lesley
　　As she gaed o'er the border?
She's gane, like Alexander,
　　To spread her conquests farther.

To see her is to love her,
　　And love but her for ever;
For nature made her what she is,
　　And ne'er made sic anither!

Thou art a queen, fair Lesley,
　　Thy subjects we, before thee;
Thou art divine, fair Lesley,
　　The hearts o' men adore thee.

The deil he could na scaith thee,
　　Or aught that wad belang thee;
He'd look into thy bonnie face,
　　And say 'I canna wrang thee!'

The Powers aboon will tent thee
　　Misfortune sha' na steer thee;
Thou'rt like themselves sae lovely
　　That ill they'll ne'er let near thee.

Return again, fair Lesley,
　　Return to Caledonie!
That we may brag we hae a lass
　　There's nane again sae bonnie.
　　　　　　　　　　R. Burns

CL

O my Luve's like a red, red rose
　　That's newly sprung in June:
O my Luve's like the melodie
　　That's sweetly play'd in tune.

As fair art thou, my bonnie lass,
    So deep in luve am I:
And I will luve thee still, my dear,
    Till a' the seas gang dry:

Till a' the seas gang dry, my dear,
    And the rocks melt wi' the sun;
I will luve thee still, my dear,
    While the sands o' life shall run.

And fare thee weel, my only Luve!
    And fare thee weel awhile!
And I will come again, my Luve,
    Tho' it were ten thousand mile.

                 R. BURNS

CLI
HIGHLAND MARY

Ye banks and braes and streams around
    The castle o' Montgomery,
Green be your woods, and fair your flowers,
    Your waters never drumlie!
There simmer first unfauld her robes,
    And there the langest tarry;
For there I took the last fareweel
    O' my sweet Highland Mary.

How sweetly bloom'd the gay green birk,
    How rich the hawthorn's blossom,
As underneath their fragrant shade
    I clasp'd her to my bosom!
The golden hours on angel wings
    Flew o'er me and my dearie;
For dear to me as light and life
    Was my sweet Highland Mary.

Wi' mony a vow and lock'd embrace
    Our parting was fu' tender;
And pledging aft to meet again,
    We tore oursels asunder;

But, O! fell Death's untimely frost,
    That nipt my flower sae early!
Now green's the sod, and cauld's the clay,
    That wraps my Highland Mary!

O pale, pale now, those rosy lips,
    I aft hae kiss'd sae fondly!
And closed for aye the sparkling glance
    That dwelt on me sae kindly;
And mouldering now in silent dust
    That heart that lo'ed me dearly!
But still within my bosom's core
    Shall live my Highland Mary.

R. Burns

CLII
AULD ROBIN GRAY

When the sheep are in the fauld, and the kye at hame,
And a' the warld to rest are gane,
The waes o' my heart fa' in showers frae my e'e,
While my gudeman lies sound by me.

Young Jamie lo'ed me weel, and sought me for his bride;
But saving a croun he had naething else beside:
To make the croun a pund, young Jamie gaed to sea;
And the croun and the pund were baith for me.

He hadna been awa' a week but only twa,
When my father brak his arm, and the cow was stown
    awa;
My mother she fell sick, and my Jamie at the sea—
And auld Robin Gray came a-courtin' me.

My father couldna work, and my mother couldna spin;
I toil'd day and night, but their bread I couldna win;
Auld Rob maintain'd them baith, and wi' tears in his e'e
Said, Jennie, for their sakes, O, marry me!

My heart it said nay; I look'd for Jamie back;
But the wind it blew high, and the ship it was a wrack;
His ship it was a wrack—why didna Jamie dee?
Or why do I live to cry, Wae's me?

My father urgit sair: my mother didna speak;
But she look'd in my face till my heart was like to break:
They gi'ed him my hand, but my heart was at the sea;
Sae auld Robin Gray he was gudeman to me.

I hadna been a wife a week but only four,
When mournfu' as I sat on the stane at the door,
I saw my Jamie's wraith, for I couldna think it he
Till he said, I'm come hame to marry thee.

O sair, sair did we greet, and muckle did we say;
We took but ae kiss, and I bad him gang away;
I wish that I were dead, but I'm no like to dee;
And why was I born to say, Wae's me!

I gang like a ghaist, and I carena to spin;
I daurna think on Jamie, for that wad be a sin;
But I'll do my best a gude wife aye to be,
For auld Robin Gray he is kind unto me.

LADY A. LINDSAY

CLIII

DUNCAN GRAY

Duncan Gray cam here to woo,
    Ha, ha, the wooing o't;
On blythe Yule night when we were fou,
    Ha, ha, the wooing o't:
Maggie coost her head fu' high,
Look'd asklent and unco skeigh,
Gart poor Duncan stand abeigh;
    Ha, ha, the wooing o't!

Duncan fleech'd, and Duncan pray'd;
Meg was deaf as Ailsa Craig;

Duncan sigh'd baith out and in,
Grat his een baith bleer't and blin',
Spak o' lowpin ower a linn!

Time and chance are but a tide,
Slighted love is sair to bide;
Shall I, like a fool, quoth he,
For a haughty hizzie dee?
She may gae to—France for me!

How it comes let doctors tell,
Meg grew sick—as he grew heal;
Something in her bosom wrings,
For relief a sigh she brings;
And O, her een, they spak sic things!

Duncan was a lad o' grace;
Maggie's was a piteous case;
Duncan couldna be her death,
Swelling pity smoor'd his wrath;
Now they're crouse and canty baith:
    Ha, ha, the wooing o't!

R. Burns

CLIV

THE SAILOR'S WIFE

And are ye sure the news is true?
    And are ye sure he's weel?
Is this a time to think o' wark?
    Ye jades, lay by your wheel;
Is this the time to spin a thread,
    When Colin's at the door?
Reach down my cloak, I'll to the quay,
    And see him come ashore.
For there's nae luck about the house,
    There's nae luck at a';
There's little pleasure in the house
    When our gudeman's awa'.

And gie to me my bigonet,
　　My bishop's satin gown;
For I maun tell the baillie's wife
　　That Colin's in the town.
My Turkey slippers maun gae on,
　　My stockins pearly blue;
It's a' to pleasure our gudeman,
　　For he's baith leal and true.

Rise, lass, and mak' a clean fireside,
　　Put on the muckle pot;
Gie little Kate her button gown
　　And Jock his Sunday coat;
And mak' their shoon as black as slaes,
　　Their hose as white as snaw;
It's a' to please my ain gudeman,
　　For he's been long awa.

There's twa fat hens upo' the coop
　　Been fed this month and mair;
Mak haste and thraw their necks about,
　　That Colin weel may fare;
And spread the table neat and clean,
　　Gar ilka thing look braw,
For wha can tell how Colin fared
　　When he was far awa?

Sae true his heart, sae smooth his speech,
　　His breath like caller air;
His very foot has music in't
　　As he comes up the stair—
And will I see his face again?
　　And will I hear him speak?
I'm downright dizzy wi' the thought,
　　In troth I'm like to greet!

If Colin's weel, and weel content,
　　I hae nae mair to crave:

And gin I live to keep him sae,
    I'm blest aboon the lave:
And will I see his face again,
    And will I hear him speak?
I'm downright dizzy wi' the thought,
    In troth I'm like to greet.
For there's nae luck about the house,
    There's nae luck at a';
There's little pleasure in the house
    When our gudeman's awa.

                  W. J. MICKLE

CLV
JEAN

Of a' the airts the wind can blaw
    I dearly like the West,
For there the bonnie lassie lives,
    The lassie I lo'e best:
There wild woods grow, and rivers row,
    And mony a hill between;
But day and night my fancy's flight
    Is ever wi' my Jean.

I see her in the dewy flowers,
    I see her sweet and fair;
I hear her in the tunefu' birds,
    I hear her charm the air:
There's not a bonnie flower that springs
    By fountain, shaw, or green,
There's not a bonnie bird that sings
    But minds me o' my Jean.

O blaw ye westlin winds, blaw saft
    Amang the leafy trees;
Wi' balmy gale, frae hill and dale
    Bring hame the laden bees;
And bring the lassie back to me
    That's aye sae neat and clean;

Ae smile o' her wad banish care,
  Sae charming is my Jean.

What sighs and vows amang the knowes
  Hae pass'd atween us twa!
How fond to meet, how wae to part
  That night she gaed awa!
The Powers aboon can only ken
  To whom the heart is seen,
That nane can be sae dear to me
  As my sweet lovely Jean!

R. Burns

CLVI
JOHN ANDERSON

John Anderson my jo, John,
When we were first acquent
Your locks were like the raven,
Your bonnie brow was brent;
But now your brow is bald, John,
Your locks are like the snow;
But blessings on your frosty pow,
John Anderson my jo.

John Anderson my jo, John,
We clamb the hill thegither,
And mony a canty day, John,
We've had wi' ane anither:
Now we maun totter down, John,
But hand in hand we'll go,
And sleep thegither at the foot,
John Anderson my jo.

R. Burns

CLVII
THE LAND O' THE LEAL

I'm wearing awa', Jean,
Like snaw when its thaw, Jean,
I'm wearing awa'
  To the land o' the leal.

There's nae sorrow there, Jean,
There's neither cauld nor care, Jean,
The day is aye fair
In the land o' the leal.

Ye were aye leal and true, Jean,
Your task's ended noo, Jean,
And I'll welcome you
To the land o' the leal.
Our bonnie bairn's there, Jean,
She was baith guid and fair, Jean;
O we grudged her right sair
To the land o' the leal!

Then dry that tearfu' e'e, Jean,
My soul langs to be free, Jean,
And angels wait on me
To the land o' the leal.
Now fare ye weel, my ain Jean,
This warld's care is vain, Jean;
We'll meet and aye be fain
In the land o' the leal.

LADY NAIRN

CLVIII

ODE ON A DISTANT PROSPECT OF ETON COLLEGE

Ye distant spires, ye antique towers,
That crown the watery glade,
Where grateful Science still adores
Her Henry's holy shade;
And ye, that from the stately brow
Of Windsor's heights th' expanse below
Of grove, of lawn, of mead survey,
Whose turf, whose shade, whose flowers among
Wanders the hoary Thames along
His silver-winding way:

Ah happy hills! ah pleasing shade!
   Ah fields beloved in vain!
When once my careless childhood stray'd,
   A stranger yet to pain!
I feel the gales that from ye blow
A momentary bliss bestow,
As waving fresh their gladsome wing
My weary soul they seem to soothe,
And, redolent of joy and youth,
   To breathe a second spring.

Say, Father Thames, for thou hast seen
   Full many a sprightly race
Disporting on thy margent green
   The paths of pleasure trace;
Who foremost now delight to cleave
With pliant arm, thy glassy wave?
The captive linnet which enthral?
What idle progeny succeed
To chase the rolling circle's speed
   Or urge the flying ball?

While some on earnest business bent
   Their murmuring labours ply
'Gainst graver hours, that bring constraint
   To sweeten liberty:
Some bold adventurers disdain
The limits of their little reign
And unknown regions dare descry:
Still as they run they look behind,
They hear a voice in every wind,
   And snatch a fearful joy.

Gay Hope is theirs by fancy fed,
   Less pleasing when possest:
The tear forgot as soon as shed,
   The sunshine of the breast:
Theirs buxom Health, of rosy hue,

Wild Wit, Invention ever new,
And lively Cheer, of Vigour born;
The thoughtless day, the easy night,
The spirits pure, the slumbers light
   That fly th' approach of morn.

Alas! regardless of their doom
   The little victims play!
No sense have they of ills to come
   Nor care beyond to-day:
Yet see how all around 'em wait
The ministers of human fate
And black Misfortune's baleful train!
Ah shew them where in ambush stand
To seize their prey, the murderous band!
   Ah, tell them they are men!

These shall the fury Passions tear,
   The vultures of the mind,
Disdainful Anger, pallid Fear,
   And Shame that skulks behind;
Or pining Love shall waste their youth,
Or Jealousy with rankling tooth
That inly gnaws the secret heart,
And Envy wan, and faded Care,
Grim-visaged comfortless Despair,
   And Sorrow's piercing dart.

Ambition this shall tempt to rise,
   Then whirl the wretch from high
To bitter Scorn a sacrifice
   And grinning Infamy.
The stings of Falsehood those shall try
And hard Unkindness' alter'd eye,
That mocks the tear it forced to flow;
And keen Remorse with blood defiled,
And moody Madness laughing wild
   Amid severest woe.

Lo, in the Vale of Years beneath
   A griesly troop are seen,
The painful family of Death,
   More hideous than their Queen:
This racks the joints, this fires the veins,
That every labouring sinew strains,
Those in the deeper vitals rage:
Lo! Poverty, to fill the band,
That numbs the soul with icy hand,
   And slow-consuming Age.

To each his sufferings: all are men,
   Condemn'd alike to groan;
The tender for another's pain,
   Th' unfeeling for his own.
Yet, ah! why should they know their fate,
Since sorrow never comes too late,
And happiness too swiftly flies?
Thought would destroy their paradise!
No more;—where ignorance is bliss,
   'Tis folly to be wise.

T. Gray

CLIX

HYMN TO ADVERSITY

Daughter of Jove, relentless power,
   Thou tamer of the human breast,
Whose iron scourge and torturing hour
   The bad affright, afflict the best!
Bound in thy adamantine chain
The proud are taught to taste of pain,
And purple tyrants vainly groan
With pangs unfelt before, unpitied and alone.

When first thy Sire to send on earth
   Virtue, his darling child, design'd,
To thee he gave the heavenly birth
   And bade to form her infant mind.

Stern, rugged Nurse! thy rigid lore
With patience many a year she bore;
What sorrow was, thou bad'st her know,
And from her own she learn'd to melt at others' woe.

Scared at thy frown terrific, fly
   Self-pleasing Folly's idle brood,
Wild Laughter, Noise, and thoughtless Joy,
   And leave us leisure to be good.
Light they disperse, and with them go
The summer Friend, the flattering Foe;
   By vain Prosperity received,
To her they vow their truth, and are again believed.

Wisdom in sable garb array'd
   Immersed in rapturous thought profound,
And Melancholy, silent maid,
   With leaden eye, that loves the ground,
Still on thy solemn steps attend:
Warm Charity, the general friend,
   With Justice, to herself severe,
And Pity dropping soft the sadly-pleasing tear.

O! gently on thy suppliant's head
   Dread Goddess, lay thy chastening hand!
Not in thy Gorgon terrors clad,
   Nor circled with the vengeful band
(As by the impious thou art seen)
With thundering voice, and threatening mien,
   With screaming Horror's funeral cry,
Despair, and fell Disease, and ghastly Poverty;—

Thy form benign, O Goddess, wear,
   Thy milder influence impart,
Thy philosophic train be there
   To soften, not to wound my heart.

The generous spark extinct revive,
Teach me to love and to forgive
Exact my own defects to scan,
What others are to feel, and know myself a Man.

T. GRAY

CLX

THE SOLITUDE
OF ALEXANDER SELKIRK

I am monarch of all I survey;
My right there is none to dispute;
From the centre all round to the sea
I am lord of the fowl and the brute.
O Solitude! where are the charms
That sages have seen in thy face?
Better dwell in the midst of alarms,
Than reign in this horrible place.

I am out of humanity's reach,
I must finish my journey alone,
Never hear the sweet music of speech;
I start at the sound of my own.
The beasts that roam over the plain
My form with indifference see;
They are so unacquainted with man,
Their tameness is shocking to me.

Society, Friendship, and Love
Divinely bestow'd upon man,
O, had I the wings of a dove
How soon would I taste you again!
My sorrows I then might assuage
In the ways of religion and truth
Might learn from the wisdom of age,
And be cheer'd by the sallies of youth.

Ye winds that have made me your sport,
Convey to this desolate shore

Some cordial endearing report
Of a land I shall visit no more:
My friends, do they now and then send
A wish or a thought after me?
O tell me I yet have a friend,
Though a friend I am never to see.

How fleet is a glance of the mind!
Compared with the speed of its flight,
The tempest itself lags behind,
And the swift-wingéd arrows of light.
When I think of my own native land
In a moment I seem to be there;
But alas! recollection at hand
Soon hurries me back to despair.

But the sea-fowl is gone to her nest,
The beast is laid down in his lair;
Even here is a season of rest,
And I to my cabin repair.
There's mercy in every place,
And mercy, encouraging thought!
Gives even affliction a grace
And reconciles man to his lot.

W. Cowper

CLXI

TO MARY UNWIN

Mary! I want a lyre with other strings,
Such aid from heaven as some have feign'd they drew,
An eloquence scarce given to mortals, new
And undebased by praise of meaner things,

That ere through age or woe I shed my wings
I may record thy worth with honour due,
In verse as musical as thou art true,
And that immortalises whom it sings:—

But thou hast little need.   There is a Book
By seraphs writ with beams of heavenly light,
On which the eyes of God not rarely look,

A chronicle of actions just and bright—
There all thy deeds, my faithful Mary, shine;
And since thou own'st that praise, I spare thee mine.

W. COWPER

CLXII

TO THE SAME

The twentieth year is well-nigh past
Since first our sky was overcast;
Ah would that this might be the last!
     My Mary!

Thy spirits have a fainter flow
I see thee daily weaker grow—
'Twas my distress that brought thee low,
     My Mary!

Thy needles, once a shining store,
For my sake restless heretofore,
Now rust disused, and shine no more;
     My Mary!

For though thou gladly wouldst fulfil
The same kind office for me still,
Thy sight now seconds not thy will,
     My Mary!

But well thou play'dst the housewife's part,
And all thy threads with magic art
Have wound themselves about this heart,
     My Mary!

Thy indistinct expressions seem
Like language utter'd in a dream;
Yet me they charm, whate'er the theme,
     My Mary!

Thy silver locks, once auburn bright,
Are still more lovely in my sight
Than golden beams of orient light,
  My Mary!

For could I view nor them nor thee,
What sight worth seeing could I see?
The sun would rise in vain for me,
  My Mary!

Partakers of thy sad decline
Thy hands their little force resign;
Yet, gently press'd, press gently mine,
  My Mary!

Such feebleness of limbs thou prov'st
That now at every step thou mov'st
Upheld by two; yet still thou lov'st,
  My Mary!

And still to love, though press'd with ill,
In wintry age to feel no chill,
With me is to be lovely still,
  My Mary!

But ah! by constant heed I know
How oft the sadness that I show
Transforms thy smiles to looks of woe,
  My Mary!

And should my future lot be cast
With much resemblance of the past,
Thy worn-out heart will break at last—
  My Mary!

W. Cowper

CLXIII

THE DYING MAN IN HIS GARDEN

Why, Damon, with the forward day
Dost thou thy little spot survey,
From tree to tree, with doubtful cheer,
Pursue the progress of the year,

What winds arise, what rains descend,
When thou before that year shalt end?

What do thy noontide walks avail,
To clear the leaf, and pick the snail,
Then wantonly to death decree
An insect usefuller than thee?
Thou and the worm are brother-kind,
As low, as earthy, and as blind.

Vain wretch! canst thou expect to see
The downy peach make court to thee?
Or that thy sense shall ever meet
The bean-flower's deep-embosom'd sweet
Exhaling with an evening blast?
Thy evenings then will all be past!

Thy narrow pride, thy fancied green
(For vanity's in little seen)
All must be left when Death appears,
In spite of wishes, groans, and tears;
Nor one of all thy plants that grow
But Rosemary will with thee go.

G. SEWELL

CLXIV
TO-MORROW

In the downhill of life when I find I'm declining,
    May my fate no less fortunate be
Than a snug elbow-chair can afford for reclining,
    And a cot that o'erlooks the wide sea;
With an ambling pad-pony to pace o'er the lawn,
    While I carol away idle sorrow,
And blithe as the lark that each day hails the dawn
    Look forward with hope for to-morrow.

With a porch at my door, both for shelter and shade too,
    As the sun-shine or rain may prevail;
And a small spot of ground for the use of the spade too,
    With a barn for the use of the flail:

A cow for my dairy, a dog for my game,
   And a purse when a friend wants to borrow;
I'll envy no nabob his riches or fame,
   Nor what honours may wait him to-morrow.

From the bleak northern blast may my cot be completely
   Secured by a neighbouring hill;
And at night may repose steal upon me more sweetly
   By the sound of a murmuring rill:
And while peace and plenty I find at my board,
   With a heart free from sickness and sorrow,
With my friends may I share what to-day may afford,
   And let them spread the table to-morrow.

And when I at last must throw off this frail covering
   Which I've worn for three-score years and ten,
On the brink of the grave I'll not seek to keep hovering,
   Nor my thread wish to spin o'er again:
But my face in the glass I'll serenely survey,
   And with smiles count each wrinkle and furrow;
And this old worn-out stuff, which is threadbare to-day,
   May become everlasting to-morrow.

                        J. Collins

CLXV

Life! I know not what thou art,
But know that thou and I must part;
And when, or how, or where we met
I own to me's a secret yet.

   Life! we've been long together
Through pleasant and through cloudy weather;
'Tis hard to part when friends are dear—
Perhaps 'twill cost a sigh, a tear;
—Then steal away, give little warning,
   Choose thine own time;
Say not Good Night,—but in some brighter clime
   Bid me Good Morning.

                     A. L. Barbauld

BOOK FOURTH

ON FIRST LOOKING INTO CHAPMAN'S HOMER

Much have I travell'd in the realms of gold
And many goodly states and kingdoms seen;
Round many western islands have I been
Which bards in fealty to Apollo hold.

Oft of one wide expanse had I been told
That deep-brow'd Homer ruled as his demesne:
Yet did I never breathe its pure serene
Till I heard Chapman speak out loud and bold:

—Then felt I like some watcher of the skies
When a new planet swims into his ken;
Or like stout Cortez—when with eagle eyes

He stared at the Pacific—and all his men
Look'd at each other with a wild surmise—
Silent, upon a peak in Darien.

J. KEATS

CLXVII

ODE ON THE POETS

Bards of Passion and of Mirth
Ye have left your souls on earth!
Have ye souls in heaven too,
Double-lived in regions new?
—Yes, and those of heaven commune
With the spheres of sun and moon;
With the noise of fountains wonderous
And the parle of voices thunderous;
With the whisper of heaven's trees
And one another, in soft ease
Seated on Elysian lawns

Browsed by none but Dian's fawns;
Underneath large blue-bells tented,
Where the daisies are rose-scented,
And the rose herself has got
Perfume which on earth is not;
Where the nightingale doth sing
Not a senseless, trancéd thing,
But divine melodious truth;
Philosophic numbers smooth;
Tales and golden histories
Of heaven and its mysteries.

Thus ye live on high, and then
On the earth ye live again;
And the souls ye left behind you
Teach us, here, the way to find you,
Where your other souls are joying,
Never slumber'd, never cloying.
Here, your earth-born souls still speak
To mortals, of their little week;
Of their sorrows and delights;
Of their passions and their spites
Of their glory and their shame;
What doth strengthen and what maim:—
Thus ye teach us, every day,
Wisdom, though fled far away.

Bards of Passion and of Mirth
Ye have left your souls on earth!
Ye have souls in heaven too,
Double-lived in regions new!

J. KEATS

CLXVIII
LOVE

All thoughts, all passions, all delights,
Whatever stirs this mortal frame,
All are but ministers of Love,
    And feed his sacred flame.

Oft in my waking dreams do I
Live o'er again that happy hour,
When midway on the mount I lay,
 Beside the ruin'd tower.

The moonshine stealing o'er the scene
Had blended with the lights of eve;
And she was there, my hope, my joy,
 My own dear Genevieve!

She lean'd against the arméd man,
The statue of the arméd knight;
She stood and listen'd to my lay,
 Amid the lingering light.

Few sorrows hath she of her own,
My hope! my joy! my Genevieve!
She loves me best, whene'er I sing
 The songs that make her grieve.

I play'd a soft and doleful air,
I sang an old and moving story—
An old rude song, that suited well
 That ruin wild and hoary.

She listen'd with a flitting blush,
With downcast eyes and modest grace;
For well she knew, I could not choose
 But gaze upon her face.

I told her of the Knight that wore
Upon his shield a burning brand;
And that for ten long years he woo'd
 The Lady of the Land.

I told her how he pined: and ah!
The deep, the low, the pleading tone
With which I sang another's love
 Interpreted my own.

She listen'd with a flitting blush,
With downcast eyes, and modest grace;
And she forgave me, that I gazed
    Too fondly on her face!

But when I told the cruel scorn
That crazed that bold and lovely Knight,
And that he cross'd the mountain-woods,
    Nor rested day nor night;

That sometimes from the savage den,
And sometimes from the darksome shade,
And sometimes starting up at once
    In green and sunny glade—

There came and look'd him in the face
An angel beautiful and bright;
And that he knew it was a Fiend,
    This miserable Knight!

And that unknowing what he did,
He leap'd amid a murderous band,
And saved from outrage worse than death
    The Lady of the Land;

And how she wept, and clasp'd his knees;
And how she tended him in vain;
And ever strove to expiate
    The scorn that crazed his brain;

And that she nursed him in a cave,
And how his madness went away,
When on the yellow forest-leaves
    A dying man he lay;

—His dying words—but when I reach'd
That tenderest strain of all the ditty,

My faltering voice and pausing harp
    Disturb'd her soul with pity!

All impulses of soul and sense
Had thrill'd my guileless Genevieve;
The music and the doleful tale,
    The rich and balmy eve;

And hopes, and fears that kindle hope,
An undistinguishable throng,
And gentle wishes long subdued,
    Subdued and cherish'd long!

She wept with pity and delight,
She blush'd with love, and virgin shame;
And like the murmur of a dream,
    I heard her breathe my name.

Her bosom heaved—she stepp'd aside,
As conscious of my look she stept—
Then suddenly, with timorous eye
    She fled to me and wept.

She half enclosed me with her arms,
She press'd me with a meek embrace;
And bending back her head, look'd up,
    And gazed upon my face.

'Twas partly love, and partly fear,
And partly 'twas a bashful art
That I might rather feel, than see,
    The swelling of her heart.

I calm'd her fears, and she was calm,
And told her love with virgin pride;
And so I won my Genevieve,
    My bright and beauteous Bride.
                S. T. COLERIDGE

ALL FOR LOVE

O talk not to me of a name great in story;
The days of our youth are the days of our glory;
And the myrtle and ivy of sweet two-and-twenty
Are worth all your laurels though ever so plenty.

What are garlands and crowns to the brow that is
    wrinkled?
'Tis but as a dead flower with May-dew besprinkled:
Then away with all such from the head that is hoary—
What care I for the wreaths that can only give glory?

Oh Fame!—if I e'er took delight in thy praises,
'Twas less for the sake of thy high-sounding phrases,
Than to see the bright eyes of the dear one discover
She thought that I was not unworthy to love her.

There chiefly I sought thee, there only I found thee;
Her glance was the best of the rays that surround thee;
When it sparkled o'er aught that was bright in my
    story,
I knew it was love, and I felt it was glory.

Lord Byron

THE OUTLAW

O Brignall banks are wild and fair,
    And Greta woods are green,
And you may gather garlands there
    Would grace a summer-queen.
And as I rode by Dalton-Hall
    Beneath the turrets high,
A Maiden on the castle-wall
    Was singing merrily:

'O Brignal Banks are fresh and fair,
  And Greta woods are green;
I'd rather rove with Edmund there
  Than reign our English queen.'

'If, Maiden, thou wouldst wend with me,
  To leave both tower and town,
Thou first must guess what life lead we
  That dwell by dale and down,
And if thou canst that riddle read,
  As read full well you may,
Then to the greenwood shalt thou speed
  As blithe as Queen of May.'
Yet sung she, 'Brignall banks are fair,
  And Greta woods are green;
I'd rather rove with Edmund there
  Than reign our English queen.

'I read you, by your bugle-horn
  And by your palfrey good,
I read you for a ranger sworn
  To keep the king's greenwood.'
'A Ranger, lady, winds his horn,
  And 'tis at peep of light;
His blast is heard at merry morn
  And mine at dead of night.'
Yet sung she, 'Brignall banks are fair,
  And Greta woods are gay;
I would I were with Edmund there
  To reign his Queen of May!

'With burnish'd brand and musketoon
  So gallantly you come,
I read you for a bold Dragoon
  That lists the tuck of drum.'
'I list no more the tuck of drum,
  No more the trumpet hear;

But when the beetle sounds his hum
    My comrades take the spear.
And O! though Brignall banks be fair
    And Greta woods be gay,
Yet mickle must the maiden dare
    Would reign my Queen of May!

'Maiden! a nameless life I lead,
    A nameless death I'll die;
The fiend whose lantern lights the mead
    Were better mate than I!
And when I'm with my comrades met
    Beneath the greenwood bough,—
What once we were we all forget,
    Nor think what we are now.'

Chorus

'Yet Brignall banks are fresh and fair,
    And Greta woods are green,
And you may gather garlands there
    Would grace a summer-queen.'

Sir W. Scott

CLXXI

There be none of Beauty's daughters
    With a magic like Thee;
And like music on the waters
    Is thy sweet voice to me:
When, as if its sound were causing
The charmed ocean's pausing,
The waves lie still and gleaming,
And the lull'd winds seem dreaming:

And the midnight moon is weaving
    Her bright chain o'er the deep,
Whose breast is gently heaving
    As an infant's asleep:

So the spirit bows before thee
To listen and adore thee;
With a full but soft emotion,
Like the swell of Summer's ocean.

Lord Byron

CLXXII

LINES TO AN INDIAN AIR

I arise from dreams of Thee
In the first sweet sleep of night,
When the winds are breathing low
And the stars are shining bright:
I arise from dreams of thee,
And a spirit in my feet
Hath led me—who knows how?
To thy chamber-window, Sweet!

The wandering airs they faint
On the dark, the silent stream—
The champak odours fail
Like sweet thoughts in a dream;
The nightingale's complaint
It dies upon her heart,
As I must die on thine
O belovéd as thou art!

O lift me from the grass!
I die, I faint, I fail!
Let thy love in kisses rain
On my lips and eyelids pale.
My cheek is cold and white, alas!
My heart beats loud and fast;
O! press it close to thine again
Where it will break at last.

P. B. Shelley

CLXXIII

She walks in beauty, like the night
Of cloudless climes and starry skies,
And all that's best of dark and bright
Meet in her aspect and her eyes;
Thus mellow'd to that tender light
Which heaven to gaudy day denies.

One shade the more, one ray the less,
Had half impair'd the nameless grace
Which waves in every raven tress
Or softly lightens o'er her face,
Where thoughts serenely sweet express
How pure, how dear their dwelling-place.

And on that cheek and o'er that brow
So soft, so calm, yet eloquent,
The smiles that win, the tints that glow
But tell of days in goodness spent,
A mind at peace with all below,
A heart whose love is innocent.

LORD BYRON

CLXXIV

She was a phantom of delight
When first she gleam'd upon my sight;
A lovely apparition, sent
To be a moment's ornament;
Her eyes as stars of twilight fair;
Like Twilight's, too, her dusky hair;
But all things else about her drawn
From May-time and the cheerful dawn;
A dancing shape, an image gay,
To haunt, to startle, and waylay.

I saw her upon nearer view,
A spirit, yet a woman too!

Her household motions light and free,
And steps of virgin-liberty;
A countenance in which did meet
Sweet records, promises as sweet;
A creature not too bright or good
For human nature's daily food,
For transient sorrows, simple wiles,
Praise, blame, love, kisses, tears, and smiles.

And now I see with eye serene
The very pulse of the machine;
A being breathing thoughtful breath,
A traveller between life and death:
The reason firm, the temperate will,
Endurance, foresight, strength, and skill;
A perfect woman, nobly plann'd
To warn, to comfort, and command;
And yet a Spirit still, and bright
With something of an angel-light.

W. WORDSWORTH

CLXXV

She is not fair to outward view
    As many maidens be;
Her loveliness I never knew
    Until she smiled on me.
O then I saw her eye was bright,
A well of love, a spring of light.

But now her looks are coy and cold,
    To mine they ne'er reply,
And yet I cease not to behold
    The love-light in her eye:
Her very frowns are fairer far
Than smiles of other maidens are.

H. COLERIDGE

I fear thy kisses, gentle maiden;
Thou needest not fear mine;
My spirit is too deeply laden
Ever to burthen thine.

I fear thy mien, thy tones, thy motion;
Thou needest not fear mine;
Innocent is the heart's devotion
With which I worship thine.

P. B. SHELLEY

THE LOST LOVE

She dwelt among the untrodden ways
    Beside the springs of Dove;
A maid whom there were none to praise,
    And very few to love.

A violet by a mossy stone
    Half-hidden from the eye!
—Fair as a star, when only one
    Is shining in the sky.

She lived unknown, and few could know
    When Lucy ceased to be;
But she is in her grave, and, O!
    The difference to me!

W. WORDSWORTH

I travell'd among unknown men
    In lands beyond the sea;
Nor, England! did I know till then
    What love I bore to thee.

'Tis past, that melancholy dream!
    Nor will I quit thy shore
A second time, for still I seem
    To love thee more and more.

Among thy mountains did I feel
　　The joy of my desire;
And she I cherish'd turn'd her wheel
　　Beside an English fire.

Thy mornings show'd, thy nights conceal'd
　　The bowers where Lucy play'd;
And thine too is the last green field
　　That Lucy's eyes survey'd.

W. WORDSWORTH

CLXXIX

THE EDUCATION OF NATURE

Three years she grew in sun and shower;
Then Nature said, 'A lovelier flower
On earth was never sown:
This child I to myself will take;
She shall be mine, and I will make
A lady of my own.

'Myself will to my darling be
Both law and impulse: and with me
The girl, in rock and plain,
In earth and heaven, in glade and bower,
Shall feel an overseeing power
To kindle or restrain.

'She shall be sportive as the fawn
That wild with glee across the lawn
Or up the mountain springs;
And her's shall be the breathing balm,
And her's the silence and the calm
Of mute insensate things.

'The floating clouds their state shall lend
To her; for her the willow bend;
Nor shall she fail to see
E'en in the motions of the storm
Grace that shall mould the maiden's form
By silent sympathy.

'The stars of midnight shall be dear
To her; and she shall lean her ear
In many a secret place
Where rivulets dance their wayward round,
And beauty born of murmuring sound
Shall pass into her face.

'And vital feelings of delight
Shall rear her form to stately height,
Her virgin bosom swell;
Such thoughts to Lucy I will give
Where she and I together live
Here in this happy dell.'

Thus Nature spake—The work was done—
How soon my Lucy's race was run!
She died, and left to me
This heath, this calm and quiet scene;
The memory of what has been,
And never more will be.

W. WORDSWORTH

CLXXX

A slumber did my spirit seal;
  I had no human fears:
She seem'd a thing that could not feel
  The touch of earthly years.

No motion has she now, no force;
  She neither hears nor sees;
Roll'd round in earth's diurnal course
  With rocks, and stones, and trees.

W. WORDSWORTH

CLXXXI

LORD ULLIN'S DAUGHTER

A Chieftain to the Highlands bound
Cries 'Boatman, do not tarry!
And I'll give thee a silver pound
To row us o'er the ferry!'

'Now who be ye, would cross Lochgyle,
This dark and stormy water?'
'O I'm the chief of Ulva's isle,
And this, Lord Ullin's daughter.

'And fast before her father's men
Three days we've fled together,
For should he find us in the glen,
My blood would stain the heather.

'His horsemen hard behind us ride—
Should they our steps discover,
Then who will cheer my bonny bride,
When they have slain her lover?'

Out spoke the hardy Highland wight,
'I'll go, my chief, I'm ready:
It is not for your silver bright,
But for your winsome lady:—

'And by my word! the bonny bird
In danger shall not tarry;
So though the waves are raging white
I'll row you o'er the ferry.'

By this the storm grew loud apace,
The water-wraith was shrieking;
And in the scowl of heaven each face
Grew dark as they were speaking.

But still as wilder blew the wind,
And as the night grew drearer,
Adown the glen rode arméd men,
Their trampling sounded nearer.

'O haste thee, haste!' the lady cries,
'Though tempests round us gather;
I'll meet the raging of the skies,
But not an angry father.'

The boat has left a stormy land,
A stormy sea before her,—
When, O! too strong for human hand
The tempest gather'd o'er her.

And still they row'd amidst the roar
Of waters fast prevailing:
Lord Ullin reach'd that fatal shore,—
His wrath was changed to wailing.

For, sore dismay'd, through storm and shade
His child he did discover:—
One lovely hand she stretch'd for aid,
And one was round her lover.

'Come back! come back!' he cried in grief,
'Across this stormy water:
And I'll forgive your Highland chief,
My daughter!—O, my daughter!'

'Twas vain: the loud waves lash'd the shore,
Return or aid preventing:
The waters wild went o'er his child,
And he was left lamenting.

T. CAMPBELL

CLXXXII

JOCK OF HAZELDEAN

'Why weep ye by the tide, ladie?
  Why weep ye by the tide?
I'll wed ye to my youngest son,
  And ye sall be his bride:
And ye sall be his bride, ladie,
  Sae comely to be seen '—
But aye she loot the tears down fa'
  For Jock of Hazeldean.

'Now let this wilfu' grief be done,
  And dry that cheek so pale;
Young Frank is chief of Errington
  And lord of Langley-dale;
His step is first in peaceful ha',
  His sword in battle keen '—
But aye she loot the tears down fa'
  For Jock of Hazeldean.

'A chain of gold ye sall not lack,
  Nor braid to bind your hair,
Nor mettled hound, nor managed hawk,
  Nor palfrey fresh and fair;
And you the foremost o' them a'
  Shall ride our forest-queen '—
But aye she loot the tears down fa'
  For Jock of Hazeldean.

The kirk was deck'd at morning-tide,
  The tapers glimmer'd fair;
The priest and bridegroom wait the bride,
  And dame and knight are there:
They sought her baith by bower and ha';
  The ladie was not seen!
She's o'er the Border, and awa'
  Wi' Jock of Hazeldean.

Sir W. Scott

CLXXXIII

FREEDOM AND LOVE

How delicious is the winning
Of a kiss at love's beginning,
When two mutual hearts are sighing
For the knot there's no untying!

Yet remember, 'midst your wooing
Love has bliss, but Love has ruing;
Other smiles may make you fickle,
Tears for other charms may trickle.

Love he comes and Love he tarries
Just as fate or fancy carries;
Longest stays, when sorest chidden;
Laughs and flies, when press'd and bidden.

Bind the sea to slumber stilly,
Bind its odour to the lily,
Bind the aspen ne'er to quiver,
Then bind Love to last for ever.

Love's a fire that needs renewal
Of fresh beauty for its fuel:
Love's wing moults when caged and captured,
Only free, he soars enraptured.

Can you keep the bee from ranging,
Or the ringdove's neck from changing?
No! nor fetter'd Love from dying
In the knot there's no untying.

J. CAMPBELL

CLXXXIV

LOVE'S PHILOSOPHY

The fountains mingle with the river
And the rivers with the ocean,
The winds of heaven mix for ever
With a sweet emotion;
Nothing in the world is single,
All things by a law divine
In one another's being mingle—
Why not I with thine?

See the mountains kiss high heaven
And the waves clasp one another;
No sister-flower would be forgiven
If it disdain'd its brother:

And the sunlight clasps the earth,
And the moonbeams kiss the sea—
What are all these kissings worth,
If thou kiss not me?

P. B. SHELLEY

CLXXXV
ECHOES

How sweet the answer Echo makes
To Music at night
When, roused by lute or horn, she wakes,
And far away o'er lawns and lakes
Goes answering light!

Yet Love hath echoes truer far
And far more sweet
Than e'er, beneath the moonlight's star,
Of horn or lute or soft guitar
The songs repeat.

'Tis when the sigh,—in youth sincere
And only then,
The sigh that's breathed for one to hear—
Is by that one, that only Dear
Breathed back again.

T. MOORE

CLXXXVI
A SERENADE

Ah! County Guy, the hour is nigh,
  The sun has left the lea,
The orange-flower perfumes the bower,
  The breeze is on the sea.
The lark, his lay who trill'd all day,
  Sits hush'd his partner nigh;
Breeze, bird, and flower confess the hour,
  But where is County Guy?

The village maid steals through the shade
  Her shepherd's suit to hear;

To Beauty shy, by lattice high,
   Sings high-born Cavalier.
The star of Love, all stars above,
   Now reigns o'er earth and sky,
And high and low the influence know—
   But where is County Guy?
Sir W. Scott

CLXXXVII

TO THE EVENING STAR

Gem of the crimson-colour'd Even,
Companion of retiring day,
Why at the closing gates of heaven,
Beloved Star, dost thou delay?

So fair thy pensile beauty burns
When soft the tear of twilight flows;
So due thy plighted love returns
To chambers brighter than the rose;

To Peace, to Pleasure, and to Love
So kind a star thou seem'st to be,
Sure some enamour'd orb above
Descends and burns to meet with thee!

Thine is the breathing, blushing hour
When all unheavenly passions fly,
Chased by the soul-subduing power
Of Love's delicious witchery.

O! sacred to the fall of day
Queen of propitious stars, appear,
And early rise, and long delay,
When Caroline herself is here!

Shine on her chosen green resort
Whose trees the sunward summit crown,
And wanton flowers, that well may court
An angel's feet to tread them down:—

Shine on her sweetly scented road
Thou star of evening's purple dome,
That lead'st the nightingale abroad,
And guid'st the pilgrim to his home.

Shine where my charmer's sweeter breath
Embalms the soft exhaling dew,
Where dying winds a sigh bequeath
To kiss the cheek of rosy hue:—

Where, winnow'd by the gentle air
Her silken tresses darkly flow
And fall upon her brow so fair,
Like shadows on the mountain snow.

Thus, ever thus, at day's decline
In converse sweet to wander far—
O bring with thee my Caroline,
And thou shalt be my Ruling Star!

T. CAMPBELL

CLXXXVIII

TO THE NIGHT

Swiftly walk over the western wave,
      Spirit of Night!
Out of the misty eastern cave
Where, all the long and lone daylight,
Thou wovest dreams of joy and fear
Which make thee terrible and dear,—
      Swift be thy flight!

Wrap thy form in a mantle gray
      Star-inwrought!
Blind with thine hair the eyes of day,
Kiss her until she be wearied out:
Then wander o'er city and sea and land,
Touching all with thine opiate wand—
      Come, long-sought!

When I arose and saw the dawn,
          I sigh'd for thee;
When light rode high, and the dew was gone,
And noon lay heavy on flower and tree,
And the weary Day turn'd to his rest
Lingering like an unloved guest,
          I sigh'd for thee.

Thy brother Death came, and cried
          Wouldst thou me?
Thy sweet child Sleep, the filmy-eyed,
Murmur'd like a noon-tide bee
Shall I nestle near thy side?
Wouldst thou me?—And I replied
          No, not thee!

Death will come when thou art dead,
          Soon, too soon—
Sleep will come when thou art fled;
Of neither would I ask the boon
I ask of thee, belovéd Night—
Swift be thine approaching flight,
          Come soon, soon!
              P. B. SHELLEY

CLXXXIX

TO A DISTANT FRIEND

Why art thou silent? Is thy love a plant
Of such weak fibre that the treacherous air
Of absence withers what was once so fair?
Is there no debt to pay, no boon to grant?

Yet have my thoughts for thee been vigilant,
Bound to thy service with unceasing care—
The mind's least generous wish a mendicant
For nought but what thy happiness could spare.

Speak!—though this soft warm heart, once free to hold
A thousand tender pleasures, thine and mine,
Be left more desolate, more dreary cold

Than a forsaken bird's-nest fill'd with snow
'Mid its own bush of leafless eglantine—
Speak, that my torturing doubts their end may know!
W. WORDSWORTH

CXC

When we two parted
In silence and tears,
Half broken-hearted,
To sever for years,
Pale grew thy cheek and cold,
Colder thy kiss;
Truly that hour foretold
Sorrow to this!

The dew of the morning
Sunk chill on my brow;
It felt like the warning
Of what I feel now.
Thy vows are all broken,
And light is thy fame:
I hear thy name spoken
And share in its shame.

They name thee before me,
A knell to mine ear;
A shudder comes o'er me—
Why wert thou so dear?
They know not I knew thee
Who knew thee too well:
Long, long shall I rue thee
Too deeply to tell.

In secret we met:
In silence I grieve
That thy heart could forget,
Thy spirit deceive.
If I should meet thee
After long years,
How should I greet thee?—
With silence and tears.

LORD BYRON

CXCI
HAPPY INSENSIBILITY

In a drear-nighted December,
Too happy, happy Tree,
Thy branches ne'er remember
Their green felicity:
The north cannot undo them
With a sleety whistle through them,
Nor frozen thawings glue them
From budding at the prime.

In a drear-nighted December,
Too happy, happy Brook,
Thy bubblings ne'er remember
Apollo's summer look;
But with a sweet forgetting
They stay their crystal fretting
Never, never petting
About the frozen time.

Ah would 'twere so with many
A gentle girl and boy!
But were there ever any
Writhed not at passèd joy?
To know the change and feel it,
When there is none to heal it
Nor numbèd sense to steal it—
Was never said in rhyme.

J. KEATS

CXCII

Where shall the lover rest
  Whom the fates sever
From his true maiden's breast
  Parted for ever?
Where, through groves deep and high
  Sounds the far billow;
Where early violets die
  Under the willow.
    Eleu loro
  Soft shall be his pillow.

There through the summer day
  Cool streams are laving:
There, while the tempests sway,
  Scarce are boughs waving;
There thy rest shalt thou take,
  Parted for ever,
Never again to wake
  Never, O never!
    Eleu loro
  Never, O never!

Where shall the traitor rest,
  He, the deceiver,
Who could win maiden's breast,
  Ruin, and leave her?
In the lost battle,
  Borne down by the flying,
Where mingles war's rattle
  With groans of the dying;
    Eleu loro
  There shall he be lying.

Her wing shall the eagle flap
  O'er the falsehearted;

His warm blood the wolf shall lap
  Ere life be parted:
Shame and dishonour sit
  By his grave ever;
Blessing shall hallow it
  Never, O never!
    Eleu loro
  Never, O never!

Sir W. Scott

CXCIII

LA BELLE DAME SANS MERCI

'O what can ail thee, knight-at-arms,
  Alone and palely loitering?
The sedge has wither'd from the lake,
  And no birds sing.

'O what can ail thee, knight-at-arms!
  So haggard and so woe-begone?
The squirrel's granary is full,
  And the harvest's done.

I see a lily on thy brow
  With anguish moist and fever-dew,
And on thy cheeks a fading rose
  Fast withereth too.'

'I met a lady in the meads,
  Full beautiful—a faery's child,
Her hair was long, her foot was light,
  And her eyes were wild.

'I made a garland for her head,
  And bracelets too, and fragrant zone;
She look'd at me as she did love,
  And made sweet moan.

'I set her on my pacing steed
  And nothing else saw all day long,

For sidelong would she bend, and sing
  A fairy's song.

'She found me roots of relish sweet
  And honey wild and manna-dew,
And sure in language strange she said
  "I love thee true."

'She took me to her elfin grot,
  And there she wept and sigh'd full sore,
And there I shut her wild wild eyes
  With kisses four.

'And there she lulléd me asleep,
  And there I dream'd—Ah! woe betide!
The latest dream I ever dream'd
  On the cold hill's side.

'I saw pale kings and princes too,
  Pale warriors, death-pale were they all,
They cried—"La belle Dame sans Merci
  Hath thee in thrall!"

'I saw their starved lips in the gloam
  With horrid warning gapéd wide,
And I awoke and found me here
  On the cold hill's side.

'And this is why I sojourn here
  Alone and palely loitering,
Though the sedge is wither'd from the lake,
  And no birds sing.'

J. KEATS

CXCIV

THE ROVER

A weary lot is thine, fair maid,
  A weary lot is thine!
To pull the thorn thy brow to braid,
  And press the rue for wine.

A lightsome eye, a soldier's mien
  A feather of the blue,
A doublet of the Lincoln green—
  No more of me you knew
      My Love!
No more of me you knew.

'This morn is merry June, I trow,
  The rose is budding fain;
But she shall bloom in winter snow
  Ere we two meet again.'
He turn'd his charger as he spake
  Upon the river shore,
He gave the bridle-reins a shake,
  Said 'Adieu for evermore
      My Love!
And adieu for evermore.'

              Sir W. Scott

CXCV

THE FLIGHT OF LOVE

When the lamp is shatter'd
The light in the dust lies dead—
When the cloud is scatter'd,
The rainbow's glory is shed.
When the lute is broken,
Sweet tones are remember'd not;
When the lips have spoken,
Loved accents are soon forgot.

As music and splendour
Survive not the lamp and the lute,
The heart's echoes render
No song when the spirit is mute—
No song but sad dirges,
Like the wind through a ruin'd cell,
Or the mournful surges
That ring the dead seaman's knell.

When hearts have once mingled,
Love first leaves the well-built nest;
The weak one is singled
To endure what it once possesst.
O Love! who bewailest
The frailty of all things here,
Why choose you the frailest
For your cradle, you home, and your bier?

Its passions will rock thee
As the storms rock the ravens on high;
Bright reason will mock thee
Like the sun from a wintry sky.
From thy nest every rafter
Will rot, and thine eagle home
Leave thee naked to laughter,
When leaves fall and cold winds come.

P. B. SHELLEY

CXCVI

THE MAID OF NEIDPATH

O lovers' eyes are sharp to see,
  And lovers' ears in hearing;
And love, in life's extremity,
  Can lend an hour of cheering.
Disease had been in Mary's bower
  And slow decay from mourning,
Though now she sits on Neidpath's tower
  To watch her Love's returning.

All sunk and dim her eyes so bright,
  Her form decay'd by pining,
Till through her wasted hand, at night,
  You saw the taper shining.
By fits a sultry hectic hue
  Across her cheek was flying;
By fits so ashy pale she grew
  Her maidens thought her dying.

Yet keenest powers to see and hear
  Seem'd in her frame residing;
Before the watch-dog prick'd his ear
  She heard her lover's riding;
Ere scarce a distant form was kenn'd
  She knew and waved to greet him,
And o'er the battlement did bend
  As on the wing to meet him.

He came—he pass'd—an heedless gaze
  As o'er some stranger glancing;
Her welcome, spoke in faltering phrase,
  Lost in his courser's prancing—
The castle-arch, whose hollow tone
  Returns each whisper spoken,
Could scarcely catch the feeble moan
  Which told her heart was broken.

Sir W. Scott

CXCVII

THE MAID OF NEIDPATH

Earl March look'd on his dying child,
  And, smit with grief to view her—
The youth, he cried, whom I exiled
  Shall be restored to woo her.

She's at the window many an hour
  His coming to discover:
And he look'd up to Ellen's bower
  And she look'd on her lover—

But ah! so pale, he knew her not,
  Though her smile on him was dwelling—
And am I then forgot—forgot?
  It broke the heart of Ellen.

In vain he weeps, in vain he sighs,
  Her cheek is cold as ashes;
Nor love's own kiss shall wake those eyes
  To lift their silken lashes.   T. Campbell

CXCVIII

Bright Star! would I were steadfast as thou art—
Not in lone splendour hung aloft the night,
And watching, with eternal lids apart,
Like Nature's patient sleepless Eremite,

The moving waters at their priest-like task
Of pure ablution round earth's human shores,
Or gazing on the new soft fallen mask
Of snow upon the mountains and the moors:—

No—yet still steadfast, still unchangeable,
Pillow'd upon my fair Love's ripening breast
To feel for ever its soft fall and swell,
Awake for ever in a sweet unrest;

Still, still to hear her tender-taken breath,
And so live ever,—or else swoon to death.

J. KEATS

CXCIX

THE TERROR OF DEATH

When I have fears that I may cease to be
Before my pen has glean'd my teeming brain,
Before high-piléd books, in charact'ry
Hold like rich garners the full-ripen'd grain;

When I behold, upon the night's starr'd face,
Huge cloudy symbols of a high romance,
And think that I may never live to trace
Their shadows, with the magic hand of chance;

And when I feel, fair Creature of an hour!
That I shall never look upon thee more,
Never have relish in the fairy power
Of unreflecting love—then on the shore

Of the wide world I stand alone, and think
Till Love and Fame to nothingness do sink.

J. KEATS

cc

DESIDERIA

Surprized by joy—impatient as the wind—
I turn'd to share the transport—O with whom
But Thee—deep buried in the silent tomb,
That spot which no vicissitude can find?

Love, faithful love recall'd thee to my mind—
But how could I forget thee? Through what power
Even for the least division of an hour
Have I been so beguiled as to be blind

To my most grievous loss—That thought's return
Was the worst pang that sorrow ever bore
Save one, one only, when I stood forlorn,

Knowing my heart's best treasure was no more;
That neither present time, nor years unborn
Could to my sight that heavenly face restore.
W. WORDSWORTH

CCI

At the mid hour of night, when stars are weeping, I fly
To the lone vale we loved, when life shone warm in
thine eye;
And I think oft, if spirits can steal from the regions
of air
To revisit past scenes of delight, thou wilt come to me
there
And tell me our love is remember'd, even in the sky!

Then I sing the wild song it once was rapture to hear
When our voices, commingling, breathed like one on
the ear;
And as Echo far off through the vale my sad orison
rolls,

I think, O my Love! 'tis thy voice, from the Kingdom
    of Souls
Faintly answering still the notes that once were so
    dear.

T. MOORE

CCII

ELEGY ON THYRZA

And thou art dead, as young and fair
    As aught of mortal birth;
And forms so soft and charms so rare
    Too soon return'd to Earth!
Though Earth received them in her bed,
And o'er the spot the crowd may tread
    In carelessness or mirth,
There is an eye which could not brook
A moment on that grave to look.

I will not ask where thou liest low
    Nor gaze upon the spot;
There flowers or weeds at will may grow
    So I behold them not:
It is enough for me to prove
That what I loved, and long must love
    Like common earth can rot;
To me there needs no stone to tell
'Tis Nothing that I loved so well.

Yet did I love thee to the last,
    As fervently as thou
Who didst not change through all the past
    And canst not alter now.
The love where Death has set his seal
Nor age can chill, nor rival steal,
    Nor falsehood disavow:
And, what were worse, thou canst not see
Or wrong, or change, or fault in me.

The better days of life were ours,
    The worst can be but mine:
The sun that cheers, the storm that lours,
    Shall never more be thine.
The silence of that dreamless sleep
I envy now too much to weep;
    Nor need I to repine
That all those charms have pass'd away
I might have watch'd through long decay.

The flower in ripen'd bloom unmatch'd
    Must fall the earliest prey;
Though by no hand untimely snatch'd,
    The leaves must drop away.
And yet it were a greater grief
To watch it withering, leaf by leaf,
    Than see it pluck'd to-day;
Since earthly eye but ill can bear
To trace the change to foul from fair.

I know not if I could have borne
    To see thy beauties fade;
The night that follow'd such a morn
    Had worn a deeper shade:
Thy day without a cloud hath past,
And thou wert lovely to the last,
    Extinguish'd, not decay'd;
As stars that shoot along the sky
Shine brightest as they fall from high.

As once I wept, if I could weep,
    My tears might well be shed
To think I was not near, to keep
    One vigil o'er thy bed:
To gaze, how fondly! on thy face,
To fold thee in a faint embrace,
    Uphold thy drooping head;

And show that love, however vain,
Nor thou nor I can feel again.

Yet how much less it were to gain,
    Though thou hast left me free,
The loveliest things that still remain
    Than thus remember thee!
The all of thine that cannot die
Through dark and dread Eternity
    Returns again to me,
And more thy buried love endears
Than aught except its living years.

LORD BYRON

CCIII

One word is too often profaned
    For me to profane it,
One feeling too falsely disdain'd
    For thee to disdain it.
One hope is too like despair
    For prudence to smother,
And Pity from thee more dear
    Than that from another.

I can give not what men call love;
    But wilt thou accept not
The worship the heart lifts above
    And the Heavens reject not:
The desire of the moth for the star,
    Of the night for the morrow,
The devotion to something afar
    From the sphere of our sorrow?

P. B. SHELLEY

GATHERING SONG OF DONALD THE
BLACK

Pibroch of Donuil Dhu
  Pibroch of Donuil
Wake thy wild voice anew,
  Summon Clan Conuil.
Come away, come away,
  Hark to the summons!
Come in your war-array,
  Gentles and commons.

Come from deep glen, and
  From mountain so rocky;
The war-pipe and pennon
  Are at Inverlochy.
Come every hill-plaid, and
  True heart that wears one,
Come every steel blade, and
  Strong hand that bears one.

Leave untended the herd,
  The flock without shelter;
Leave the corpse uninterr'd,
  The bride at the altar;
Leave the deer, leave the steer,
  Leave nets and barges:
Come with your fighting gear,
  Broadswords and targes.

Come as the winds come, when
  Forests are rended,
Come as the waves come, when
  Navies are stranded:

Faster come, faster come,
  Faster and faster,
Chief, vassal, page and groom,
  Tenant and master.

Fast they come, fast they come;
  See how they gather!
Wide waves the eagle plume
  Blended with heather.
Cast your plaids, draw your blades,
  Forward each man set!
Pibroch of Donuil Dhu
  Knell for the onset!

SIR W. SCOTT

CCV

A wet sheet and a flowing sea,
  A wind that follows fast
And fills the white and rustling sail
  And bends the gallant mast;
And bends the gallant mast, my boys,
  While like the eagle free
Away the good ship flies, and leaves
  Old England on the lee.

O for a soft and gentle wind!
  I heard a fair one cry;
But give to me the snoring breeze
  And white waves heaving high;
And white waves heaving high, my lads,
  The good ship tight and free—
The world of waters is our home,
  And merry men are we.

There's tempest in yon hornéd moon,
  And lightning in yon cloud;
But hark the music, mariners!
  The wind is piping loud;

The wind is piping loud, my boys,
  The lightning flashes free—
While the hollow oak our palace is,
  Our heritage the sea.
                    A. CUNNINGHAM

CCVI

Ye Mariners of England
That guard our native seas!
Whose flag has braved, a thousand years,
The battle and the breeze!
Your glorious standard launch again
To match another foe:
  And sweep through the deep,
  While the stormy winds do blow;
While the battle rages loud and long
And the stormy winds do blow.

The spirits of your fathers
Shall start from every wave—
For the deck it was their field of fame,
And Ocean was their grave:
Where Blake and mighty Nelson fell
Your manly hearts shall glow,
  As ye sweep through the deep,
  While the stormy winds do blow;
While the battle rages loud and long
And the stormy winds do blow.

Britannia needs no bulwarks,
No towers along the steep;
Her march is o'er the mountain-waves,
Her home is on the deep.
With thunders from her native oak
She quells the floods below—
  As they roar on the shore,
  When the stormy winds do blow;
When the battle rages loud and long,
And the stormy winds do blow.

The meteor flag of England
Shall yet terrific burn;
Till danger's troubled night depart
And the star of peace return.
Then, then, ye ocean-warriors!
Our song and feast shall flow
To the fame of your name,
When the storm has ceased to blow;
When the fiery fight is heard no more,
And the storm has ceased to blow.

T. CAMPBELL

CCVII

BATTLE OF THE BALTIC

Of Nelson and the North
Sing the glorious day's renown,
When to battle fierce came forth
All the might of Denmark's crown,
And her arms along the deep proudly shone;
By each gun the lighted brand
In a bold determined hand,
And the Prince of all the land
Led them on.

Like leviathans afloat
Lay their bulwarks on the brine;
While the sign of battle flew
On the lofty British line:
It was ten of April morn by the chime:
As they drifted on their path
There was silence deep as death;
And the boldest held his breath
For a time.

But the might of England flush'd
To anticipate the scene;

And her van the fleeter rush'd
O'er the deadly space between.
'Hearts of oak!' our captains cried, when each gun
From its adamantine lips
Spread a death-shade round the ships,
Like the hurricane eclipse
Of the sun.

Again! again! again!
And the havoc did not slack,
Till a feeble cheer the Dane
To our cheering sent us back;—
Their shots along the deep slowly boom:—
Then ceased—and all is wail,
As they strike the shatter'd sail;
Or in conflagration pale
Light the gloom.

Out spoke the victor then
As he hail'd them o'er the wave,
'Ye are brothers! ye are men!
And we conquer but to save:—
So peace instead of death let us bring:
But yield, proud foe, thy fleet
With the crews, at England's feet,
And make submission meet
To our King.'

Then Denmark bless'd our chief
That he gave her wounds repose;
And the sounds of joy and grief
From her people wildly rose,
As death withdrew his shades from the day;
While the sun look'd smiling bright
O'er a wide and woeful sight,
Where the fires of funeral light
Died away.

Now joy, old England, raise!
For the tidings of thy might,
By the festal cities' blaze,
Whilst the wine-cup shines in light;
And yet amidst that joy and uproar,
Let us think of them that sleep
Full many a fathom deep
By thy wild and stormy steep,
Elsinore!

Brave hearts! to Britain's pride
Once so faithful and so true,
On the deck of fame that died,
With the gallant good Riou:
Soft sigh the winds of Heaven o'er their grave!
While the billow mournful rolls
And the mermaid's song condoles
Singing glory to the souls
Of the brave!

T. CAMPBELL

CCVIII

ODE TO DUTY

Stern Daughter of the voice of God!
O Duty! if that name thou love
Who art a light to guide, a rod
To check the erring, and reprove;
Thou who art victory and law
When empty terrors overawe;
From vain temptations dost set free,
And calm'st the weary strife of frail humanity!

There are who ask not if thine eye
Be on them; who, in love and truth
Where no misgiving is, rely
Upon the genial sense of youth:

Glad hearts! without reproach or blot,
Who do thy work, and know it not:
O! if through confidence misplaced
They fail, thy saving arms, dread Power! around
  them cast.

Serene will be our days and bright
And happy will our nature be
When love is an unerring light,
And joy its own security.
And they a blissful course may hold
Ev'n now, who, not unwisely bold,
Live in the spirit of this creed;
Yet seek thy firm support according to their need.

I, loving freedom, and untried,
No sport of every random gust,
Yet being to myself a guide,
Too blindly have reposed my trust:
And oft, when in my heart was heard
Thy timely mandate, I deferr'd
The task, in smoother walks to stray;
But thee I now would serve more strictly, if I may.

Through no disturbance of my soul
Or strong compunction in me wrought,
I supplicate for thy controul,
But in the quietness of thought:
Me this uncharter'd freedom tires;
I feel the weight of chance-desires:
My hopes no more must change their name;
I long for a repose that ever is the same.

Stern lawgiver! yet thou dost wear
The Godhead's most benignant grace;
Nor know we anything so fair
As is the smile upon thy face:

Flowers laugh before thee on their beds,
And fragrance in thy footing treads;
Thou dost preserve the Stars from wrong;
And the most ancient Heavens, through thee, are
  fresh and strong.

To humbler functions, awful Power!
I call thee: I myself commend
Unto thy guidance from this hour;
O let my weakness have an end!
Give unto me, made lowly wise,
The spirit of self-sacrifice;
The confidence of reason give;
And in the light of Truth thy bondman let me live.
                                    W. WORDSWORTH

CCIX

ON THE CASTLE OF CHILLON

Eternal Spirit of the chainless Mind!
Brightest in dungeons, Liberty, thou art,—
For there thy habitation is the heart—
The heart which love of Thee alone can bind;

And when thy sons to fetters are consign'd,
To fetters, and the damp vault's dayless gloom,
Their country conquers with their martyrdom,
And Freedom's fame finds wings on every wind.

Chillon! thy prison is a holy place
And thy sad floor an altar, for 'twas trod,
Until his very steps have left a trace

Worn as if thy cold pavement were a sod,
By Bonnivard! May none those marks efface!
For they appeal from tyranny to God.
                                    LORD BYRON

CCX

ENGLAND AND SWITZERLAND, 1802

Two Voices are there, one is of the Sea,
One of the Mountains, each a mighty voice:
In both from age to age thou didst rejoice,
They were thy chosen music, Liberty!

There came a tyrant, and with holy glee
Thou fought'st against him,—but hast vainly striven:
Thou from thy Alpine holds at length art driven
Where not a torrent murmurs heard by thee.

—Of one deep bliss thine ear hath been bereft;
Then cleave, O cleave to that which still is left—
For high-soul'd Maid, what sorrow would it be

That Mountain floods should thunder as before,
And Ocean bellow from his rocky shore,
And neither awful Voice be heard by Thee!

W. WORDSWORTH

CCXI

ON THE EXTINCTION OF THE VENETIAN
REPUBLIC

Once did She hold the gorgeous East in fee
And was the safeguard of the West; the worth
Of Venice did not fall below her birth,
Venice, the eldest child of liberty.

She was a maiden city, bright and free;
No guile seduced, no force could violate;
And when she took unto herself a mate,
She must espouse the everlasting Sea.

And what if she had seen those glories fade,
Those titles vanish, and that strength decay,—
Yet shall some tribute of regret be paid

When her long life hath reach'd its final day:
Men are we, and must grieve when even the shade
Of that which once was great has pass'd away.

W. WORDSWORTH

CCXII

LONDON, MDCCCII

O Friend! I know not which way I must look
For comfort, being, as I am, opprest
To think that now our life is only drest
For show; mean handi-work of craftsman, cook,

Or groom!—We must run glittering like a brook
In the open sunshine, or we are unblest;
The wealthiest man among us is the best:
No grandeur now in nature or in book

Delights us. Rapine, avarice, expense,
This is idolatry; and these we adore:
Plain living and high thinking are no more:

The homely beauty of the good old cause
Is gone; our peace, our fearful innocence,
And pure religion breathing household laws.

W. WORDSWORTH

CCXIII

THE SAME

Milton! thou shouldst be living at this hour:
England hath need of thee: she is a fen
Of stagnant waters: altar, sword, and pen,
Fireside, the heroic wealth of hall and bower,

Have forfeited their ancient English dower
Of inward happiness. We are selfish men:
O! raise us up, return to us again;
And give us manners, virtue, freedom, power.

Thy soul was like a Star, and dwelt apart:
Thou hadst a voice whose sound was like the sea,
Pure as the naked heavens, majestic, free;

So didst thou travel on life's common way
In cheerful godliness; and yet thy heart
The lowliest duties on herself did lay.

W. WORDSWORTH

CCXIV

When I have borne in memory what has tamed
Great nations; how ennobling thoughts depart
When men change swords for ledgers, and desert
The student's bower for gold,—some fears unnamed

I had, my Country!—am I to be blamed?
Now, when I think of thee, and what thou art,
Verily, in the bottom of my heart
Of those unfilial fears I am ashamed.

For dearly must we prize thee; we who find
In thee a bulwark for the cause of men;
And I by my affection was beguiled:

What wonder if a Poet now and then,
Among the many movements of his mind,
Felt for thee as a lover or a child!

W. WORDSWORTH

CCXV

HOHENLINDEN

On Linden, when the sun was low,
All bloodless lay the untrodden snow;
And dark as winter was the flow
      Of Iser, rolling rapidly.

But Linden saw another sight,
When the drum beat at dead of night
Commanding fires of death to light
      The darkness of her scenery.

By torch and trumpet fast array'd
Each horseman drew his battle-blade,
And furious every charger neigh'd
    To join the dreadful revelry.

Then shook the hills with thunder riven;
Then rush'd the steed, to battle driven;
And louder than the bolts of Heaven
    Far flash'd the red artillery.

But redder yet that light shall glow
On Linden's hills of stainéd snow;
And bloodier yet the torrent flow
    Of Iser, rolling rapidly.

'Tis morn; but scarce yon level sun
Can pierce the war-clouds, rolling dun,
Where furious Frank and fiery Hun
    Shout in their sulphurous canopy.

The combat deepens. On, ye Brave
Who rush to glory, or the grave!
Wave, Munich, all thy banners wave,
    And charge with all thy chivalry!

Few, few shall part, where many meet!
The snow shall be their winding-sheet,
And every turf beneath their feet
    Shall be a soldier's sepulchre.

T. Campbell

CCXVI

AFTER BLENHEIM

It was a summer evening,
    Old Kaspar's work was done,
And he before his cottage door
    Was sitting in the sun;
And by him sported on the green
His little grandchild Wilhelmine.

She saw her brother Peterkin
   Roll something large and round
Which he beside the rivulet
   In playing there had found;
He came to ask what he had found
That was so large and smooth and round.

Old Kaspar took it from the boy
   Who stood expectant by;
And then the old man shook his head,
   And with a natural sigh
' 'Tis some poor fellow's skull," said he,
' Who fell in the great victory.

' I find them in the garden,
   For there's many here about;
And often when I go to plough
   The ploughshare turns them out.
For many thousand men,' said he,
' Were slain in that great victory.'

' Now tell us what 'twas all about '
   Young Peterkin he cries;
And little Wilhelmine looks up
   With wonder-waiting eyes;
' Now tell us all about the war,
And what they fought each other for.'

' It was the English,' Kaspar cried,
   ' Who put the French to rout;
But what they fought each other for
   I could not well make out.
But every body said,' quoth he,
' That 'twas a famous victory.

' My father lived at Blenheim then,
   Yon little stream hard by;

They burnt his dwelling to the ground,
   And he was forced to fly:
So with his wife and child he fled,
Nor had he where to rest his head.

'With fire and sword the country round
   Was wasted far and wide,
And many a childing mother then
   And newborn baby died:
But things like that, you know, must be
At every famous victory.

'They say it was a shocking sight
   After the field was won;
For many thousand bodies here
   Lay rotting in the sun:
But things like that, you know, must be
After a famous victory.

'Great praise the Duke of Marlbro' won
   And our good Prince Eugene;'
'Why 'twas a very wicked thing!'
   Said little Wilhelmine;
'Nay . . nay . . my little girl," quoth he,
'It was a famous victory.

'And every body praised the Duke
   Who this great fight did win.'
'But what good came of it at last?'
   Quoth little Peterkin:—
'Why that I cannot tell,' said he,
'But 'twas a famous victory.'

R. Southey

CCXVII

PRO PATRIA MORI

When he who adores thee has left but the name
   Of his fault and his sorrows behind,
O! say wilt thou weep, when they darken the fame
   Of a life that for thee was resign'd!

Yes, weep, and however my foes may condemn,
    Thy tears shall efface their decree;
For, Heaven can witness, though guilty to them,
    I have been but too faithful to thee.

With thee were the dreams of my earliest love;
    Every thought of my reason was thine:
In my last humble prayer to the Spirit above
    Thy name shall be mingled with mine!
O! blest are the lovers and friends who shall live
    The days of thy glory to see;
But the next dearest blessing that Heaven can give
    Is the pride of thus dying for thee.

T. MOORE

CCXVIII

THE BURIAL OF SIR JOHN MOORE
AT CORUNNA

Not a drum was heard, not a funeral note,
    As his corpse to the rampart we hurried;
Not a soldier discharged his farewell shot
    O'er the grave where our hero we buried.

We buried him darkly at dead of night,
    The sods with our bayonets turning;
By the struggling moonbeam's misty light
    And the lantern dimly burning.

No useless coffin enclosed his breast,
    Not in sheet or in shroud we wound him;
But he lay like a warrior taking his rest,
    With his martial cloak around him.

Few and short were the prayers we said,
    And we spoke not a word of sorrow;
But we steadfastly gazed on the face that was dead,
    And we bitterly thought of the morrow.

We thought, as we hollow'd his narrow bed
   And smoothed down his lonely pillow,
That the foe and the stranger would tread o'er his head,
   And we far away on the billow!

Lightly they'll talk of the spirit that's gone
   And o'er his cold ashes upbraid him,—
But little he'll reck, if they let him sleep on
   In the grave where a Briton has laid him.

But half of our heavy task was done
   When the clock struck the hour for retiring
And we heard the distant and random gun
   That the foe was sullenly firing.

Slowly and sadly we laid him down,
   From the field of his fame fresh and gory;
We carved not a line, and we raised not a stone,
   But we left him alone with his glory.

C. WOLFE

CCXIX

SIMON LEE THE OLD HUNTSMAN

In the sweet shire of Cardigan,
Not far from pleasant Ivor Hall,
An old man dwells, a little man,
I've heard he once was tall.
Full five-and-thirty years he lived
A running huntsman merry;
And still the centre of his cheek
Is red as a ripe cherry.

No man like him the horn could sound,
And hill and valley rang with glee,
When Echo bandied, round and round,
The halloo of Simon Lee.
In those proud days he little cared
For husbandry or tillage;

To blither tasks did Simon rouse
The sleepers of the village.

He all the country could outrun,
Could leave both man and horse behind;
And often, ere the chase was done,
He reel'd and was stone-blind.
And still there's something in the world
At which his heart rejoices;
For when the chiming hounds are out,
He dearly loves their voices.

But O the heavy change!—bereft
Of health, strength, friends and kindred, see
Old Simon to the world is left
In liveried poverty:
His master's dead, and no one now
Dwells in the Hall of Ivor;
Men, dogs, and horses, all are dead;
He is the sole survivor.

And he is lean, and he is sick,
His body, dwindled and awry,
Rests upon ankles swoln and thick;
His legs are thin and dry.
One prop he has, and only one,
His wife, an aged woman,
Lives with him, near the waterfall,
Upon the village common.

Beside their moss-grown hut of clay,
Not twenty paces from the door,
A scrap of land they have, but they
Are poorest of the poor.
This scrap of land he from the heath
Enclosed when he was stronger;
But what avails the land to them
Which he can till no longer?

Oft, working by her husband's side,
Ruth does what Simon cannot do;
For she, with scanty cause for pride,
Is stouter of the two.
And, though you with your utmost skill
From labour could not wean them,
'Tis little, very little, all
That they can do between them.

Few months of life has he in store
As he to you will tell,
For still, the more he works, the more
Do his weak ankles swell.
My gentle reader, I perceive
How patiently you've waited,
And now I fear that you expect
Some tale will be related.

O reader! had you in your mind
Such stores as silent thought can bring,
O gentle reader! you would find
A tale in everything.
What more I have to say is short,
And you must kindly take it:
It is no tale; but, should you think,
Perhaps a tale you'll make it.

One summer-day I chanced to see
This old man doing all he could
To unearth the root of an old tree,
A stump of rotten wood.
The mattock totter'd in his hand;
So vain was his endeavour
That at the root of the old tree
He might have work'd for ever.

'You're overtask'd, good Simon Lee,
Give me your tool,' to him I said;

And at the word right gladly he
Received my proffer'd aid.
I struck, and with a single blow
The tangled root I sever'd,
At which the poor old man so long
And vainly had endeavour'd.

The tears into his eyes were brought,
And thanks and praises seem'd to run
So fast out of his heart, I thought
They never would have done.
—I've heard of hearts unkind, kind deeds
With coldness still returning;
Alas! the gratitude of men
Hath oftener left me mourning.

W. WORDSWORTH

CCXX

THE OLD FAMILIAR FACES

I have had playmates, I have had companions
In my days of childhood, in my joyful school-days;
All, all are gone, the old familiar faces.

I have been laughing, I have been carousing,
Drinking late, sitting late, with my bosom cronies;
All, all are gone, the old familiar faces.

I loved a Love once, fairest among women:
Closed are her doors on me, I must not see her—
All, all are gone, the old familiar faces.

I have a friend, a kinder friend has no man:
Like an ingrate, I left my friend abruptly;
Left him, to muse on the old familiar faces.

Ghost-like I paced round the haunts of my childhood,
Earth seem'd a desert I was bound to traverse,
Seeking to find the old familiar faces.

Friend of my bosom, thou more than a brother,
Why wert not thou born in my father's dwelling?
So might we talk of the old familiar faces,

How some they have died, and some they have left me,
And some are taken from me; all are departed;
All, all are gone, the old familiar faces.

C. LAMB

CCXXI
THE JOURNEY ONWARDS

As slow our ship her foamy track
    Against the wind was cleaving,
Her trembling pennant still look'd back
    To that dear isle 'twas leaving.
So loth we part from all we love,
    From all the links that bind us;
So turn our hearts, as on we rove,
    To those we've left behind us!

When, round the bowl, of vanish'd years
    We talk with joyous seeming—
With smiles that might as well be tears,
    So faint, so sad their beaming;
While memory brings us back again
    Each early tie that twined us,
O, sweet's the cup that circles then
    To those we've left behind us!

And when, in other climes, we meet
    Some isle or vale enchanting,
Where all looks flowery, wild and sweet,
    And nought but love is wanting;
We think how great had been our bliss
    If Heaven had but assign'd us
To live and die in scenes like this,
    With some we've left behind us!

As travellers oft look back at eve
    When eastward darkly going,
To gaze upon that light they leave
    Still faint behind them glowing,—
So, when the close of pleasure's day
    To gloom hath near consign'd us,
We turn to catch one fading ray
    Of joy that's left behind us.

T. MOORE

CCXXII
YOUTH AND AGE

There's not a joy the world can give like that it takes
    away
When the glow of early thought declines in feeling's
    dull decay;
'Tis not on youth's smooth cheek the blush alone,
    which fades so fast,
But the tender bloom of heart is gone, ere youth itself
    be past.

Then the few whose spirits float above the wreck of
    happiness
Are driven o'er the shoals of guilt, or ocean of excess:
The magnet of their course is gone, or only points in
    vain
The shore to which their shiver'd sail shall never
    stretch again.

Then the mortal coldness of the soul like death itself
    comes down;
It cannot feel for others' woes, it dare not dream its own;
That heavy chill has frozen o'er the fountain of our
    tears,
And though the eye may sparkle still, 'tis where the
    ice appears.

Though wit may flash from fluent lips, and mirth
    distract the breast,

Through midnight hours that yield no more their
    former hope of rest;
'Tis but as ivy-leaves around the ruin'd turret wreathe,
All green and wildly fresh without, but worn and gray
    beneath.

O could I feel as I have felt, or be what I have been,
Or weep as I could once have wept o'er many a
    vanish'd scene,—
As springs in deserts found seem sweet, all brackish
    though they be,
So midst the wither'd waste of life, those tears would
    flow to me!

Lord Byron

CCXXIII

A LESSON

There is a flower, the Lesser Celandine,
That shrinks like many more from cold and rain,
And the first moment that the sun may shine,
Bright as the sun himself, 'tis out again!

When hailstones have been falling, swarm on swarm,
Or blasts the green field and the trees distrest,
Oft have I seen it muffled up from harm
In close self-shelter, like a thing at rest.

But lately, one rough day, this flower I past,
And recognized it, though an alter'd form,
Now standing forth an offering to the blast,
And buffeted at will by rain and storm.

I stopp'd and said, with inly-mutter'd voice,
' It doth not love the shower, nor seek the cold;
This neither is its courage nor its choice,
But its necessity in being old.

' The sunshine may not cheer it, nor the dew;
It cannot help itself in its decay;

Stiff in its members, wither'd, changed of hue,'—
And, in my spleen, I smiled that it was gray.

To be a prodigal's favourite—then, worse truth,
A miser's pensioner—behold our lot!
O Man! that from thy fair and shining youth
Age might but take the things Youth needed not!

W. WORDSWORTH

CCXXIV
PAST AND PRESENT

I remember, I remember
The house where I was born,
The little window where the sun
Came peeping in at morn;
He never came a wink too soon
Nor brought too long a day;
But now, I often wish the night
Had borne my breath away.

I remember, I remember
The roses, red and white,
The violets, and the lily-cups—
Those flowers made of light!
The lilacs where the robin built,
And where my brother set
The laburnum on his birthday,—
The tree is living yet!

I remember, I remember
Where I was used to swing,
And thought the air must rush as fresh
To swallows on the wing;
My spirit flew in feathers then
That is so heavy now,
And summer pools could hardly cool
The fever on my brow.

I remember, I remember
The fir-trees dark and high;
I used to think their slender tops
Were close against the sky:
It was a childish ignorance,
But now 'tis little joy
To know I'm farther off from Heaven
Than when I was a boy.

T. HOOD

CCXXV

THE LIGHT OF OTHER DAYS

Oft in the stilly night
  Ere slumber's chain has bound me,
Fond Memory brings the light
  Of other days around me:
    The smiles, the tears
    Of boyhood's years,
  The words of love then spoken;
    The eyes that shone,
    Now dimm'd and gone,
  The cheerful hearts now broken!
Thus in the stilly night
  Ere slumber's chain has bound me,
Sad Memory brings the light
  Of other days around me.

When I remember all
  The friends so link'd together
I've seen around me fall
  Like leaves in wintry weather,
    I feel like one
    Who treads alone
  Some banquet-hall deserted,
    Whose lights are fled
    Whose garlands dead,
  And all but he departed!

Thus in the stilly night
   Ere slumber's chain has bound me,
Sad Memory brings the light
   Of other days around me.

T. Moore

CCXXVI

INVOCATION

Rarely, rarely comest thou,
   Spirit of Delight!
Wherefore hast thou left me now
   Many a day and night?
Many a weary night and day
'Tis since thou art fled away.

How shall ever one like me
   Win thee back again?
With the joyous and the free
   Thou wilt scoff at pain.
Spirit false! thou hast forgot
All but those who need thee not.

As a lizard with the shade
   Of a trembling leaf,
Thou with sorrow art dismay'd;
   Even the sighs of grief
Reproach thee, that thou art not near,
And reproach thou wilt not hear.

Let me set my mournful ditty
   To a merry measure;—
Thou wilt never come for pity,
   Thou wilt come for pleasure;—
Pity thou wilt cut away
Those cruel wings, and thou wilt stay.

I love all that thou lovest,
   Spirit of Delight!

The fresh Earth in new leaves drest
   And the starry night;
Autumn evening, and the morn
When the golden mists are born.

I love snow and all the forms
   Of the radiant frost;
I love waves, and winds, and storms,
   Everything almost
Which is Nature's, and may be
Untainted by man's misery.

I love tranquil solitude,
   And such society
As is quiet, wise, and good;
   Between thee and me
What diff'rence? but thou dost possess
The things I seek, nor love them less.

I love Love—though he has wings,
   And like light can flee,
But above all other things,
   Spirit, I love thee—
Thou art love and life! O come!
Make once more my heart thy home!

P. B. SHELLEY

CCXXVII

STANZAS WRITTEN IN DEJECTION
NEAR NAPLES

The sun is warm, the sky is clear,
The waves are dancing fast and bright,
Blue isles and snowy mountains wear
The purple noon's transparent light:
The breath of the moist earth is light
Around its unexpanded buds;
Like many a voice of one delight—
The winds', the birds', the ocean-floods'—
The City's voice itself is soft like Solitude's.

I see the Deep's untrampled floor
With green and purple sea-weeds strown;
I see the waves upon the shore
Like light dissolved in star-showers thrown:
I sit upon the sands alone;
The lightning of the noon-tide ocean
Is flashing round me, and a tone
Arises from its measured motion—
How sweet! did any heart now share in my emotion?

Alas! I have nor hope nor health,
Nor peace within nor calm around,
Nor that Content, surpassing wealth,
The sage in meditation found,
And walk'd with inward glory crown'd—
Nor fame, nor power, nor love, nor leisure;
Others I see whom these surround—
Smiling they live, and call life pleasure;
To me that cup has been dealt in another measure.

Yet now despair itself is mild
Even as the winds and waters are;
I could lie down like a tired child,
And weep away the life of care
Which I have borne, and yet must bear,
Till death like sleep might steal on me,
And I might feel in the warm air
My cheek grow cold, and hear the sea
Breathe o'er my dying brain its last monotony.

P. B. SHELLEY

CCXXVIII

THE SCHOLAR

My days among the Dead are past;
Around me I behold,
Where'er these casual eyes are cast,
The mighty minds of old:
My never-failing friends are they,
With whom I converse day by day.

With them I take delight in weal
And seek relief in woe;
And while I understand and feel
How much to them I owe,
My cheeks have often been bedew'd
With tears of thoughtful gratitude.

My thoughts are with the Dead; with them
I live in long-past years,
Their virtues love, their faults condemn,
Partake their hopes and fears,
And from their lessons seek and find
Instruction with an humble mind.

My hopes are with the Dead; anon
My place with them will be,
And I with them shall travel on
Through all Futurity;
Yet leaving here a name, I trust,
That will not perish in the dust.

R. SOUTHEY

CCXXIX

THE MERMAID TAVERN

Souls of Poets dead and gone,
What Elysium have ye known,
Happy field or mossy cavern,
Choicer than the Mermaid Tavern?
Have ye tippled drink more fine
Than mine host's Canary wine?
Or are fruits of Paradise
Sweeter than those dainty pies
Of Venison? O generous food!
Drest as though bold Robin Hood
Would, with his Maid Marian,
Sup and bowse from horn and can.

I have heard that on a day
Mine host's sign-board flew away
Nobody knew whither, till
An astrologer's old quill
To a sheepskin gave the story—
Said he saw you in your glory
Underneath a new-old Sign
Sipping beverage divine,
And pledging with contented smack
The Mermaid in the Zodiac!

Souls of Poets dead and gone,
What Elysium have ye known—
Happy field of mossy cavern—
Choicer than the Mermaid Tavern?

J. KEATS

ccxxx
THE PRIDE OF YOUTH

Proud Maisie is in the wood,
  Walking so early;
Sweet Robin sits on the bush
  Singing so rarely.

'Tell me, thou bonny bird,
  When shall I marry me?'
—'When six braw gentlemen
  Kirkward shall carry ye.'

'Who makes the bridal bed,
  Birdie, say truly?'
—'The gray-headed sexton
  That delves the grave duly

'The glowworm o'er grave and stone
  Shall light thee steady;
The owl from the steeple sing,
  Welcome, proud lady.'

SIR W. SCOTT.

CCXXXI
THE BRIDGE OF SIGHS

One more Unfortunate
Weary of breath
Rashly importunate,
Gone to her death!

Take her up tenderly,
Lift her with care;
Fashion'd so slenderly,
Young, and so fair!

Look at her garments
Clinging like cerements;
Whilst the wave constantly
Drips from her clothing;
Take her up instantly,
Loving, not loathing.

Touch her not scornfully;
Think of her mournfully,
Gently and humanly;
Not of the stains of her—
All that remains of her
Now is pure womanly.

Make no deep scrutiny
Into her mutiny
Rash and undutiful:
Past all dishonour,
Death has left on her
Only the beautiful.

Still, for all slips of hers,
One of Eve's family—
Wipe those poor lips of hers
Oozing so clammily.

Loop up her tresses
Escaped from the comb,
Her fair auburn tresses;
Whilst wonderment guesses
Where was her home?

Who was her father?
Who was her mother?
Had she a sister?
Had she a brother?
Or was there a dearer one
Still, and a nearer one
Yet, than all other?

Alas! for the rarity
Of Christian charity
Under the sun!
O! it was pitiful!
Near a whole city full,
Home she had none.

Sisterly, brotherly,
Fatherly, motherly
Feelings had changed:
Love, by harsh evidence,
Thrown from its eminence;
Even God's providence
Seeming estranged.

Where the lamps quiver
So far in the river,
With many a light
From window and casement,
From garret to basement,
She stood, with amazement,
Houseless by night.

The bleak wind of March
Made her tremble and shiver;

But not the dark arch,
Or the black flowing river:
Mad from life's history,
Glad to death's mystery
Swift to be hurl'd—
Any where, any where
Out of the world!

In she plunged boldly,
No matter how coldly
The rough river ran,
Over the brink of it,—
Picture it, think of it,
Dissolute Man!
Lave in it, drink of it,
Then, if you can!

Take her up tenderly,
Lift her with care;
Fashion'd so slenderly,
Young, and so fair!

Ere her limbs frigidly
Stiffen too rigidly,
Decently, kindly,
Smooth and compose them;
And her eyes, close them,
Staring so blindly!

Dreadfully staring
Thro' muddy impurity,
As when with the daring
Last look of despairing
Fix'd on futurity.

Perishing gloomily,
Spurr'd by contumely,

Cold inhumanity,
Burning insanity,
Into her rest.
—Cross her hands humbly
As if praying dumbly,
Over her breast!

Owning her weakness,
Her evil behaviour,
And leaving, with meekness,
Her sins to her Saviour.   T. Hood

CCXXXII
ELEGY

O snatch'd away in beauty's bloom!
On thee shall press no ponderous tomb;
But on thy turf shall roses rear
Their leaves, the earliest of the year,
And the wild cypress wave in tender gloom:

And oft by yon blue gushing stream
Shall Sorrow lean her drooping head,
And feed deep thought with many a dream,
And lingering pause and lightly tread;
Fond wretch! as if her step disturb'd the dead.

Away! we know that tears are vain,
That Death nor heeds nor hears distress:
Will this unteach us to complain?
Or make one mourner weep the less?
And thou, who tell'st me to forget,
Thy looks are wan, thine eyes are wet.
                                   Lord Byron

CCXXXIII
HESTER

When maidens such as Hester die
Their place ye may not well supply,
Though ye among a thousand try
          With vain endeavour.

A month or more hath she been dead,
Yet cannot I by force be led
To think upon the wormy bed
  And her together.

A springy motion in her gait.
A rising step, did indicate
Of pride and joy no common rate
  That flush'd her spirit:
I know not by what name beside
I shall it call: if 'twas not pride,
It was a joy to that allied
  She did inherit.

Her parents held the Quaker rule,
Which doth the human feeling cool;
But she was train'd in Nature's school,
  Nature had blest her.
A waking eye, a prying mind,
A heart that stirs, is hard to bind;
A hawk's keen sight ye cannot blind,
  Ye could not Hester.

My sprightly neighbour! gone before
To that unknown and silent shore,
Shall we not meet, as heretofore
  Some summer morning—
When from thy cheerful eyes a ray
Hath struck a bliss upon the day,
A bliss that would not go away,
  A sweet fore-warning?

         C. LAMB

CCXXXIV

CORONACH

He is gone on the mountain,
 He is lost to the forest,
Like a summer-dried fountain,
 When our need was the sorest.

The font reappearing
  From the raindrops shall borrow,
But to us comes no cheering,
  To Duncan no morrow!

The hand of the reaper
  Takes the ears that are hoary,
But the voice of the weeper
  Wails manhood in glory.
The autumn winds rushing
  Waft the leaves that are serest,
But our flower was in flushing
  When blighting was nearest.

Fleet foot on the correi,
  Sage counsel in cumber,
Red hand in the foray,
  How sound is thy slumber!
Like the dew on the mountain,
  Like the foam on the river
Like the bubble on the fountain,
  Thou art gone, and for ever!

Sir W. Scott

ccxxxv

THE DEATH BED

We watch'd her breathing thro' the night,
  Her breathing soft and low,
As in her breast the wave of life
  Kept heaving to and fro.

But when the morn came dim and sad
  And chill with early showers,
Her quiet eyelids closed—she had
  Another morn than ours.

T. Hood

ROSABELLE

O listen, listen, ladies gay!
  No haughty feat of arms I tell;
Soft is the note, and sad the lay
  That mourns the lovely Rosabelle.

' Moor, moor the barge, ye gallant crew!
  And, gentle lady, deign to stay!
Rest thee in Castle Ravensheuch,
  Nor tempt the stormy firth to-day.

' The blackening wave is edged with white;
  To inch and rock the sea-mews fly;
The fishers have heard the Water-Sprite,
  Whose screams forebode that wreck is nigh.

' Last night the gifted Seer did view
  A wet shroud swathed round ladye gay;
Then stay thee, Fair, in Ravensheuch;
  Why cross the gloomy firth to-day?'

' 'Tis not because Lord Lindesay's heir
  To-night at Roslin leads the ball,
But that my lady-mother there
  Sits lonely in her castle-hall.

' 'Tis not because the ring they ride,
  And Lindesay at the ring rides well,
But that my sire the wine will chide
  If 'tis not fill'd by Rosabelle.'

—O'er Roslin all that dreary night
  A wondrous blaze was seen to gleam;
'Twas broader than the watch-fire's light,
  And redder than the bright moonbeam.

It glared on Roslin's castled rock,
  It ruddied all the copse-wood glen;
'Twas seen from Dryden's groves of oak,
  And seen from cavern'd Hawthornden.

Seem'd all on fire that chapel proud
  Where Roslin's chiefs uncoffin'd lie,
Each Baron, for a sable shroud,
  Sheathed in his iron panoply.

Seem'd all on fire within, around,
  Deep sacristy and altar's pale;
Shone every pillar foliage-bound,
  And glimmer'd all the dead men's mail.

Blazed battlement and pinnet high,
  Blazed every rose-carved buttress fair—
So still they blaze, when fate is nigh
  The lordly line of high Saint Clair.

There are twenty of Roslin's barons bold
  Lie buried within that proud chapelle;
Each one the holy vault doth hold
  But the sea holds lovely Rosabelle!

And each Saint Clair was buried there
  With candle, with book, and with knell;
But the sea-caves rung, and the wild winds sung
  The dirge of lovely Rosabelle.

SIR W. SCOTT

CCXXXVII

ON AN INFANT DYING AS SOON AS BORN

I saw where in the shroud did lurk
A curious frame of Nature's work;
A flow'ret crushéd in the bud,
A nameless piece of Babyhood,

Was in her cradle-coffin lying;
Extinct, with scarce the sense of dying:
So soon to exchange the imprisoning womb
For darker closets of the tomb!
She did but ope an eye, and put
A clear beam forth, then straight up shut
For the long dark: ne'er more to see
Through glasses of mortality.
Riddle of destiny, who can show
What thy short visit meant, or know
What thy errand here below?
Shall we say, that Nature blind
Check'd her hand, and changed her mind
Just when she had exactly wrought
A finish'd pattern without fault?
Could she flag, or could she tire,
Or lack'd she the Promethean fire
(With her nine moons' long workings sicken'd)
That should thy little limbs have quicken'd?
Limbs so firm, they seem'd to assure
Life of health, and days mature:
Woman's self in miniature!
Limbs so fair, they might supply
(Themselves now but cold imagery)
The sculptor to make Beauty by.
Or did the stern-eyed Fate descry
That babe or mother, one must die;
So in mercy left the stock
And cut the branch; to save the shock
Of young years widow'd, and the pain
When Single State comes back again
To the lone man who, reft of wife,
Thenceforward drags a maiméd life?
The economy of Heaven is dark,
And wisest clerks have miss'd the mark
Why human buds, like this, should fall,
More brief than fly ephemeral

That has his day; while shrivell'd crones
Stiffen with age to stocks and stones;
And crabbed use the conscience sears
In sinners of an hundred years.
—Mother's prattle, mother's kiss,
Baby fond, thou ne'er wilt miss:
Rites, which custom does impose,
Silver bells, and baby clothes;
Coral redder than those lips
Which pale death did late eclipse;
Music framed for infants' glee,
Whistle never tuned for thee;
Though thou want'st not, thou shalt have them,
Loving hearts were they which gave them.
Let not one be missing; nurse,
See them laid upon the hearse
Of infant slain by doom perverse.
Why should kings and nobles have
Pictured trophies to their grave,
And we, churls, to thee deny
Thy pretty toys with thee to lie—
A more harmless vanity?

C. LAMB

CCXXXVIII

THE AFFLICTION OF MARGARET

Where art thou, my beloved Son,
Where art thou, worse to me than dead!
O find me, prosperous or undone!
Or if the grave be now thy bed,
Why am I ignorant of the same
That I may rest; and neither blame
Nor sorrow may attend thy name?

Seven years, alas! to have received
No tidings of an only child—
To have despair'd, have hoped, believed,

And been for evermore beguiled,—
Sometimes with thoughts of very bliss
I catch at them, and then I miss;
Was ever darkness like to this?

He was among the prime in worth,
An object beauteous to behold;
Well born, well bred; I sent him forth
Ingenuous, innocent, and bold:
If things ensued that wanted grace
As hath been said, they were not base;
And never blush was on my face.

Ah! little doth the young-one dream
When full of play and childish cares,
What power is in his wildest scream
Heard by his mother unawares!
He knows it not, he cannot guess;
Years to a mother bring distress;
But do not make her love the less.

Neglect me! no, I suffer'd long
From that ill thought; and being blind
Said 'Pride shall help me in my wrong:
Kind mother have I been, as kind
As ever breathed:' and that is true;
I've wet my path with tears like dew,
Weeping for him when no one knew.

My Son, if thou be humbled, poor,
Hopeless of honour and of gain,
O! do not dread thy mother's door;
Think not of me with grief and pain:
I now can see with better eyes;
And worldly grandeur I despise
And fortune with her gifts and lies.

Alas! the fowls of heaven have wings,
And blasts of heaven will aid their flight;

They mount—how short a voyage brings
The wanderers back to their delight!
Chains tie us down by land and sea;
And wishes, vain as mine, may be
All that is left to comfort thee.

Perhaps some dungeon hears thee groan
Maim'd, mangled by inhuman men;
Or thou upon a desert thrown
Inheritest the lion's den;
Or hast been summon'd to the deep
Thou, thou, and all thy mates, to keep
An incommunicable sleep.

I look for ghosts: but none will force
Their way to me; 'tis falsely said
That there was ever intercourse
Between the living and the dead;
For surely then I should have sight
Of him I wait for day and night
With love and longings infinite.

My apprehensions come in crowds;
I dread the rustling of the grass;
The very shadows of the clouds
Have power to shake me as they pass;
I question things, and do not find
One that will answer to my mind;
And all the world appears unkind.

Beyond participation lie
My troubles, and beyond relief:
If any chance to heave a sigh
They pity me, and not my grief.
Then come to me, my Son, or send
Some tidings that my woes may end!
I have no other earthly friend.

W. WORDSWORTH

CCXXXIX

HUNTING SONG

Waken, lords and ladies gay,
On the mountain dawns the day;
All the jolly chase is here
With hawk and horse and hunting-spear;
Hounds are in their couples yelling,
Hawks are whistling, horns are knelling,
Merrily merrily mingle they,
' Waken, lords and ladies gay.'

Waken, lords and ladies gay,
The mist has left the mountain gray,
Springlets in the dawn are streaming,
Diamonds on the brake are gleaming;
And foresters have busy been
To track the buck in thicket green;
Now we come to chant our lay
' Waken, lords and ladies gay.'

Waken, lords and ladies gay,
To the greenwood haste away;
We can show you where he lies,
Fleet of foot and tall of size;
We can show the marks he made
When 'gainst the oak his antlers fray'd;
You shall see him brought to bay;
' Waken, lords and ladies gay.'

Louder, louder chant the lay,
Waken, lords and ladies gay!
Tell them youth and mirth and glee
Run a course as well as we;
Time, stern huntsman! who can baulk,
Stanch as hound and fleet as hawk;
Think of this, and rise with day
Gentle lords and ladies gay!

Sir W. Scott

CCXL

TO THE SKYLARK

Ethereal minstrel! pilgrim of the sky!
Dost thou despise the earth where cares abound?
Or while the wings aspire, are heart and eye
Both with thy nest upon the dewy ground?
Thy nest which thou canst drop into at will,
Those quivering wings composed, that music still!

To the last point of vision, and beyond
Mount, daring warbler!—that love-prompted strain
—'Twixt thee and thine a never-failing bond—
Thrills not the less the bosom of the plain:
Yet might'st thou seem, proud privilege! to sing
All independent of the leafy Spring.

Leave to the nightingale her shady wood;
A privacy of glorious light is thine,
Whence thou dost pour upon the world a flood
Of harmony, with instinct more divine;
Type of the wise, who soar, but never roam—
True to the kindred points of Heaven and Home.

W. WORDSWORTH

CCXLI

TO A SKYLARK

Hail to thee, blithe Spirit!
  Bird thou never wert,
That from heaven, or near it
  Pourest thy full heart
In profuse strains of unpremeditated art.

  Higher still and higher
    From the earth thou springest
  Like a cloud of fire;
    The blue deep thou wingest,
And singing still dost soar, and soaring ever singest.

In the golden lightning
    Of the sunken sun
O'er which clouds are brightening,
    Thou dost float and run,
Like an embodied joy whose race is just begun.

The pale purple even
    Melts around thy flight;
Like a star of heaven
    In the broad daylight
Thou art unseen, but yet I hear thy shrill delight:

Keen as are the arrows
    Of that silver sphere,
Whose intense lamp narrows
    In the white dawn clear
Until we hardly see, we feel that it is there.

All the earth and air
    With thy voice is loud,
As, when night is bare,
    From one lonely cloud
The moon rains out her beams, and heaven is over-
      flow'd.

What thou art we know not;
    What is most like thee?
From rainbow clouds there flow not
    Drops so bright to see
As from thy presence showers a rain of melody.

Like a poet hidden
    In the light of thought,
Singing hymns unbidden,
    Till the world is wrought
To sympathy with hopes and fears it heeded not:

Like a high-born maiden
In a palace tower,
Soothing her love-laden
Soul in secret hour
With music sweet as love, which overflows her bower:

Like a glow-worm golden
In a dell of dew,
Scattering unbeholden
Its aerial hue
Among the flowers and grass, which screen it from the
view:

Like a rose embower'd
In its own green leaves,
By warm winds deflower'd,
Till the scent it gives
Makes faint with too much sweet these heavy-winged
thieves.

Sound of vernal showers
On the twinkling grass,
Rain-awaken'd flowers,
All that ever was
Joyous, and clear, and fresh, thy music doth surpass.

Teach us, sprite or bird,
What sweet thoughts are thine:
I have never heard
Praise of love or wine
That panted forth a flood of rapture so divine.

Chorus hymeneal
Or triumphal chaunt
Match'd with thine, would be all
But an empty vaunt—
A thing wherein we feel there is some hidden want.

What objects are the fountains
   Of thy happy strain?
What fields, or waves, or mountains?
   What shapes of sky or plain?
What love of thine own kind? what ignorance of pain?

With thy clear keen joyance
   Languor cannot be:
Shadow of annoyance
   Never came near thee:
Thou lovest; but ne'er knew love's sad satiety.

Waking or asleep
   Thou of death must deem
Things more true and deep
   Than we mortals dream,
Or how could thy notes flow in such a crystal
     stream?

We look before and after,
   And pine for what is not:
Our sincerest laughter
   With some pain is fraught;
Our sweetest songs are those that tell of saddest
     thought.

Yet if we could scorn
   Hate, and pride, and fear;
If we were things born
   Not to shed a tear,
I know not how thy joy we ever should come near.

Better than all measures
   Of delightful sound,
Better than all treasures
   That in books are found,
Thy skill to poet were, thou scorner of the ground!

Teach me half the gladness
  That thy brain must know,
Such harmonious madness
  From my lips would flow
The world should listen then, as I am listening now!
                                        P. B. SHELLEY

CCXLII
THE GREEN LINNET

Beneath these fruit-tree boughs that shed
Their snow-white blossoms on my head,
With brightest sunshine round me spread
  Of Spring's unclouded weather,
In this sequester'd nook how sweet
To sit upon my orchard-seat!
And flowers and birds once more to greet,
  My last year's friends together.

One have I mark'd, the happiest guest
In all this covert of the blest:
Hail to Thee, far above the rest
  In joy of voice and pinion!
Thou, Linnet! in thy green array
Presiding Spirit here to-day
Dost lead the revels of the May,
  And this is thy dominion.

While birds, and butterflies, and flowers,
Make all one band of paramours,
Thou, ranging up and down the bowers
  Art sole in thy employment;
A Life, a Presence like the air,
Scattering thy gladness without care,
Too blest with any one to pair,
  Thyself thy own enjoyment.

Amid yon tuft of hazel trees
That twinkle to the gusty breeze,

Behold him perch'd in ecstasies
Yet seeming still to hover;
There, where the flutter of his wings
Upon his back and body flings
Shadows and sunny glimmerings,
That cover him all over.

My dazzled sight he oft deceives—
A brother of the dancing leaves;
Then flits, and from the cottage-eaves
Pours forth his song in gushes,
As if by that exulting strain
He mock'd and treated with disdain
The voiceless Form he chose to feign,
While fluttering in the bushes.

W. WORDSWORTH

CCXLIII

TO THE CUCKOO

O blithe new-comer! I have heard,
I hear thee and rejoice:
O Cuckoo! shall I call thee bird,
Or but a wandering Voice?

While I am lying on the grass
Thy twofold shout I hear;
From hill to hill it seems to pass,
At once far off and near.

Though babbling only to the vale
Of sunshine and of flowers,
Thou bringest unto me a tale
Of visionary hours.

Thrice welcome, darling of the Spring!
Even yet thou art to me
No bird, but an invisible thing,
A voice, a mystery;

The same whom in my school-boy days
I listen'd to; that Cry
Which made me look a thousand ways
In bush, and tree, and sky.

To seek thee did I often rove
Through woods and on the green;
And thou wert still a hope, a love;
Still long'd for, never seen!

And I can listen to thee yet;
Can lie upon the plain
And listen, till I do beget
That golden time again.

O blesséd Bird! the earth we pace
Again appears to be
An unsubstantial, fairy place,
That is fit home for Thee!

W. WORDSWORTH

CCXLIV

ODE TO A NIGHTINGALE

My heart aches, and a drowsy numbness pains
  My sense, as though of hemlock I had drunk,
Or emptied some dull opiate to the drains
  One minute past, and Lethe-wards had sunk:
'Tis not through envy of thy happy lot,
  But being too happy in thy happiness,—
    That thou, light-wingéd Dryad of the trees,
      In some melodious plot
Of beechen green, and shadows numberless,
  Singest of summer in full-throated ease.

O, for a draught of vintage, that hath been
  Cool'd a long age in the deep-delvéd earth,
Tasting of Flora and the country green,
  Dance, and Provençal song, and sun-burnt mirth:

O for a beaker full of the warm South,
  Full of the true, the blushful Hippocrene,
    With beaded bubbles winking at the brim,
      And purple-stainéd mouth;
That I might drink, and leave the world unseen,
  And with thee fade away into the forest dim:

Fade far away, dissolve, and quite forget
  What thou among the leaves hast never known,
The weariness, the fever, and the fret
  Here, where men sit and hear each other groan;
Where palsy shakes a few, sad, last gray hairs,
  Where youth grows pale, and spectre-thin, and dies;
    Where but to think is to be full of sorrow
      And leaden-eyed despairs;
Where Beauty cannot keep her lustrous eyes,
  Or new Love pine at them beyond to-morrow.

Away! away! for I will fly to thee,
  Not charioted by Bacchus and his pards,
But on the viewless wings of Poesy,
  Though the dull brain perplexes and retards:
Already with thee! tender is the night,
  And haply the Queen-Moon is on her throne,
    Cluster'd around by all her starry Fays;
      But here there is no light
Save what from heaven is with the breezes blown
  Through verdurous glooms and winding mossy
    ways.

I cannot see what flowers are at my feet,
  Nor what soft incense hangs upon the boughs,
But, in embalméd darkness, guess each sweet
  Wherewith the seasonable month endows
The grass, the thicket, and the fruit-tree wild;
  White hawthorn, and the pastoral eglantine;
    Fast fading violets cover'd up in leaves;
      And mid-May's eldest child,

The coming musk-rose, full of dewy wine,
  The murmurous haunt of flies on summer eves.

Darkling I listen; and for many a time
  I have been half in love with easeful Death,
Call'd him soft names in many a muséd rhyme,
  To take into the air my quiet breath;
Now more than ever seems it rich to die,
  To cease upon the midnight with no pain,
    While thou art pouring forth thy soul abroad
      In such an ecstasy!
  Still wouldst thou sing, and I have ears in vain—
    To thy high requiem become a sod.

Thou wast not born for death, immortal Bird!
  No hungry generations tread thee down;
The voice I hear this passing night was heard
  In ancient days by emperor and clown:
Perhaps the self-same song that found a path
  Through the sad heart of Ruth, when, sick for home,
    She stood in tears amid the alien corn;
      The same that oft-times hath
  Charm'd magic casements, opening on the foam
    Of perilous seas, in faery lands forlorn.

Forlorn! the very word is like a bell
  To toll me back from thee to my sole self!
Adieu! the fancy cannot cheat so well
  As she is famed to do, deceiving elf.
Adieu! adieu! thy plaintive anthem fades
  Past the near meadows, over the still stream,
    Up the hill-side; and now 'tis buried deep
      In the next valley-glades:
  Was it a vision, or a waking dream?
    Fled is that music:—do I wake or sleep?
                                J. KEATS

UPON WESTMINSTER BRIDGE
Sept. 3, 1802

Earth has not anything to show more fair:
Dull would he be of soul who could pass by
A sight so touching in its majesty:
This City now doth like a garment wear

The beauty of the morning: silent, bare,
Ships, towers, domes, theatres, and temples lie
Open unto the fields, and to the sky,
All bright and glittering in the smokeless air.

Never did sun more beautifully steep
In his first splendour valley, rock, or hill;
Ne'er saw I, never felt, a calm so deep!

The river glideth at his own sweet will:
Dear God! the very houses seem asleep;
And all that mighty heart is lying still!
W. Wordsworth

OZYMANDIAS OF EGYPT

I met a traveller from an antique land
Who said: Two vast and trunkless legs of stone
Stand in the desert. Near them on the sand
Half sunk, a shatter'd visage lies, whose frown
And wrinkled lip and sneer of cold command
Tell that its sculptor well those passions read
Which yet survive, stamp'd on these lifeless things,
The hand that mock'd them and the heart that fed;
And on the pedestal these words appear:
' My name is Ozymandias, king of kings:

Look on my works, ye Mighty, and despair!'
Nothing beside remains.   Round the decay
Of that colossal wreck, boundless and bare,
The lone and level sands stretch far away.

P. B. SHELLEY

CCXLVII

COMPOSED AT NEIDPATH CASTLE, THE PROPERTY OF LORD QUEENSBERRY,

1803

Degenerate Douglas! oh, the unworthy lord!
Whom mere despite of heart could so far please
And love of havoc, (for with such disease
Fame taxes him,) that he could send forth word

To level with the dust a noble horde,
A brotherhood of venerable trees,
Leaving an ancient dome, and towers like these,
Beggar'd and outraged!—Many hearts deplored

The fate of those old trees; and oft with pain
The traveller at this day will stop and gaze
On wrongs, which Nature scarcely seems to heed:

For shelter'd places, bosoms, nooks, and bays,
And the pure mountains, and the gentle Tweed,
And the green silent pastures, yet remain.

W. WORDSWORTH

CCXLVIII

ADMONITION TO A TRAVELLER

Yes, there is holy pleasure in thine eye!
—The lovely cottage in the guardian nook
Hath stirr'd thee deeply; with its own dear brook,
Its own small pasture, almost its own sky!

But covet not the abode; O do not sigh
As many do, repining while they look;
Intruders who would tear from Nature's book
This precious leaf with harsh impiety:

—Think what the home must be if it were thine,
Even thine, though few thy wants!—Roof, window,
    door,
The very flowers are sacred to the Poor,

The roses to the porch which they entwine:
Yea, all that now enchants thee, from the day
On which it should be touch'd would melt away!

W. Wordsworth

ccxlix

TO THE HIGHLAND GIRL OF
INVERSNEYDE

Sweet Highland Girl, a very shower
Of beauty is thy earthly dower!
Twice seven consenting years have shed
Their utmost bounty on thy head:
And these gray rocks, this household lawn,
These trees—a veil just half withdrawn,
This fall of water that doth make
A murmur near the silent lake,
This little bay, a quiet road
That holds in shelter thy abode;
In truth together ye do seem
Like something fashion'd in a dream;
Such forms as from their covert peep
When earthly cares are laid asleep!
But O fair Creature! in the light
Of common day, so heavenly bright
I bless Thee, Vision as thou art,
I bless thee with a human heart:

God shield thee to thy latest years!
I neither know thee nor thy peers:
And yet my eyes are fill'd with tears.

With earnest feeling I shall pray
For thee when I am far away;
For never saw I mien or face
In which more plainly I could trace
Benignity and home-bred sense
Ripening in perfect innocence.
Here scatter'd, like a random seed,
Remote from men, Thou dost not need
The embarrass'd look of shy distress,
And maidenly shamefacédness:
Thou wear'st upon thy forehead clear
The freedom of a mountaineer:
A face with gladness overspread,
Soft smiles, by human kindness bred;
And seemliness complete, that sways
Thy courtesies, about thee plays;
With no restraint, but such as springs
From quick and eager visitings
Of thoughts that lie beyond the reach
Of thy few words of English speech:
A bondage sweetly brook'd, a strife
That gives thy gestures grace and life!
So have I, not unmoved in mind,
Seen birds of tempest-loving kind,
Thus beating up against the wind.

What hand but would a garland cull
For thee who art so beautiful?
O happy pleasure! here to dwell
Beside thee in some heathy dell;
Adopt your homely ways, and dress,
A shepherd, thou a shepherdess!
But I could frame a wish for thee

More like a grave reality:
Thou art to me but as a wave
Of the wild sea: and I would have
Some claim upon thee, if I could,
Though but of common neighbourhood.
What joy to hear thee, and to see!
Thy elder brother I would be,
Thy father, anything to thee.
Now thanks to Heaven! that of its grace
Hath led me to this lonely place;
Joy have I had; and going hence
I bear away my recompense.
In spots like these it is we prize
Our memory, feel that she hath eyes:
Then why should I be loth to stir?
I feel this place was made for her;
To give new pleasure like the past,
Continued long as life shall last.
Nor am I loth, though pleased at heart,
Sweet Highland Girl! from thee to part;
For I, methinks, till I grow old
As fair before me shall behold
As I do now, the cabin small,
The lake, the bay, the waterfall;
And Thee, the spirit of them all!

W. Wordsworth

CCL

THE REAPER

Behold her, single in the field,
Yon solitary Highland Lass!
Reaping and singing by herself;
Stop here, or gently pass!
Alone she cuts and binds the grain,
And sings a melancholy strain;
O listen! for the vale profound
Is overflowing with the sound.

No nightingale did ever chaunt
More welcome notes to weary bands
Of travellers in some shady haunt,
Among Arabian sands:
A voice so thrilling ne'er was heard
In spring-time from the cuckoo-bird,
Breaking the silence of the seas
Among the farthest Hebrides.

Will no one tell me what she sings?
Perhaps the plaintive numbers flow
For old, unhappy, far-off things,
And battles long ago:
Or is it some more humble lay,
Familiar matter of to-day?
Some natural sorrow, loss, or pain,
That has been, and may be again!

Whate'er the theme, the maiden sang
As if her song could have no ending;
I saw her singing at her work,
And o'er the sickle bending;
I listen'd, motionless and still;
And, as I mounted up the hill,
The music in my heart I bore
Long after it was heard no more.

W. WORDSWORTH

THE REVERIE OF POOR SUSAN

At the corner of Wood Street, when daylight appears,
Hangs a Thrush that sings loud, it has sung for three
    years:
Poor Susan has pass'd by the spot, and has heard
In the silence of morning the song of the bird.

'Tis a note of enchantment; what ails her? She sees
A mountain ascending, a vision of trees;
Bright volumes of vapour through Lothbury glide.
And a river flows on through the vale of Cheapside.

Green pastures she views in the midst of the dale
Down which she so often has tripp'd with her pail;
And a single small cottage, a nest like a dove's,
The one only dwelling on earth that she loves.

She looks, and her heart is in heaven: but they fade,
The mist and the river, the hill and the shade;
The stream will not flow, and the hill will not rise,
And the colours have all pass'd away from her eyes!

W. WORDSWORTH

CCLII

TO A LADY WITH A GUITAR

Ariel to Miranda:—Take
This slave of music, for the sake
Of him, who is the slave of thee;
And teach it all the harmony
In which thou canst, and only thou,
Make the delighted spirit glow,
Till joy denies itself again
And, too intense, is turn'd to pain.
For by permission and command
Of thine own Prince Ferdinand,
Poor Ariel sends this silent token
Of more than ever can be spoken;
Your guardian spirit, Ariel, who
From life to life must still pursue
Your happiness, for thus alone
Can Ariel ever find his own;
From Prospero's enchanted cell,
As the mighty verses tell,

To the throne of Naples he
Lit you o'er the trackless sea,
Flitting on, your prow before,
Like a living meteor.

When you die, the silent Moon
In her interlunar swoon
Is not sadder in her cell
Than deserted Ariel;
When you live again on earth,
Like an unseen Star of birth
Ariel guides you o'er the sea
Of life from your nativity:
Many changes have been run
Since Ferdinand and you begun
Your course of love, and Ariel still
Has track'd your steps and served your will.
Now in humbler, happier lot,
This is all remember'd not;
And now, alas! the poor sprite is
Imprison'd for some fault of his
In a body like a grave—
From you he only dares to crave
For his service and his sorrow
A smile to-day, a song to-morrow.

The artist who this idol wrought
To echo all harmonious thought,
Fell'd a tree, while on the steep
The woods were in their winter sleep,
Rock'd in that repose divine
On the wind-swept Apennine;
And dreaming, some of autumn past,
And some of spring approaching fast,
And some of April buds and showers,
And some of songs in July bowers,
And all of love: And so this tree,—
Oh that such our death may be!—

Died in sleep, and felt no pain,
To live in happier form again:
From which, beneath Heaven's fairest star,
The artist wrought this loved Guitar;
And taught it justly to reply
To all who question skilfully
In language gentle as thine own;
Whispering in enamour'd tone
Sweet oracles of woods and dells,
And summer winds in sylvan cells;
—For it had learnt all harmonies
Of the plains and of the skies,
Of the forests and the mountains,
And the many-voicéd fountains;
The clearest echoes of the hills,
The softest notes of falling rills,
The melodies of birds and bees,
The murmuring of summer seas,
And pattering rain, and breathing dew
And airs of evening; and it knew
That seldom-heard mysterious sound
Which, driven on its diurnal round,
As it floats through boundless day,
Our world enkindles on its way:
—All this it knows, but will not tell
To those who cannot question well
The spirit that inhabits it;
It talks according to the wit
Of its companions; and no more
Is heard than has been felt before
By those who tempt it to betray
These secrets of an elder day.
But, sweetly as its answers will
Flatter hands of perfect skill,
It keeps its highest holiest tone
For our beloved Friend alone.

P. B. SHELLEY

CCLIII
THE DAFFODILS

I wander'd lonely as a cloud
That floats on high o'er vales and hills,
When all at once I saw a crowd,
A host of golden daffodils,
Beside the lake, beneath the trees
Fluttering and dancing in the breeze.

Continuous as the stars that shine
And twinkle on the milky way,
They stretched in never-ending line
Along the margin of a bay:
Ten thousand saw I at a glance
Tossing their heads in sprightly dance.

The waves beside them danced, but they
Out-did the sparkling waves in glee:—
A Poet could not but be gay
In such a jocund company!
I gazed—and gazed—but little thought
What wealth the show to me had brought;

For oft, when on my couch I lie
In vacant or in pensive mood,
They flash upon that inward eye
Which is the bliss of solitude;
And then my heart with pleasure fills,
And dances with the daffodils.

                              W. WORDSWORTH

TO THE DAISY

With little here to do or see
Of things that in the great world be,
Sweet Daisy! oft I talk to thee
　　　For thou art worthy,
Thou unassuming commonplace
Of Nature, with that homely face,
And yet with something of a grace
　　　Which love makes for thee!

Oft on the dappled turf at ease
I sit and play with similes,
Loose types of things through all degrees,
　　　Thoughts of thy raising;
And many a fond and idle name
I give to thee, for praise or blame
As is the humour of the game,
　　　While I am gazing.

A nun demure, of lowly port;
Or sprightly maiden, of Love's court,
In thy simplicity the sport
　　　Of all temptations;
A queen in crown of rubies drest;
A starveling in a scanty vest;
Are all, as seems to suit thee best,
　　　Thy appellations.

A little Cyclops, with one eye
Staring to threaten and defy,
That thought comes next—and instantly
　　　The freak is over,
The shape will vanish, and behold!
A silver shield with boss of gold
That spreads itself, some fairy bold
　　　In fight to cover.

I see thee glittering from afar—
And then thou art a pretty star,
Not quite so fair as many are
    In heaven above thee!
Yet like a star, with glittering crest,
Self-poised in air thou seem'st to rest;—
May peace come never to his nest
    Who shall reprove thee!

Sweet Flower! for by that name at last
When all my reveries are past
I call thee, and to that cleave fast,
    Sweet silent Creature!
That breath'st with me in sun and air,
Do thou, as thou art wont, repair
My heart with gladness, and a share
    Of thy meek nature!
             W. WORDSWORTH

CCLV

ODE TO AUTUMN

Season of mists and mellow fruitfulness,
Close bosom-friend of the maturing sun;
Conspiring with him how to load and bless
With fruit the vines that round the thatch-eaves run;
To bend with apples the moss'd cottage-trees,
And fill all fruit with ripeness to the core;
To swell the gourd, and plump the hazel shells
With a sweet kernel; to set budding more,
And still more, later flowers for the bees,
Until they think warm days will never cease;
For Summer has o'erbrimm'd their clammy cells.

Who hath not seen Thee oft amid thy store?
Sometimes whoever seeks abroad may find
Thee sitting careless on a granary floor,

Thy hair soft-lifted by the winnowing wind;
Or on a half-reap'd furrow sound asleep,
Drowsed with the fume of poppies, while thy hook
Spares the next swath and all its twinéd flowers;
And sometimes like a gleaner thou dost keep
Steady thy laden head across a brook;
Or by a cider-press, with patient look,
Thou watchest the last oozings, hours by hours.

Where are the songs of Spring?　Ay, where are they?
Think not of them, thou hast thy music too,
While barréd clouds bloom the soft-dying day
And touch the stubble-plains with rosy hue;
Then in a wailful choir the small gnats mourn
Among the river-sallows, borne aloft
Or sinking as the light wind lives or dies;
And full-grown lambs loud bleat from hilly bourn;
Hedge-crickets sing, and now with treble soft
The redbreast whistles from a garden-croft;
And gathering swallows twitter in the skies.

J. KEATS

CCLVI

ODE TO WINTER

Germany, December, 1800

When first the fiery-mantled Sun
His heavenly race began to run,
Round the earth and ocean blue
His children four the Seasons flew:—
　　First, in green apparel dancing,
The young Spring smiled with angel-grace;
　　Rosy Summer next advancing,
Rush'd into her sire's embrace—
Her bright-hair'd sire, who bade her keep
　　For ever nearest to his smiles,
On Calpe's olive-shaded steep
　　Or India's citron-cover'd isles.

More remote, and buxom-brown,
  The Queen of vintage bow'd before his throne;
A rich pomegranate gemm'd her crown,
  A ripe sheaf bound her zone.

But howling Winter fled afar
To hills that prop the polar star;
And loves on deer-borne car to ride
With barren darkness at his side,
Round the shore where loud Lofoden
  Whirls to death the roaring whale,
Round the hall where Runic Odin
  Howls his war-song to the gale—
Save when adown the ravaged globe
  He travels on his native storm,
Deflowering Nature's grassy robe
  And trampling on her faded form;
Till light's returning Lord assume
  The shaft that drives him to his northern field,
Of power to pierce his raven plume
  And crystal-cover'd shield.

O, sire of storms! whose savage ear
The Lapland drum delights to hear,
When Frenzy with her bloodshot eye
Implores thy dreadful deity—
Archangel! Power of desolation!
  Fast descending as thou art,
Say, hath mortal invocation
  Spells to touch thy stony heart:
Then, sullen Winter! hear my prayer,
And gently rule the ruin'd year;
Nor chill the wanderer's bosom bare
Nor freeze the wretch's falling tear:
To shuddering Want's unmantled bed
  Thy horror-breathing agues cease to lend,
And gently on the orphan head
  Of Innocence descend.

But chiefly spare, O king of clouds!
The sailor on his airy shrouds,
When wrecks and beacons strew the steep,
And spectres walk along the deep.
Milder yet thy snowy breezes
   Pour on yonder tented shores,
Where the Rhine's broad billow freezes,
   Or the dark-brown Danube roars.
O, winds of Winter! list ye there
   To many a deep and dying groan?
Or start, ye demons of the midnight air,
   At shrieks and thunders louder than your own?
Alas! e'en your unhallow'd breath
   May spare the victim fallen low;
But Man will ask no truce to death,
   No bounds to human woe.

T. Campbell

CCLVII

YARROW UNVISITED

1803

From Stirling Castle we had seen
The mazy Forth unravell'd,
Had trod the banks of Clyde and Tay,
And with the Tweed had travell'd;
And when we came to Clovenford,
Then said my ' winsome Marrow,'
' Whate'er betide, we'll turn aside,
And see the Braes of Yarrow.'

' Let Yarrow folk, frae Selkirk town,
Who have been buying, selling,
Go back to Yarrow, 'tis their own,
Each maiden to her dwelling!
On Yarrow's banks let herons feed,
Hares couch, and rabbits burrow;

But we will downward with the Tweed,
Nor turn aside to Yarrow.

' There's Galla Water, Leader Haughs,
Both lying right before us;
And Dryburgh, where with chiming Tweed
The lintwhites sing in chorus;
There's pleasant Tiviotdale, a land
Made blythe with plough and harrow:
Why throw away a needful day
To go in search of Yarrow?

' What's Yarrow but a river bare
That glides the dark hills under?
There are a thousand such elsewhere
As worthy of your wonder.'
—Strange words they seem'd of slight and scorn;
My true-love sigh'd for sorrow,
And look'd me in the face, to think
I thus could speak of Yarrow!

' O green,' said I, ' are Yarrow's holms,
And sweet is Yarrow flowing!
Fair hangs the apple frae the rock,
But we will leave it growing.
O'er hilly path and open strath
We'll wander Scotland thorough;
But, though so near, we will not turn
Into the dale of Yarrow.

' Let beeves and home-bred kine partake
The sweets of Burn-mill meadow;
The swan on still Saint Mary's Lake
Float double, swan and shadow!
We will not see them; will not go
To-day, nor yet to-morrow;

Enough if in our hearts we know
There's such a place as Yarrow.

' Be Yarrow stream unseen, unknown;
It must, or we shall rue it:
We have a vision of our own,
Ah! why should we undo it?
The treasured dreams of times long past,
We'll keep them, winsome Marrow!
For when we're there, although 'tis fair,
'Twill be another Yarrow!

' If care with freezing years should come
And wandering seem but folly,—
Should we be loth to stir from home,
And yet be melancholy;
Should life be dull, and spirits low,
'Twill soothe us in our sorrow
That earth has something yet to show,
The bonny Holms of Yarrow!'

W. WORDSWORTH

CCLVIII

YARROW VISITED

September, 1814

And is this—Yarrow?—This the stream
Of which my fancy cherish'd
So faithfully, a waking dream,
An image that hath perish'd?
O that some minstrel's harp were near
To utter notes of gladness
And chase this silence from the air,
That fills my heart with sadness.

Yet why?—a silvery current flows
With uncontroll'd meanderings;

Nor have these eyes by greener hills
Been soothed, in all my wanderings.
And, through her depths, Saint Mary's Lake
Is visibly delighted;
For not a feature of those hills
Is in the mirror slighted.

A blue sky bends o'er Yarrow Vale,
Save where that pearly whiteness
Is round the rising sun diffused,
A tender hazy brightness;
Mild dawn of promise! that excludes
All profitless dejection;
Though not unwilling here to admit
A pensive recollection.

Where was it that the famous flower
Of Yarrow Vale lay bleeding?
His bed perchance was yon smooth mound
On which the herd is feeding:
And haply from this crystal pool
Now peaceful as the morning,
The water-Wraith ascended thrice,
And gave his doleful warning.

Delicious is the Lay that sings
The haunts of happy lovers,
The path that leads them to the grove,
The leafy grove that covers:
And pity sanctifies the verse
That paints, by strength of sorrow,
The unconquerable strength of love;
Bear witness, rueful Yarrow!

But thou that didst appear so fair
To fond imagination

Dost rival in the light of day
Her delicate creation:
Meek loveliness is round thee spread,
A softness still and holy:
The grace of forest charms decay'd,
And pastoral melancholy.

That region left, the vale unfolds
Rich groves of lofty stature,
With Yarrow winding through the pomp
Of cultivated Nature;
And rising from those lofty groves
Behold a ruin hoary,
The shatter'd front of Newark's Towers,
Renown'd in Border story.

Fair scenes for childhood's opening bloom,
For sportive youth to stray in,
For manhood to enjoy his strength,
And age to wear away in!
Yon cottage seems a bower of bliss,
A covert for protection
Of studious ease and generous cares
And every chaste affection!

How sweet on this autumnal day
The wild-wood fruits to gather,
And on my true-love's forehead plant
A crest of blooming heather!
And what if I enwreathed my own?
'Twere no offence to reason;
The sober hills thus deck their brows
To meet the wintry season.

I see—but not by sight alone,
Loved Yarrow, have I won thee;

A ray of Fancy still survives—
Her sunshine plays upon thee!
Thy ever-youthful waters keep
A course of lively pleasure;
And gladsome notes my lips can breathe
Accordant to the measure.

The vapours linger round the heights,
They melt, and soon must vanish;
One hour is theirs, nor more is mine—
Sad thought! which I would banish,
But that I know, where'er I go,
Thy genuine image, Yarrow!
Will dwell with me, to heighten joy
And cheer my mind in sorrow.

W. WORDSWORTH

CCLIX

THE INVITATION

Best and Brightest, come away,
Fairer far than this fair day,
Which, like thee, to those in sorrow
Comes to bid a sweet good-morrow
To the rough year just awake
In its cradle on the brake.
The brightest hour of unborn Spring
Through the winter wandering,
Found, it seems, the halcyon morn
To hoar February born;
Bending from Heaven, in azure mirth,
It kiss'd the forehead of the earth,
And smiled upon the silent sea,
And bade the frozen streams be free,
And waked to music all their fountains,
And breathed upon the frozen mountains,
And like a prophetess of May
Strew'd flowers upon the barren way,

Making the wintry world appear
Like one on whom thou smilest, Dear.

   Away, away, from men and towns,
To the wild wood and the downs—
To the silent wilderness
Where the soul need not repress
Its music, lest it should not find
An echo in another's mind,
While the touch of Nature's art
Harmonizes heart to heart.

   Radiant Sister of the Day
Awake! arise! and come away!
To the wild woods and the plains,
To the pools where winter rains
Image all their roof of leaves,
Where the pine its garland weaves
Of sapless green, and ivy dun,
Round stems that never kiss the sun,
Where the lawns and pastures be
And the sandhills of the sea,
Where the melting hoar-frost wets
The daisy-star that never sets,
And wind-flowers and violets
Which yet join not scent to hue
Crown the pale year weak and new;
When the night is left behind
In the deep east, dim and blind,
And the blue noon is over us,
And the multitudinous
Billows murmur at our feet,
Where the earth and ocean meet,
And all things seem only one
In the universal Sun.

P. B. SHELLEY

CCLX

THE RECOLLECTION

Now the last day of many days
All beautiful and bright as thou,
The loveliest and the last, is dead:
Rise, Memory, and write its praise!
Up, do thy wonted work! come, trace
The epitaph of glory fled,
For now the earth has changed its face,
A frown is on the Heaven's brow.

We wander'd to the Pine Forest
　That skirts the Ocean's foam;
The lightest wind was in its nest,
　The tempest in its home.
The whispering waves were half asleep,
　The clouds were gone to play,
And on the bosom of the deep
　The smile of Heaven lay;
It seem'd as if the hour were one
　Sent from beyond the skies
Which scatter'd from above the sun
　A light of Paradise!

We paused amid the pines that stood
　The giants of the waste,
Tortured by storms to shape as rude
　As serpents interlaced,—
And soothed by every azure breath
　That under heaven is blown
To harmonies and hues beneath,
　As tender as its own:
Now all the tree-tops lay asleep
　Like green waves on the sea,
As still as in the silent deep
　The ocean-woods may be.

How calm it was!—the silence there
    By such a chain was bound,
That even the busy woodpecker
    Made stiller by her sound
The inviolable quietness;
    The breath of peace we drew
With its soft motion made not less
    The calm that round us grew.
There seem'd, from the remotest seat
    Of the wide mountain waste
To the soft flower beneath our feet
    A magic circle traced,
A spirit interfused around,
    A thrilling silent life;
To momentary peace it bound
    Our mortal nature's strife;—
And still I felt the centre of
    The magic circle there
Was one fair Form that fill'd with love
    The lifeless atmosphere.

We paused beside the pools that lie
    Under the forest bough;
Each seem'd as 'twere a little sky
    Gulf'd in a world below;
A firmament of purple light
    Which in the dark earth lay,
More boundless than the depth of night
    And purer than the day—
In which the lovely forests grew
    As in the upper air,
More perfect both in shape and hue
    Than any spreading there.
There lay the glade and neighbouring lawn,
    And through the dark-green wood
The white sun twinkling like the dawn
    Out of a speckled cloud.

Sweet views which in our world above
　　Can never well be seen
Were imaged by the water's love
　　Of that fair forest green:
And all was interfused beneath
　　With an Elysian glow,
An atmosphere without a breath,
　　A softer day below.
Like one beloved, the scene had lent
　　To the dark water's breast
Its every leaf and lineament
　　With more than truth exprest;
Until an envious wind crept by,
　　Like an unwelcome thought
Which from the mind's too faithful eye
　　Blots one dear image out.
—Though Thou art ever fair and kind,
　　The forests ever green,
Less oft is peace in Shelley's mind
　　Than calm in waters seen!

P. B. SHELLEY

CCLXI

BY THE SEA

It is a beauteous evening, calm and free;
The holy time is quiet as a nun
Breathless with adoration; the broad sun
Is sinking down in its tranquillity;

The gentleness of heaven is on the Sea:
Listen! the mighty being is awake,
And doth with his eternal motion make
A sound like thunder—everlastingly.

Dear child! dear girl! that walkest with me here,
If thou appear untouch'd by solemn thought
Thy nature is not therefore less divine:

Thou liest in Abraham's bosom all the year,
And worship'st at the Temple's inner shrine,
God being with thee when we know it not.
                              W. WORDSWORTH

CCLXII

TO THE EVENING STAR

Star that bringest home the bee,
And sett'st the weary labourer free!
If any star shed peace, 'tis Thou
    That send'st it from above,
Appearing when Heaven's breath and brow
    Are sweet as hers we love.

Come to the luxuriant skies,
Whilst the landscape's odours rise,
Whilst far-off lowing herds are heard
    And songs when toil is done,
From cottages whose smoke unstirr'd
    Curls yellow in the sun.

Star of love's soft interviews,
Parted lovers on thee muse;
Their remembrancer in Heaven
    Of thrilling vows thou art,
Too delicious to be riven
    By absence from the heart.
                              T. CAMPBELL

CCLXIII

DATUR HORA QUIETI

The sun upon the lake is low,
    The wild birds hush their song,
The hills have evening's deepest glow,
    Yet Leonard tarries long.

Now all whom varied toil and care
  From home and love divide,
In the calm sunset may repair
  Each to the loved one's side.

The noble dame, on turret high,
  Who waits her gallant knight,
Looks to the western beam to spy
  The flash of armour bright.
The village maid, with hand on brow
  The level ray to shade,
Upon the footpath watches now
  For Colin's darkening plaid.

Now to their mates the wild swans row,
  By day they swam apart,
And to the thicket wanders slow
  The hind beside the hart.
The woodlark at his partner's side
  Twitters his closing song—
All meet whom day and care divide,
  But Leonard tarries long!

Sir W. Scott

CCLXIV

TO THE MOON

Art thou pale for weariness
Of climbing heaven, and gazing on the earth,
  Wandering companionless
Among the stars that have a different birth,—
And ever-changing, like a joyless eye
That finds no object worth its constancy?

P. B. Shelley

CCLXV

A widow bird sate mourning for her Love
    Upon a wintry bough;
The frozen wind crept on above
    The freezing stream below.

There was no leaf upon the forest bare,
    No flower upon the ground,
And little motion in the air
    Except the mill-wheel's sound.

P. B. SHELLEY

CCLXVI

TO SLEEP

A flock of sheep that leisurely pass by
One after one; the sound of rain, and bees
Murmuring; the fall of rivers, winds and seas,
Smooth fields, white sheets of water, and pure sky;—

I've thought of all by turns, and still I lie
Sleepless; and soon the small birds' melodies
Must hear, first utter'd from my orchard trees,
And the first cuckoo's melancholy cry.

Even thus last night, and two nights more I lay,
And could not win thee, Sleep! by any stealth:
So do not let me wear to-night away:

Without Thee what is all the morning's wealth?
Come, blessèd barrier between day and day,
Dear mother of fresh thoughts and joyous health!

W. WORDSWORTH

CCLXVII

THE SOLDIER'S DREAM

Our bugles sang truce, for the night-cloud had
    lower'd,
  And the sentinel stars set their watch in the sky;
And thousands had sunk on the ground overpower'd,
  The weary to sleep, and the wounded to die.

When reposing that night on my pallet of straw
  By the wolf-scaring faggot that guarded the slain,
At the dead of the night a sweet Vision I saw;
  And thrice ere the morning I dreamt it again.

Methought from the battle-field's dreadful array
  Far, far, I had roam'd on a desolate track:
'Twas Autumn,—and sunshine arose on the way
  To the home of my fathers, that welcomed me back.

I flew to the pleasant fields traversed so oft
  In life's morning march, when my bosom was young;
I heard my own mountain-goats bleating aloft,
  And knew the sweet strain that the corn-reapers
    sung.

Then pledged we the wine-cup, and fondly I swore
  From my home and my weeping friends never to
    part;
My little ones kiss'd me a thousand times o'er,
  And my wife sobb'd aloud in her fulness of heart.

' Stay—stay with us!—rest!—thou art weary and
    worn! '—
  And fain was their war-broken soldier to stay;—
But sorrow return'd with the dawning of morn,
  And the voice in my dreaming ear melted away.

                         T. CAMPBELL

A DREAM OF THE UNKNOWN

I dream'd that as I wander'd by the way
   Bare Winter suddenly was changed to Spring,
And gentle odours led my steps astray,
   Mix'd with a sound of waters murmuring
Along a shelving bank of turf, which lay
   Under a copse, and hardly dared to fling
Its green arms round the bosom of the stream,
But kiss'd it and then fled, as Thou mightest in dream.

There grew pied wind-flowers and violets,
   Daisies, those pearl'd Arcturi of the earth,
The constellated flower that never sets;
   Faint oxlips; tender blue-bells, at whose birth
The sod scarce heaved; and that tall flower that wets
   It's mother's face with heaven-collected tears,
When the low wind, its playmate's voice, it hears.

And in the warm hedge grew lush eglantine,
   Green cow-bind and the moonlight-colour'd May,
And cherry-blossoms, and white cups, whose wine
   Was the bright dew yet drain'd not by the day;
And wild roses, and ivy serpentine
   With its dark buds and leaves, wandering astray;
And flowers azure, black, and streak'd with gold,
Fairer than any waken'd eyes behold.

And nearer to the river's trembling edge
   There grew broad flag-flowers, purple prank't with
      white,
And starry river-buds among the sedge,
   And floating water-lilies, broad and bright,
Which lit the oak that overhung the hedge
   With moonlight beams of their own watery light;

And bulrushes, and reeds of such deep green
As soothed the dazzled eye with sober sheen.

Methought that of these visionary flowers
   I made a nosegay, bound in such a way
That the same hues, which in their natural bowers
   Were mingled or opposed, the like array
Kept these imprison'd children of the Hours
   Within my hand,—and then, elate and gay,
I hasten'd to the spot whence I had come
That I might there present it—O! to Whom?
P. B. SHELLEY

CCLXIX

THE INNER VISION

Most sweet it is with unuplifted eyes
To pace the ground, if path there be or none,
While a fair region round the Traveller lies
Which he forbears again to look upon;

Pleased rather with some soft ideal scene
The work of Fancy, or some happy tone
Of meditation, slipping in between
The beauty coming and the beauty gone.

—If Thought and Love desert us, from that day
Let us break off all commerce with the Muse:
With Thought and Love companions of our way—

What'er the senses take or may refuse,—
The Mind's internal heaven shall shed her dews
Of inspiration on the humblest lay.
W. WORDSWORTH

THE REALM OF FANCY

Ever let the Fancy roam!
Pleasure never is at home:
At a touch sweet Pleasure melteth,
Like to bubbles when rain pelteth;
Then let wingéd Fancy wander
Through the thought still spread beyond her:
Open wide the mind's cage-door,
She'll dart forth, and cloudward soar.
O sweet Fancy! let her loose;
Summer's joys are spoilt by use,
And the enjoying of the Spring
Fades as does its blossoming:
Autumn's red-lipp'd fruitage too,
Blushing through the mist and dew
Cloys with tasting: What do then?
Sit thee by the ingle, when
The sear faggot blazes bright,
Spirit of a winter's night;
When the soundless earth is muffled,
And the cakéd snow is shuffled
From the ploughboy's heavy shoon;
When the Night doth meet the Noon
In a dark conspiracy
To banish Even from her sky.
—Sit thee there, and send abroad,
With a mind self-overaw'd,
Fancy, high-commission'd:—send her!
She has vassals to attend her;
She will bring, in spite of frost,
Beauties that the earth hath lost;
She will bring thee, all together,
All delights of summer weather;
All the buds and bells of May

From dewy sward or thorny spray;
All the heapéd Autumn's wealth,
With a still, mysterious stealth:
She will mix these pleasures up
Like three fit wines in a cup,
And thou shalt quaff it:—thou shalt hear
Distant harvest-carols clear;
Rustle of the reapéd corn;
Sweet birds antheming the morn:
And, in the same moment—hark!
'Tis the early April lark,
Or the rooks, with busy caw,
Foraging for sticks and straw.
Thou shalt, at one glance, behold
The daisy and the marigold;
White-plumed lilies, and the first
Hedge-grown primrose that hath burst;
Shaded hyacinth, alway
Sapphire queen of the mid-May;
And every leaf, and every flower
Pearléd with the self-same shower.
Thou shalt see the field-mouse peep
Meagre from its celléd sleep;
And the snake all winter-thin
Cast on sunny bank its skin;
Freckled nest-eggs thou shalt see
Hatching in the hawthorn-tree,
When the hen-bird's wing doth rest
Quiet on her mossy nest;
Then the hurry and alarm
When the bee-hive casts its swarm;
Acorns ripe down-pattering,
While the autumn breezes sing.

  Oh, sweet Fancy! let her loose!
Everything is spoilt by use:
Where's the cheek that doth not fade,

Too much gazed at? Where's the maid
Whose lip mature is ever new?
Where's the eye, however blue,
Doth not weary? Where's the face
One would meet in every place?
Where's the voice, however soft,
One would hear so very oft?
At a touch sweet Pleasure melteth
Like to bubbles when rain pelteth.
Let then wingéd Fancy find
Thee a mistress to thy mind:
Dulcet-eyed as Ceres' daughter,
Ere the God of Torment taught her
How to frown and how to chide;
With a waist and with a side
White as Hebe's, when her zone
Slipt its golden clasp, and down
Fell her kirtle to her feet,
While she held the goblet sweet,
And Jove grew languid.—Break the mesh
Of the Fancy's silken leash;
Quickly break her prison-string,
And such joys as these she'll bring:
—Let the wingéd Fancy roam!
Pleasure never is at home.

J. KEATS

CCLXXI

HYMN TO THE SPIRIT OF NATURE

Life of Life! Thy lips enkindle
With their love the breath between them;
And thy smiles before they dwindle
Make the cold air fire; then screen them
In those locks, where whoso gazes
Faints, entangled in their mazes.

Child of Light! Thy limbs are burning
Through the veil which seems to hide them,
As the radiant lines of morning
Through thin clouds, ere they divide them;
And this atmosphere divinest
Shrouds thee wheresoe'er thou shinest.

Fair are others: none beholds Thee;
But thy voice sounds low and tender
Like the fairest, for it folds thee
From the sight, that liquid splendour;
And all feel, yet see thee never,—
As I feel now, lost for ever!

Lamp of Earth! where'er thou movest
Its dim shapes are clad with brightness,
And the souls of whom thou lovest
Walk upon the winds with lightness
Till they fail, as I am failing,
Dizzy, lost, yet unbewailing!

P. B. SHELLEY

CCLXXII
WRITTEN IN EARLY SPRING

I heard a thousand blended notes
While in a grove I sate reclined,
In that sweet mood when pleasant thoughts
Bring sad thoughts to the mind.

To her fair works did Nature link
The human soul that through me ran;
And much it grieved my heart to think
What Man has made of Man.

Through primrose tufts, in that sweet bower,
The periwinkle trail'd its wreaths;

And 'tis my faith that every flower
Enjoys the air it breathes.

The birds around me hopp'd and play'd,
Their thoughts I cannot measure,—
But the least motion which they made
It seem'd a thrill of pleasure.

The budding twigs spread out their fan
To catch the breezy air;
And I must think, do all I can,
That there was pleasure there.

If this belief from heaven be sent,
If such be Nature's holy plan,
Have I not reason to lament
What Man has made of Man?

W. WORDSWORTH

CCLXXIII

RUTH: OR THE INFLUENCES OF NATURE

When Ruth was left half desolate
Her father took another mate;
And Ruth, not seven years old,
A slighted child, at her own will
Went wandering over dale and hill,
In thoughtless freedom bold.

And she had made a pipe of straw,
And music from that pipe could draw
Like sounds of winds and floods;
Had built a bower upon the green,
As if she from her birth had been
An infant of the woods.

Beneath her father's roof, alone
She seem'd to live; her thoughts her own;
Herself her own delight:
Pleased with herself, nor sad nor gay,
And, passing thus the live-long day,
She grew to woman's height.

There came a youth from Georgia's shore—
A military casque he wore
With splendid feathers drest;
He brought them from the Cherokees;
The feathers nodded in the breeze
And made a gallant crest.

From Indian blood you deem him sprung:
But no! he spake the English tongue
And bore a soldier's name;
And, when America was free
From battle and from jeopardy,
He 'cross the ocean came.

With hues of genius on his cheek,
In finest tones the youth could speak:
—While he was yet a boy
The moon, the glory of the sun,
And streams that murmur as they run
Had been his dearest joy.

He was a lovely youth! I guess
The panther in the wilderness
Was not so fair as he;
And when he chose to sport and play,
No dolphin ever was so gay
Upon the tropic sea.

Among the Indians he had fought;
And with him many tales he brought

Of pleasure and of fear;
Such tales as, told to any maid
By such a youth, in the green shade,
Were perilous to hear.

He told of girls, a happy rout!
Who quit their fold with dance and shout.
Their pleasant Indian town,
To gather strawberries all day long;
Returning with a choral song
When daylight is gone down.

He spake of plants that hourly change
Their blossoms, through a boundless range
Of intermingling hues;
With budding, fading, faded flowers,
They stand the wonder of the bowers
From morn to evening dews.

He told of the Magnolia, spread
High as a cloud, high over head!
The cypress and her spire;
—Of flowers that with one scarlet gleam
Cover a hundred leagues, and seem
To set the hills on fire.

The youth of green savannahs spake,
And many an endless, endless lake
With all its fairy crowds
Of islands, that together lie
As quietly as spots of sky
Among the evening clouds.

' And,' then he said, ' how sweet it were
A fisher or a hunter there,
In sunshine or in shade
To wander with an easy mind,

And build a household fire, and find
A home in every glade!

'What days and what bright years! Ah me!
Our life were life indeed, with Thee
So pass'd in quiet bliss;
And all the while,' said he, ' to know
That we were in a world of woe,
On such an earth as this! '

And then he sometimes interwove
Fond thoughts about a father's love,
' For there,' said he, ' are spun
Around the heart such tender ties,
That our own children to our eyes
Are dearer than the sun.

'Sweet Ruth! and could you go with me
My helpmate in the woods to be,
Our shed at night to rear;
Or run, my own adopted bride,
A sylvan huntress at my side,
And drive the flying deer!

'Beloved Ruth! '—No more he said.
The wakeful Ruth at midnight shed
A solitary tear:
She thought again—and did agree
With him to sail across the sea,
And drive the flying deer.

'And now, as fitting is and right,
We in the church our faith will plight,
A husband and a wife.'
Even so they did; and I may say
That to sweet Ruth that happy day
Was more than human life.

Through dream and vision did she sink,
Delighted all the while to think
That, on those lonesome floods
And green savannahs, she should share
His board with lawful joy, and bear
His name in the wild woods.

But, as you have before been told,
This Stripling, sportive, gay, and bold,
And with his dancing crest
So beautiful, through savage lands
Had roam'd about, with vagrant bands
Of Indians in the West.

The wind, the tempest roaring high,
The tumult of a tropic sky
Might well be dangerous food
For him, a youth to whom was given
So much of earth—so much of heaven,
And such impetuous blood.

Whatever in those climes he found
Irregular in sight or sound
Did to his mind impart
A kindred impulse, seem'd allied
To his own powers, and justified
The workings of his heart.

Nor less, to feed voluptuous thought,
The beauteous forms of Nature wrought,—
Fair trees and gorgeous flowers;
The breezes their own languor lent;
The stars had feelings, which they sent
Into those favour'd bowers.

Yet, in his worst pursuits, I ween
That sometimes there did intervene

Pure hopes of high intent:
For passions link'd to forms so fair
And stately, needs must have their share
Of noble sentiment.

But ill he lived, much evil saw,
With men to whom no better law
Nor better life was known;
Deliberately and undeceived
Those wild men's vices he received,
And gave them back his own.

His genius and his moral frame
Were thus impair'd, and he became
The slave of low desires;
A man who without self-control
Would seek what the degraded soul
Unworthily admires.

And yet he with no feign'd delight
Had woo'd the maiden, day and night
Had loved her, night and morn:
What could he less than love a maid
Whose heart with so much nature play'd—
So kind and so forlorn?

Sometimes most earnestly he said,
'O Ruth! I have been worse than dead;
False thoughts, thoughts bold and vain
Encompass'd me on every side
When I, in confidence and pride,
Had cross'd the Atlantic main.

'Before me shone a glorious world
Fresh as a banner bright, unfurl'd
To music suddenly:
I look'd upon those hills and plains,

And seem'd as if let loose from chains
To live at liberty!

'No more of this—for now, by thee,
Dear Ruth! more happily set free,
With nobler zeal I burn;
My soul from darkness is released
Like the whole sky when to the east
The morning doth return.'

Full soon that better mind was gone;
No hope, no wish remain'd, not one,
They stirr'd him now no more;
New objects did new pleasure give,
And once again he wish'd to live
As lawless as before.

Meanwhile, as thus with him it fared,
They for the voyage were prepared,
And went to the sea-shore:
But, when they thither came, the youth
Deserted his poor bride, and Ruth
Could never find him more.

God help thee, Ruth!—Such pains she had
That she in half a year was mad
And in a prison housed;
And there, exulting in her wrongs
Among the music of her songs
She fearfully caroused.

Yet sometimes milder hours she knew,
Nor wanted sun, nor rain, nor dew,
Nor pastimes of the May,
—They all were with her in her cell;
And a clear brook with cheerful knell
Did o'er the pebbles play.

When Ruth three seasons thus had lain,
There came a respite to her pain;
She from her prison fled;
But of the vagrant none took thought;
And where it liked her best she sought
Her shelter and her bread.

Among the fields she breathed again:
The master-current of her brain
Ran permanent and free;
And, coming to the banks of Tone,
There did she rest; and dwell alone
Under the greenwood tree.

The engines of her pain, the tools
That shaped her sorrow, rocks and pools,
And airs that gently stir
The vernal leaves—she loved them still,
Nor ever tax'd them with the ill
Which had been done to her.

A barn her Winter bed supplies;
But, till the warmth of Summer skies
And Summer days is gone,
(And all do in this tale agree)
She sleeps beneath the greenwood tree,
And other home hath none.

An innocent life, yet far astray!
And Ruth will, long before her day,
Be broken down and old.
Sore aches she needs must have! but less
Of mind, than body's wretchedness,
From damp, and rain, and cold.

If she is prest by want of food
She from her dwelling in the wood

Repairs to a road-side;
And there she begs at one steep place,
Where up and down with easy pace
The horsemen-travellers ride.

That oaten pipe of hers is mute
Or thrown away: but with a flute
Her loneliness she cheers;
This flute, made of a hemlock stalk,
At evening in his homeward walk
The Quantock woodman hears.

I, too, have pass'd her on the hills
Setting her little water-mills
By spouts and fountains wild—
Such small machinery as she turn'd
Ere she had wept, ere she had mourn'd,
A young and happy child!

Farewell! and when thy days are told,
Ill-fated Ruth! in hallow'd mould
Thy corpse shall buried be;
For thee a funeral bell shall ring,
And all the congregation sing
A Christian psalm for thee.

W. WORDSWORTH

CCLXXIV
WRITTEN AMONG THE EUGANEAN HILLS, NORTH ITALY

Many a green isle needs must be
In the deep wide sea of misery,
Or the mariner, worn and wan,
Never thus could voyage on
Day and night, and night and day,
Drifting on his dreary way,

With the solid darkness black
Closing round his vessel's track;
Whilst above, the sunless sky
Big with clouds, hangs heavily,
And behind the tempest fleet
Hurries on with lightning feet,
Riving sail, and cord, and plank,
Till the ship has almost drank
Death from the o'er-brimming deep;
And sinks down, down, like that sleep
When the dreamer seems to be
Weltering through eternity;
And the dim low line before
Of a dark and distant shore
Still recedes, as ever still
Longing with divided will,
But no power to seek or shun,
He is ever drifted on
O'er the unreposing wave,
To the haven of the grave.

Ah, many flowering islands lie
In the waters of wide agony:
To such a one this morn was led
My bark, by soft winds piloted.
—'Mid the mountains Euganean
I stood listening to the paean
With which the legion'd rooks did hail
The Sun's uprise majestical:
Gathering round with wings all hoar,
Through the dewy mist they soar
Like gray shades, till the eastern heaven
Bursts, and then,—as clouds of even
Fleck'd with fire and azure, lie
In the unfathomable sky,—
So their plumes of purple grain
Starr'd with drops of golden rain

Gleam above the sunlight woods,
As in silent multitudes
On the morning's fitful gale
Through the broken mist they sail;
And the vapours cloven and gleaming
Follow down the dark steep streaming,
Till all is bright, and clear, and still
Round the solitary hill.

Beneath is spread like a green sea
The waveless plain of Lombardy,
Bounded by the vaporous air,
Islanded by cities fair;
Underneath day's azure eyes,
Ocean's nursling, Venice lies,—
A peopled labyrinth of walls,
Amphitrite's destined halls,
Which her hoary sire now paves
With his blue and beaming waves.
Lo! the sun upsprings behind,
Broad, red, radiant, half-reclined
On the level quivering line
Of the waters crystalline;
And before that chasm of light,
As within a furnace bright,
Column, tower, and dome, and spire,
Shine like obelisks of fire,
Pointing with inconstant motion
From the altar of dark ocean
To the sapphire-tinted skies;
As the flames of sacrifice
From the marble shrines did rise
As to pierce the dome of gold
Where Apollo spoke of old.

Sun-girt City! thou hast been
Ocean's child, and then his queen;

Now is come a darker day,
And thou soon must be his prey,
If the power that raised thee here
Hallow so thy watery bier.
A less drear ruin then than now
With thy conquest-branded brow
Stooping to the slave of slaves
From thy throne among the waves,
Wilt thou be,—when the sea-mew
Flies, as once before it flew,
O'er thine isles depopulate,
And all is in its ancient state,
Save where many a palace-gate
With green sea-flowers overgrown
Like a rock of ocean's own,
Topples o'er the abandon'd sea
As the tides change sullenly.
The fisher on his watery way
Wandering at the close of day,
Will spread his sail and seize his oar
Till he pass the gloomy shore,
Lest thy dead should, from their sleep,
Bursting o'er the starlight deep,
Lead a rapid masque of death
O'er the waters of his path.

Noon descends around me now:
'Tis the noon of autumn's glow,
When a soft and purple mist
Like a vaporous amethyst,
Or an air-dissolvéd star
Mingling light and fragrance, far
From the curved horizon's bound
To the point of heaven's profound,
Fills the overflowing sky;
And the plains that silent lie
Underneath; the leaves unsodden

Where the infant frost has trodden
With his morning-wingéd feet
Whose bright print is gleaming yet;
And the red and golden vines
Piercing with their trellised lines
The rough, dark-skirted wilderness;
The dun and bladed grass no less,
Pointing from this hoary tower
In the windless air; the flower
Glimmering at my feet; the line
Of the olive-sandall'd Apennine
In the south dimly islanded;
And the Alps, whose snows are spread
High between the clouds and sun;
And of living things each one;
And my spirit, which so long
Darken'd this swift stream of song,—
Interpenetrated lie
By the glory of the sky;
Be it love, light, harmony,
Odour, or the soul of all
Which from heaven like dew doth fall,
Or the mind which feels this verse,
Peopling the lone universe.

Noon descends, and after noon
Autumn's evening meets me soon,
Leading the infantine moon
And that one star, which to her
Almost seems to minister
Half the crimson light she brings
From the sunset's radiant springs:
And the soft dreams of the morn
(Which like wingéd winds had borne
To that silent isle, which lies
'Mid remember'd agonies,
The frail bark of this lone being),

Pass, to other sufferers fleeing,
And its ancient pilot, Pain,
Sits beside the helm again.

Other flowering isles must be
In the sea of life and agony:
Other spirits float and flee
O'er that gulf: ev'n now, perhaps,
On some rock the wild wave wraps,
With folding wings they waiting sit
For my bark, to pilot it
To some calm and blooming cove,
Where for me, and those I love,
May a windless bower be built,
Far from passion, pain, and guilt,
In a dell 'mid lawny hills
Which the wild sea-murmur fills,
And soft sunshine, and the sound
Of old forests echoing round,
And the light and smell divine
Of all flowers that breathe and shine
—We may live so happy there,
That the spirits of the air
Envying us, may even entice
To our healing paradise
The polluting multitude;
But their rage would be subdued
By that clime divine and calm,
And the winds whose wings rain balm
On the uplifted soul, and leaves
Under which the bright sea heaves;
While each breathless interval
In their whisperings musical
The inspired soul supplies
With its own deep melodies;
And the Love which heals all strife
Circling, like the breath of life,

All things in that sweet abode
With its own mild brotherhood.
They, not it, would change; and soon
Every sprite beneath the moon
Would repent its envy vain,
And the Earth grow young again!

P. B. Shelley

CCLXXV

ODE TO THE WEST WIND

O wild West Wind, thou breath of Autumn's being,
Thou, from whose unseen presence the leaves dead
Are driven, like ghosts from an enchanter fleeing,
Yellow, and black, and pale, and hectic red,
Pestilence-stricken multitudes: O thou
Who chariotest to their dark wintry bed
The wingéd seeds, where they lie cold and low,
Each like a corpse within its grave, until
Thine azure sister of the spring shall blow
Her clarion o'er the dreaming earth, and fill
(Driving sweet buds like flocks to feed in air)
With living hues and odours plain and hill:
Wild Spirit, which art moving everywhere;
Destroyer and Preserver; Hear, O hear!

Thou on whose stream, 'mid the steep sky's com-
    motion,
Loose clouds like earth's decaying leaves are shed,
Shook from the tangled boughs of Heaven and Ocean,
Angels of rain and lightning; there are spread
On the blue surface of thine airy surge,
Like the bright hair uplifted from the head
Of some fierce Maenad, ev'n from the dim verge
Of the horizon to the zenith's height—
The locks of the approaching storm.   Thou dirge
Of the dying year, to which this closing night

Will be the dome of a vast sepulchre,
Vaulted with all thy congregated might
Of vapours, from whose solid atmosphere
Black rain, and fire, and hail, will burst: O hear!

Thou who didst waken from his summer-dreams
The blue Mediterranean, where he lay
Lull'd by the coil of his crystalline streams,
Beside a pumice isle in Baiae's bay,
And saw in sleep old palaces and towers
Quivering within the wave's intenser day,
All overgrown with azure moss and flowers
So sweet, the sense faints picturing them!   Thou
For whose path the Atlantic's level powers
Cleave themselves into chasms, while far below
The sea-blooms and the oozy woods which wear
The sapless foliage of the ocean, know
Thy voice, and suddenly grow gray with fear
And tremble and despoil themselves: O hear!

If I were a dead leaf thou mightest bear;
If I were a swift cloud to fly with thee;
A wave to pant beneath thy power, and share
The impulse of thy strength, only less free
Than Thou, O uncontrollable!   If even
I were as in my boyhood, and could be
The comrade of thy wanderings over heaven,
As then, when to outstrip thy skyey speed
Scarce seem'd a vision, I would ne'er have striven
As thus with thee in prayer in my sore need.
O lift me as a wave, a leaf, a cloud!
I fall upon the thorns of life!   I bleed!
A heavy weight of hours has chain'd and bow'd
One too like thee: tameless, and swift, and proud.

Make me thy lyre, ev'n as the forest is:
What if my leaves are falling like its own!

The tumult of thy mighty harmonies
Will take from both a deep autumnal tone,
Sweet though in sadness.   Be thou, Spirit fierce,
My spirit! be thou me, impetuous one!
Drive my dead thoughts over the universe
Like wither'd leaves, to quicken a new birth;
And, by the incantation of this verse,
Scatter, as from an unextinguish'd hearth
Ashes and sparks, my words among mankind!
Be through my lips to unawaken'd earth
The trumpet of a prophecy!   O Wind,
If Winter comes, can Spring be far behind?

P. B. SHELLEY

CCLXXVI

NATURE AND THE POET

*Suggested by a Picture of Peele Castle in a Storm,
painted by Sir George Beaumont*

I was thy neighbour once, thou rugged Pile!
Four summer weeks I dwelt in sight of thee:
I saw thee every day; and all the while
Thy form was sleeping on a glassy sea.

So pure the sky, so quiet was the air!
So like, so very like, was day to day!
Whene'er I look'd, thy image still was there;
It trembled, but it never pass'd away.

How perfect was the calm!   It seem'd no sleep,
No mood, which season takes away, or brings:
I could have fancied that the mighty Deep
Was even the gentlest of all gentle things.

Ah! then if mine had been the painter's hand
To express what then I saw; and add the gleam,

The light that never was on sea or land,
The consecration, and the Poet's dream,—

I would have planted thee, thou hoary pile,
Amid a world how different from this!
Beside a sea that could not cease to smile;
On tranquil land, beneath a sky of bliss.

. . .

A picture had it been of lasting ease,
Elysian quiet, without toil or strife;
No motion but the moving tide, a breeze,
Or merely silent Nature's breathing life.

Such, in the fond illusion of my heart,
Such picture would I at that time have made;
And seen the soul of truth in every part,
A steadfast peace that might not be betray'd.

So once it would have been,—'tis so no more;
I have submitted to a new control:
A power is gone, which nothing can restore;
A deep distress hath humanized my soul.

Not for a moment could I now behold
A smiling sea, and be what I have been:
The feeling of my loss will ne'er be old;
This, which I know, I speak with mind serene.

Then, Beaumont, Friend! who would have been the
        friend
If he had lived, of him whom I deplore,
This work of thine I blame not, but commend;
This sea in anger, and that dismal shore.

O 'tis a passionate work!—yet wise and well,
Well chosen is the spirit that is here;

That hulk which labours in the deadly swell,
This rueful sky, this pageantry of fear!

And this huge Castle, standing here sublime,
I love to see the look with which it braves,
—Cased in the unfeeling armour of old time—
The lightning, the fierce wind, and trampling waves.

—Farewell, farewell the heart that lives alone,
Housed in a dream, at distance from the Kind!
Such happiness, wherever it be known
Is to be pitied; for 'tis surely blind.

But welcome fortitude, and patient cheer,
And frequent sights of what is to be borne!
Such sights, or worse, as are before me here:—
Not without hope we suffer and we mourn.

W. WORDSWORTH

CCLXXVII

THE POET'S DREAM

On a Poet's lips I slept
Dreaming like a love-adept
In the sound his breathing kept;
Nor seeks nor finds he mortal blisses,
But feeds on the aërial kisses
Of shapes that haunt Thought's wildernesses.
He will watch from dawn to gloom
The lake-reflected sun illume
The yellow bees in the ivy-bloom,
    Nor heed nor see what things they be—
But from these create he can
Forms more real than living Man,
    Nurslings of Immortality!

P. B. SHELLEY

CCLXXVIII

The World is too much with us; late and soon,
Getting and spending, we lay waste our powers;
Little we see in Nature that is ours;
We have given our hearts away, a sordid boon!

This Sea that bares her bosom to the moon,
The winds that will be howling at all hours
And are up-gather'd now like sleeping flowers,
For this, for everything, we are out of tune;

It moves us not.—Great God! I'd rather be
A Pagan suckled in a creed outworn,—
So might I, standing on this pleasant lea,

Have glimpses that would make me less forlorn;
Have sight of Proteus rising from the sea;
Or hear old Triton blow his wreathéd horn.
                                W. WORDSWORTH

CCLXXIX

WITHIN KING'S COLLEGE CHAPEL, CAMBRIDGE

Tax not the royal Saint with vain expense,
With ill-match'd aims the Architect who plann'd
(Albeit labouring for a scanty band
Of white-robed Scholars only) this immense

And glorious work of fine intelligence!
—Give all thou canst; high Heaven rejects the lore
Of nicely-calculated less or more:—
So deem'd the man who fashion'd for the sense

These lofty pillars, spread that branching roof
Self-poised, and scoop'd into ten thousand cells
Where light and shade repose, where music dwells

Lingering and wandering on as loth to die—
Like thoughts whose very sweetness yieldeth proof
That they were born for immortality.

W. WORDSWORTH

CCLXXX

YOUTH AND AGE

Verse, a breeze 'mid blossoms straying,
Where Hope clung feeding, like a bee—
Both were mine! Life went a-maying
     With Nature, Hope, and Poesy,
        When I was young!
When I was young?—Ah, woful when!
Ah! for the change 'twixt Now and Then!
This breathing house not built with hands,
This body that does me grievous wrong,
O'er aery cliffs and glittering sands
How lightly then it flash'd along:
Like those trim skiffs, unknown of yore,
On winding lakes and rivers wide,
That ask no aid of sail or oar,
That fear no spite of wind or tide!
Nought cared this body for wind or weather
When Youth and I lived in't together.

    Flowers are lovely; Love is flower-like;
Friendship is a sheltering tree;
O! the joys, that came down shower-like,
Of Friendship, Love, and Liberty,
        Ere I was old!
Ere I was old? Ah woful Ere,
Which tells me, Youth's no longer here!
O Youth! for years so many and sweet,
'Tis known that Thou and I were one,
I'll think it but a fond conceit—
It cannot be, that Thou art gone!

Thy vesper-bell hath not yet toll'd:—
And thou wert aye a masker bold!
What strange disguise hast now put on
To make believe that Thou art gone?
I see these locks in silvery slips,
This drooping gait, this alter'd size:
But Springtide blossoms on thy lips,
And tears take sunshine from thine eyes!
Life is but Thought: so think I will
That Youth and I are housemates still.

Dew-drops are the gems of morning,
But the tears of mournful eve!
Where no hope is, life's a warning
That only serves to make us grieve
   When we are old:
—That only serves to make us grieve
With oft and tedious taking-leave,
Like some poor nigh-related guest
That may not rudely be dismist,
Yet hath out-stay'd his welcome while,
And tells the jest without the smile.
     S. T. COLERIDGE

CCLXXXI

THE TWO APRIL MORNINGS

We walk'd along, while bright and red
Uprose the morning sun;
And Matthew stopp'd, he look'd, and said,
'The will of God be done!'

A village schoolmaster was he,
With hair of glittering gray;
As blithe a man as you could see
On a spring holiday.

And on that morning, through the grass
And by the steaming rills
We travell'd merrily, to pass
A day among the hills.

' Our work,' said I, ' was well begun;
Then, from thy breast what thought,
Beneath so beautiful a sun,
So sad a sigh has brought?'

A second time did Matthew stop;
And fixing still his eye
Upon the eastern mountain-top,
To me he made reply:

' Yon cloud with that long purple cleft
Brings fresh into my mind
A day like this, which I have left
Full thirty years behind.

' And just above yon slope of corn
Such colours, and no other,
Were in the sky that April morn
Of this the very brother.

' With rod and line I sued the sport
Which that sweet season gave,
And coming to the church, stopp'd short
Beside my daughter's grave.

' Nine summers had she scarcely seen,
The pride of all the vale;
And then she sang:—she would have been
A very nightingale.

' Six feet in earth my Emma lay;
And yet I loved her more—

For so it seem'd,—than till that day
I e'er had loved before.

' And turning from her grave, I met,
Beside the churchyard yew,
A blooming Girl, whose hair was wet
With points of morning dew.

' A basket on her head she bare;
Her brow was smooth and white:
To see a child so very fair,
It was a pure delight!

' No fountain from its rocky cave
E'er tripp'd with foot so free;
She seem'd as happy as a wave
That dances on the sea.

' There came from me a sigh of pain
Which I could ill confine;
I look'd at her, and look'd again:
And did not wish her mine! '

—Matthew is in his grave, yet now
Methinks I see him stand
As at that moment, with a bough
Of wilding in his hand.

W. WORDSWORTH

CCLXXXII

THE FOUNTAIN

A Conversation

We talk'd with open heart, and tongue
Affectionate and true,
A pair of friends, though I was young,
And Matthew seventy-two

We lay beneath a spreading oak,
Beside a mossy seat;
And from the turf a fountain broke
And gurgled at our feet.

'Now, Matthew!' said I, 'let us match
This water's pleasant tune
With some old border-song, or catch
That suits a summer's noon.

'Or of the church-clock and the chimes
Sing here beneath the shade
That half-mad thing of witty rhymes
Which you last April made!'

In silence Matthew lay, and eyed
The spring beneath the tree;
And thus the dear old man replied,
The gray-hair'd man of glee:

'No check, no stay, this Streamlet fears,
How merrily it goes!
'Twill murmur on a thousand years
And flow as now it flows.

'And here, on this delightful day,
I cannot choose but think
How oft, a vigorous man, I lay
Beside this fountain's brink.

'My eyes are dim with childish tears,
My heart is idly stirr'd,
For the same sound is in my ears
Which in those days I heard.

'Thus fares it still in our decay:
And yet the wiser mind
Mourns less for what Age takes away,
Than what it leaves behind.

' The blackbird amid leafy trees,
The lark above the hill,
Let loose their carols when they please,
Are quiet when they will.

' With Nature never do they wage
A foolish strife; they see
A happy youth, and their old age
Is beautiful and free:

' But we are press'd by heavy laws;
And often, glad no more,
We wear a face of joy, because
We have been glad of yore.

' If there be one who need bemoan
His kindred laid in earth,
The household hearts that were his own,—
It is the man of mirth.

' My days, my friend, are almost gone,
My life has been approved,
And many love me; but by none
Am I enough beloved.'

' Now both himself and me he wrongs,
The man who thus complains!
I live and sing my idle songs
Upon these happy plains:

' And Matthew, for thy children dead
I'll be a son to thee!'
At this he grasp'd my hand and said,
' Alas! that cannot be.'

We rose up from the fountain-side;
And down the smooth descent

Of the green sheep-track did we glide;
And through the wood we went;

And ere we came to Leonard's rock
He sang those witty rhymes
About the crazy old church-clock,
And the bewilder'd chimes.

W. WORDSWORTH

CCLXXXIII

THE RIVER OF LIFE

The more we live, more brief appear
　　Our life's succeeding stages:
A day to childhood seems a year,
　　And years like passing ages.

The gladsome current of our youth,
　　Ere passion yet disorders,
Steals lingering like a river smooth
　　Along its grassy borders.

But as the care-worn cheeks grow wan,
　　And sorrow's shafts fly thicker,
Ye Stars, that measure life to man,
　　Why seem your courses quicker?

When joys have lost their bloom and breath
　　And life itself is vapid,
Why, as we reach the Falls of Death,
　　Feel we its tide more rapid?

It may be strange—yet who would change
　　Time's course to slower speeding,
When one by one our friends have gone
　　And left our bosoms bleeding?

Heaven gives our years of fading strength
　Indemnifying fleetness;
And those of youth, a seeming length,
　Proportion'd to their sweetness.

T. CAMPBELL

CCLXXXIV

THE HUMAN SEASONS

Four Seasons fill the measure of the year;
There are four seasons in the mind of Man:
He has his lusty Spring, when fancy clear
Takes in all beauty with an easy span:

He has his Summer, when luxuriously
Spring's honey'd cud of youthful thought he loves
To ruminate, and by such dreaming high
Is nearest unto heaven: quiet coves

His soul has in its Autumn, when his wings
He furleth close; contented so to look
On mists in idleness—to let fair things
Pass by unheeded as a threshold brook:—

He has his Winter too of pale misfeature,
Or else he would forego his mortal nature.

J. KEATS

CCLXXXV

A LAMENT

O World! O Life! O Time!
On whose last steps I climb,
　Trembling at that where I had stood before;
When will return the glory of your prime?
　　No more—O never more!

Out of the day and night
A joy has taken flight:
    Fresh spring, and summer, and winter hoar
Move my faint heart with grief, but with delight
        No more—O never more!

                                P. B. SHELLEY

CCLXXXVI

My heart leaps up when I behold
    A rainbow in the sky:
So was it when my life began,
So is it now I am a man,
So be it when I shall grow old
        Or let me die!
The Child is father of the Man:
And I could wish my days to be
Bound each to each by natural piety.

                            W. WORDSWORTH

CCLXXXVII

ODE ON INTIMATIONS OF IMMORTALITY
FROM RECOLLECTIONS OF EARLY
CHILDHOOD

There was a time when meadow, grove, and stream,
The earth, and every common sight
            To me did seem
        Apparell'd in celestial light,
The glory and the freshness of a dream.
It is not now as it has been of yore;—
        Turn wheresoe'er I may,
            By night or day,
The things which I have seen I now can see no more!

        The rainbow comes and goes,
        And lovely is the rose;
        The moon doth with delight

Look round her when the heavens are bare;
    Waters on a starry night
    Are beautiful and fair;
The sunshine is a glorious birth;
But yet I know, where'er I go,
That there hath pass'd away a glory from the earth.

Now, while the birds thus sing a joyous song,
    And while the young lambs bound
    As to the tabor's sound,
To me alone there came a thought of grief:
A timely utterance gave that thought relief,
    And I again am strong.
The cataracts blow their trumpets from the steep,—
No more shall grief of mine the season wrong:
I hear the echoes through the mountains throng,
The winds come to me from the fields of sleep,
    And all the earth is gay;
    Land and sea
    Give themselves up to jollity,
    And with the heart of May
Doth every beast keep holiday;—
    Thou child of joy
Shout round me, let me hear thy shouts, thou happy
    Shepherd-boy!

Ye blessèd creatures, I have heard the call
    Ye to each other make; I see
The heavens laugh with you in your jubilee;
    My heart is at your festival,
    My head hath its coronal,
The fulness of your bliss, I feel—I feel it all.
    O evil day! if I were sullen
    While Earth herself is adorning
    This sweet May morning;
    And the children are pulling
    On every side

In a thousand valleys far and wide,
    Fresh flowers; while the sun shines warm,
And the babe leaps up on his mother's arm:—
    I hear, I hear, with joy I hear!
    —But there's a tree, of many, one,
A single field which I have look'd upon,
Both of them speak of something that is gone:
    The pansy at my feet
    Doth the same tale repeat:
Whither is fled the visionary gleam?
Where is it now, the glory and the dream?

Our birth is but a sleep and a forgetting;
The Soul that rises with us, our life's Star,
    Hath had elsewhere its setting
    And cometh from afar;
    Not in entire forgetfulness,
    And not in utter nakedness,
But trailing clouds of glory do we come
    From God, who is our home:
Heaven lies about us in our infancy!
Shades of the prison-house begin to close
    Upon the growing boy,
But he beholds the light, and whence it flows,
    He sees it in his joy;
The youth, who daily farther from the east
    Must travel, still is Nature's priest,
    And by the vision splendid
    Is on his way attended;
At length the man perceives it die away,
And fade into the light of common day.

Earth fills her lap with pleasures of her own;
Yearnings she hath in her own natural kind,
And, even with something of a mother's mind
    And no unworthy aim,
    The homely nurse doth all she can

To make her foster-child, her inmate, Man,
>> Forget the glories he hath known
And that imperial palace whence he came.

Behold the Child among his new-born blisses,
A six years' darling of a pigmy size!
See, where 'mid work of his own hand he lies,
Fretted by sallies of his mother's kisses,
With light upon him from his father's eyes!
See, at his feet, some little plan or chart,
Some fragment from his dream of human life,
Shaped by himself with newly-learnéd art;
>> A wedding or a festival,
>> A mourning or a funeral;
>>> And this hath now his heart,
>> And unto this he frames his song:
>>> Then will he fit his tongue
To dialogues of business, love, or strife;
>>> But it will not be long
>>> Ere this be thrown aside,
>>> And with new joy and pride
The little actor cons another part;
Filling from time to time his ' humorous stage
With all the Persons, down to palsied Age,
That life brings with her in her equipage;
>>> As if his whole vocation
>>> Were endless imitation.

Thou, whose exterior semblance doth belie
>>> Thy soul's immensity;
Thou best philosopher, who yet dost keep
Thy heritage, thou eye among the blind,
That, deaf and silent, read'st the eternal deep,
Haunted for ever by the eternal Mind,—
>>> Mighty Prophet!   Seer blest!
>>> On whom those truths do rest
Which we are toiling all our lives to find,
In darkness lost, the darkness of the grave;

Thou, over whom thy immortality
Broods like the day, a master o'er a slave,
A presence which is not to be put by;
Thou little child, yet glorious in the might
Of heaven-born freedom on thy being's height,
Why with such earnest pains dost thou provoke
The years to bring the inevitable yoke,
Thus blindly with thy blessedness at strife?
Full soon thy soul shall have her earthly freight,
And custom lie upon thee with a weight
Heavy as frost, and deep almost as life!

    O joy! that in our embers
    Is something that doth live,
    That Nature yet remembers
    What was so fugitive!
The thought of our past years in me doth breed
Perpetual benediction: not indeed
For that which is most worthy to be blest,
Delight and liberty, the simple creed
Of childhood, whether busy or at rest,
With new-fledged hope still fluttering in his breast:
    —Not for these I raise
    The song of thanks and praise;
    But for those obstinate questionings
    Of sense and outward things,
    Fallings from us, vanishings,
    Blank misgivings of a creature
Moving about in worlds not realized,
High instincts, before which our mortal nature
Did tremble like a guilty thing surprized:
    But for those first affections,
    Those shadowy recollections,
      Which, be they what they may,
Are yet the fountain-light of all our day,
Are yet a master-light of all our seeing;
    Uphold us—cherish—and have power to make

Our noisy years seem moments in the being
Of the eternal silence: truths that wake,
      To perish never;
Which neither listlessness, nor mad endeavour,
      Nor man nor boy,
Nor all that is at enmity with joy,
Can utterly abolish or destroy!
    Hence, in a season of calm weather
      Though inland far we be,
Our souls have sight of that immortal sea
      Which brought us hither;
    Can in a moment travel thither—
And see the children sport upon the shore,
And hear the mighty waters rolling evermore.

Then sing, ye birds, sing, sing a joyous song!
      And let the young lambs bound
      As to the tabor's sound!
We, in thought, will join your throng
      Ye that pipe and ye that play,
      Ye that through your hearts to-day
      Feel the gladness of the May!
What though the radiance which was once so bright
Be now for ever taken from my sight,
    Though nothing can bring back the hour
Of splendour in the grass, of glory in the flower:
      We will grieve not, rather find
      Strength in what remains behind,
      In the primal sympathy
      Which having been must ever be,
      In the soothing thoughts that spring
      Out of human suffering,
      In the faith that looks through death,
In years that bring the philosophic mind.

And O, ye Fountains, Meadows, Hills, and Groves,
Forbode not any severing of our loves!

Yet in my heart of hearts I feel your might;
I only have relinquish'd one delight
To live beneath your more habitual sway;
I love the brooks which down their channels fret
Even more than when I tripp'd lightly as they;
The innocent brightness of a new-born day
        Is lovely yet;
The clouds that gather round the setting sun
Do take a sober colouring from an eye
That hath kept watch o'er man's mortality;
Another race hath been, and other palms are won.
Thanks to the human heart by which we live,
Thanks to its tenderness, its joys and fears,
To me the meanest flower that blows can give
Thoughts that do often lie too deep for tears.

W. Wordsworth

CCLXXXVIII

Music, when soft voices die,
Vibrates in the memory—
Odours, when sweet violets sicken,
Live within the sense they quicken.

Rose leaves, when the rose is dead,
Are heap'd for the beloved's bed;
And so thy thoughts, when Thou art gone,
Love itself shall slumber on.

P. B. Shelley

SUPPLEMENTARY BOOK

CCLXXXIX

I strove with none, for none was worth my strife;
   Nature I loved, and, next to Nature, Art:
I warmed both hands before the fire of life;
   It sinks, and I am ready to depart.

W. S. LANDOR

CCXC
RONDEAU

Jenny kissed me when we met,
   Jumping from the chair she sat in;
Time, you thief, who love to get
   Sweets into your list, put that in!
Say I'm weary, say I'm sad,
   Say that health and wealth have missed me,
Say I'm growing old, but add,
   Jenny kiss'd me.

J. H. LEIGH HUNT

CCXCI
THE WOOD-CUTTER'S NIGHT SONG

Welcome, red and roundy sun,
   Dropping lowly in the west;
Now my hard day's work is done,
   I'm as happy as the best.

Joyful are the thoughts of home,
   Now I'm ready for my chair,
So, till morrow-morning's come,
   Bill and mittens, lie ye there!

Though to leave your pretty song,
  Little birds, it gives me pain,
Yet to-morrow is not long,
  Then I'm with you all again.

If I stop, and stand about,
  Well I know how things will be,
Judy will be looking out
  Every now-and-then for me.

So fare ye well! and hold your tongues,
  Sing no more until I come;
They're not worthy of your songs
  That never care to drop a crumb.

All day long I love the oaks,
  But, at nights, yon little cot,
Where I see the chimney smokes,
  Is by far the prettiest spot.

Wife and children all are there,
  To revive with pleasant looks,
Table ready set, and chair,
  Supper hanging on the hooks.

Soon as ever I get in,
  Where my faggot down I fling,
Little prattlers they begin
  Teasing me to talk and sing.

Welcome, red and roundy sun,
  Dropping lowly in the west;
Now my hard day's work is done,
  I'm as happy as the best.

Joyful are the thoughts of home,
    Now I'm ready for my chair,
So, till morrow-morning's come,
    Bill and mittens, lie ye there!

                                    J. CLARE

CCXCII

WRITTEN IN NORTHAMPTON COUNTY ASYLUM

I am! yet what I am who cares, or knows?
    My friends forsake me like a memory lost.
I am the self-consumer of my woes;
    They rise and vanish, an oblivious host,
Shadows of life, whose very soul is lost,
And yet I am—I live—though I am toss'd

Into the nothingness of scorn and noise,
    Into the living sea of waking dream,
Where there is neither sense of life, nor joys,
    But the huge shipwreck of my own esteem
And all that's dear.   Even those I loved the best
Are strange—nay, they are stranger than the rest.

I long for scenes where man has never trod—
    For scenes where woman never smiled or wept—
There to abide with my Creator, God,
    And sleep as I in childhood sweetly slept,
Full of high thoughts, unborn.   So let me lie.—
The grass below; above, the vaulted sky.

                                    J. CLARE

THE BATTLE OF NASEBY

*By Obadiah Bind-their-king-in-chains-and-their-nobles-
    with-links-of-iron, serjeant in Ireton's regiment*

Oh! wherefore come ye forth, in triumph from the
        North,
  With your hands, and your feet, and your raiment
        all red?
And wherefore doth your rout send forth a joyous
        shout?
  And whence be the grapes of the wine-press which
        ye tread?

Oh, evil was the root, and bitter was the fruit,
  And crimson was the juice of the vintage that we
        trod;
For we trampled on the throng of the haughty and
        the strong,
  Who sate in the high places, and slew the saints of
        God.

It was about the noon of a glorious day of June,
  That we saw their banners dance and their cuirasses
        shine,
And the Man of Blood was there, with his long essenced
        hair,
  And Astley, and Sir Marmaduke, and Rupert of
        the Rhine.

Like a servant of the Lord, with his Bible and his
        sword,
  The General rode along us to form us to the fight,
When a murmuring sound broke out, and swell'd into
        a shout,
  Among the godless horsemen upon the tyrant's
        right.

And hark! like the roar of the billows on the shore,
   The cry of battle rises along their charging line!
For God! for the Cause! for the Church! for the Laws!
   For Charles King of England, and Rupert of the
      Rhine!

The furious German comes, with his clarions and his
      drums,
   His bravoes of Alsatia, and pages of Whitehall;
They are bursting on our flanks. Grasp your pikes,
   close your ranks;
   For Rupert never comes but to conquer or to fall.

They are here! They rush on! We are broken!
   We are gone!
   Our left is borne before them like stubble on the blast.
O Lord, put forth thy might! O Lord, defend the
   right!
   Stand back to back, in God's name, and fight it to
   the last.

Stout Skippon hath a wound; the centre hath given
      ground:
   Hark! hark!—What means the trampling of horse-
   men on our rear?
Whose banner do I see, boys?   'Tis he, thank God!
   'tis he, boys.
   Bear up another minute: brave Oliver is here.

Their heads all stooping low, their points all in a row,
   Like a whirlwind on the trees, like a deluge on the
   dykes,
Our cuirassiers have burst on the ranks of the Accurst,
   And at a shock have scattered the forest of his pikes.

Fast, fast, the gallants ride, in some safe nook to hide
    Their coward heads, predestined to rot on Temple
        Bar:
And he—he turns, he flies:—shame on those cruel eyes
    That bore to look on torture, and dare not look on
        war.

Ho! comrades, scour the plain; and, ere ye strip the
        slain,
    First give another stab to make your search secure,
Then shake from sleeves and pockets their broad-
        pieces and lockets,
    The tokens of the wanton, the plunder of the poor.

Fools! your doublets shone with gold, and your hearts
        were gay and bold,
    When you kissed your lily hands to your lemans
        to-day;
And to-morrow shall the fox, from her chambers in
        the rocks,
    Lead forth her tawny cubs to howl above the prey.

Where be your tongues that late mocked at heaven
        and hell and fate,
    And the fingers that once were so busy with your
        blades,
Your perfum'd satin clothes, your catches and your
        oaths,
    Your stage-plays and your sonnets, your diamonds
        and your spades?

Down, down, for ever down with the mitre and the
        crown,
    With the Belial of the Court, and the Mammon of
        the Pope;
There is woe in Oxford Halls; there is wail in Durham's
        Stalls:
    The Jesuit smites his bosom; the Bishop rends his cope.

And She of the seven hills shall mourn her children's
      ills,
   And tremble when she thinks on the edge of Eng-
      land's sword;
And the Kings of earth in fear shall shudder when
      they hear
   What the hand of God hath wrought for the Houses
      and the Word.

LORD MACAULAY

CCXCIV

LINDEN LEA

'Ithin the woodlands, flow'ry gleäded,
   By the woak tree's mossy moot,
The sheenèn grass bleädes, timber-sheäded,
   Now do quiver under voot;
An' birds do whissle auver head,
An' water's bubblèn in its bed,
An' there vor me the apple tree
Do leän down low in Linden Lea.

When leaves that leätely wer a-springèn
   Now do feäde 'ithin the copse,
An' païnted birds do hush ther zingèn
   Up upon the timber's tops;
An' brown-leav'd fruit's a-turnèn red,
In cloudless zunsheen, auver head,
Wi' fruit vor me the apple tree
Do leän down low in Linden Lea.

Let other vo'k meäke money vaster
   In the aïr o' dark-room'd towns,
I don't dread a peevish meäster;
   Though noo man do heed my frowns,

I be free to goo abrode,
Or teäke ageän my hwomeward road
To where vor me the apple tree
Do leän down low in Linden Lea.

W. BARNES

CCXCV

BRAHMA

If the red slayer think he slays,
  Or if the slain think he is slain,
They know not well the subtle ways
  I keep, and pass, and turn again.

Far or forgot to me is near;
  Shadow and sunlight are the same;
The vanished gods to me appear;
  And one to me are shame and fame.

They reckon ill who leave me out;
  When me they fly, I am the wings;
I am the doubter and the doubt,
  And I the hymn the Brahmin sings.

The strong gods pine for my abode,
  And pine in vain the sacred Seven;
But thou, meek lover of the good!
  Find me, and turn thy back on heaven.

R. W. EMERSON

CCXCVI

TO EVA

O fair and stately maid, whose eyes
Were kindled in the upper skies
 At the same torch that lighted mine;
For so I must interpret still
Thy sweet dominion o'er my will,
 A sympathy divine.

Ah! let me blameless gaze upon
Features that seem at heart my own;
 Nor fear those watchful sentinels,
Who charm the more their glance forbids.
Chaste-glowing, underneath their lids,
 With fire that draws while it repels.

R. W. EMERSON

CCXCVII

AND SHALL TRELAWNY DIE?

A good sword and a trusty hand!
 A merry heart and true!
King James's men shall understand
 What Cornish lads can do.

And have they fixed the where and when?
 And shall Trelawny die?
Here's twenty thousand Cornish men
 Will know the reason why!

Out spake their captain brave and bold,
 A merry wight was he:
'If London Tower were Michael's hold,
 We'll set Trelawny free!

'We'll cross the Tamar, land to land,
    The Severn is no stay,—
With "one and all," and hand in hand,
    And who shall bid us nay?

'And when we come to London Wall,
    A pleasant sight to view,
Come forth! Come forth, ye cowards all,
    Here's men as good as you.

'Trelawny he's in keep and hold
    Trelawny he may die;—
But here's twenty thousand Cornish bold
    Will know the reason why!'

R. S. HAWKER

CCXCVIII

DARK ROSALEEN

O my Dark Rosaleen,
    Do not sigh, do not weep!
The priests are on the ocean green,
    They march along the deep.
There's wine from the royal Pope,
    Upon the ocean green;
And Spanish ale shall give you hope,
    My Dark Rosaleen!
    My own Rosaleen!
Shall glad your heart, shall give you hope,
Shall give you health, and help, and hope,
    My Dark Rosaleen!

Over hills, and thro' dales,
    Have I roam'd for your sake;
All yesterday I sail'd with sails
    On river and on lake.

The Erne, at its highest flood,
  I dash'd across unseen.
For there was lightning in my blood,
  My Dark Rosaleen!
  My own Rosaleen!
O, there was lightning in my blood,
Red lightning lighten'd thro' my blood,
  My Dark Rosaleen!

All day long, in unrest,
  To and fro do I move.
The very soul within my breast
  Is wasted for you, love!
The heart in my bosom faints
  To think of you, my Queen,
My life of life, my saint of saints,
  My Dark Rosaleen!
  My own Rosaleen!
To hear your sweet and sad complaints,
My life, my love, my saint of saints,
  My Dark Rosaleen!

Woe and pain, pain and woe,
  Are my lot, night and noon,
To see your bright face clouded so,
  Like to the mournful moon.
But yet will I rear your throne
  Again in golden sheen;
'Tis you shall reign, shall reign alone,
  My Dark Rosaleen!
  My own Rosaleen!
'Tis you shall have the golden throne,
'Tis you shall reign, and reign alone,
  My Dark Rosaleen!

Over dews, over sands,
  Will I fly, for your weal:

Your holy delicate white hands
 Shall girdle me with steel.
At home, in your emerald bowers,
 From morning's dawn till e'en,
You'll pray for me, my flower of flowers,
 My Dark Rosaleen!
 My fond Rosaleen!
You'll think of me thro' daylight hours,
My virgin flower, my flower of flowers,
 My Dark Rosaleen!

I could scale the blue air,
 I could plough the high hills,
O, I could kneel all night in prayer,
 To heal your many ills!
And one beamy smile from you
 Would float like light between
My toils and me, my own, my true,
 My Dark Rosaleen!
 My fond Rosaleen!
Would give me life and soul anew,
A second life, a soul anew,
 My Dark Rosaleen!

O, the Erne shall run red,
 With redundance of blood,
The earth shall rock beneath our tread,
 And flames wrap hill and wood,
And gun-peal and slogan-cry
 Wake many a glen serene,
Ere you shall fade, ere you shall die,
 My Dark Rosaleen!
 My own Rosaleen!
The Judgment Hour must first be nigh,
Ere you can fade, ere you can die,
 My Dark Rosaleen!

       J. C. MANGAN

THE SHANDON BELLS

With deep affection,
And recollection,
I often think of
    Those Shandon bells,
Whose sounds so wild would,
In the days of childhood,
Fling round my cradle
    Their magic spells.
On this I ponder
Where'er I wander,
And thus grow fonder,
    Sweet Cork, of thee;
With thy bells of Shandon,
That sound so grand on
The pleasant waters
    Of the River Lee.

I've heard bells chiming
Full many a clime in,
Tolling sublime in
    Cathedral shrine,
While at a glibe rate
Brass tongues would vibrate—
But all their music
    Spoke naught like thine;
For memory, dwelling
On each proud swelling
Of thy belfrey knelling
    Its bold notes free,
Made the bells of Shandon
Sound far more grand on
The pleasant waters
    Of the River Lee.

I've heard bells tolling
Old Adrian's Mole in,
Their thunder rolling
 From the Vatican,
And cymbals glorious
Swinging uproarious
In the gorgeous turrets
 Of Notre Dame;
But thy sounds were sweeter
Than the dome of Peter
Flings o'er the Tiber,
 Pealing solemnly;—
O! the bells of Shandon
Sound far more grand on
The pleasant waters
 Of the River Lee.

There's a bell in Moscow,
While on tower and kiosk O
In Saint Sophia
 The Turkman gets;
And loud in air
Calls men to prayer
From the tapering summit
 Of tall minarets.
Such empty phantom
I freely grant them;
But there is an anthem
 More dear to me,—
'Tis the bells of Shandon
That sound so grand on
The pleasant waters
 Of the River Lee.

F. Mahony (Father Prout)

ccc

SONNET FROM THE PORTUGUESE

When our two souls stand up erect and strong,
  Face to face, silent, drawing nigh and nigher,
  Until the lengthening wings break into fire
At either curving point,—what bitter wrong
Can the earth do us, that we should not long
  Be here contented?   Think!   In mounting higher,
  The angels would press on us, and aspire
To drop some golden orb of perfect song
Into our deep, dear silence.   Let us stay
  Rather on earth, Belovèd—where the unfit
Contrarious moods of men recoil away
  And isolate pure spirits, and permit
A place to stand and love in for a day,
  With darkness and the death-hour rounding it.

E. B. BROWNING

ccci

THE WAYS OF LOVE

How do I love thee?   Let me count the ways.
I love thee to the depth and breadth and height
My soul can reach, when feeling out of sight
For the ends of Being and ideal Grace.
I love thee to the level of every day's
Most quiet need, by sun and candlelight.
I love thee freely, as men strive for Right:
I love thee purely, as they turn from Praise.

I love thee with the passion put to use
In my old griefs, and with my childhood's faith.
I love thee with a love I seemed to lose
With my lost saints,—I love thee with the breath,
Smiles, tears, of all my life!—and, if God choose,
I shall but love thee better after death.

E. B. BROWNING

CCCII

THE VILLAGE BLACKSMITH

Under a spreading chestnut tree
  The village smithy stands;
The smith, a mighty man is he,
  With large and sinewy hands;
And the muscles of his brawny arms
  Are strong as iron bands.

His hair is crisp, and black, and long,
  His face is like the tan;
His brow is wet with honest sweat,
  He earns whate'er he can,
And looks the whole world in the face,
  For he owes not any man.

Week in, week out, from morn till night,
  You can hear his bellows blow;
You can hear him swing his heavy sledge,
  With measured beat and slow,
Like a sexton ringing the village bell,
  When the evening sun is low.

And children coming home from school
   Look in at the open door;
They love to see the flaming forge,
   And hear the bellows roar,
And catch the burning sparks that fly
   Like chaff from a threshing floor.

He goes on Sunday to the church,
   And sits among his boys;
He hears the parson pray and preach,
   He hears his daughter's voice,
Singing in the village choir,
   And it makes his heart rejoice.

It sounds to him like her mother's voice,
   Singing in Paradise!
He needs must think of her once more,
   How in the grave she lies;
And with his hard, rough hand he wipes
   A tear out of his eyes.

Toiling,—rejoicing,—sorrowing,
   Onward through life he goes;
Each morning sees some task begin,
   Each evening sees it close;
Something attempted, something done,
   Has earned a night's repose.

Thanks, thanks to thee, my worthy friend,
   For the lesson thou hast taught!
Thus at the flaming forge of life
   Our fortunes must be wrought;
Thus on its sounding anvil shaped
   Each burning deed and thought!

H. W. Longfellow

CCCIII

THE LADDER OF ST. AUGUSTINE

Saint Augustine! well hast thou said,
  That of our vices we can frame
A ladder,[1] if we will but tread
  Beneath our feet each deed of shame!

All common things, each day's events,
  That with the hour begin and end,
Our pleasures and our discontents,
  Are rounds by which we may ascend.

The low desire, the base design,
  That makes another's virtues less;
The revel of the ruddy wine,
  And all occasions of excess;

The longing for ignoble things;
  The strife for triumph more than truth;
The hardening of the heart, that brings
  Irreverence for the dreams of youth;

All thoughts of ill; all evil deeds,
  That have their root in thoughts of ill;
Whatever hinders or impedes
  The action of the nobler will;—

All these must first be trampled down
  Beneath our feet, if we would gain
In the bright fields of fair renown
  The right of eminent domain.

We have not wings, we cannot soar;
  But we have feet to scale and climb
By slow degrees, by more and more,
  The cloudy summits of our time.

[1] The words of St. Augustine are, 'De vitiis nostris scalam nobis facimus, si vitia ipsa calcamus.' Sermon III, *De Ascensione*.

The mighty pyramids of stone
  That wedge-like cleave the desert airs,
When nearer seen, and better known,
  Are but gigantic flights of stairs.

The distant mountains, that uprear
  Their solid bastions to the skies,
Are crossed by pathways, that appear
  As we to higher levels rise.

The heights by great men reached and kept
  Were not attained by sudden flight,
But they, while their companions slept,
  Were toiling upward in the night.

Standing on what too long we bore
  With shoulders bent and downcast eyes,
We may discern—unseen before—
  A path to higher destinies.

Nor deem the irrevocable Past,
  As wholly wasted, wholly vain,
If, rising on its wrecks, at last
  To something nobler we attain.

H. W. Longfellow

CCCIV

OMAR AND DEATH [1]

Ah, with the Grape my fading Life provide,
And wash my Body whence the Life has died,
  And in a Winding-sheet of Vine-leaf wrapt,
So bury me by some sweet Garden-side.

That ev'n my buried Ashes such a Snare
Of Perfume shall fling up into the Air,
  As not a True Believer passing by
But shall be overtaken unaware.

[1] From *The Rubáiyát of Omar Khayyám.*

Indeed the Idols I have loved so long
Have done my Credit in Men's Eye much wrong:
    Have drown'd my Honour in a shallow Cup,
And sold my Reputation for a Song.

Indeed, indeed, Repentance oft before
I swore—but was I sober when I swore?
    And then and then came Spring, and Rose-in-hand
My thread-bare Penitence apieces tore.

And much as Wine has play'd the Infidel,
And Robb'd me of my Robe of Honour—well,
    I often wonder what the Vintners buy
One half so precious as the Goods they sell.

Alas, that Spring should vanish with the Rose!
That Youth's sweet-scented Manuscript should close!
    The Nightingale that in the Branches sang,
Ah, whence, and whither flown again, who knows!

Ah Love! could thou and I with Fate conspire
To grasp this sorry Scheme of Things entire,
    Would not we shatter it to bits—and then
Re-mould it nearer to the Heart's Desire!

Ah, Moon of my Delight, who know'st no wane,
The Moon of Heav'n is rising once again:
    How oft hereafter rising shall she look
Through this same Garden after me—in vain!

And when Thyself with shining Foot shall pass
Among the Guests Star-scatter'd on the Grass,
    And in thy joyous Errand reach the Spot
Where I made one—turn down an empty Glass!

                    TAMÁM SHUD

                                    E. FITZGERALD

THE LADY OF SHALOTT

Part I

On either side the river lie
Long fields of barley and of rye,
That clothe the wold and meet the sky;
And thro' the field the road runs by
        To many-tower'd Camelot;
And up and down the people go,
Gazing where the lilies blow
Round an island there below,
        The island of Shalott.

Willows whiten, aspens quiver,
Little breezes dusk and shiver
Thro' the wave that runs for ever
By the island in the river
        Flowing down to Camelot.
Four gray walls, and four gray towers,
Overlook a space of flowers,
And the silent isle imbowers
        The Lady of Shalott.

By the margin, willow-veil'd,
Slide the heavy barges trail'd
By slow horses; and unhail'd
The shallop flitteth silken-sail'd
        Skimming down to Camelot:
But who hath seen her wave her hand?
Or at the casement seen her stand?
Or is she known in all the land,
        The Lady of Shalott?

Only reapers, reaping early
In among the bearded barley,
Hear a song that echoes cheerly
From the river winding clearly,
   Down to tower'd Camelot:
And by the moon the reaper weary,
Piling sheaves in uplands airy,
Listening, whispers ''Tis the fairy
   Lady of Shalott.'

Part II

There she weaves by night and day
A magic web with colours gay.
She has heard a whisper say,
A curse is on her if she stay
   To look down to Camelot.
She knows not what the curse may be,
And so she weaveth steadily,
And little other care hath she,
   The Lady of Shalott.

And moving thro' a mirror clear
That hangs before her all the year,
Shadows of the world appear.
There she sees the highway near
   Winding down to Camelot:
There the river eddy whirls,
And there the surly village-churls,
And the red cloaks of market girls,
   Pass onward from Shalott.

Sometimes a troop of damsels glad,
An abbot on an ambling pad,
Sometimes a curly shepherd-lad,
Or long-hair'd page in crimson clad,
   Goes by to tower'd Camelot;

And sometimes thro' the mirror blue
The knights come riding two and two:
She hath no loyal knight and true,
    The Lady of Shalott.

But in her web she still delights
To weave the mirror's magic sights,
For often thro' the silent nights
A funeral, with plumes and lights,
        And music, went to Camelot:
Or when the moon was overhead,
Came two young lovers lately wed;
'I am half sick of shadows,' said
    The Lady of Shalott.

PART III

A bow-shot from her bower-eaves,
He rode between the barley-sheaves,
The sun came dazzling thro' the leaves,
And flamed upon the brazen greaves
        Of bold Sir Lancelot.
A red-cross knight for ever kneel'd
To a lady in his shield,
That sparkled on the yellow field,
    Beside remote Shalott.

The gemmy bridle glitter'd free,
Like to some branch of stars we see
Hung in the golden Galaxy.
The bridle bells rang merrily
        As he rode down to Camelot:
And from his blazon'd baldric slung
A mighty silver bugle hung,
And as he rode his armour rung,
    Beside remote Shalott.

All in the blue unclouded weather
Thick-jewell'd shone the saddle-leather,
The helmet and the helmet-feather
Burn'd like one burning flame together,
   As he rode down to Camelot.
As often thro' the purple night,
Below the starry clusters bright,
Some bearded meteor, trailing light,
   Moves over still Shalott.

His broad clear brow in sunlight glow'd;
On burnish'd hooves his war-horse trode;
From underneath his helmet flow'd
His coal-black curls as on he rode,
   As he rode down to Camelot.
From the bank and from the river
He flash'd into the crystal mirror,
'Tirra lirra,' by the river
   Sang Sir Lancelot.

She left the web, she left the loom,
She made three paces thro' the room,
She saw the water-lily bloom,
She saw the helmet and the plume,
   She look'd down to Camelot.
Out flew the web and floated wide;
The mirror crack'd from side to side;
'The curse is come upon me!' cried
   The Lady of Shalott.

Part IV

In the stormy east-wind straining,
The pale yellow woods were waning,
The broad stream in his banks complaining,
Heavily the low sky raining
   Over tower'd Camelot;

Down she came and found a boat
Beneath a willow left afloat,
And round about the prow she wrote
    The Lady of Shalott.

And down the river's dim expanse—
Like some bold seer in a trance,
Seeing all his own mischance—
With a glassy countenance
    Did she look to Camelot.
And at the closing of the day
She loosed the chain, and down she lay;
The broad stream bore her far away,
    The Lady of Shalott.

Lying, robed in snowy white
That loosely flew to left and right—
The leaves upon her falling light—
Thro' the noises of the night
    She floated down to Camelot:
And as the boat-head wound along
The willowy hills and fields among,
They heard her singing her last song,
    The Lady of Shalott.

Heard a carol, mournful, holy,
Chanted loudly, chanted lowly,
Till her blood was frozen slowly,
And her eyes were darken'd wholly,
    Turn'd to tower'd Camelot;
For ere she reach'd upon the tide
The first house by the water-side,
Singing in her song she died,
    The Lady of Shalott.

Under tower and balcony,
By garden-wall and gallery,
A gleaming shape she floated by,
Dead-pale between the houses high,
　　　　Silent into Camelot.
Out upon the wharfs they came,
Knight and burgher, lord and dame,
And round the prow they read her name,
　　　The Lady of Shalott.

Who is this? and what is here?
And in the lighted palace near
Died the sound of royal cheer;
And they cross'd themselves for fear,
　　　　All the knights at Camelot:
But Lancelot mused a little space;
He said, 'She has a lovely face;
God in His mercy lend her grace,
　　　　The Lady of Shalott.'

　　　　　　　　　LORD TENNYSON

CCCVI

BREAK, BREAK, BREAK

Break, break, break,
　On thy cold grey stones, O Sea!
And I would that my tongue could utter
　The thoughts that arise in me.

O well for the fisherman's boy,
　That he shouts with his sister at play!
O well for the sailor lad,
　That he sings in his boat on the bay!

And the stately ships go on
　　To their haven under the hill;
But O for the touch of a vanish'd hand,
　　And the sound of a voice that is still!

Break, break, break,
　　At the foot of thy crags, O Sea!
But the tender grace of a day that is dead
　　Will never come back to me.

　　　　　　　　　　　　LORD TENNYSON

CCCVII

THE BROOK

I come from haunts of coot and hern,
　　I make a sudden sally
And sparkle out among the fern,
　　To bicker down a valley.

By thirty hills I hurry down,
　　Or slip between the ridges,
By twenty thorps, a little town,
　　And half a hundred bridges.

Till last by Philip's farm I flow
　　To join the brimming river,
For men may come and men may go,
　　But I go on for ever.

I chatter over stony ways,
　　In little sharps and trebles,
I bubble into eddying bays,
　　I babble on the pebbles.

With many a curve my banks I fret
  By many a field and fallow,
And many a fairy foreland set
  With willow-weed and mallow.

I chatter, chatter, as I flow
  To join the brimming river,
For men may come and men may go,
  But I go on for ever.

I wind about, and in and out,
  With here a blossom sailing,
And here and there a lusty trout,
  And here and there a grayling,

And here and there a foamy flake
  Upon me, as I travel
With many a silvery waterbreak
  Above the golden gravel,

And draw them all along, and flow
  To join the brimming river,
For men may come and men may go,
  But I go on for ever.

I steal by lawns and grassy plots,
  I slide by hazel covers;
I move the sweet forget-me-nots
  That grow for happy lovers.

I slip, I slide, I gloom, I glance,
  Among my skimming swallows;
I make the netted sunbeam dance
  Against my sandy shallows.

I murmur under moon and stars
  In brambly wildernesses;
I linger by my shingly bars;
  I loiter round my cresses;

And out again I curve and flow
    To join the brimming river,
For men may come and men may go,
    But I go on for ever.

LORD TENNYSON

CCCVIII

Tears, idle tears, I know not what they mean,
Tears from the depth of some divine despair
Rise in the heart, and gather to the eyes,
In looking on the happy Autumn-fields,
And thinking of the days that are no more.

Fresh as the first beam glittering on a sail,
That brings our friends up from the underworld,
Sad as the last which reddens over one
That sinks with all we love below the verge;
So sad, so fresh, the days that are no more.

Ah, sad and strange as in dark summer dawns
The earliest pipe of half-awaken'd birds
To dying ears, when unto dying eyes
The casement slowly grows a glimmering square;
So sad, so strange, the days that are no more.

Dear as remember'd kisses after death,
And sweet as those by hopeless fancy feign'd
On lips that are for others; deep as love,
Deep as first love, and wild with all regret;
O Death in Life, the days that are no more.

LORD TENNYSON

CCCIX

CROSSING THE BAR

Sunset and evening star,
  And one clear call for me!
And may there be no moaning of the bar,
  When I put out to sea,

But such a tide as moving seems asleep,
  Too full for sound and foam,
When that which drew from out the boundless deep
  Turns again home.

Twilight and evening bell,
  And after that the dark!
And may there be no sadness of farewell,
  When I embark;

For tho' from out our bourne of Time and Place
  The flood may bear me far,
I hope to see my Pilot face to face
  When I have crost the bar.

LORD TENNYSON

CCCX

PIPPA'S SONG

The year's at the spring,
And day's at the morn;
Morning's at seven;
The hill-side's dew-pearl'd;
The lark's on the wing;
The snail's on the thorn;
God's in His heaven—
All's right with the world!

R. BROWNING

CCCXI

HOME THOUGHTS, FROM ABROAD

Oh, to be in England,
Now that April's there,
And whoever wakes in England
Sees, some morning, unaware,
That the lowest boughs and the brushwood sheaf
Round the elm-tree bole are in tiny leaf,
While the chaffinch sings on the orchard bough
In England—now!

And after April, when May follows,
And the whitethroat builds, and all the swallows!
Hark, where my blossomed pear-tree in the hedge
Leans to the field and scatters on the clover
Blossoms and dewdrops—at the bent spray's edge—
That's the wise thrush; he sings each song twice over,
Lest you should think he never could recapture
The first fine careless rapture!
And though the fields look rough with hoary dew
All will be gay when noontide wakes anew
The buttercups, the little children's dower—
Far brighter than this gaudy melon-flower.

R. BROWNING

CCCXII

PARTING AT MORNING

Round the cape of a sudden came the sea,
And the sun looked over the mountain's rim:
And straight was a path of gold for him,
And the need of a world of men for me.

R. BROWNING

LOVE AMONG THE RUINS

Where the quiet-coloured end of evening smiles,
    Miles and miles
On the solitary pastures where our sheep
    Half-asleep
Tinkle homeward thro' the twilight, stray or stop
    As they crop—
Was the site once of a city great and gay,
    (So they say)
Of our country's very capital, its prince
    Ages since
Held his court in, gathered councils, wielding far
    Peace or war.

Now—the country does not even boast a tree,
    As you see,
To distinguish slopes of verdure, certain rills
    From the hills
Intersect and give a name to (else they run
    Into one)
Where the domed and daring palace shot its spires
    Up like fires
O'er the hundred-gated circuit of a wall
    Bounding all,
Made of marble, men might march on nor be pressed,
    Twelve abreast.

And such plenty and perfection, see, of grass
    Never was!
Such a carpet as, this summer-time, o'erspreads
    And embeds
Every vestige of the city, guessed alone,
    Stock or stone—

Where a multitude of men breathed joy and woe
      Long ago;
Lust of glory pricked their hearts up, dread of shame
      Struck them tame;
And that glory and that shame alike, the gold
      Bought and sold.

Now,—the single little turret that remains
      On the plains,
By the caper overrooted, by the gourd
      Overscored,
While the patching houseleek's head of blossom winks
      Through the chinks—
Marks the basement whence a tower in ancient time
      Sprang sublime,
And a burning ring, all round, the chariots traced
      As they raced,
And the monarch and his minions and his dames
      Viewed the games.

And I know, while thus the quiet-coloured eve
      Smiles to leave
To their folding, all our many-tinkling fleece
      In such peace,
And the slopes and rills in undistinguished grey
      Melt away—
That a girl with eager eyes and yellow hair
      Waits me there
In the turret whence the charioteers caught soul
      For the goal,
When the king looked, where she looks now, breath-
        less, dumb
      Till I come.

But he looked upon the city, every side,
      Far and wide,

All the mountains topped with temples, all the glades'
      Colonnades,
All the causeys, bridges, aqueducts,—and then,
      All the men!
When I do come, she will speak not, she will stand,
      Either hand
On my shoulder, give her eyes the first embrace
      Of my face,
Ere we rush, ere we extinguish sight and speech
      Each on each.

In one year they sent a million fighters forth
      South and North,
And they built their gods a brazen pillar high
      As the sky,
Yet reserved a thousand chariots in full force—
      Gold, of course.
Oh heart! oh blood that freezes, blood that burns!
      Earth's returns
For whole centuries of folly, noise and sin!
      Shut them in,
With their triumphs and their glories and the rest!
      Love is best.

                R. BROWNING

CCCXIV

PROSPICE

Fear death?—to feel the fog in my throat,
    The mist in my face,
When the snows begin, and the blasts denote
    I am nearing the place,
The power of the night, the press of the storm,
    The post of the foe;
Where he stands, the Arch Fear in a visible form,
    Yet the strong man must go:

For the journey is done and the summit attained
    And the barriers fall,
Though a battle's to fight ere the guerdon be gained,
    The reward of it all.
I was ever a fighter, so—one fight more,
    The best and the last!
I would hate that death bandaged my eyes, and
        forbore,
    And bade me creep past.
No! let me taste the whole of it, fare like my peers,
    The heroes of old,
Bear the brunt, in a minute pay glad life's arrears
    Of pain, darkness, and cold.
For sudden the worst turns the best to the brave,
    The black minute's at end,
And the elements' rage, the fiend voices that rave,
    Shall dwindle, shall blend,
Shall change, shall become first a peace out of pain,
    Then a light, then thy breast,
O thou soul of my soul!   I shall clasp thee again,
    And with God be the rest!

                    R. BROWNING

CCCXV

RABBI BEN EZRA

I

    Grow old along with me!
    The best is yet to be,
The last of life, for which the first was made:
    Our times are in His hand
    Who saith 'A whole I planned,
Youth shows but half; trust God: see all, nor be
        afraid!'

2

Not that, amassing flowers,
Youth sighed 'Which rose make ours,
Which lily leave and then as best recall?'
Not that, admiring stars,
It yearned 'Nor Jove, nor Mars;
Mine be some figured flame which blends, transcends
them all!'

3

Not for such hopes and fears
Annulling youth's brief years,
Do I remonstrate: folly wide the mark!
Rather I prize the doubt
Low kinds exist without,
Finished and finite clods, untroubled by a spark.

4

Poor vaunt of life indeed,
Were man but formed to feed
On joy, to solely seek and find and feast:
Such feasting ended, then
As sure an end to men;
Irks care the crop-full bird? Frets doubt the maw-
crammed beast?

5

Rejoice we are allied
To That which doth provide
And not partake, effect and not receive!
A spark disturbs our clod;
Nearer we hold of God
Who gives, than of His tribes that take, I must believe

6

Then, welcome each rebuff
    That turns earth's smoothness rough,
Each sting that bids nor sit nor stand but go!
    Be our joys three-parts pain!
    Strive, and hold cheap the strain;
Learn, nor account the pang; dare, never grudge the
      throe!

7

For thence,—a paradox
    Which comforts while it mocks,—
Shall life succeed in that it seems to fail:
    What I aspired to be,
    And was not, comforts me:
A brute I might have been, but would not sink i' the
      scale.

8

What is he but a brute
    Whose flesh hath soul to suit,
Whose spirit works lest arms and legs want play?
    To man, propose this test—
    Thy body at its best,
How far can that project thy soul on its lone way?

9

Yet gifts should prove their use:
    I own the Past profuse
Of power each side, perfection every turn:
    Eyes, ears took in their dole,
    Brain treasured up the whole;
Should not the heart beat once 'How good to live and
      learn'?

10

Not once beat 'Praise be Thine!
   I see the whole design,
I, who saw power, see now Love perfect too:
   Perfect I call Thy plan:
   Thanks that I was a man!
Maker, remake, complete,—I trust what Thou shalt
      do!'

11

For pleasant is this flesh;
   Our soul in its rose-mesh
Pulled ever to the earth, still yearns for rest:
   Would we some prize might hold
   To match those manifold
Possessions of the brute,—gain most, as we did best!

12

Let us not always say
   'Spite of this flesh to-day
I strove, made head, gained ground upon the whole!'
   As the bird wings and sings,
   Let us cry 'All good things
Are ours, nor soul helps flesh more, now, than flesh
      helps soul!'

13

Therefore I summon age
   To grant youth's heritage,
Life's struggle having so far reached its term:
   Thence shall I pass, approved
   A man, for ay removed
From the developed brute; a God though in the germ.

14

And I shall thereupon
Take rest, ere I be gone
Once more on my adventure brave and new:
    Fearless and unperplexed,
    When I wage battle next,
What weapons to select, what armour to indue.

15

Youth ended, I shall try
My gain or loss thereby;
Leave the fire ashes, what survives is gold:
    And I shall weigh the same,
    Give life its praise or blame:
Young, all lay in dispute; I shall know, being old.

16

For note, when evening shuts,
A certain moment cuts
The deed off, calls the glory from the grey:
    A whisper from the west
    Shoots—'Add this to the rest,
Take it and try its worth: here dies another day.'

17

So, still within this life,
Though lifted o'er its strife,
Let me discern, compare, pronounce at last,
    'This rage was right i' the main,
    That acquiescence vain:
The Future I may face now I have proved the Past.'

18

For more is not reserved
To man, with soul just nerved
To act to-morrow what he learns to-day:

Here, work enough to watch
The master work, and catch
Hints of the proper craft, tricks of the tool's true play.

19

As it was better, youth
Should strive, through acts uncouth,
Toward making, than repose on aught found made;
So, better, age, exempt
From strife, should know, than tempt
Further. Thou waitedst age; wait death nor be
afraid!

20

Enough now, if the Right
And Good and Infinite
Be named here, as thou callest thy hand thine own,
With knowledge absolute,
Subject to no dispute
From fools that crowded youth, or let thee feel alone.

21

Be there, for once and all,
Severed great minds from small,
Announced to each his station in the Past!
Was I, the world arraigned,
Were they, my soul disdained,
Right? Let age speak the truth and give us peace
at last!

22

Now, who shall arbitrate?
Ten men love what I hate,
Shun what I follow, slight what I receive;
Ten, who in ears and eyes
Match me: we all surmise,
They, this thing, and I, that: whom shall my soul
believe?

23

Not on the vulgar mass
  Called 'work,' must sentence pass,
Things done, that took the eye and had the price;
  O'er which, from level stand,
  The low world laid its hand,
Found straightway to its mind, could value in a trice:

24

But all the world's coarse thumb
  And finger failed to plumb,
So passed in making up the main account;
  All instincts immature,
  All purposes unsure,
That weighed not as his work, yet swelled the man's
      amount:

25

Thoughts hardly to be packed
  Into a narrow act,
Fancies that broke through language and escaped;
  All I could never be,
  All men ignored in me.
This, I was worth to God, whose wheel the pitcher
      shaped.

26

Aye, note that Potter's wheel,
  That metaphor! and feel
Why time spins fast, why passive lies our clay,—
  Thou, to whom fools propound,
  When the wine makes its round,
'Since life fleets, all is change; the Past gone, seize
      to-day!'

27

Fool!   All that is, at all,
    Lasts ever, past recall;
Earth changes, but thy soul and God stand sure:
    What entered into thee,
    That was, is, and shall be:
Time's wheel runs back or stops; Potter and clay
        endure.

28

He fixed thee mid this dance
    Of plastic circumstance,
This Present, thou, forsooth, wouldst fain arrest:
    Machinery just meant
    To give thy soul its bent,
Try thee and turn thee forth, sufficiently impressed.

29

What though the earlier grooves
    Which ran the laughing loves
Around thy base, no longer pause and press?
    What though, about thy rim,
    Skull-things in order grim
Grow out, in graver mood, obey the sterner stress?

30

Look not thou down but up!
    To uses of a cup,
The festal board, lamp's flash and trumpet's peal,
    The new wine's foaming flow,
    The Master's lips aglow!
Thou, heaven's consummate cup, what needst thou
        with earth's wheel?

31

But I need, now as then,
    Thee, God, who mouldest men;
And since, not even while the whirl was worst,
    Did I,—to the wheel of life
    With shapes and colours rife,
Bound dizzily,—mistake my end, to slake Thy thirst:

32

So, take and use Thy work!
    Amend what flaws may lurk,
What strain o' the stuff, what warpings past the aim!
    My times be in Thy hand!
    Perfect the cup as planned!
Let age approve of youth, and' death complete the
        same!

R. BROWNING

CCCXVI

REMEMBRANCE

Cold in the earth—and the deep snow piled above thee,
Far, far, removed, cold in the dreary grave!
Have I forgot, my only Love, to love thee,
Severed at last by Time's all-severing wave?

Now, when alone, do my thoughts no longer hover
Over the mountains, on that northern shore,
Resting their wings where heath and fern-leaves cover
Thy noble heart for ever, ever more?

Cold in the earth—and fifteen wild Decembers,
From those brown hills, have melted into spring:
Faithful, indeed, is the spirit that remembers
After such years of change and suffering!

Sweet Love of youth, forgive, if I forget thee,
While the world's tide is bearing me along;
Other desires and other hopes beset me,
Hopes which obscure, but cannot do thee wrong!

No later light has lightened up my heaven,
No second morn has ever shone for me;
All my life's bliss from thy dear life was given,
All my life's bliss is in the grave with thee.

But, when the days of golden dreams had perished,
And even Despair was powerless to destroy;
Then did I learn how existence could be cherished,
Strengthened and fed without the aid of joy.

Then did I check the tears of useless passion—
Weaned my young soul from yearning after thine;
Sternly denied its burning wish to hasten
Down to that tomb already more than mine.

And, even yet, I dare not let it languish,
Dare not indulge in memory's rapturous pain;
Once drinking deep of that divinest anguish,
How could I seek the empty world again?

E. Brontë

CCCXVII

No coward soul is mine,
No trembler in the world's storm-troubled sphere:
I see Heaven's glories shine,
And faith shines equal, arming me from fear.

O God within my breast,
Almighty, ever-present Deity!
Life—that in me has rest,
As I—undying Life—have power in Thee!

Vain are the thousand creeds
That move men's hearts: unutterably vain;
Worthless as withered weeds,
Or idlest froth amid the boundless main,

To waken doubt in one
Holding so fast by Thine infinity;
So surely anchored on
The steadfast rock of immortality.

With wide-embracing love
Thy Spirit animates eternal years,
Pervades and broods above,
Changes, sustains, dissolves, creates, and rears.

Though earth and man were gone,
And suns and universes ceased to be,
And Thou were left alone,
Every existence would exist in Thee.

There is not room for Death,
Nor atom that his might could render void:
Thou—THOU art Being and Breath,
And what THOU art may never be destroyed.

E. BRONTË

CCCXVIII

THE SANDS OF DEE

'O Mary, go and call the cattle home,
    And call the cattle home,
    And call the cattle home
  Across the sands of Dee';
The western wind was wild and dank with foam
  And all alone went she.

The western tide crept up along the sand,
    And o'er and o'er the sand,
    And round and round the sand,
  As far as eye could see.
The rolling mist came down and hid the land:
  And never home came she.

'Oh! is it weed, or fish, or floating hair—
    A tress of golden hair,
    A drownèd maiden's hair
  Above the nets at sea?
Was never salmon yet that shone so fair
  Among the stakes on Dee.'

They rowed her in across the rolling foam,
    The cruel crawling foam,
    The cruel hungry foam,
  To her grave beside the sea:
But still the boatmen hear her call the cattle home
  Across the sands of Dee.
                                C. KINGSLEY

CCCXIX

O CAPTAIN! MY CAPTAIN!

O Captain! my Captain! our fearful trip is done,
The ship has weather'd every rack, the prize we sought
    is won,
The port is near, the bells I hear, the people all
    exulting,
While follow eyes the steady keel, the vessel grim
    and daring,
        But O heart! heart! heart!
          O the bleeding drops of red!
            Where on the deck my Captain lies,
              Fallen cold and dead.

O Captain! my Captain! rise up and hear the bells;
Rise up—for you the flag is flung—for you the bugle
    trills,
For you bouquets and ribbon'd wreaths—for you the
    shores a-crowding,
For you they call, the swaying mass, their eager faces
    turning;
      Here Captain! dear father!
        This arm beneath your head!
          It is some dream that on the deck
            You 've fallen cold and dead.

My Captain does not answer, his lips are pale and still,
My father does not feel my arm, he has no pulse nor
    will;
The ship is anchor'd safe and sound, its voyage closed
    and done,
From fearful trip the victor ship comes in with object
    won;
      Exult, O shores, and ring, O bells!
        But I, with mournful tread,
          Walk the deck my Captain lies,
           Fallen cold and dead.

                  WALT WHITMAN

CCCXX

Say not the struggle nought availeth,
    The labour and the wounds are vain,
The enemy faints not, nor faileth,
    And as things have been they remain.

If hopes were dupes, fears may be liars;
    It may be, in yon smoke concealed,
Your comrades chase e'en now the fliers,
    And, but for you, possess the field.

For while the tired waves, vainly breaking,
   Seem here no painful inch to gain,
Far back, through creeks and inlets making,
   Comes silent, flooding in, the main.

And not by eastern windows only,
   When daylight comes, comes in the light,
In front, the sun climbs slow, how slowly,
   But westward, look, the land is bright!

A. H. Clough

CCCXXI

THE HIGH TIDE ON THE COAST OF LINCOLNSHIRE (1571)

The old mayor climbed the belfry tower,
   The ringers ran by two, by three;
'Pull, if ye never pulled before;
   Good ringers, pull your best,' quoth he.
'Play uppe, play uppe, O Boston bells!
Ply all your changes, all your swells,
   Play uppe "The Brides of Enderby."'

Men say it was a stolen tyde—
   The Lord that sent it, He knows all;
But in myne ears doth still abide
   The message that the bells let fall:
And there was naught of strange, beside
The flight of mews and peewits pied
   By millions crouched on the old sea wall.

I sat and spun within the doore,
   My thread brake off, I raised myne eyes;
The level sun, like ruddy ore,
   Lay sinking in the barren skies;

And dark against day's golden death
She moved where Lindis wandereth,
My sonne's faire wife, Elizabeth.

'Cusha! Cusha! Cusha!' calling,
Ere the early dews were falling,
Farre away I heard her song,
'Cusha! Cusha!' all along;
Where the reedy Lindis floweth,
    Floweth, floweth,
From the meads where melick groweth
Faintly came her milking song.

'Cusha! Cusha! Cusha!' calling,
'For the dews will soone be falling;
Leave your meadow grasses mellow,
    Mellow, mellow;
Quit your cowslips, cowslips yellow;
Come uppe Whitefoot, come uppe Lightfoot,
Quit the stalks of parsley hollow,
    Hollow, hollow;
Come uppe Jetty, rise and follow,
  From the clovers lift your head;
Come uppe Whitefoot, come uppe Lightfoot,
Come uppe Jetty, rise and follow,
    Jetty, to the milking shed.'

If it be long, aye, long ago,
  When I beginne to think howe long,
Againe I hear the Lindis flow,
  Swift as an arrowe, sharp and strong;
And all the aire, it seemeth mee,
Bin full of floating bells (sayth shee),
That ring the tune of Enderby.

Alle fresh the level pasture lay,
   And not a shadowe mote be seene,
Save where full fyve good miles away
   The steeple towered from out the greene;
And lo! the great bell farre and wide
Was heard in all the country side
That Saturday at eventide.

The swanherds where their sedges are
   Moved on in sunset's golden breath,
The shepherde lads I heard afarre,
   And my sonne's wife, Elizabeth;
Till floating o'er the grassy sea
Came downe that kyndly message free,
The 'Brides of Mavis Enderby.'

Then some looked uppe into the sky,
   And all along where Lindis flows
To where the goodly vessels lie,
   And where the lordly steeple shows.
They sayde, 'And why should this thing be?
What danger lowers by land or sea?
They ring the tune of Enderby!

'For evil news from Mablethorpe,
   Of pyrate galleys warping down;
For shippes ashore beyond the scorpe,
   They have not spared to wake the towne:
But while the west bin red to see,
And storms be none, and pyrates flee,
Why ring "The Brides of Enderby"?'

I looked without, and lo! my sonne
   Came riding downe with might and main:
He raised a shout as he drew on,
   Till all the welkin rang again,

'Elizabeth! Elizabeth!'
(A sweeter woman ne'er drew breath
Than my sonne's wife, Elizabeth.)

'The olde sea wall (he cried) is downe,
   The rising tide comes on apace,
And boats adrift in yonder towne
   Go sailing uppe the market-place.'
He shook as one that looks on death:
'God save you, mother!' straight he saith;
'Where is my wife, Elizabeth?'

'Good sonne, where Lindis winds away,
   With her two bairns I marked her long;
And ere yon bells beganne to play
   Afar I heard her milking song.'
He looked across the grassy lea,
To right, to left, 'Ho Enderby!'
They rang 'The Brides of Enderby!'

With that he cried and beat his breast;
   For, lo! along the river's bed
A mighty eygre reared his crest,
   And uppe the Lindis raging sped.
It swept with thunderous noises loud;
Shaped like a curling snow-white cloud,
Or like a demon in a shroud.

And rearing Lindis backward pressed
   Shook all her trembling bankes amaine;
Then madly at the eygre's breast
   Flung uppe her weltering walls again.
Then bankes came downe with ruin and rout—
Then beaten foam flew round about—
Then all the mighty floods were out.

So farre, so fast the eygre drave,
  The heart had hardly time to beat,
Before a shallow seething wave
  Sobbed in the grasses at oure feet:
The feet had hardly time to flee
Before it brake against the knee,
And all the world was in the sea.

Upon the roofe we sate that night,
  The noise of bells went sweeping by:
I marked the lofty beacon light
  Stream from the church tower, red and high—
A lurid mark and dread to see;
And awesome bells they were to mee,
That in the dark rang 'Enderby.'

They rang the sailor lads to guide
  From roofe to roofe who fearless rowed;
And I—my sonne was at my side,
  And yet the ruddy beacon glowed:
And yet he moaned beneath his breath,
'O come in life, or come in death!
O lost! my love, Elizabeth.'

And didst thou visit him no more?
  Thou didst, thou didst, my daughter deare;
The waters laid thee at his doore,
  Ere yet the early dawn was clear,
Thy pretty bairns in fast embrace,
The lifted sun shone on thy face,
Downe drifted to thy dwelling-place.

That flow strewed wrecks about the grass,
  That ebbe swept out the flocks to sea;
A fatal ebbe and flow, alas!

To manye more than myne and mee:
But each will mourn his own (she saith),
And sweeter woman ne'er drew breath
Than my sonne's wife, Elizabeth.

I shall never hear her more
By the reedy Lindis shore,
'Cusha! Cusha! Cusha!' calling,
Ere the early dews be falling;
I shall never hear her song,
'Cusha! Cusha' all along
Where the sunny Lindis floweth,
    Goeth, floweth;
From the meads where melick groweth,
When the water winding down,
Onward floweth to the town.

I shall never see her more
Where the reeds and rushes quiver,
    Shiver, quiver;
Stand beside the sobbing river,
Sobbing, throbbing, in its falling
To the sandy lonesome shore;

I shall never hear her calling,
'Leave your meadow grasses mellow,
    Mellow, mellow;
Quit your cowslips, cowslips yellow;
Come uppe Whitefoot, come uppe Lightfoot,
Quit your pipes of parsley hollow,
    Hollow, hollow;
Come uppe Lightfoot, rise and follow;
    Lightfoot, Whitefoot,
  From your clovers lift the head;
Come uppe Jetty, follow, follow,
  Jetty, to the milking shed.'

JEAN INGELOW

CCCXXII

DOVER BEACH

The sea is calm to-night.
The tide is full, the moon lies fair
Upon the straits;—on the French coast the light
Gleams and is gone; the cliffs of England stand,
Glimmering and vast, out in the tranquil bay.
Come to the window, sweet is the night air!
Only, from the long line of spray
Where the sea meets the moon-blanch'd land,
Listen! you hear the grating roar
Of pebbles which the waves draw back, and fling,
At their return, up the high strand,
Begin, and cease, and then again begin,
With tremulous cadence slow, and bring
The eternal note of sadness in.

Sophocles long ago
Heard it on the Aegean, and it brought
Into his mind the turbid ebb and flow
Of human misery; we
Find also in the sound a thought,
Hearing it by this distant northern sea.

The sea of faith
Was once, too, at the full, and round earth's shore
Lay like the folds of a bright girdle furl'd.
But now I only hear
Its melancholy, long, withdrawing roar,
Retreating, to the breath
Of the night wind, down the vast edges drear
And naked shingles of the world.

Ah, love, let us be true
To one another! for the world, which seems
To lie before us like a land of dreams,
So various, so beautiful, so new,
Hath really neither joy, nor love, nor light,
Nor certitude, nor peace, nor help for pain;
And we are here as on a darkling plain
Swept with confused alarms of struggle and flight
Where ignorant armies clash by night.

M. Arnold

CCCXXIII

THE FORSAKEN MERMAN

Come, dear children, let us away:
   Down and away below!
Now my brothers call from the bay;
   Now the great winds shoreward blow;
   Now the salt tides seaward flow;
Now the wild white horses play,
Champ and chafe and toss in the spray.
Children dear, let us away!
   This way, this way!

Call her once before you go.
   Call once yet.
In a voice that she will know:
   'Margaret! Margaret!'
Children's voices should be dear
(Call once more) to a mother's ear:
Children's voices, wild with pain—
Surely she will come again.
Call her once and come away;
   This way, this way!
'Mother dear, we cannot stay.'
The wild white horses foam and fret.
   Margeret! Margaret!

Come, dear children, come away down!
    Call no more!
One last look at the white-walled town,
And the little grey church on the windy shore.
    Then come down.
She will not come though you call all day.
    Come away, come away!

Children dear, was it yesterday
We heard the sweet bells over the bay?
In the caverns where we lay,
Through the surf and through the swell,
The far-off sound of a silver bell?
Sand-strewn caverns, cool and deep,
Where the winds are all asleep;
Where the spent lights quiver and gleam;
Where the salt weed sways in the stream;
Where the sea-beasts ranged all round
Feed in the ooze of their pasture-ground;
Where the sea-snakes coil and twine,
Dry their mail and bask in the brine;
Where great whales come sailing by,
Sail and sail, with unshut eye,
Round the world for ever and ay?
When did music come this way?
Children dear, was it yesterday?

Children dear, was it yesterday
(Call yet once) that she went away?
Once she sate with you and me,
On a red gold throne in the heart of the sea,
And the youngest sate on her knee.
She comb'd its bright hair, and she tended it well,
When down swung the sound of the far-off bell.
She sigh'd, she look'd up through the clear green sea;
She said: 'I must go, for my kinsfolk pray
In the little grey church on the shore to-day.

'Twill be Easter-time in the world—ah me!
And I lose my poor soul, Merman, here with thee.'
I said: 'Go up, dear heart, through the waves!
Say thy prayer, and come back to the kind sea-caves!'
She smiled, she went up through the surf in the bay.
Children dear, was it yesterday?

Children dear, were we long alone?
'The sea grows stormy, the little ones moan.
Long prayers,' I said, 'in the world they say.
Come!' I said, and we rose through the surf in the bay.
We went up the beach, by the sandy down
Where the sea-stocks bloom, to the white-walled town.
Through the narrow paved streets, where all was still,
To the little grey church on the windy hill.
From the church came a murmur of folk at their
        prayers,
But we stood without in the cold blowing airs.
We climbed on the graves, on the stones, worn with
        rains,
And we gazed up the aisle through the small-leaded
        panes.
She sate by the pillar; we saw her clear:
'Margaret, hist! come quick, we are here.
Dear heart,' I said, 'we are long alone.
The sea grows stormy, the little ones moan.'
But, ah, she gave me never a look,
For her eyes were sealed to the holy book!
Loud prays the priest; shut stands the door.
Come away, children, call no more!
Come away, come down, call no more!

Down, down, down!
  Down to the depths of the sea!
She sits at her wheel in the humming town,
  Singing most joyfully.

Hark, what she sings: 'O joy, O joy,
For the humming street, and the child with its toy!
For the priest, and the bell, and the holy well—
　　For the wheel where I spun,
　　And the blessed light of the sun!'
　　And so she sings her fill,
　　Singing most joyfully,
Till the shuttle falls from her hand,
　　And the whizzing wheel stands still.
She steals to the window, and looks at the sand,
　　And over the sand at the sea;
And her eyes are set in a stare;
　　And anon there breaks a sigh,
And anon there drops a tear,
　　From a sorrow-clouded eye,
And a heart sorrow-laden,
　　A long, long sigh;
For the cold strange eyes of a little Mermaiden,
　　And the gleam of her golden hair.

Come away, away children!
　　Come children, come down!
The hoarse wind blows colder;
　　Lights shine in the town.
She will start from her slumber
　　When gusts shake the door;
She will hear the winds howling,
　　Will hear the waves roar.
We shall see, while above us
　　The waves roar and whirl,
A ceiling of amber,
　　A pavement of pearl.
Singing: 'Here came a mortal,
　　But faithless was she!
And alone dwell for ever
　　The kings of the sea.'

But, children, at midnight,
  When soft the winds blow,
When clear falls the moonlight,
  When spring-tides are low;
When sweet airs come seaward
  From heaths starred with broom,
And high rocks throw mildly
  On the blanched sands a gloom;
Up the still, glistening beaches,
  Up the creeks we will hie,
Over banks of bright seaweed
  The ebb-tide leaves dry.
We will gaze, from the sand-hills,
At the white, sleeping town;
At the church on the hill-side—
  And then come back down.
Singing: 'There dwells a loved one,
  But cruel is she!
She left lonely for ever
  The kings of the sea.'

M. Arnold

CCCXXIV

RUGBY CHAPEL
November 1857

Coldly, sadly descends
The autumn evening!   The field
Strewn with its dank yellow drifts
Of withered leaves, and the elms,
Fade into dimness apace,
Silent;—hardly a shout
From a few boys late at their play!
The lights come out in the street,
In the school-room windows; but cold,

Solemn, unlighted, austere,
Through the gathering darkness, arise
The chapel-walls, in whose bound
Thou, my father! art laid.

There thou dost lie, in the gloom
Of the autumn evening.   But ah!
That word, *gloom*, to my mind
Brings thee back in the light
Of thy radiant vigour again!
In the gloom of November we pass'd
Days not of gloom at thy side;
Seasons impair'd not the ray
Of thine even cheerfulness clear.
Such thou wast! and I stand
In the autumn evening, and think
Of bygone autumns with thee.

Fifteen years have gone round
Since thou arosest to tread,
In the summer morning, the road
Of death, at a call unforeseen,
Sudden!   For fifteen years,
We who till then in thy shade
Rested as under the boughs
Of a mighty oak, have endured
Sunshine and rain as we might,
Bare, unshaded, alone,
Lacking the shelter of thee!

O strong soul, by what shore
Tarriest thou now?   For that force,
Surely, has not been left vain!
Somewhere, surely, afar,
In the sounding labour-house vast
Of being, is practised that strength,
Zealous, beneficent, firm!

Yes, in some far-shining sphere,
Conscious or not of the past,
Still thou performest the word
Of the Spirit in whom thou dost live—
Prompt, unwearied, as here!
Still thou upraisest with zeal
The humble good from the ground,
Sternly repressest the bad!
Still, like a trumpet, dost rouse
Those who with half-open eyes
Tread the border-land dim
'Twixt vice and virtue; reviv'st,
Succourest!—this was thy work,
This was thy life upon earth.

What is the course of the life
Of mortal men on the earth?—
Most men eddy about
Here and there—eat and drink,
Chatter and love and hate,
Gather and squander, are raised
Aloft, are hurl'd in the dust,
Striving blindly, achieving
Nothing; and then they die—
Perish! and no one asks
Who or what they have been,
More than he asks what waves,
In the moonlit solitudes mild
Of the midmost Ocean, have swell'd,
Foam'd for a moment and gone.

And there are some, whom a thirst
Ardent, unquenchable, fires,
Not with the crowd to be spent—
Not without aim to go round
In an eddy of purposeless dust,
Effort unmeaning and vain.
Ah yes, some of us strive

Not without action to die
Fruitless, but something to snatch
From dull oblivion, nor all
Glut the devouring grave!
We, we have chosen our path—
Path to a clear-purposed goal,
Path of advance!—but it leads
A long, steep journey, through sunk
Gorges, o'er mountains in snow!
Cheerful, with friends, we set forth—
Then, on the height, comes the storm!
Thunder crashes from rock
To rock, the cataracts reply;
Lightnings dazzle our eyes;
Roaring torrents have breach'd
The track—the stream-bed descends
In the place where the wayfarer once
Planted his footstep—the spray
Boils o'er its borders! aloft,
The unseen snow-beds dislodge
Their hanging ruin;—alas,
Havoc is made in our train!
Friends who set forth at our side
Falter, are lost in the storm!
We, we only, are left!
With frowning foreheads, with lips
Sternly compress'd, we strain on,
On—and at nightfall, at last,
Come to the end of our way,
To the lonely inn 'mid the rocks;
Where the gaunt and taciturn host
Stands on the threshold, the wind
Shaking his thin white hairs—
Holds his lantern to scan
Our storm-beat figures, and asks:
Whom in our party we bring?
Whom we have left in the snow?

Sadly we answer: We bring
Only ourselves! we lost
Sight of the rest in the storm!
Hardly ourselves we fought through,
Stripp'd, without friends, as we are!
Friends, companions, and train
The avalanche swept from our side.

But thou would'st not *alone*
Be saved, my father! *alone*
Conquer and come to thy goal,
Leaving the rest in the wild.
We were weary, and we
Fearful, and we, in our march,
Fain to drop down and to die.
Still thou turnedst, and still
Beckonedst the trembler, and still
Gavest the weary thy hand!
If, in the paths of the world,
Stones might have wounded thy feet,
Toil or dejection have tried
Thy spirit, of that we saw
Nothing! to us thou wert still
Cheerful, and helpful, and firm.
Therefore to thee it was given
Many to save with thyself;
And, at the end of thy day,
O faithful shepherd! to come,
Bringing thy sheep in thy hand.

And through thee I believe
In the noble and great who are gone;
Pure souls honour'd and blest
By former ages, who else—
Such, so soulless, so poor,
Is the race of men whom I see—
Seem'd but a dream of the heart,
Seem'd but a cry of desire.

Yes! I believe that there lived
Others like thee in the past,
Not like the men of the crowd
Who all round me to-day
Bluster or cringe, and make life
Hideous, and arid, and vile;
But souls temper'd with fire,
Fervent, heroic, and good,
Helpers and friends of mankind.

Servants of God!—or sons
Shall I not call you? because
Not as servants ye knew
Your Father's innermost mind,
His, who unwillingly sees
One of his little ones lost—
Yours is the praise, if mankind
Hath not as yet in its march
Fainted, and fallen, and died!

See! in the rocks of the world
Marches the host of mankind,
A feeble, wavering line!
Where are they tending?—A God
Marshall'd them, gave them their goal.—
Ah, but the way is so long!
Years they have been in the wild!
Sore thirst plagues them; the rocks,
Rising all round, overawe.
Factions divide them—their host
Threatens to break, to dissolve.—
Ah, keep, keep them combined!
Else, of the myriads who fill
That army, not one shall arrive!
Sole they shall stray; in the rocks
Labour for ever in vain,
Die one by one in the waste.

Then, in such hour of need
Of your fainting, dispirited race,
Ye, like angels, appear,
Radiant with ardour divine.
Beacons of hope, ye appear!
Languor is not in your heart,
Weakness is not in your word,
Weariness not on your brow.
Ye alight in our van! at your voice,
Panic, despair, flee away.
Ye move through the ranks, recall
The stragglers, refresh the outworn,
Praise, re-inspire the brave!
Order, courage, return.
Eyes rekindling, and prayers,
Follow your steps as ye go.
Ye fill up the gaps in our files,
Strengthen the wavering line,
Stablish, continue our march,
Oh, to the bound of the waste,
On, to the City of God!

M. ARNOLD

CCCXXV

ST. VALENTINE'S DAY

Well dost thou, Love, thy solemn Feast to hold
In vestal February;
Not rather choosing out some rosy day
From the rich coronet of the coming May,
When all things meet to marry!
  O quick, praevernal Power
That signall'st punctual through the sleepy mould
The Snowdrop's time to flower,
Fair as the rash oath of virginity

Which is first-love's first cry;
O, Baby spring,
That flutter'st sudden 'neath the breast of Earth
A month before the birth;
Whence is the peaceful poignancy,
The joy contrite,
Sadder than sorrow, sweeter than delight,
That burthens now the breath of everything,
Though each one sighs as if to each alone
The cherish'd pang were known?
At dusk of dawn, on his dark spray apart,
With it the Blackbird breaks the young Day's heart;
In evening's hush
About it talks the heavenly-minded Thrush;
The hill with like remorse
Smiles to the Sun's smile in his westering course;
The fisher's drooping skiff
In yonder sheltering bay;
The choughs that call about the shining cliff;
The children, noisy in the setting ray;
Own the sweet season, each thing as it may;
Thoughts of strange kindness and forgotten peace
In me increase;
And tears arise
Within my happy, happy Mistress' eyes,
And, lo, her lips, averted from my kiss,
Ask from Love's bounty, ah, much more than bliss!
  Is't the sequester'd and exceeding sweet
Of dear Desire electing his defeat?
Is't the waked Earth now to yon purpling cope
Uttering first-love's first cry,
Vainly renouncing, with a seraph's sigh,
Love's natural hope?
Fair-meaning Earth, foredoom'd to perjury!
Behold, all amorous May,
With roses heap'd upon her laughing brows,
Avoids thee of thy vows!

Were it for thee, with her warm bosom near,
To abide the sharpness of the Seraph's sphere?
Forget thy foolish words,
Go to her summons gay,
Thy heart with dead, wing'd Innocencies fill'd,
Ev'n as a nest with birds
After the old ones by the hawk are kill'd.
    Well dost thou, Love, to celebrate
The noon of thy soft ecstasy,
Or e'er it be too late,
Or e'er the Snowdrop die!

C. PATMORE

CCCXXVI

THE TOYS

My little son, who look'd from thoughtful eyes
And moved and spoke in quiet grown-up wise,
Having my law the seventh time disobey'd,
I struck him, and dismiss'd
With hard words and unkiss'd,
His Mother, who was patient, being dead.
Then, fearing lest his grief should hinder sleep,
I visited his bed,
But found him slumbering deep,
With darken'd eyelids, and their lashes yet
From his late sobbing wet.
And I, with moan,
Kissing away his tears, left others of my own;
For, on a table drawn beside his head,
He had put, within his reach,
A box of counters and a red-vein'd stone,
A piece of glass abraded by the beach
And six or seven shells,
A bottle with bluebells,

And two French copper coins, ranged there with
    careful art,
To comfort his sad heart.
So when that night I pray'd
To God, I wept, and said:
Ah, when at last we lie with trancèd breath,
    Not vexing Thee in death,
And thou rememberest of what toys
    We made our joys,
How weakly understood,
Thy great commanded good,
Then, fatherly not less
Than I whom thou hast moulded from the clay,
Thou'lt leave Thy wrath, and say,
'I will be sorry for their childishness.'

C. PATMORE

CCCXXVII

THE BLESSED DAMOZEL

The blessed damozel leaned out
    From the gold bar of Heaven;
Her eyes were deeper than the depth
    Of waters stilled at even;
She had three lilies in her hand,
    And the stars in her hair were seven.

Her robe, ungirt from clasp to hem,
    No wrought flowers did adorn,
But a white rose of Mary's gift,
    For service meetly worn;
Her hair that lay along her back
    Was yellow like ripe corn.

Herseemed she scarce had been a day
    One of God's choristers;
The wonder was not yet quite gone
    From that still look of hers;

Albeit, to them she left, her day
   Had counted as ten years.

(To one, it is ten years of years.
   . . . Yet now, and in this place,
Surely she leaned o'er me—her hair
   Fell all about my face. . . .
Nothing: the autumn-fall of leaves.
   The whole year sets apace.)

It was the rampart of God's house
   That she was standing on;
By God built over the sheer depth
   The which is Space begun;
So high, that looking downward thence
   She scarce could see the sun.

It lies in Heaven, across the flood
   Of ether, as a bridge.
Beneath, the tides of day and night
   With flame and darkness ridge
The void, as low as where this earth
   Spins like a fretful midge.

Around her, lovers, newly met
   'Mid deathless love's acclaims,
Spoke evermore among themselves
   Their heart-remembered names;
And the souls mounting up to God
   Went by her like thin flames.

And still she bowed herself and stooped
   Out of the circling charm;
Until her bosom must have made
   The bar she leaned on warm,
And the lilies lay as if asleep
   Along her bended arm.

From the fixed place of Heaven she saw
    Time like a pulse shake fierce
Through all the worlds.   Her gaze still strove
    Within the gulf to pierce
Its path; and now she spoke as when
    The stars sang in their spheres.

The sun was gone now; the curled moon
    Was like a little feather
Fluttering far down the gulf; and now
    She spoke through the still weather.
Her voice was like the voice the stars
    Had when they sang together.

(Ah sweet! Even now, in that bird's song
    Strove not her accents there,
Fain to be hearkened? When those bells
    Possessed the midday air,
Strove not her steps to reach my side
    Down all the echoing stair?)

'I wish that he were come to me,
    For he will come,' she said.
'Have I not prayed in Heaven?—on earth,
    Lord, Lord, has he not pray'd?
Are not two prayers a perfect strength?
    And shall I feel afraid?

'When round his head the aureole clings,
    And he is clothed in white,
I'll take his hand and go with him
    To the deep wells of light;
As unto a stream we will step down,
    And bathe there in God's sight.

'We two will stand beside that shrine,
    Occult, withheld, untrod,
Whose lamps are stirred continually
    With prayer sent up to God;

And see our old prayers, granted, melt
    Each like a little cloud.

'We two will lie i' the shadow of
    That living mystic tree
Within whose secret growth the Dove
    Is sometimes felt to be,
While every leaf that His plumes touch
    Saith his Name audibly.

'And I myself will teach to him,
    I myself, lying so,
The songs I sing here; which his voice
    Shall pause in, hushed and slow,
And find some knowledge at each pause,
    Or some new thing to know.'

(Alas! we two, we two, thou say'st!
    Yea, one wast thou with me,
That once of old.   But shall God lift
    To endless unity
The soul whose likeness with thy soul
    Was but its love for thee?)

'We two,' she said, 'will seek the groves
    Where the lady Mary is,
With her five handmaidens, whose names
    Are five sweet symphonies,
Cecily, Gertrude, Magdalen.
    Margaret and Rosalys.

'Circlewise sit they, with bound locks
    And foreheads garlanded;
Into the fine cloth white like flame
    Weaving the golden thread,
To fashion the birth-robes for them
    Who are just born, being dead.

'He shall fear, haply, and be dumb
  Then will I lay my cheek
To his, and tell about our love,
  Not once abashed or weak;
And the dear Mother will approve
  My pride, and let me speak.

'Herself shall bring us, hand in hand,
  To Him round whom all souls
Kneel, the clear-ranged unnumbered heads
  Bowed with their aureoles:
And angels meeting us shall sing
  To their citherns and citoles.

'There will I ask of Christ the Lord
  Thus much for him and me:—
Only to live as once on earth
  With Love,—only to be,
As then awhile, for ever now
  Together, I and he.'

She gazed and listened and then said,
  Less sad of speech than mild,—
'All this is when he comes.' She ceased.
  The light thrilled towards her, fill'd
With angels in strong level flight.
  Her eyes prayed, and she smil'd.

(I saw her smile.) But soon their path
  Was vague in distant spheres:
And then she cast her arms along
  The golden barriers,
And laid her face between her hands,
  And wept. (I heard her tears.)

D. G. ROSSETTI

CCCXXVIII

SILENT NOON

Your hands lie open in the long fresh grass,—
　The finger-points look through like rosy blooms:
　Your eyes smile peace.　The pasture gleams and
　　　glooms
'Neath billowing skies that scatter and amass.
All round our nest, far as the eye can pass,
　Are golden kingcup-fields with silver edge
　Where the cow-parsley skirts the hawthorn-hedge.
'Tis visible silence, still as the hour-glass.

Deep in the sun-searched growths the dragon-fly
Hangs like a blue thread loosened from the sky:—
　So this wing'd hour is dropt to us from above.
Oh! clasp we to our hearts, for deathless dower,
This close-companioned inarticulate hour
　When twofold silence was the song of love.

D. G. Rossetti

CCCXXIX

UP-HILL

Does the road wind up-hill all the way?
　　Yes, to the very end.
Will the day's journey take the whole long day?
　　From morn to night, my friend.

But is there for the night a resting-place?
　　A roof for when the slow dark hours begin.
May not the darkness hide it from my face?
　　You cannot miss that inn.

Shall I meet other wayfarers at night?
    Those who have gone before.
Then must I knock, or call when just in sight?
    They will not keep you standing at that door.

Shall I find comfort, travel-sore and weak?
    Of labour you shall find the sum.
Will there be beds for me and all who seek?
    Yea, beds for all who come.

C. G. ROSSETTI

CCCXXX

A BIRTHDAY

My heart is like a singing bird
    Whose nest is in a watered shoot;
My heart is like an apple-tree
    Whose boughs are bent with thickset fruit;
My heart is like a rainbow shell
    That paddles in a halcyon sea;
My heart is gladder than all these
    Because my love is come to me.

Raise me a dais of silk and down;
    Hang it with vair and purple dyes;
Carve it in doves, and pomegranates,
    And peacocks with a hundred eyes;
Work it in gold and silver grapes,
    In leaves, and silver fleurs-de-lys;
Because the birthday of my life
    Is come, my love is come to me.

C. G. ROSSETTI

CCCXXXI

I know a little garden close
Set thick with lily and red rose,
Where I would wander if I might
From dewy dawn to dewy night,
And have one with me wandering.

And though within it no birds sing,
And though no pillared house is there,
And though the apple boughs are bare
Of fruit and blossom, would to God,
Her feet upon the green grass trod,
And I beheld them as before.

There comes a murmur from the shore,
And in the place two fair streams are,
Drawn from the purple hills afar,
Drawn down unto the restless sea;
The hills whose flowers ne'er fed the bee,
The shore no ship has ever seen,
Still beaten by the billows green,
Whose murmur comes unceasingly
Unto the place for which I cry.

For which I cry both day and night,
For which I let slip all delight,
That maketh me both deaf and blind,
Careless to win, unskilled to find,
And quick to lose what all men seek.

Yet tottering as I am, and weak,
Still have I left a little breath
To seek within the jaws of death
An entrance to that happy place,
To seek the unforgotten face
Once seen, once kissed. once reft from me
Anigh the murmuring of the sea.

W. MORRIS

ITYLUS

Swallow, my sister, O sister swallow,
　　How can thine heart be full of the spring?
　　　A thousand summers are over and dead.
What hast thou found in the spring to follow?
　　What hast thou found in thine heart to sing?
　　　What wilt thou do when the summer is shed?

O swallow, sister, O fair swift swallow,
　　Why wilt thou fly after spring to the south,
　　　The soft south whither thine heart is set?
Shall not the grief of the old time follow?
　　Shall not the song thereof cleave to thy mouth?
　　　Hast thou forgotten ere I forget?

Sister, my sister, O fleet sweet swallow,
　　Thy way is long to the sun and the south;
　　　But I, fulfilled of my heart's desire,
Shedding my song upon height, upon hollow,
　　From tawny body and sweet small mouth
　　　Feed the heart of the night with fire.

I the nightingale all spring through,
　　O swallow, sister, O changing swallow,
　　　All spring through till the spring be done,
Clothed with the light of the night on the dew,
　　Sing, while the hours and the wild birds follow,
　　　Take flight and follow and find the sun.

Sister, my sister, O soft light swallow,
　　Though all things feast in the spring's guest-chamber,
　　　How hast thou heart to be glad thereof yet?
For where thou fliest I shall not follow,
　　Till life forget and death remember,
　　　Till thou remember and I forget.

Swallow, my sister, O singing swallow,
   I know not how thou hast heart to sing.
      Hast thou the heart? is it all past over?
Thy lord the summer is good to follow,
   And fair the feet of thy lover the spring:
      But what wilt thou say to the spring thy lover?

O swallow, sister, O fleeting swallow,
   My heart in me is a molten ember
      And over my head the waves have met.
But thou wouldst tarry or I would follow,
   Could I forget or thou remember,
      Couldst thou remember and I forget.

O sweet stray sister, O shifting swallow,
   The heart's division divideth us.
      Thy heart is light as a leaf of a tree;
But mine goes forth among sea-gulfs hollow
   To the place of the slaying of Itylus,
      The feast of Daulis, the Thracian sea.

O swallow, sister, O rapid swallow,
   I pray thee sing not a little space.
      Are not the roofs and the lintels wet?
The woven web that was plain to follow,
   The small slain body, the flowerlike face,
      Can I remember if thou forget?

O sister, sister, thy first-begotten!
   The hands that cling and the feet that follow,
      The voice of the child's blood crying yet,
Who hath remembered me? who hath forgotten?
   Thou hast forgotten, O summer swallow,
      But the world shall end when I forget.

A. C. SWINBURNE

CCCXXXIII

THE GARDEN OF PROSERPINE

Here, where the world is quiet;
  Here, where all trouble seems
Dead winds' and spent waves' riot
  In doubtful dreams of dreams;
I watch the green field growing
For reaping folk and sowing,
For harvest-time and mowing,
  A sleepy world of streams.

I am tired of tears and laughter,
  And men that laugh and weep;
Of what may come hereafter
  For men that sow to reap:
I am weary of days and hours
Brown buds of barren flowers,
Desires and dreams and powers
  And everything but sleep.

Here life has death for neighbour,
  And far from eye or ear
Wan waves and wet winds labour,
  Weak ships and spirits steer;
They drive adrift, and whither
They wot not who make thither;
But no such winds blow hither,
  And no such things grow here.

No growth of moor or coppice,
  No heather-flower or vine,
But bloomless buds of poppies,
  Green grapes of Proserpine,
Pale beds of blowing rushes,
Where no leaf blooms or blushes
Save this whereout she crushes
  For dead men deadly wine.

Pale, without name or number,
   In fruitless fields of corn,
They bow themselves and slumber
   All night till light is born;
And like a soul belated,
In hell and heaven unmated,
By cloud and mist abated
   Comes out of darkness morn.

Though one were strong as seven,
   He too with death shall dwell,
Nor wake with wings in heaven,
   Nor weep for pains in hell;
Though one were fair as roses,
His beauty clouds and closes;
And well though love reposes,
   In the end it is not well.

Pale, beyond porch and portal,
   Crowned with calm leaves, she stands
Who gathers all things mortal
   With cold immortal hands;
Her languid lips are sweeter
Than love's who fears to greet her
To men that mix and meet her
   From many times and lands.

She waits for each and other,
   She waits for all men born;
Forgets the earth her mother,
   The life of fruits and corn;
And spring and seed and swallow
Take wing for her and follow
Where summer song rings hollow
   And flowers are put to scorn.

There go the loves that wither,
    The old loves with wearier wings;
And all dead years draw thither,
    And all disastrous things;
Dead dreams of days forsaken,
Blind buds that snows have shaken,
Wild leaves that winds have taken,
    Red strays of ruined springs.

We are not sure of sorrow,
    And joy was never sure;
To-day will die to-morrow;
    Time stoops to no man's lure;
And love, grown faint and fretful,
With lips but half regretful
Sighs, and with eyes forgetful
    Weeps that no loves endure.

From too much love of living,
    From hope and fear set free,
We thank with brief thanksgiving
    Whatever gods may be
That no life lives for ever;
That dead men rise up never;
That even the weariest river
    Winds somewhere safe to sea.

Then star nor sun shall waken,
    Nor any change of light:
Nor sound of waters shaken,
    Nor any sound or sight:
Nor wintry leaves nor vernal,
Nor days nor things diurnal;
Only the sleep eternal
    In an eternal night.

                              A. C. SWINBURNE

THE HOUNDS OF SPRING

When the hounds of spring are on winter's traces,
　The mother of months in meadow or plain
Fills the shadows and windy places
　With lisp of leaves and ripple of rain;
And the brown bright nightingale amorous
Is half assuaged for Itylus,
For the Thracian ships and the foreign faces,
　　The tongueless vigil, and all the pain.

Come with bows bent and with emptying of quivers,
　Maiden most perfect, lady of light,
With a noise of winds and many rivers,
　With a clamour of waters, and with might;
Bind on thy sandals, O thou most fleet,
Over the splendour and speed of thy feet;
For the faint east quickens, the wan west shivers,
　Round the feet of the day and the feet of the night.

Where shall we find her, how shall we sing to her,
　Fold our hands round her knees, and cling?
O that man's heart were as fire and could spring to her,
　Fire, or the strength of the streams that spring!
For the stars and the winds are unto her
As raiment, as songs of the harp-player;
For the risen stars and the fallen cling to her,
　And the south-west wind and the west wind sing.

For winter's rains and ruins are over,
　And all the season of snows and sins;
The days dividing lover and lover,
　The light that loses, the night that wins;

And time remembered is grief forgotten.
And frosts are slain and flowers begotten,
And in green underwood and cover
    Blossom by blossom the spring begins.

The full streams feed on flower of rushes,
Ripe grasses trammel a travelling foot,
The faint fresh flame of the young year flushes
    From leaf to flower and flower to fruit;
And fruit and leaf are as gold and fire,
And the oat is heard above the lyre,
And the hoofèd heel of a satyr crushes
    The chestnut-husk at the chestnut-root.

And Pan by noon and Bacchus by night,
    Fleeter of foot than the fleet-foot kid,
Follows with dancing and fills with delight
    The Maenad and the Bassarid;
And soft as lips that laugh and hide
The laughing leaves of the trees divide,
And screen from seeing and leave in sight
    The god pursuing, the maiden hid.

The ivy falls with the Bacchanal's hair
    Over her eyebrows hiding her eyes;
The wild vine slipping down leaves bare
    Her bright breast shortening into sighs;
The wild vine slips with the weight of its leaves,
But the berried ivy catches and cleaves
To the limbs that glitter, the feet that scare
    The wolf that follows, the fawn that flies.

A. C. SWINBURNE

A GARDEN SONG

Here in this sequestered close
Bloom the hyacinth and rose,
Here beside the modest stock
Flaunts the flaring hollyhock;
Here, without a pang, one sees
Ranks, conditions, and degrees.

All the seasons run their race
In this quiet resting-place;
Peach and apricot and fig
Here will ripen and grow big;
Here is store and overplus,—
More had not Alcinoüs!

Here, in alleys cool and green,
Far ahead the thrush is seen;
Here along the southern wall
Keeps the bee his festival;
All is quiet else—afar
Sounds of toil and turmoil are.

Here be shadows large and long;
Here be spaces meet for song;
Grant, O garden-god, that I,
Now that none profane is nigh,—
Now that mood and moment please,—
Find the fair Pierides!

A. DOBSON

CCCXXXVI

When I set out for Lyonesse,
　　A hundred miles away,
　　The rime was on the spray,
And starlight lit my lonesomeness
When I set out for Lyonesse
　　A hundred miles away.

What would bechance at Lyonesse
　　While I should sojourn there
　　No prophet durst declare,
Nor did the wisest wizard guess
What would bechance at Lyonesse
　　While I should sojourn there.

When I came back from Lyonesse
　　With magic in my eyes,
　　All marked with mute surprise
My radiance rare and fathomless,
When I came back from Lyonesse
　　With magic in my eyes!

T. HARDY

CCCXXXVII

THE OXEN

Christmas Eve, and twelve of the clock.
　　'Now they are all on their knees,'
An elder said as we sat in a flock
　　By the embers in hearthside ease.

We pictured the meek mild creatures where
  They dwelt in their strawy pen,
Nor did it occur to one of us there
  To doubt they were kneeling then.

So fair a fancy few would weave
  In these years!   Yet, I feel,
If someone said on Christmas Eve,
  'Come; see the oxen kneel

'In the lonely barton by yonder coomb
  Our childhood used to know,'
I should go with him in the gloom,
  Hoping it might be so.

T. HARDY

CCCXXXVIII

NIGHTINGALES

Beautiful must be the mountains whence ye come,
And bright in the fruitful valleys the streams, where-
    from
        Ye learn your song:
Where are those starry woods?   O might I wander
    there,
  Among the flowers, which in that heavenly air
        Bloom the year long!

Nay, barren are those mountains and spent the
    streams:
  Our song is the voice of desire, that haunts our
    dreams,
        A throe of the heart,
Whose pining visions dim, forbidden hopes profound,
  No dying cadence nor long sigh can sound,
        For all our art.

Alone, aloud in the raptured ear of men
We pour our dark nocturnal secret; and then,
　　　As night is withdrawn
From these sweet-springing meads and bursting
　　boughs of May,
　Dream, while the innumerable choir of day
　　　Welcome the dawn.

R. Bridges

CCCXXXIX

A PASSER-BY

Whither, O splendid ship, thy white sails crowding,
　Leaning across the bosom of the urgent West,
That fearest nor sea rising, nor sky clouding,
　Whither away, fair rover, and what thy quest?
　Ah! soon, when Winter has all our vales opprest,
When skies are cold and misty, and hail is hurling,
　Wilt thou glide on the blue Pacific, or rest
In a summer haven asleep, thy white sails furling.

I there before thee, in the country that well thou
　　knowest,
　Already arrived am inhaling the odorous air:
I watch thee enter unerringly where thou goest,
　And anchor queen of the strange shipping there,
　Thy sails for awnings spread, thy masts bare:
Nor is aught from the foaming reef to the snow-capped,
　　grandest
　Peak, that is over the feathery palms more fair
Than thou, so upright, so stately, and still thou
　　standest.

And yet, O splendid ship, unhailed and nameless,
　I know not if, aiming a fancy, I rightly divine
That thou hast a purpose joyful, a courage blameless,
　Thy port assured in a happier land than mine.

But for all I have given thee, beauty enough is thine,
As thou, aslant with trim tackle and shrouding,
   From the proud nostril curve of a prow's line
In the offing scatterest foam, thy white sails crowding.

R. BRIDGES

CCCXL

PIED BEAUTY

Glory be to God for dappled things—
   For skies of couple-colour as a brinded cow;
      For rose-moles all in stipple upon trout that swim;
Fresh-firecoal chestnut-falls; finches' wings;
   Landscape plotted and pieced—fold, fallow, and
      plough;
      And àll tràdes, their gear and tackle and trim.

All things counter, original, spare, strange;
   Whatever is fickle, freckled (who knows how?)
      With swift, slow; sweet, sour; adazzle, dim;
He fathers-forth whose beauty is past change:
      Praise him.

G. M. HOPKINS

CCCXLI

THE HABIT OF PERFECTION

Elected Silence, sing to me
And beat upon my whorlèd ear,
Pipe me to pastures still and be
The music that I care to hear.

Shape nothing, lips; be lovely-dumb:
It is the shut, the curfew sent
From there where all surrenders come
Which only makes you eloquent.

Be shellèd, eyes, with double dark
And find the uncreated light:
This ruck and reel which you remark
Coils, keeps, and teases simple sight.

Palate, the hutch of tasty lust,
Desire not to be rinsed with wine:
The can must be so sweet, the crust
So fresh that come in fasts divine!

Nostrils, your careless breath that spend
Upon the stir and keep of pride,
What relish shall the censers send
Along the sanctuary side!

O feel-of-primrose hands, O feet
That want the yield of plushy sward,
But you shall walk the golden street
And you unhouse and house the Lord.

And, Poverty, be thou the bride
And now the marriage feast begun,
And lily-coloured clothes provide
Your spouse not laboured-at nor spun.

G. M. HOPKINS

CCCXLII

ODE

We are the music-makers,
    And we are the dreamers of dreams,
Wandering by lone sea-breakers,
    And sitting by desolate streams;
World-losers and world-forsakers,
    On whom the pale moon gleams:
Yet we are the movers and shakers
    Of the world for ever, it seems.

With wonderful deathless ditties
We build up the world's great cities,
  And out of a fabulous story
  We fashion an empire's glory:
One man with a dream, at pleasure,
  Shall go forth and conquer a crown;
And three with a new song's measure
  Can trample an empire down.

We, in the ages lying
  In the buried past of the earth,
Built Nineveh with our sighing,
  And Babel itself with our mirth;
And o'erthrew them with prophesying
  To the old of the new world's worth;
For each age is a dream that is dying,
  Or one that is coming to birth.

A breath of our inspiration
Is the life of each generation;
  A wondrous thing of our dreaming
  Unearthly, impossible seeming—
The soldier, the king, and the peasant
  Are working together in one,
Till our dream shall become their present,
  And their work in the world be done.

They had no vision amazing
Of the goodly house they are raising;
  They had no divine foreshowing
  Of the land to which they are going:
But on one man's soul it hath broken,
  A light that doth not depart;
And his look, or a word he hath spoken,
  Wrought flame in another man's heart.

And therefore to-day is thrilling
With a past day's late fulfilling;
    And the multitudes are enlisted
    In the faith that their fathers resisted,
And, scorning the dream of to-morrow,
    And bringing to pass, as they may,
In the world, for its joy or its sorrow,
    The dream that was scorned yesterday

But we, with our dreaming and singing,
    Ceaseless and sorrowless we!
The glory about us clinging
    Of the glorious futures we see,
Our souls with high music ringing:
    O men! it must ever be
That we dwell, in our dreaming and singing,
    A little apart from ye.

For we are afar with the dawning
    And the suns that are not yet high,
And out of the infinite morning
    Intrepid you hear us cry—
How, spite of your human scorning,
    Once more God's future draws nigh,
And already goes forth the warning
    That ye of the past must die.

Great hail! we cry to the comers
    From the dazzling unknown shore;
Bring us hither your sun and your summers,
    And renew our world as of yore;
You shall teach us your song's new numbers,
    And things that we dreamed not before:
Yea, in spite of a dreamer who slumbers,
    And a singer who sings no more.

A. W. E. O'SHAUGHNESSY

INVICTUS

Out of the night that covers me,
　　Black as the pit from pole to pole,
I thank whatever gods may be
　　For my unconquerable soul.

In the fell clutch of circumstance
　　I have not winced nor cried aloud;
Under the bludgeonings of chance
　　My head is bloody, but unbow'd.

Beyond this place of wrath and tears
　　Looms but the Horror of the shade,
And yet the menace of the years
　　Finds and shall find me unafraid.

It matters not how strait the gate,
　　How charged with punishments the scroll,
I am the master of my fate:
　　I am the captain of my soul.

W. E. HENLEY

THE SHEPHERDESS

She walks—the lady of my delight—
　　A shepherdess of sheep.
Her flocks are thoughts.　She keeps them white;
　　She guards them from the steep.
She feeds them on the fragrant height,
　　And folds them in for sleep.

She roams maternal hills and bright,
  Dark valleys soft and deep.
Into that tender breast at night
  The chastest stars may peep.
She walks—the lady of my delight—
  A shepherdess of sheep.

She holds her little thoughts in sight,
  Though gay they run and leap.
She is so circumspect and right;
  She has her soul to keep.
She walks—the lady of my delight—
  A shepherdess of sheep.

A. MEYNELL

CCCXLV

THE VAGABOND

Give to me the life I love,
  Let the lave go by me,
Give the jolly heaven above
  And the by-way nigh me.
Bed in the bush with stars to see—
  Bread I dip in the river—
There's the life for a man like me,
  There's the life for ever.

Let the blow fall soon or late,
  Let what will be o'er me;
Give the face of earth around
  And the road before me.
Wealth I seek not, hope nor love,
  Nor a friend to know me;
All I seek, the heaven above
  And the road below me.

Or let autumn fall on me
  Where afield I linger,
Silencing the bird on tree,
  Biting the blue finger.
White as meal the frosty field—
  Warm the fireside haven—
Not to autumn will I yield,
  Not to winter even;

Let the blow fall soon or late,
  Let what will be o'er me;
Give the face of earth around
  And the road before me.
Wealth I ask not, hope nor love,
  Not a friend to know me.
All I ask, the heaven above,
  And the road below me.

R. L. STEVENSON

CCCXLVI

REQUIEM

Under the wide and starry sky,
Dig the grave and let me lie.
Glad did I live and gladly die
  And I laid me down with a will.

This be the verse you grave for me:
Here he lies where he longed to be;
Home is the sailor, home from sea,
  And the hunter home from the hill

R. L. STEVENSON

THE NIGHT HAS A THOUSAND EYES

The night has a thousand eyes,
　And the day but one;
Yet the light of the bright world dies
　With the dying sun.

The mind has a thousand eyes,
　And the heart but one;
Yet the light of a whole life dies
　When love is done.

F. W. Bourdillon

DAISY

Where the thistle lifts a purple crown
　Six foot out of the turf,
And the harebell shakes on the windy hill—
　O the breath of the distant surf!—

The hills look over on the South,
　And southward dreams the sea;
And, with the sea-breeze hand in hand,
　Came innocence and she.

Where 'mid the gorse the raspberry
　Red for the gatherer springs,
Two children did we stray and talk
　Wise, idle, childish things.

She listened with big-lipped surprise,
　　Breast-deep 'mid flower and spine:
Her skin was like a grape, whose veins
　　Run snow instead of wine.

She knew not those sweet words she spake,
　　Nor knew her own sweet way;
But there's never a bird, so sweet a song
　　Thronged in whose throat that day!

Oh, there were flowers in Storrington
　　On the turf and on the spray;
But the sweetest flower on Sussex hills
　　Was the Daisy-flower that day!

Her beauty smoothed earth's furrowed face!
　　She gave me tokens three:—
A look, a word of her winsome mouth,
　　And a wild raspberry.

A berry red, a guileless look,
　　A still word,—strings of sand!
And yet they made my wild, wild heart
　　Fly down to her little hand.

For, standing artless as the air,
　　And candid as the skies,
She took the berries with her hand,
　　And the love with her sweet eyes.

The fairest things have fleetest end:
　　Their scent survives their close,
But the rose's scent is bitterness
　　To him that loved the rose!

She looked a little wistfully,
  Then went her sunshine way:—
The sea's eye had a mist on it,
  And the leaves fell from the day.

She went her unremembering way;
  She went, and left in me
The pang of all the partings gone,
  And the partings yet to be.

She left me marvelling why my soul
  Was sad that she was glad;
At all the sadness in the sweet,
  The sweetness in the sad.

Still, still I seemed to see her, still
  Look up with soft replies,
And take the berries with her hand,
  And the love with her lovely eyes.

Nothing begins, and nothing ends,
  That is not paid with moan;
For we are born in other's pain,
  And perish in our own.

F. THOMPSON

CCCXLIX

'IN NO STRANGE LAND'

'The Kingdom of God is within you.'

O world invisible, we view thee,
O world intangible, we touch thee,
O world unknowable, we know thee,
Inapprehensible, we clutch thee!

Does the fish soar to find the ocean,
The eagle plunge to find the air—
That we ask of the stars in motion
If they have rumour of thee there?

Not where the wheeling systems darken,
And our benumbed conceiving soars!—
The drift of pinions, would we hearken,
Beats at our own clay-shuttered doors.

The angels keep their ancient places;—
Turn but a stone, and start a wing!
'Tis ye, 'tis your estrangèd faces,
That miss the many-splendoured thing.

But (when so sad thou canst not sadder)
Cry;—and upon thy so sore loss
Shall shine the traffic of Jacob's ladder
Pitched betwixt Heaven and Charing Cross.

Yea, in the night, my Soul, my daughter,
Cry,—clinging Heaven by the hems;
And lo, Christ walking on the water,
Not of Gennesareth, but Thames!

F. Thompson

CCCL

Loveliest of trees, the cherry now
Is hung with bloom along the bough,
And stands about the woodland ride
Wearing white for Eastertide.

Now, of my threescore years and ten,
Twenty will not come again,
And take from seventy springs a score,
It only leaves me fifty more.

And since to look at things in bloom
Fifty springs are little room,
About the woodlands I will go
To see the cherry hung with snow.

A. E. HOUSMAN

CCCLI

On the idle hill of summer,
  Sleepy with the flow of streams,
Far I hear the steady drummer
  Drumming like a noise in dreams.

Far and near and low and louder
  On the roads of earth go by,
Dear to friends and food for powder,
  Soldiers marching, all to die.

East and west on fields forgotten
  Bleach the bones of comrades slain,
Lovely lads and dead and rotten;
  None that go return again.

Far the calling bugles hollo,
  High the screaming fife replies,
Gay the files of scarlet follow:
  Woman bore me, I will rise.

A. E. HOUSMAN

CCCLII

REVEILLE

Wake: the silver dusk returning
  Up the beach of darkness brims,
And the ship of sunrise burning
  Strands upon the eastern rims.

Wake: the vaulted shadow shatters,
  Trampled to the floor it spanned,
And the tent of night in tatters
  Straws the sky-pavilioned land.

Up, lad, up, 'tis late for lying:
  Hear the drums of morning play;
Hark, the empty highways crying
  'Who'll beyond the hills away?'

Towns and countries woo together,
  Forelands beacon, belfries call;
Never lad that trod on leather
  Lived to feast his heart with all.

Up, lad: thews that lie and cumber
  Sunlit pallets never thrive;
Morns abed and daylight slumber
  Were not meant for man alive.

Clay lies still, but blood's a rover;
  Breath's a ware that will not keep.
Up, lad: when the journey's over
  There'll be time enough to sleep.

A. E. HOUSMAN

CCCLIII

UNWELCOME

We were young, we were merry, we were very very
    wise,
    And the door stood open at our feast,
When there passed us a woman with the West in her
    eyes,
    And a man with his back to the East.

O, still grew the hearts that were beating so fast,
    The loudest voice was still.
The jest died away on our lips as they passed,
    And the rays of July struck chill.

The cups of red wine turn'd pale on the board,
    The white bread black as soot.
The hound forgot the hand of her lord,
    She fell down at his foot.

Low let me lie, where the dead dog lies,
    Ere I sit me down again at a feast,
When there passes a woman with the West in her eyes,
    And a man with his back to the East.

MARY COLERIDGE

CCCLIV

DRAKE'S DRUM

Drake he's in his hammock an' a thousand mile away,
    (Capten, art tha sleepin' there below?),
Slung atween the round shot in Nombre Dios Bay,
    An' dreamin' arl the time o' Plymouth Hoe.

Yarnder lumes the Island, yarnder lie the ships,
    Wi' sailor lads a-dancin' heel-an'-toe,
An' the shore-lights flashin', an' the night-tide dashin',
    He sees et arl so plainly as he saw et long ago.

Drake he was a Devon man, an' rüled the Devon seas,
    (Capten, art tha sleepin' there below?),
Rovin' tho' his death fell, he went wi' heart at ease,
    An' dreamin' arl the time o' Plymouth Hoe.
'Take my drum to England, hang et by the shore,
    Strike et when your powder's runnin' low;
If the Dons sight Devon, I'll quit the port o' Heaven,
    An' drum them up the Channel as we drummed
      them long ago.'

Drake he's in his hammock till the great Armadas
    come,
    (Capten, art tha sleepin' there below?),
Slung atween the round shot, listenin' for the drum,
    An' dreamin' arl the time o' Plymouth Hoe.
Call him on the deep sea, call him up the Sound,
    Call him when ye sail to meet the foe;
Where the old trade's plyin' an' the old flag flyin'
    They shall find him ware an' wakin', as they found
      him long ago!

Sir Henry Newbolt

CCCLV

VITAÏ LAMPADA

There's a breathless hush in the Close to-night—
    Ten to make and the match to win—
A bumping pitch and a blinding light,
    An hour to play and the last man in.

And it's not for the sake of a ribboned coat,
   Or the selfish hope of a season's fame,
But his Captain's hand on his shoulder smote—
'Play up! play up! and play the game!'

The sand of the desert is sodden red,—
   Red with the wreck of a square that broke;—
The Gatling's jammed and the Colonel dead,
   And the regiment blind with dust and smoke.
The river of death has brimmed his banks,
   And England's far, and Honour a name,
But the voice of a schoolboy rallies the ranks:
'Play up! play up! and play the game!'

This is the word that year by year,
   While in her place the School is set,
Every one of her sons must hear,
   And none that hears it dare forget.
This they all with a joyful mind
   Bear through life like a torch in flame,
And falling fling to the host behind—
.'Play up! play up! and play the game!'

                        HENRY NEWBOLT

CCCLVI

IF

If you can keep your head when all about you
   Are losing theirs and blaming it on you;
If you can trust yourself when all men doubt you,
   But make allowance for their doubting too;
If you can wait and not be tired by waiting,
   Or being lied about, don't deal in lies,
Or being hated don't give way to hating,
   And yet don't look too good, nor talk too wise;

If you can dream—and not make dreams your master;
   If you can think—and not make thoughts your aim,
If you can meet with Triumph and Disaster
   And treat those two impostors just the same;
If you can bear to hear the truth you've spoken
   Twisted by knaves to make a trap for fools,
Or watch the things you gave your life to, broken,
   And stoop and build 'em up with worn-out tools;

If you can make one heap of all your winnings
   And risk it on one turn of pitch-and-toss,
And lose, and start again at your beginnings
   And never breathe a word about your loss;
If you can force your heart and nerve and sinew
   To serve your turn long after they are gone,
And so hold on when there is nothing in you
   Except the Will which says to them: 'Hold on!'

If you can talk with crowds and keep your virtue,
   Or walk with Kings—nor lose the common touch,
If neither foes nor loving friends can hurt you,
   If all men count with you, but none too much;
If you can fill the unforgiving minute
   With sixty seconds' worth of distance run,
Yours is the Earth and everything that's in it,
   And—which is more—you'll be a Man, my son!

R. KIPLING

CCCLVII

RECESSIONAL

(1897)

God of our fathers, known of old,
   Lord of our far-flung battle-line,
Beneath whose awful Hand we hold
   Dominion over palm and pine—

Lord God of Hosts, be with us yet,
Lest we forget—lest we forget!

The tumult and the shouting dies;
    The captains and the kings depart:
Still stands Thine ancient sacrifice,
    An humble and a contrite heart.
Lord God of Hosts, be with us yet,
Lest we forget—lest we forget!

Far-called, our navies melt away;
    On dune and headland sinks the fire:
Lo, all our pomp of yesterday
    Is one with Nineveh and Tyre!
Judge of the Nations, spare us yet,
Lest we forget—lest we forget!

If, drunk with sight of power, we loose
    Wild tongues that have not Thee in awe,
Such boastings as the Gentiles use,
    Or lesser breeds without the Law—
Lord God of Hosts, be with us yet,
Lest we forget—lest we forget!

For heathen heart that puts her trust
    In reeking tube and iron shard,
All valiant dust that builds on dust,
    And guarding, calls not Thee to guard,
For frantic boast and foolish word—
Thy mercy on Thy People, Lord!

                                Amen.

                        R. KIPLING

CCCLVIII

When you are old and gray and full of sleep,
　And nodding by the fire, take down this book,
　And slowly read, and dream of the soft look
Your eyes had once, and of their shadows deep;

How many loved your moments of glad grace,
　And loved your beauty with love false or true;
　But one man loved the pilgrim soul in you,
And loved the sorrows of your changing face.

And bending down beside the glowing bars
　Murmur, a little sadly, how love fled
　And paced upon the mountains overhead,
And hid his face amid a crowd of stars.

W. B. YEATS

CCCLIX

DOWN BY THE SALLEY GARDENS

Down by the salley gardens my love and I did meet;
She passed the salley gardens with little snow-white
　feet.
She bid me take love easy, as the leaves grow on the
　tree;
But I, being young and foolish, with her would not
　agree.

In a field by the river my love and I did stand,
And on my leaning shoulder she laid her snow-white
　hand
She bid me take life easy, as the grass grows on the
　weirs;
But I was young and foolish, and now am full of tears.

W. B. YEATS

CCCLX

THE LAKE ISLE OF INNISFREE

I will arise and go now, and go to Innisfree,
And a small cabin build there, of clay and wattles
    made:
Nine bean-rows will I have there, a hive for the honey-
    bee,
And live alone in the bee-loud glade.

And I shall have some peace there, for peace comes
    dropping slow,
Dropping from the veils of the morning to where the
    cricket sings;
There midnight's all a-glimmer, and noon a purple
    glow,
And evening full of the linnet's wings.

I will arise and go now, for always night and day
I hear lake water lapping with low sounds by the shore;
While I stand on the roadway, or on the pavements
    grey,
I hear it in the deep heart's core.

W. B. YEATS

CCCLXI

BY THE MARGIN OF THE GREAT DEEP

When the breath of twilight blows to flame the misty
    skies,
All its vaporous sapphire, violet glow and silver gleam,
With their magic flood me through the gateway of the
    eyes;
    I am one with the twilight's dream.

When the trees and skies and fields are one in dusky
      mood,
Every heart of man is rapt within the mother's breast:
Full of peace and sleep and dreams in the vasty
      quietude,
    I am one with their hearts at rest.

From our immemorial joys of hearth and home and
      love
Stray'd away along the margin of the unknown tide,
All its reach of soundless calm can thrill me far above
    Word or touch from the lips beside.

Aye, and deep and deep and deeper let me drink and
      draw
From the olden fountain more than light or peace or
      dream,
Such primaeval being as o'erfills the heart with awe,
    Growing one with its silent stream.

G. W. Russell ('Æ')

CCCLXII

CADGWITH

My windows open to the autumn night,
In vain I watched for sleep to visit me;
How should sleep dull mine ears, and dim my sight,
Who saw the stars, and listened to the sea?

Ah, how the City of our God is fair!
If, without sea, and starless though it be,
For joy of the majestic beauty there,
Men shall not miss the stars, nor mourn the sea.

L. Johnson

FOR THE FALLEN

With proud thanksgiving, a mother for her children,
England mourns for her dead across the sea.
Flesh of her flesh they were, spirit of her spirit,
Fallen in the cause of the free.

Solemn the drums thrill: Death august and royal
Sings sorrow up into immortal spheres.
There is music in the midst of desolation
And glory that shines upon our tears.

They went with songs to the battle, they were young,
Straight of limb, true of eye, steady and aglow,
They were staunch to the end against odds uncounted,
They fell with their faces to the foe.

They shall grow not old, as we that are left grow old:
Age shall not weary them, nor the years condemn.
At the going down of the sun and in the morning
We will remember them.

They mingle not with their laughing comrades again;
They sit no more at familiar tables of home;
They have no lot in our labour of the day-time;
They sleep beyond England's foam.

But where our desires are and our hopes profound,
Felt as a well-spring that is hidden from sight,
To the innermost heart of their own land they are
    known
As the stars are known to the Night;

As the stars that shall be bright when we are dust,
Moving in marches upon the heavenly plain,
As the stars that are starry in the time of our darkness
To the end, to the end they remain.

L. BINYON

THE SOUTH COUNTRY

When I am living in the Midlands
   That are sodden and unkind,
I light my lamp in the evening:
   My work is left behind;
And the great hills of the South Country
   Come back into my mind.

The great hills of the South Country
   They stand along the sea;
And it's there walking in the high woods
   That I could wish to be,
And the men that were boys when I was a boy
   Walking along with me.

The men that live in North England
   I saw them for a day:
Their hearts are set upon the waste fells,
   Their skies are fast and grey;
From their castle-walls a man may see
   The mountains far away.

The men that live in West England
   They see the Severn strong,
A-rolling on rough water brown
   Light aspen leaves along.
They have the secret of the Rocks,
   And the oldest kind of song.

But the men that live in the South Country
   Are the kindest and most wise,
They get their laughter from the loud surf,
   And the faith in their happy eyes

Comes surely from our Sister the Spring
　　When over the sea she flies;
The violets suddenly bloom at her feet,
　　She blesses us with surprise.

I never get between the pines
　　But I smell the Sussex air;
Nor I never come on a belt of sand
　　But my home is there.
And along the sky the line of the Downs
　　So noble and so bare.

A lost thing could I never find,
　　Nor a broken thing mend:
And I fear I shall be all alone
　　When I get towards the end.
Who will there be to comfort me
　　Or who will be my friend?

I will gather and carefully make my friends
　　Of the men of the Sussex Weald,
They watch the stars from silent folds,
　　They stiffly plough the field.
By them and the God of the South Country
　　My poor soul shall be healed.

If I ever become a rich man,
　　Or if ever I grow to be old,
I will build a house with deep thatch
　　To shelter me from the cold,
And there shall the Sussex songs be sung
　　And the story of Sussex told.

I will hold my house in the high wood
　　Within a walk of the sea,
And the men that were boys when I was a boy
　　Shall sit and drink with me.

H. BELLOC

CCCLXV

LEISURE

What is this life if, full of care,
We have no time to stand and stare.

No time to stand beneath the boughs
And stare as long as sheep or cows.

No time to see, when woods we pass,
Where squirrels hide their nuts in grass

No time to see, in broad daylight,
Streams full of stars, like skies at night.

No time to turn at Beauty's glance,
And watch her feet, how they can dance.

No time to wait till her mouth can
Enrich that smile her eyes began.

A poor life this if, full of care,
We have no time to stand and stare.

W. H. DAVIES

CCCLXVI

THE DONKEY

When fishes flew and forests walked
    And figs grew upon thorn,
Some moment when the moon was blood
    Then surely I was born;

With monstrous head and sickening cry
　　And ears like errant wings,
The devil's walking parody
　　On all four-footed things.

The tattered outlaw of the earth,
　　Of ancient, crooked will;
Starve, scourge, deride me: I am dumb,
　　I keep my secret still.

Fools!　For I also had my hour;
　　One far fierce hour and sweet:
There was a shout about my ears,
　　And palms before my feet.

G. K. CHESTERTON

CCCLXVII

A HYMN

O God of earth and altar,
　　Bow down and hear our cry,
Our earthly rulers falter,
　　Our people drift and die:
The walls of gold entomb us,
　　The swords of scorn divide,
Take not thy thunder from us,
　　But take away our pride.

From all that terror teaches,
　　From lies of tongue and pen,
From all the easy speeches
　　That comfort cruel men,

From sale and profanation
  Of honour and the sword,
From sleep and from damnation,
  Deliver us, good Lord!

Tie in a living tether
  The prince and priest and thrall,
Bind all our lives together,
  Smite us and save us all;
In ire and exultation
  Aflame with faith, and free,
Lift up a living nation,
  A single sword to thee.

G. K. CHESTERTON

CCCLXVIII

MANY A MICKLE

A little sound—
Only a little, a little—
The breath in a reed,
A trembling fiddle;
The trumpet's ring,
The shuddering drum;
So all the glory, bravery, hush
Of music come.

A little sound—
Only a stir and a sigh
Of each green leaf
Its fluttering neighbour by;

Oak on to oak,
The wide, dark forest through—
So o'er the watery wheeling world
The night-winds go.

A little sound—
Only a little, a little,
The thin high drone
Of the simmering kettle,
The gathering frost,
The click of needle and thread;
Mother, the fading wall, the dream,
The drowsy bed.

W. De La Mare

CCCLXIX

THE LISTENERS

'Is there anybody there?' said the Traveller,
    Knocking on the moonlit door;
And his horse in the silence champed the grasses
    Of the forest's ferny floor:
And a bird flew up out of the turret,
    Above the Traveller's head:
And he smote upon the door again a second time;
    'Is there anybody there?' he said.
But no one descended to the Traveller;
    No head from the leaf-fringed sill
Leaned over and looked into his grey eyes,
    Where he stood perplexed and still.
But only a host of phantom listeners
    That dwelt in the lone house then
Stood listening in the quiet of the moonlight
    To that voice from the world of men:

Stood thronging the faint moonbeams on the dark stair,
    That goes down to the empty hall,
Hearkening in an air stirred and shaken
    By the lonely Traveller's call.
And he felt in his heart their strangeness,
    Their stillness answering his cry,
While his horse moved, cropping the dark turf,
    'Neath the starred and leafy sky;
For he suddenly smote on the door, even
    Louder, and lifted his head:—
'Tell them I came, and no one answered,
    That I kept my word!' he said.
Never the least stir made the listeners,
    Though every word he spake
Fell echoing through the shadowiness of the still house
    From the one man left awake;
Ay, they heard his foot upon the stirrup,
    And the sound of iron on stone,
And how the silence surged softly backward,
    When the plunging hoofs were gone.

                  W. De La Mare

CCCLXX

THE CALL OF THE WILD

Have you gazed on naked grandeur when there's
        nothing else to gaze on,
    Set pieces and drop-curtain scenes galore,
Big mountains heaved to heaven, which the blinding
        sunsets blazon,
    Black canyons where the rapids rip and roar?
Have you swept the visioned valley with the green
        stream streaking through it,
    Searched the Vastness for a something you have
        lost?

Have you strung your soul to silence? Then for
    God's sake go and do it;
  Hear the challenge, learn the lesson, pay the cost.

Have you wandered in the wilderness, the sage-brush
    desolation,
  The bunch-grass levels where the cattle graze?
Have you whistled bits of rag-time at the end of all
    creation,
  And learned to know the desert's little ways?
Have you camped upon the foothills, have you gal-
    loped o'er the ranges,
  Have you roamed the arid sun-lands through and
    through?
Have you chummed up with the mesa?   Do you know
    its moods and changes?
  Then listen to the wild—it's calling you.

Have you known the Great White Silence, not a snow-
    gemmed twig aquiver?
  (Eternal truths that shame our soothing lies.)
Have you broken trail on snowshoes? mushed your
    huskies up the river,
  Dared the unknown, led the way, and clutched the
    prize?
Have you marked the map's void spaces, mingled with
    the mongrel races,
  Felt the savage strength of brute in every thew?
And though grim as hell the worst is, can you round
    if off with curses?
  Then hearken to the wild—it's wanting you.

Have you suffered, starved and triumphed, grovelled
    down, yet grasped at glory,
  Grown bigger in the bigness of the whole?
'Done things' just for the doing, letting babblers tell
    the story,

Seeing through the nice veneer the naked soul?
Have you seen God in His splendours, heard the text
  that nature renders?
  (You'll never hear it in the family pew.)
The simple things, the true things, the silent men who
  do things—
  Then listen to the wild—it's calling you.

They have cradled you in custom, they have primed
  you with their preaching,
  They have soaked you in convention through and
  through;
They have put you in a showcase; you're a credit to
  their teaching—
  But can't you hear the wild?—it's calling you.
Let us probe the silent places, let us seek what luck
  betide us;
  Let us journey to a lonely land I know.
There's a whisper on the night-wind, there's a star
  agleam to guide us,
  And the wild is calling, calling . . . let us go.

R. W. Service

CCCLXXI

SEA-FEVER

I must down to the seas again, to the lonely sea and the
  sky,
And all I ask is a tall ship and a star to steer her by,
And the wheel's kick and the wind's song and the white
  sail's shaking,
And a grey mist on the sea's face and a grey dawn
  breaking.

I must down to the seas again, for the call of the
running tide
Is a wild call and a clear call that may not be denied;
And all I ask is a windy day with the white clouds
flying,
And the flung spray and the blown spume, and the
sea-gulls crying.

I must down to the seas again, to the vagrant gipsy
life,
To the gull's way and the whale's way where the
wind's like a whetted knife;
And all I ask is a merry yarn from a laughing fellow-
rover,
And quiet sleep and a sweet dream when the long
trick's over.

J. MASEFIELD

CCCLXXII

SPANISH WATERS

Spanish waters, Spanish waters, you are ringing in my
ears,
Like a slow sweet piece of music from the grey forgotten years;
Telling tales, and beating tunes, and bringing weary
thoughts to me
Of the sandy beach at Muertos, where I would that I
could be.

There's a surf breaks on Los Muertos, and it never
stops to roar,
And it's there we came to anchor, and it's there we
went ashore,

Where the blue lagoon is silent amid snags of rotting
    trees,
Dropping like the clothes of corpses cast up by the
    seas.

We anchored at Los Muertos when the dipping sun
    was red,
We left her half a mile to sea, to west of Nigger Head;
And before the mist was on the Cay, before the day
    was done,
We were all ashore on Muertos with the gold that we
    had won.

We bore it through the marshes in a half-score battered
    chests,
Sinking, in the sucking quagmires to the sunburn on
    our breasts,
Heaving over tree-trunks, gasping, damning at the
    flies and heat,
Longing for a long drink, out of silver, in the ship's
    cool lazareet.

The moon came white and ghostly as we laid the
    treasure down,
There was gear there'd make a beggarman as rich as
    Lima Town,
Copper charms and silven trinkets from the chests of
    Spanish crews,
Gold doubloons and double moidores, louis d'ors and
    portagues,

Clumsy yellow-metal earrings from the Indians of
    Brazil,
Uncut emeralds out of Rio, bezoar stones from
    Guayaquil;
Silver, in the crude and fashioned, pots of old Arica
    bronze,
Jewels from the bones of Incas desecrated by the Dons.

We smoothed the place with mattocks, and we took
    and blazed the tree.
Which marks yon where the gear is hid that none will
    ever see,
And we laid aboard the ship again, and south away we
    steers,
Through the loud surf of Los Muertos which is beating
    in my ears.

I'm the last alive that knows it. All the rest have
    gone their ways
Killed, or died, or come to anchor in the old Mulatas
    Cays,
And I go singing, fiddling, old and starved and in
    despair,
And I know where all that gold is hid, if I were only
    there.

It's not the way to end it all. I'm old, and nearly
    blind,
And an old man's past's a strange thing, for it never
    leaves his mind.
And I see in dreams, awhiles, the beach, the sun's disc
    dipping red,
And the tall ship, under topsails, swaying in past
    Nigger Head.

I'd be glad to step ashore there. Glad to take a pick
    and go
To the lone blazed coco-palm tree in the place no
    others know,
And lift the gold and silver that has mouldered there
    for years
By the loud surf of Los Muertos which is beating in
    my ears.

J. MASEFIELD

CCCLXXIII

THE NEW HOUSE

Now first, as I shut the door,
　　I was alone
In the new house; and the wind
　　Began to moan.

Old at once was the house,
　　And I was old;
My ears were teased with the dread
　　Of what was foretold,

Nights of storm, days of mist, without end;
　　Sad days when the sun
Shone in vain: old griefs and griefs
　　Not yet begun.

All was foretold me; naught
　　Could I foresee;
But I learnt how the wind would sound
　　After these things should be.

E. THOMAS

CCCLXXIV

THE OLD WOMAN

As a white candle
In a holy place,
So is the beauty
Of an agèd face.

As the spent radiance
Of the winter sun,
So is a woman
With her travail done,

Her brood gone from her,
And her thoughts as still
As the waters under
A ruined mill.

J. CAMPBELL

CCCLXXV

THE STREAM'S SONG

Make way, make way,
You thwarting stones;
Room for my play,
Serious ones.

Do you fear,
O rocks and boulders,
To feel my laughter
On your grave shoulders?

Do you not know
My joy at length
Will all wear out
Your solemn strength?

You will not for ever
Cumber my play;
With joy and a song
I clear my way.

Your faith of rock
Shall yield to me,
And be carried away
By the song of my glee.

Crumble, crumble,
Voiceless things;
No faith can last
That never sings.

For the last hour
To joy belongs;
The steadfast perish,
But not the songs.

Yet for a while
Thwart me, O boulders;
I need for laughter
Your serious shoulders.

And when my singing
Has razed you quite,
I shall have lost
Half my delight.

L. ABERCROMBIE

CCCLXXVI

THE SNARE

I hear a sudden cry of pain!
There is a rabbit in a snare:
Now I hear the cry again,
But I cannot tell from where.

But I cannot tell from where
He is calling out for aid!
Crying on the frightened air,
Making everything afraid!

Making everything afraid!
Wrinkling up his little face!
As he cries again for aid;
—And I cannot find the place!

And I cannot find the place
Where his paw is in the snare!
Little One!   Oh, Little One!
I am searching everywhere!

J. STEPHENS

CCCLXXVII

LITTLE THINGS

Little things, that run, and quail,
And die, in silence and despair!

Little things, that fight, and fail,
And fall, on sea, and earth, and air!

All trapped and frightened little things,
The mouse, the coney, hear our prayer!

As we forgive those done to us,
... The lamb, the linnet, and the hare—

Forgive us all our trespasses,
Little creatures, everywhere!

J. STEPHENS

THE SOLDIER

If I should die, think only this of me:
That there's some corner of a foreign field
That is for ever England.   There shall be
In that rich earth a richer dust concealed;
A dust whom England bore, shaped, made aware,
Gave, once, her flowers to love, her ways to roam,
A body of England's, breathing English air,
Washed by the rivers, blest by suns of home.

And think, this heart, all evil shed away,
A pulse in the eternal mind, no less
Gives somewhere back the thoughts by England given:
Her sights and sounds; dreams happy as her day;
And laughter, learnt of friends; and gentleness,
In hearts at peace, under an English heaven.

R. BROOKE

CLOUDS

Down the blue night the unending columns press
In noiseless tumult, break and wave and flow,
Now tread the far South, or lift rounds of snow
Up to the white moon's hidden loveliness.
Some pause in their grave wandering comradeless,
And turn with profound gesture vague and slow,
As who would pray good for the world, but know
Their benediction empty as they bless.

They say that the Dead die not, but remain
Near to the rich heirs of their grief and mirth.
I think they ride the calm mid-heaven, as these,
In wise majestic melancholy train,
And watch the moon, and the still raging seas,
And men, coming and going on the earth.

R. BROOKE

CCCLXXX

A SAXON SONG

Tools with the comely names,
    Mattock and scythe and spade,
    Couth and bitter as flames,
    Clean, and bowed in the blade,—
A man and his tools make a man and his trade.

Breadth of the English shires,
    Hummock and kame and mead,
    Tang of the reeking byres,
    Land of the English breed,—
A man and his land make a man and his creed.

Leisurely flocks and herds,
    Cool-eyed cattle that come
    Mildly to wonted words,
    Swine that in orchards roam,—
A man and his beasts make a man and his home.

Children sturdy and flaxen
    Shouting in brotherly strife,
    Like the land they are Saxon,
    Sons of a man and his wife,—
For a man and his loves make a man and his life

V. SACKVILLE-WEST

INDEX OF AUTHORS AND TITLES

INDEX OF AUTHORS AND TITLES

INDEX OF FIRST LINES